For Angelina, to whom I owe more than I can ever say

THE COOK

AJAY CHOWDHURY

VINTAGE

1 3 5 7 9 10 8 6 4 2

Vintage is part of the Penguin Random House group of companies
whose addresses can be found at global.penguinrandomhouse.com

Penguin
Random House
UK

First published in Vintage in 2023
First published in hardback by Harvill Secker in 2022

penguin.co.uk/vintage

A CIP catalogue record for this book is available from the British Library

ISBN 9781529115390

Printed and bound in Great Britain by Clays Ltd, Elcograf S.p.A.

The authorised representative in the EEA is Penguin Random House Ireland,
Morrison Chambers, 32 Nassau Street, Dublin D02 YH68

Penguin Random House is committed to a sustainable future for
our business, our readers and our planet. This book is made from
Forest Stewardship Council® certified paper.

MIX
Paper from
responsible sources
FSC
www.fsc.org   FSC® C018179

Once, in finesse of fiddles found I ecstasy,
In the flash of gold heels on the hard pavement.
Now see I
That warmth's the very stuff of poesy.
Oh, God, make small
The old star-eaten blanket of the sky,
That I may fold it round me and in comfort lie.

T. E. Hulme, 'The Embankment (The fantasia of a fallen
gentleman on a cold, bitter night)' 1908–9

Prologue

Two years ago. Lahore, Pakistan.

He was always more dangerous when sober.

She used to find it romantic, this prelude to a kiss. First, a whisper filled with insatiable longing – *Jaan*; then, hands hovering a millimetre away from her face, so she felt the heat of his palms, his stare drilling into her, trying to see into the soul she kept sealed away behind her green eyes.

She wanted to squeeze them shut as he probed, 'So what did you do today, my Jaan? Where did you go? Tell me. I love you so much I want to share every second of every minute of every day with you.'

The first time he had said this, she'd felt warm and loved. He desired her so much he couldn't bear to be without her! Wasn't that what every young girl dreamed of? A tall, handsome, educated man who loved her with all his being.

It was a few months after their wedding when she realised this wasn't the tender questioning of a lover, it was the subtle interrogation of a jailer – she was his inmate, not his soulmate and the fortress they had built against the world had become her prison. Sure, she could go where she pleased (as long as his driver took her), buy what she desired (as long as she used his credit card), call who she wanted (as long as she used the mobile he'd given her) and meet who she liked (as long as she didn't go to their homes).

She didn't notice the bonds tightening inch by tiny inch, until, to her surprise, one morning she couldn't move. That's when she struggled, desperate to break the engirdling chains.

Divorce was out of the question. For a woman to divorce her husband in Pakistan he had to have either abandoned her, married someone else, contracted a venereal disease or consorted with immoral females. As far as she knew, he had done none of those. In the eyes of the law, being *too* loving and *too* caring weren't adequate grounds for ending a marriage.

She tried to broach her difficulties with Daddy, but found it hard to explain. He didn't beat her, did he? No. Looked after her? Yes. Then what was the problem? The marriage had been her choice, although he and her mother had counselled against it. She was just eighteen. She had always been too impulsive, too headstrong. She needed to settle into the real world.

She couldn't express how the walls were closing in, how her essential self was being erased. She'd given up her dreams of being a nurse, of helping others, to marry this man. And now she was . . . nothing. Like a used car, with one signature on a marriage form, her ownership had been transferred. She needed to belong to herself. To fill the blank pages ahead with love and warmth and fulfilling adventures . . . not this cold, planned, inevitability. There were no words she could find to make them understand.

And then she found the ledger.

The idea came to her while working out on the treadmill as she pushed herself to her limit, legs pumping, lungs bursting, Beyoncé exploding in her headphones. That's when she realised: I will be *stronger* without him, not weaker.

The ledger was her golden ticket.

She had one shot at escape. She had to play it with care. It had to be *his* idea, done in a way to save face and continue the public projection of their perfect marriage. He had to believe her leaving was temporary. That she would return to be his again.

Where would she go?

London. The nursing capital of the world. Florence Nightingale, Mary Seacole, Edith Cavell. She would follow the path they had blazed. She had the money her grandfather had left her; Imran couldn't touch that. And Salim Uncle was there, she could stay with him.

She made her preparations.

And tonight, in their home, at the celebrations for her nineteenth birthday, she would light the touch paper.

Heart threatening to break loose from her ribcage, she stood after dinner and began her rehearsed speech. 'My darling Imran wanted me to keep this a secret, but I can't – I have to share his amazing generosity and love with you. He has given me the best present I could ever hope for – on top of the diamond earrings! He has always known how much I want to be a nurse and has agreed to let me get my degree in the best nursing college in the world – King's in London. I applied and got accepted! So, I will study hard for my qualifications and come back to my beloved country, where clinics are so in need of qualified medical professionals. Thank you, my Jaan. You are the best husband in the world, and I feel blessed every day that I'm your wife.'

She wrapped her arms around him in a showy embrace and passed round her acceptance letter for all to read. Daddy's army officer friends clapped, and his parents said what a great husband their son was to let his wife go to college in the UK and how she was a diamond on his ring.

And Imran smiled and accepted the congratulations for his generosity, but his dark eyes said, 'Wait, just wait. You may *think* you have escaped, but you haven't. Just wait.'

Somehow, she made her way through the rest of the party as the fuse burned down. And now, when the door closed behind the last guest, she prepared for the detonation.

Would the ledger give her the protection she needed?

She'd find out soon enough.

Because if it didn't, she'd be dead.

He wasn't drunk tonight.

Mouth dry, she stuck on her best smile and walked into the bedroom, Beyoncé's words giving her strength.

She *was* a survivor. She *would* make it.

Chapter 1

May. Tuesday. London.

They say your most profound memories are anchored in sensory experience. For me, it was the shocking crackle and explosive smack of aromatics that made me salivate and choked my lungs with savoury smoke as, with deceptive simplicity, Suresh added a dash of tiny black seeds, then a spoonful of red powder, followed by a pinch of something orange to the pot.

It's one of the few childhood memories I can muster while lying in bed, staring out of my tiny window at the flashing neon sign of the Jolly Rajah restaurant opposite. 'I am making your phavourite dish today, Baba, chicken curry' he would say as I stared at him with all the immediate intensity only a six-year-old boy can summon. Ma would come in and remonstrate – why did he spend so much on vegetables and was he cheating her, and did he want her to fire him and get another cook? Suresh would nod and smile at this weekly ritual as he stirred his pot, hypnotising me with every one of his economical movements. Then I'd get bored and move on to something else that the intervening quarter-century has blurred out of focus.

The kitchen in Tandoori Knights was stifling. The extractor fan wheezed its complaints as it competed with the sizzling hiss from the pans, trying to funnel out the smoke from the pot of frying onions, ginger and garlic that was making my eyes tear up. I downed a pint of water, dabbed at my face with a sleeve and threw in a handful of lamb chunks. As I tossed the pieces around with a wooden spoon to brown them, I considered the dramas this ancient, blackened pot must have witnessed since the restaurant first opened on Brick Lane thirty years ago. The cooking pan was almost as old as I was, and had stoically accepted a litany of flames, vegetables, flesh, bones and spices while I was taking my first wobbly steps, crying on my first day of school, having my first ecstatic kiss. I added a couple of spoonfuls of yoghurt, a handful of fresh, chopped fenugreek, and mixed it all up with a well-practised twist of the wrist. Suresh would be proud if he could see me now – 'Baba can make his phavourite food himself, no need for old Suresh any more'.

No need for my old Kolkata life any more. No need to be a detective any more. No need for clues, witnesses, evidence statements. Just mounds of spices from which to conjure up the magic that made our guests happy to pay their bills without complaint. I no longer missed my old life – I was busy driving towards my new future, appreciating the road ahead instead of navigating via a rear-view mirror.

'Baingan bhuna, extra kajoo.' Salim Mian waddled into the kitchen, voice booming over the hubbub, ever present pristine white napkin over his arm and order book tucked into the upper left pocket of his waiter's outfit.

'Naila in da house!' Anjoli yanked my chain from across the kitchen, where she appeared to be molesting a dead chicken. 'Your girlfriend's here, Kamil; make sure you cook that aubergine with extra love.'

'Piss off,' I said, but my heart gave a tell-tale flutter. Naila was the only person I knew who ordered cashews with everything. I glanced at my watch – 9.45; she was on day shifts this week at the hospital. Must have run long.

'That's piss off, *boss*, to you.' Anjoli deboned her chicken breast with delicate cuts.

'Just keep torturing that chicken, *Boss* – maybe she'll confess where she hid her eggs.' I chopped the aubergine for Naila's meal, the contrasting purple skin and firm white flesh turning brown and soggy as I threw them into the pool of hot oil in the pan. I chucked in the extra red chillies I knew she liked, enjoying their sharp, sinus-piercing sizzle.

'What is this girlfriend business, Kamil? Naila is in London to study, not have boyfriend.' Salim Mian's usual warm tone had sharpened.

'Nothing, Salim Mian. Anjoli's making a stupid joke. We're just friends, you know that. She's been very helpful in getting me settled here.'

Salim Mian was our head waiter and Naila's uncle. Diabetic and overweight, he was fond of me but not supposed to know I was semi-sort-of-kind-of going out with his twenty-one-year-old niece. Naila lived with him, having come over from Lahore two years ago to study nursing at King's, and we'd agreed to keep our non-relationship quiet so as not to cause consternation back in Pakistan.

'Mmm-hmm.' He looked at Anjoli with suspicion, who realised she had screwed up.

'I was just kidding,' she said with a laugh, trying to rescue the situation. 'Anyway, who'd want Kamil as their boyfriend?'

'I'll take the food out, Salim Mian. You sit and have a rest,' I said.

'I will rest when I am dead.' He wagged an accusatory finger at me and sailed back into the restaurant to share his views on the terrible state of the country with the regulars.

'Thanks so much, Anjoli, that was helpful.' I wiped my hands and glanced at my reflection in a shiny new pan hanging on the wall. Just about presentable.

'Any time, lover boy.' Anjoli watched me with an amused expression as I plated the aubergine and cashew dish, threw a naan into a basket and strode into the restaurant.

Tuesdays were quiet and only a few tables were occupied, diners speaking in low tones over their food, the soft piano music and dim lighting giving our East End eatery the air of what I imagined a chic European club was like. Our customers knew nothing of the clanging confusion and chaos that occurred on the other side of the wall where chefs produced their perfect Malabar prawn masala and harra murgh; as far as the guests were concerned those dishes were enchanted out of the air, delectable and Instagram ready.

There she was.

Dressed in her blue and white striped student nurse uniform with the red embroidered King's College London emblem, *Naila Alvi* name badge on display, she tapped away at her phone with a smile on her lips that could speed up global warming. I placed the plate in front of her and slid in opposite, enjoying the relief of sitting, feeling the soft velour of the booth seat under my thighs, that were cramping after hours of standing in the kitchen.

'Hello, Kamil, waitering *and* cooking tonight?' she said, her soft Punjabi accent and affectionate look having its usual effect on my pulse rate.

'You get the full service, Naila.' I returned her smile, astonished as always by the piercing green eyes gazing at me under cinnamon lashes, a relic of a goat-herding ancestor violated in the mountains of the Khyber by an officer in Alexander the Great's army two thousand years ago.

Chapter 2

Tuesday.

'Tum woh detective ho,' were the first words Naila had said to me nine months earlier when I'd first moved from Kolkata to become a waiter in London. 'Tell me your story.'

'And you're the socialite from Pakistan who wants to be a nurse – I already know yours,' I said, Anjoli having filled me in.

'I thought good detectives looked under the skin, not just at the surface, no? *Such* a disappointment.'

Hypnotised by those eyes and unable to think of a good comeback, I grinned like an idiot. 'Sorry to let you down.'

She took pity on me. 'Come, sit with me while Uncle packs his things.'

We'd have the occasional chat when she came into the restaurant. I'd quiz her about her life in Pakistan and she would question me about my past as a detective, my present job holding no interest for her. Then, with Anjoli's encouragement, I asked her out for a drink. We'd gone to the Big Chill, shared a Caesar salad (with extra cashews) sitting side by side on a squashy sofa and revealed to each other what *was* under our skins, the actual things that mattered and what drove us. We shared the loneliness of being the only children of domineering fathers – hers a high-ranking officer in the Pakistani army and mine a retired Kolkata Police commissioner – both worshipping and resenting them in equal measure, knowing we had big boots to fill.

9

'Daddy helped the country so much, did so much good. But it was hard, you know. We would move to a cantonment where I would settle and make friends and then . . . off again after two years. Punjab, Sindh, Baluchistan, Khyber – I saw all of Pakistan. No, that's not even true; I saw only the garrisons, as we were not allowed out much. When I was sixteen, we settled in Lahore, and I suppose that's where my life really began.'

'Well, your dad was a general by then; it must have been pretty comfortable?'

'Ya, we had a big house, servants, the lot and then . . .'

'And then?'

She looked away.

'Nothing. Then I came to London.'

We had many common reference points. I'd been brought up to believe Pakistani and Bengali Muslims were very different, us Bengalis being tolerant, easy-going and cultured while they were rigid, obsessed with money and status. I couldn't be more wrong – Naila had traded in her life of cleaners, chauffeurs and cooks for scrubs, SARS and stethoscopes, seeming to endure student life with a cheery curiosity. I enjoyed unburdening myself, her gentle probing eliciting confessions I had shared with few people, including the break-up of my engagement with Maliha, how I'd given up my career in the police, and my feelings about living in London. I hadn't been able to glean much about *her* past relationships, and trawling through Facebook and Instagram yielded nothing about her life in Pakistan – just a few anodyne selfies with hospital colleagues (#Nightingales) and London landmarks (#Londonlife).

These intermittent conversations (I didn't dare to call them dates) petered out as I got caught up in the Rakesh Sharma death and its fallout and our lives went their separate ways, with me ruminating now and then about what might have been.

Then four weeks ago.

'It's my twenty-first tomorrow and I'm celebrating with friends at this club in the West End. You and Anjoli are coming.'

'I don't know, Naila. I'm not a dancing kind of guy and . . .'

'Such a mood breaker, yaar. You *are* coming.'

So, it was off to Tiger Tiger to hang out with her college friends till, after a few cocktails, she dragged me away from the table, laughing at my pathetic attempts to seem cool on the dance floor. Destiny's Child's 'Survivor' came on and she yelled, 'My favourite song!' put an arm around my shoulders and took a selfie. The mirrorball lit up her eyes as Beyoncé vibrated in the air and she said, 'Well, if you're not going to, I have to.'

The kiss seemed to go on for ever as we held each other, the still point of the crowds of people swirling around us. The last chants of the song faded, and we floated back to the table, where she acted as if nothing had happened. But my world had been rocked on its axis.

The very occasional snog was as far as we had gone since then, our living arrangements making it difficult to take things further. Maybe that was a good thing. She was a different generation from me and I was still figuring out my feelings for Anjoli that had germinated during the Sharma killing.

Who was I kidding! It was frustrating as hell. Naila was the most stunning woman I'd been out with – not that I had much of a track record in that respect. Besides the intelligent cardamom-green eyes with the laughter lines, she was tall with chai latte skin, hazelnut hair tumbling around her face and a wide strawberry-red mouth that always seemed on the edge of a smile. The polar opposite of Anjoli, who was petite with skin the colour of cappuccino (with an extra shot), rounded features, big chocolate manga eyes and plum lips pursed, always ready for an argument. I guess I didn't have a 'type' – other than that they were describable in food terms. In the desert of my love life, I'd have latched on to any woman who showed interest in me. But I'd struck lucky with Naila, although she was not only way out of my league, we weren't even playing the same sport.

Chapter 3

Tuesday.

With Salim Mian hovering around, I painted a 'just friends' expression on my face and watched Naila dig into her food.

'Long day?'

Before she could reply, the phone lying next to her plate buzzed, *Imran* came up on the screen. Lips compressed, she rejected it, turning it face down. After a few seconds, it buzzed again, and she clicked it off without looking.

'It *was* a long day, but . . .' The smile in her eyes told me she was about to launch into one of her improbable tales of life on the front line of the NHS. She didn't disappoint. 'So, remember I told you I was starting my placement in Emergency Medicine, because Respiratory finished last week? Well, it was quite a first day. This fellow came in with an agonising kidney stone, so I left him with a jug and told him to drink as much water as possible so we could treat him. After a few minutes, I smelled something funny and found him smoking a joint! Ward mein! In the actual ward! He looked at me all innocent and said it was all he had to stop the pain. Can you *imagine*?'

I was never sure whether to believe these stories of Naila's. This one was amusing – her tales of being vomited on or split colostomy bags less so.

'Did you ask for a puff?'

She laughed and slapped my hand, her touch sending an electric charge through me. 'Hardly, yaar! I'd be rusticated! No, I just took it off him before the head nurse could see. We treated him, and as he was leaving, he asked if he could have it back. What a cheek!'

'Do you still have it? We can have a party later.'

'Tauba! And here I thought you were a nice, law-abiding detective.'

A voice interrupted. 'He's not a detective, he's a cook! Who's not doing his job. Shove up, I need a break too. Naila, we haven't seen you in a while. All okay?'

Anjoli, carrying a sheaf of menus and deciding I could do with more of her hilarious ribbing, had deigned to join us. I shuffled across the booth as she slid in next to me, tossing the menus in front of her.

'Ya, been crazy busy. I love the work, but it's *so* emotionally and physically exhausting. Had to hit the library after classes because the end-of-term exams are coming up. Then I thought I would grab a bite to wind down so I could take Uncle home at the end of his shift.'

'I don't know how you do it, Naila,' said Anjoli. 'I thought my psych course was tough, but this? My hat goes off to you.'

'Well, I need to go home with a first to show the family it was worth all the money. I absolutely adore that T-shirt, Anj.'

Anjoli looked down at her top, which read *A Working Class Heroine Is Something To Be.* 'Thanks, I can make you one if you like.'

'That would be amazing. You're quite the artist.'

'But *are* you working class though, Anjoli?' I said. 'What with your private school education and all.'

She shot me a look. 'I work and I have class as opposed to *certain* cooks I know.'

Naila stepped in, her trademark Urdu-English-Millennialese

amusing me. 'Yeh redecoration peng hai. How do Saibal Uncle and Maya Aunty like it?'

Anjoli looked around with a hint of pride at the white walls, arty black and white abstract photos, polished wooden floor and bright red and blue tablecloths. Tearing down the faded wallpaper, the fake chandelier and the worn carpet with decades of food ground into it had been cathartic for her. And good for business.

'Yeah, with them away in India, I thought I would exercise my managerial privileges and modernise the place. The old decor was a little too "Look at us, we're brown" for me. Baba hasn't seen it yet, but I sent him pictures and he came back with "Very nice but looks expensive" so I'll take that as approval. Although, to be honest, maybe I did spend too much. We're stretched thin as it is. I had to take a loan from the bank.'

Anjoli's parents were in Kolkata for six months to look after her uncle who hadn't been keeping well, and with reluctance she'd given up her new market research job to join the family business. Once she stopped grousing about having to waste a psychology degree on 'lookin' after a bloomin' restaurant in Brick Lane' she had thrown all her frustrations into the project – redecorating, changing the menu, building a presence on social media – and it was paying off. We were getting a different type of diner – younger, richer, less prone to get drunk and cause trouble – and were doing ever more covers a night as our reputation grew. She'd even considered changing the name of the restaurant ('Tandoori Knights is so naff') but worried her father would consider that a step too far. She pulled strings to get a positive review in the *Evening Standard* ('An authentic serving of Kolkata in Brick Lane'), which turbocharged the business. It was still hand to mouth, but a few grains of rice were now dropping out of the hand to be squirrelled away.

I had tried to talk to Anjoli about how she felt in the aftermath of the previous year's murder, but she always brushed me off – 'It's done Kamil, let's not dwell on it.' Sometimes, when she thought I wasn't looking, I would see a hint of the emotional scars that remained. A tendril of sadness would blow across her face as her attention shifted inwards, and I knew she was reliving the traumatic incarceration of her best friend, Neha. At other times it was more obvious when her mood dropped from mountain peak to valley trough in the space of a brief conversation. I wanted to help, but couldn't find a way in.

I'd changed too. Solving the case saw the return of my self-esteem. I left the trauma of being fired from the Kolkata Police behind and discovered a flair for cooking ('The Kashmiri rogan josh is the best I've ever eaten'), earning a decent wage, enjoying life in London. I'd even made friends – the imam at my mosque and Sergeant Tahir Ismail, an old pal of Anjoli's. He would come for dinner with his Tinder dates once a week, and we'd swap war stories about the similarities and differences in the Kolkata and Met Police and our mutual love of detective stories. 'Once a cop always a cop, Kamil, even if you try to hide it under a chef's hat. You should think about applying to the Met. We need more diversity around here.' But being a 'diversity hire' didn't appeal; my spare time was now spent researching new dishes on YouTube to justify my self-generated head chef title.

'Hello! Brick Lane to Kamil!' Anjoli waved a menu in my face and jarred me back to the restaurant; Naila looking at me from across the table, segment of naan in hand.

'Sorry, was miles away,' I said as the bell at the door tinkled, signalling a customer.

'I was just telling Anjoli that— Salma! Hello!' said Naila, a note of surprise entering her voice as she looked across to the young woman who had come in.

'Oh. Naila. What are you doing here?'

'My uncle works here; I was having a bite before taking him

home. I thought you said you were going back to yours? I would have given you a lift if I'd known you were coming here too.' She turned to us. 'Salma's my batchmate in college and we're placed together at Tommy's.'

'Hi, I'm Kamil.' I waved at Salma as she gave me a thin smile and waggled a hand holding a phone, seeming twitchy and ill at ease. Smaller than Naila, with a round Bangla face, she had a shocking-pink hijab draped over her head and shoulders, hiding all her hair and contrasting with the stripy nursing student's uniform that covered her stocky frame.

'I ordered takeaway,' she said, fiddling with the end of her headscarf, looking around for a waiter.

'Oh yes, I took the order. Nice to see you again. Salma, right? Sit here, I'll check.' Anjoli scooted into the kitchen.

Salma hesitated for a moment, then perched at the extreme edge of the booth as if I had a communicable disease, clutching at her phone like a security blanket, eyes drilling a hole into the menu on the table. There was an awkward silence as Naila and I looked at each other, mouths smiling, brows puzzled.

Salma's phone squawked into life and I got a glimpse of Z flashing up on the screen as her face tightened and her thumb snapped off the call. After a few seconds it rang again; she rejected it once more and slapped the phone on the table in front of her. What *was* it with these women not answering their phones?

'Everything okay, Salma?' said Naila.

Salma's head shot up as if surprised she wasn't alone. She seemed about to speak, gave a brief nod, then looked back down at the menu.

Naila raised a 'Well, I tried' eyebrow at me and carried on eating, the clink of her cutlery sounding overly loud as Anjoli returned with a brown paper bag containing Salma's takeaway.

'Let's see, one chicken biryani and one dal makhani. Was that it? Seventeen pounds fifty, please.'

Salma grabbed her handbag and scuttled out of the booth, the menu sliding to the floor under the table. She extracted a twenty from her purse, tossed it on the tablecloth, said, 'Keep the change,' snatched the food and rushed out of the restaurant.

Anjoli shouted after her, 'See you again . . . soon,' her voice fading as the door drifted shut and the three of us stared at the space where Salma had been.

Naila shook her head. 'She is a strange girl, that one.'

'She seemed nervous. Are the two of you friends?'

'We have a few classes together. But she's always like that. Jumpy one minute, like she expects to be attacked, and aggressive the next. Anyway,' she smiled and pushed away her plate, 'maybe I'll treat myself to rusgulla while I wait for Uncle. Kamil, would you mind?'

'Sure.' I picked up her dishes, clean as always, and went into the kitchen as she got back to her phone.

I brought her the super-sweet dessert, nodded to the last diners as they left, turned the sign on the door to CLOSED FOR NOW. PLEASE COME BACK AS YOU HAVE JUST MISSED THE BEST MEAL YOU NEVER HAD (another Anjolism) and helped Anjoli, Salim Mian and the other waiters clear the tables, prior to tackling the kitchen, which Anjoli insisted be left 'spick-span' every night, borrowing a phrase from her mother. We were an excellent team, all in our well-practised roles, working in harmony, wiping things down, replacing tablecloths, shuttling dirty dishes back to the kitchen. A convivial silence had descended on the restaurant when the warm voice of Bob Marley telling us to get up and stand up for our rights shattered the quiet.

I tracked the sound to under Naila's table and bent to find a mobile warbling at me, the oversized clock on the screen showing 10:47 p.m. I picked it up. 'Hello?'

A panicked voice. 'Is that Tandoori Knights restaurant?'

'Yes. How can I help?'

'Oh, thank God. My name is Salma Ali. I just picked up my takeaway and left my phone. Can I come and get it?'

Appearances could be deceptive – that twitchy woman hadn't struck me as a Marley fan.

'Hi, it's Kamil; we just met. Yes, I have the phone; it must have dropped under the table. Shall I give it to Naila to give you in college tomorrow?'

A pause. 'I really need it tonight. Can I please come for it?'

This was a pain. I was ready for bed and didn't fancy hanging around waiting for her.

'We're about to close. How long will you be? I can just get Naila to—'

'I'm only twenty minutes away. Please. It's important.'

'Hang on.' I covered the phone and said to Anjoli. 'Salma left her mobile. She wants to pick it up. Says she'll be twenty minutes.'

'That's fine,' said Anjoli. 'We'll still be here.'

'She lives in Bethnal Green,' said Naila. 'She'll never be here in twenty minutes; the night bus takes ages. If she's so desperate, I'll drive over and give it back while you finish here. Uncle, I can be there and back in fifteen, otherwise who knows how long you will have to stay and Alaya Aunty is alone at home.'

'That is a lot of problem, Naila,' said Salim Mian. 'It's late; I don't want you to go alone to a strange place at night. Wait for me to finish and we can drop it off on the way home.'

'All right.' Naila went back to picking at the last bits of her dessert.

I was about to pass this on to Salma when I realised this was an ideal opportunity for me to spend alone time with Naila. 'That will make it very late for Salma, Salim Mian. Tell you what, *I'll* drive over with Naila to make sure she's okay, and we'll be back soon.' Naila hid a smile at my transparent ruse as her uncle gave me a suspicious look but then nodded and went back to clearing up.

'Okay. Salma give me your address,' I said. 'We'll drop it off. No, it's no problem. You relax and eat your biryani before it gets cold.'

I stood over Naila's shoulder and recited the address while Naila tapped it into her phone. As I hung up, Naila's phone rang, *Imran* popping up on her screen again. She glanced at me, expressionless. 'I have to take this. Hello? Wait a minute.'

'I'll change and be back in a sec,' I said.

She nodded and made her way to the toilet decorated with the stylised image of a pair of thick-lashed eyes (another instance of Anjoli's frenzied creativity). I dashed upstairs through the inner door from the restaurant storeroom to the flat I shared with Anjoli, tore off my chef's whites and shrugged on a pair of jeans, eagerly anticipating my night drive with Naila.

When I came down, she still hadn't emerged from the loo, so I helped Salim Mian wash up in the kitchen as Anjoli sat behind the bar and totted up the day's takings. Naila came out at a few minutes past eleven, face stony. She forced a smile and gave a twenty-pound note to Anjoli. 'Thanks for dinner, delicious as always.'

'Naila, why are you giving money to her? You are insulting me in my restaurant,' grumbled Salim Mian.

'Please Uncle, you do everything for me already, you are like my father; let me have this bit of independence. Here, I brought your cholesterol tablets from the hospital; take them before we leave, otherwise you'll forget. See you shortly. Chalo, Kamil.'

'Be careful,' Salim Mian called after us, pocketing the tablets.

We walked out into the soft May Brick Lane night.

Chapter 4

Tuesday.

Walking to Naila's car, we passed the orange brick facade of the East London Mosque. The white minarets reached up to embrace the deep purple night sky as a thin new moon far above reflected the metal crescent of the Adhan tower floating overhead. It was quiet now, waiting for the muezzin to call the faithful to prayer.

I have a complicated relationship with religion. While I'm not faith*less,* neither am I among the faith*ful,* I'm more of a *have-faith-when-it-suits-me* kind of guy. Years of traipsing around masjids and being inculcated into the rituals of Islam by my parents had the opposite effect to the one they'd intended – at fifteen I'd rebelled, proclaimed, 'All organised religion is evil,' and, much to Ma's dismay, stopped visiting all mosques.

But last year, at one of the lowest points in my life, I rediscovered the comforts of worship. I'd been searching for a direction, feeling abandoned by my family and people I'd loved, so wandered back into the easy familiarity of rituals that allowed me to slow my mind and breathe in thirteen hundred years of community and warmth. Imam Masroor and I met every couple of weeks, when he would try to guide me back to the path he thought I needed, while I enjoyed his company and sharp intelligence.

'Your jihad will continue,' he said.

'What jihad? I'm not struggling with anything. I'm happy.'

He looked at me with his usual inscrutable gaze. 'Outside you are happy, Kamil. Inside, you are struggling.'

Such gnomic comments had turned me away from mosques in the first place, but I let this one pass. I wasn't on the path yet; I was perhaps on a trail leading to a track that might get me to the path.

A voice called: 'Hello, Kamil.'

Yasir.

Huddled under a worn blanket in the mosque's doorway, Yasir was a rough sleeper who had staked out this spot as his own. Anjoli and I would bring him leftovers from the restaurant a few times a week, and he would accept them, nodding a benediction to us as though the cartons of korma and dal were his due, and it was right and just that we should make offerings to him, seated like a venerable caliph in front of the mosque. We'd bring him to the restaurant from time to time, where he'd tell us about his life in Syria.

He'd been a chemical engineer in Aleppo, married, with two grown-up children. And then the bombing started, rebels fighting the Syrian government. As Anjoli cajoled, feeding him tea, samosas and desserts, the words emerged as if they were being extracted like teeth, one by one. 'This gulab jamun is nice, Anjoli, but nothing like the awameh Rima used to make. She made the best desserts – our neighbours used to come on Friday mornings to try her zlebiye. That taste, I never forget it. I do not know, Anjoli, how to tell you. I do not know how much else I remember. Or want to remember. All I have left are . . . little pieces. Fragments. Aleppo was a beautiful city. Peaceful. We used to go to the Umayyad mosque at night for prayers. All lit up. Meet our friends. The entire family. Or the souk al-Zarab. Buy things to eat. When the children were small, they loved the noise and the colours. All the normal things we took for granted. Then the bombing started . . .'

His eyes drilled through the walls of Anjoli's kitchen, and instead of Brick Lane, it was as though he could see rubble, smoke and screaming children. He took a sip of tea and continued: 'She and I used to lie in bed at night, just waiting for the next explosion. Was that nearer? Further? Trying to calculate from the noise. Would the next mortar land on our house? Imagine, Anjoli. Just imagine. We were helpless. Last November in London. The fireworks. People were going ooh and aah, but for me . . . the noise . . . Then that day. I went to get food. A little bread here. Cheese there. I came back and . . .'

The intensity vanished, and his voice became toneless. Eyes blank.

Anjoli looked at me. Should we ask him to stop? Perhaps he felt he *had* to tell us this because we had fed him. I felt like a vampire sucking at his misery.

Yasir brushed a speck of dust off the sleeve of the grubby blue suit he always wore. 'It was all destroyed. Our full apartment block. I searched and searched the rubble, but never found them. Not Rima. Not Jamal. Not Saad. Not Rima. Not Jamal. Not Saad.' It sounded like an invocation. 'They were gone. Obliterated like they had never been. Of course, not just them. My neighbours and friends. Some alive. Most dead. The screams. Then the quiet. I remember the silence after the screaming. I looked for them for days. Something to bury. But there was nothing. Nothing. Not Rima. Not Jamal. Not Saad.'

His voice trailed away. Anjoli, eyes moist, put her hand on his.

On another day over rice, dal and spinach he told us about the horrors of leaving the city of his birth to make the treacherous journey in a tiny boat on the Mediterranean, crammed with other refugees, buffeted by wind and waves, hoping to make landfall in Europe.

He was one of the lucky ones. He made it to Italy and from there to the UK. He was vague on the details of *that* trip – the people smugglers he had to deal with and the desperation he had seen along the way. England was his dream. It was where he had studied for his degree – at Southampton University all those years ago – and where he now hoped to rebuild a shattered life.

But that vision ended in a web of bureaucracy.

Not eligible for asylum.

No explanation.

He showed us the Home Office letter that stated, 'You are liable to be detained as it has been ascertained that you are liable for deportation,' then folded it with care and put it in his pocket as if it was a holy relic. Without legal immigration status, he was classified as 'No Recourse to Public Funds' and not allowed any benefits or access to official services. And so he had ended up in the mosque's doorway, relying on the kindness of strangers and dreaming of times with Rima, Jamal and Saad in the souk al-Zarab.

He smiled as Naila and I passed, teeth white in a weathered face that could have been anywhere from forty to eighty. I tossed a fifty-pence coin into the cup in front of him and said, 'Hi, Yasir. Sorry, no food today.'

He nodded his thanks. 'Money is food, food is life, so money is life.'

Naila reached into her handbag and a pound coin rattled in, joining my fifty p. 'Here's more life for you then. You know him?' she said as we walked on.

'He's a friend of Anjoli's. She's adopted several homeless people around here. Saibal-da used to give our leftovers to the Whitechapel Mission, but now Anjoli prefers to give it straight to the people on the street. Cutting out the middleman, she says.'

I told Naila Yasir's story, ending with '... the imam at the mosque lets him sleep here and we feed him when we can. Nice guy, always smiling. Amazing he can, given the suffering he's experienced. I would be raging.'

Naila fell silent for a moment before turning to look at Yasir, who waved. Then she said, 'It's terrible that aaj kal there are so many homeless around London. The lives they lead are worse than in Lahore. At least there people have families to care for them, even if they live in slums. At the hospital we are told not to admit certain homeless people because they fake illnesses to get a bed for the night – their pictures are on the walls in admissions and everything. Can you believe that? Hospitals are meant to care.'

'I know. Sometimes this area is like the worst bits of Kolkata.'

We arrived at Salim Mian's battered Vauxhall Astra and I punched Salma's address into Waze as Naila put the car into gear. 'Eleven minutes.'

I glanced at her profile, sharp against the shop lights of Mile End Road as we drove in silence through stop-start traffic. 'You okay?'

'Sorry, I was just thinking.'

'Of what?'

She hesitated. 'Maloom nahin. Just wondering what I am doing here. Did I make the right decision or was I too impulsive? My life in Lahore was very different.'

'Who's Imran?' I said, curious about the call she had not wanted to take.

A shadow flickered across her face. 'Someone from . . . home. It doesn't matter.'

'Must be, what, three in the morning in Pakistan? Is everything all right?'

'Fine.'

'How *was* your life in Lahore different from here?'

'There were bad times, but . . . there were good times too. I forget those sometimes. Here I just spend my time in lectures, slaving away in the hospital, studying in my tiny room at Salim Uncle's. London isn't all I thought it would be, to be honest. It's exhausting.'

25

'Oh?' A chill built in my belly as I essayed a casualness I didn't feel. 'Are you thinking of quitting and going back to Pakistan?'

'I don't know if I can.'

'Why?'

Her face hardened and some remembered pain floated into her eyes.

'I can't be myself there. It's ... constricting. If I hadn't left when I did, I don't know what would have happened to me. I'm ... freer here.'

This made no sense to me, after what she had just said about being stuck in college, hospital and her room. How was that freedom? There was a darkness in her I hadn't seen before.

I tried to lighten the mood. 'All that high-society life in Lahore got too much for you?'

She rewarded me with a grateful waggle of her head.

'Ya. Something like that. Although clubs and kitty parties and gossipy afternoons were not my style. But when I am changing catheters in the hospital, the thought of a beer in Lahore Gymkhana is very tempting.' She smiled, shutting off further questioning. 'But *you* make up for the problems of living in London. I'm happy we are friends.'

Friends? I reached out and squeezed the hand she had extended, churning inside. I sneaked a look at her again; the soft vulnerability on her face.

She caught me looking. 'Maybe more than friends.'

A warm rush to my head.

We drove the rest of the way in silence.

Chapter 5

Tuesday.

The address Salma had given me was an unprepossessing cul-de-sac called Usk Street off Lilac Lane off Smart Street – the town planner appeared to have been influenced by *Noddy in Toyland*. Naila parked on a double yellow line and said, 'You stay in the car in case there are any traffic wardens; I'll give her the phone and be right back.'

Her 'more than friends' line still ringing in my head, I said, 'What's the hurry, Naila? Salma can wait a few more minutes for her phone. We get so little time on our own, come and sit in the back seat with me.'

A moment's silence as she considered this, then a crooked smile edged its way across her face. 'Oh, you had an *ulterior* motive. I'd never have guessed!' Taking a quick look around, she followed me into the back.

We looked into each other's eyes for a moment, then I took her face in my hands and kissed her, the taste of her strawberry lip gloss and her flowery perfume filling my senses. I closed my eyes, relishing the moment. But something felt off, and she didn't seem into it. I pulled away reluctantly and took her hand instead. 'Are you okay?'

'Sorry, Kamil. It's not you, I promise. Just have a few things on my mind.'

'You can talk to me, you know.'

'I know. I will. Just not now. Not . . .' she gestured at our grim surroundings, '. . . here.'

I seized the moment. 'We need to make the most of our time. Especially if you're seriously thinking of going back to Pakistan.'

'What do you mean?'

In for a rupee . . . 'Basically, I was thinking we could go away for a weekend. The coast, maybe? See the sea? Anjoli and Salim Mian's flats are not an ideal . . . situation.'

Silence. Could she hear my heart hammering? It sounded like it was echoing through the car. Was it time to disentangle my fingers?

Then a squeeze.

'I miss the sea. Let's find a weekend soon.'

Eid, Christmas and Diwali arrived simultaneously.

'Great. I'll organise something.'

She kissed her fingertips and brushed my lips with them. 'I look forward to it. Now let me give Salma her phone or Salim Uncle will send out a search party of relatives.'

'No, I'll do it. You wait here. Lock your doors.'

I leaped out of the car and strode towards the two-storey block of flats, sitting squat and ugly like a toad guarding its patch on a murky lily pond. I could hear music from a television set above me and the hum of traffic from the main road as I picked my way through the crisp packets and lager cans that littered the path. The night was warm, edging on oppressive, and a pervasive smell of rotting rubbish from the bins slimed sinuously around me as I approached the main entrance door to the block. *Noddy Goes Dumpster Diving.*

A harsh blast of techno music shattered the night. A group of teenagers were sitting on a low wall a few metres away, one of them fiddling with a phone and a speaker as a couple nodded along with the music, lit roll-ups in their fingers creating comet trails as the sweet smell of weed drifted over to me. The light over the doorway was broken, so I held up my phone to locate the buzzer to Flat 12. Just then the door slammed open and a figure dashed past, catching my shoulder and causing me to stumble. I glimpsed a hunched frame, pale yellow hoodie pulled low over a face, and it was gone.

I darted in through the closing door – it wasn't surprising Salma was jittery, living in a place like this. A sign pointing up the stairs said, FLATS 7–12, and I walked up, my phone torch providing a cone of security, flashing off the graffitied walls of the stairwell.

Flat 12 was at the end of a covered walkway overlooking the street. The techno music was still audible. A mother yelled at a child to go to sleep inside a flat, startling me. Over the railings I saw Naila cocooned in the car, face lit by her phone, tapping away as usual. Good thing she hadn't come up. This place would have terrified her into booking the next flight back to Lahore.

I got to the end of the walkway and rapped on the door.

'Hi, Salma, it's Kamil. I've got your phone.'

To my surprise, my knock caused the door to creak open, and a shaft of light from the flat coupled with the sound of laughter from a television programme enveloped me.

Then I felt it.

That part of my reptile brain telling me something was very wrong. I'd learned to pay attention to it from my cop days – the ice cube tingling in the back of my neck that spread down my spine and arms, making my fingers twitch, all my senses on high alert – danger, danger . . .

I stepped into a neat, well-painted hallway, taking in everything with the clarity of a high-definition movie camera – small table with a set of keys in a bowl, coats hanging on hooks on the wall, framed print of a mountain scene – all in distinct contrast to the grubbiness outside. I moved further into the flat, shouting over the TV, 'Salma, your door was open,' but there was no response.

The open door of a bedroom on my left, the inside empty save for a made-up bed. At the end of the corridor, a tiny kitchenette and a living room with a sofa, the TV tuned to a rowdy game show splashing colours on the wall.

And on the face of the dead woman lying on the carpeted floor.

Salma.

Eyes open, staring at the ceiling, face twisted, tongue protruding from her mouth. Red blotches under her eyes where blood vessels had burst. Dressed in the same nurse's uniform I'd seen her in at the restaurant just ninety minutes ago. But her pink hijab was now knotted around her neck instead of covering the hair which was fanned around her white face.

In death she looked twenty years older.

I panned around to make sure the room was empty, then, heart beating like syncopated tablas and finding it hard to breathe, I knelt and put a hand to her cheek. Still warm. I felt for a heartbeat. Nothing.

Was the killer still here? Unlikely. I had seen pretty much all there was of this minuscule flat. The open door meant they had left in a hurry. The figure that had pushed past me, just a few minutes ago . . . My God, was that the murderer? Had I just seen him?

I wiped my hand on my jeans and stood. My phone informed me it was 11.37 as I dialled 999. I gave them the details and was told to wait where I was and not touch anything. I hung up and looked around where Salma had lived a tiny part of her brief life. Through force of habit, I took out my phone and documented the scene, starting with the corpse.

The living room was simple, just a threadbare red sofa, a non-matching armchair, an overturned blue-painted crate that had played the part of a coffee table, a few black hairpins scattered on the carpet and the TV. There was a small window overlooking what seemed to be a courtyard, with lit windows opposite. Salma had tried to brighten up her home with colourful prints on the wall, but nothing took away from the flat's depressing air of having given up. The kitchen had four cabinets on the wall, a tiny cooker and an even tinier table with two folding chairs. There was a plate with a partially eaten portion of biryani on the table, takeaway cartons from Tandoori Knights next to it. I felt a shaft of sadness as I remembered telling Salma to enjoy her biryani before it got cold and imagined her starting her meal as she waited for me to come and return her phone.

Then someone else had come calling.

I made my way into her bedroom, which was as neat as the rest of the flat, continuing to take photographs as I moved. Just a single bed with a side table, a copy of the Holy Koran and a handful of black pins similar to the ones on the carpet in the living room. For her hijab, I guessed. A door led to a bathroom with a shower and a toilet, a few cosmetics beside the wash-basin. I looked in the medicine cabinet but there was nothing out of the ordinary.

A voice at the door. 'Salma, are you there? Kamil? What is taking so long? I have to pick up Salim Uncle.'

Damn. I had forgotten about Naila.

'Naila, don't . . .' I rushed into the hall to stop her entering, but it was too late.

She was in the living room, mouth open in an O of horror, staring at the body.

'W-what . . .'

'Naila, come away from there. Salma's been murdered.' I took her arm.

'Murdered!' She jerked away from me to crouch next to the corpse, slipped her fingers under the scarf tied around Salma's neck, felt for a pulse, then put her ear to her chest. Hearing nothing, she stayed on her knees and stared at Salma's face. She seemed to be looking deep into her eyes as if the picture of the killer might be imprinted there, the last thing the dead girl had seen.

She shook her head then put her hands on Salma's chest, pressing down rhythmically, counting under her breath, 'Ek, do, teen, char . . .' When she reached thirty, she bent and breathed into Salma's mouth and then started the CPR again: 'Ek, do, teen, char . . .'

She gave up, desolation covering her face. 'She has expired.'

I eased her hand away from the body, put my arms under her shoulders and pulled her up. 'We have to go. We can't contaminate the crime scene. The police will be here any minute. I saw someone leave as I came in. That might have been the killer.'

'Who was it? A woman with a shopping bag coming into the flats let me in. Was it her?'

'Was she in a yellow hoodie?'

'No.'

'Then it was someone else, I couldn't make out who. It was dark. Come, let's stand outside.'

Naila took another look at Salma's body and stumbled out after me. We stood outside the flat, looking over the railing for any sign of the police but just seeing the teenagers dancing to their music and Naila's car, flashing its hazard lights forlornly into the night.

'Are you okay?'

'No, of course not.' Her voice shook. 'Y'Allah, who has done this?'

'In the restaurant you said she was strange. What did you mean?'

'What? I don't know. She liked to get involved in causes. Always sure she was right. Complained a lot. Oh no!' She

32

clapped a palm over her mouth. 'I'm speaking ill of the dead, I don't mean to. And . . . Kamil, we were *kissing* downstairs while she was . . . she was . . .'

I put my arms around her and held her close. She pulled away.

'Salim Uncle. He'll be waiting for me. I have to call him.'

'What are you going to say?'

She dialled.

'Salim Uncle? It's Naila. I'm sorry, but something terrible has happened. We came to give Salma her phone and Kamil found her dead. Yes, dead. It's awful. We are waiting for the police. You better go home on your own by Uber, I don't know how long they will keep us.' I heard Salim Mian squawking at the other end. 'No, I'm fine. I'll see you soon.'

She hung up, hands trembling, staring at the road below.

My phone rang. Anjoli. She had heard Salim Mian's side of the conversation and wanted to know what was going on. I told her as much as I could and said I'd be home as soon as the police had finished with us.

I put a hand on Naila's to comfort her as we heard the sounds of a siren, and an unmarked car, lights flashing, screeched to a halt below us. Two men got out, and I shouted, 'Up here! Wait, I'll let you in.'

I ran down the steps and opened the door. 'I'm the one who phoned 999. Follow me.'

'I'm DI Rogers and this is DS Ismail,' said the older of the two plain-clothes police officers. 'Please step back, sir.'

Tall, toned, square-jawed with deep-set eyes, Tahir Ismail looked at me in surprise. 'Kamil, what are you doing here?'

'Oh, Tahir. I found the body.'

'I know him, guv,' said Tahir. 'He's a cook at Tandoori Knights. He used to be a copper. In India. Helped clear up the Bishops Avenue killing last year. Show us, Kamil.'

I stepped back as they entered and looked around the stair-well, Tahir's wiry body a contrast to his flabbier boss. They followed me up to Naila standing at the end of the walkway, Rogers breathing hard with the effort.

'This is Naila Alvi,' I said. 'Let me show you . . .'

'That's all right, sir,' said Rogers. 'We can find our way from here. Will the two of you please wait outside?'

They went into the flat and I heard the crackling of a radio with Rogers saying, 'IC-4, female, twenties. No sign of life, 1151 hours. Please inform LAS, SOCO, on duty CID and the duty officer. Flat 12, Jane Harrington House, Usk Street.'

It was odd being a bystander at a crime scene. In Kolkata I would have been the one calling the shots, directing my team. Here I was . . . nothing. It was a relief in a way. I stood next to Naila, holding her hand.

After some time, Tahir and Rogers came back out and questioned us about the events of the night. I told them all I knew, handing them Salma's mobile, which was still in my pocket.

'I found the body and called 999 at 11.37.'

'Is that when the two of you arrived at the flats?' said Rogers.

I glanced at Naila. 'We must have got here around 11.20 maybe?'

'Oh? And what were you doing for seventeen minutes?'

Naila looked down at the floor as I said, 'Actually . . . Naila's my girlfriend and we were . . . well, cuddling in the car.'

Tahir smothered a smile as I tried to redeem myself. 'But I may have seen the killer leave. As I was coming in, someone rushed out. Just before I came up – after 11.30.'

'Can you describe them, sir?' said Rogers.

'Medium height and build. Yellow hoodie pulled down over their face. Dark jeans. I couldn't say if it was a man or a woman. Naila saw a woman arrive.'

'White? Asian? Black?' said Tahir, notebook at the ready.

'I don't know, I didn't see their face.'

'Did you notice their hands?' said Rogers.

I tried to focus on the moment the figure had collided with me. Nothing. I shook my head.

Tahir made a note as Rogers nodded. 'Can you please continue to wait; we'll tell you when you can leave.'

By now about a dozen neighbours had figured out something was happening and were gathering, a buzz of speculation filling the air as they watched Tahir unroll crime scene tape, stick it across the door of Flat 12 and then angle it to the railing to form a barrier between them and the end of the walkway. I could see them wondering who the hell Naila and I were and why we were standing inside the taped-off zone.

They pushed towards the tape, the older ones groggy with sleep, the younger with cameras in their hands recording what was going on. Lights clicked on in windows around the block, silhouettes appearing. All death was public property now to be tweeted and Facebooked and Instagrammed with the pride of 'I was there.'

'Hey, did something happen to the girl who lived here?' called a woman in her forties wearing a faded, flower-print dressing gown, pushing against the tape, threatening to break it.

'What makes you think it's the girl?' I said.

'She lived in the end flat. She's a sweet thing but complained about my TV being too loud when she was trying to study. Is she okay?'

Naila nudged me. 'That was the woman who let me in.' Before I could respond the *nee-naw* of an ambulance filled the air and blue lights flashed across the faces of the onlookers as they turned away en masse from gawking at Salma's door to stare greedily over the railing at the arrival of the ambulance and car below. Tahir ducked under the tape, pushed past the crowd and ran down, returning with four men. One of them, carrying a large case, smiled at DI Rogers, who had emerged from the flat. 'Sorry for the delay, Paul. Turned out to be a fight night.'

'Tell me about it,' said the DI, shaking hands with them.

'Gillies, CID.'

'Jackson, LAS.'

'Rogers, Bethnal Green nick.'

I watched three of the men troop after Rogers into the flat, ducking under the red tape as the fourth, a constable, kept people away from the scene. 'So, you SOCO guys asleep as usual? Got you out of your bed, did we? Ruin your Tuesday night?' Rogers said.

'Yeah, yeah. You've been sitting on your arse scoffing doughnuts and coffee,' said the scene of crime officer, 'while we're hard at work . . .' His voice faded into the flat.

The constable and Tahir started taking details of the neighbours as the London Ambulance Service man who had gone into the flat with Rogers emerged, speaking into his radio, 'Jackson here. Victim deceased,' and left.

I gave Tahir a side look to make sure he was occupied, then walked over to the woman in the dressing gown. 'Did you see anything out of the ordinary?'

'No, I just popped out to get fags and milk. I let *her* into the building.' She pointed at Naila. 'Did something happen to the girl? I heard her arguing with someone earlier.'

'When?'

'Let me see, my husband was watching the footie highlights. Just after eleven, maybe?'

'Was it a man or woman you heard?'

'A man. They were shouting, but I couldn't hear what because of the telly. There was a young guy who came to her flat now and then. It may have been him.'

'What did he look like, this young guy?'

'Asian chap. Mid-twenties, maybe? Thin. I saw him here on a few evenings. Is she dead? Are you a cop?'

'Inspector Rahman. And you are . . .'

'Pam. Pam Longfellow.'

'Thank you, Mrs Longfellow.'

Tahir made his way to us. 'You guys can go now, unless you want to *cuddle* some more. We'll need a formal statement, but I'll take that later.'

'I'll be at TK,' I said. 'Impressive interview technique.'

'Piss off. Say hi to Anj. Look after yourself, yeah? If you need a support officer, let me know.'

As we got into the car, the four teenagers around the boombox pointed their phones at us – we would be on Twitter before the night was out.

Naila drove fast, eyes focused on the road, silent.

'If you need to talk later, just call me, okay?' I said. 'The shock will creep up on you.'

She shivered. 'I just want to go home and get into my bed.'

We reached the restaurant, and I jumped out. 'Come by Anjoli's for breakfast in the morning on your way to college.'

She nodded and drove away, taillights disappearing down the now empty street.

I thought my past had sped away in *my* side mirrors but had forgotten that 'Objects in the mirror are closer than they appear.'

Chapter 6

Tuesday.

I kicked off my shoes and collapsed next to Anjoli, who was watching something trashy on television in her worn #SELFIESH T-shirt and pyjama shorts, brown legs tucked under her and cradling a half-empty glass of red wine. She switched the TV off and poured another for me.

'What *happened*?'

I shook my head, trying to find the words. The enormity of what I had experienced was hitting me. I'd eaten nothing since lunch; my brain was mush and I needed my bed.

'She was so young,' I said.

'*You* found the body?'

I nodded. I didn't want to go into everything again, but she'd waited up to find out. I gave her the bare facts, leaving out our 'cuddle'.

'And you can't remember *any* details of the person in the hoodie?' she said when I finished speaking.

'No. I've been racking my brains for the slightest thing, but I didn't pay much attention. Just wanted to give Salma her phone and enjoy the rest of my time alone with Naila.'

'That poor girl. Imagine, if she hadn't left her phone downstairs, she'd still be lying there, undiscovered. She lived alone, right?' She shivered. 'It might have been days. What an awful thought.'

'Although if I'd let her come to pick it up, like she wanted . . .'

Anjoli stared at me.

'Bloody hell, Kamil.'

We lapsed into silence. Then she said, 'Anyway, you can't think like that. It literally wasn't your fault. The killer would have just waited for her to come back and—'

'They might have. But it feels like I'm responsible for what happened . . . I don't know. I'm exhausted. I need to go to bed.'

I got up as she said, 'Don't feel guilty about it, Kamil – it'll drive you crazy. Believe me, I know. Given what happened last year.'

Her voice trailed off.

'Nothing that happened last year was your fault, Anjoli.'

'I know that. But guilt isn't rational, is it? There we were playing cops and robbers and . . .'

'Well, we got there in the end. Everything worked out.'

'It did. All because of you. You were – are – a skilled detective. How is Naila taking it?'

'Pretty shook up. I told her to come by in the morning. This kind of thing can mess you up.'

'She must see worse in the hospital, though?'

I looked at her. 'It doesn't compare. This is someone she *knows*. Who was *strangled*!'

She looked abashed. 'You're right. Sorry. That was thoughtless.'

I turned to leave, and she said, 'You like her, don't you?'

I faced her again. 'Naila?'

'Yes.'

Her question unsettled me.

'I guess so. I mean, I don't know her that well. It's difficult, given the circumstances. Why do you ask?'

She looked down at her wine. 'No reason. You make a delightful couple.'

This disconcerted me even further. 'I'm not sure about that.

39

She's much younger than I am. And who knows if this will lead to anything. She's quite conservative under her bubbly college girl persona. Anyway, I'm not even sure she's what I'm looking for and . . .'

I realised I was babbling and shut up. What was wrong with me?

'You're quite the hopeless romantic, aren't you?'

'Hope*ful* romantic. All romantics are hopeful.'

The silence between us was electric, thrumming with things unsaid. I couldn't take it any more and walked off, but she said, 'Does that make you a better or worse detective?'

'What?'

'Being a romantic.'

I stopped to consider her comment. 'Um, I've no idea. Look I'm knackered, and . . .'

'Well, if you're a hopeful romantic, you must believe everything will work out. Doesn't that get in the way of being an effective cop?'

I was getting exasperated now and not in the mood for a philosophical discussion about policing procedure.

'I don't know.'

'Don't you have to believe everyone is capable of the worst?'

She wasn't going to give up. I took a breath. 'I've always been quite trusting. Maybe I'm too quick to believe people. As opposed to starting from *Why is this bastard lying to me?*'

Her face creased into a smile. 'Kamil, that's why you're so good at it. You have faith in people and excellent instincts – I saw it first hand. You're empathetic – people open up to you. Because you trust them, they trust you. So maybe . . .'

'Maybe what?'

'Maybe *you* should look into what happened to Salma? You and Naila. Like you and I did last year.'

'Why?'

'How happy are you being a cook, Kamil?'

Where was she going with this? I really couldn't deal with Anjoli in psychologist mode.

'I'm happy.'

'Come on, Kamil. You *are* an excellent cook; I'll give you that. But do you want to spend the rest of your life doing this? Any more than I want to be managing this bloody restaurant? Maybe this is your chance? Look into Salma's death, help the police. Tahir knows you. He can vouch for you. Maybe you can find your way back to doing what you love. You said the neighbour heard an argument and saw a young Asian guy visiting Salma. Maybe he was in her class? If you see him, you might be able to tell if it was the same guy running out? You can help solve the crime.'

'I don't even know if it *was* a guy I saw. I'm sure the police will question him, and I can do an identification if they ask me.'

She stood and faced me.

'Or you could try to get ahead of them and check him out yourself?'

This annoyed me. I had settled into a rhythm over the last few months. Had reached a kind of . . . contentment? No, not quite that, but I wasn't *dis*contented. I'd given up my dreams of being a brilliant detective. And now . . . this? And all this talk of romance. What the hell did Anjoli think she was doing?

'*No!*' The word came out harsher than I'd intended. I moderated my tone. 'No. I'm not doing all of that again. Look what happened last time . . . Tahir Ismail's very capable. Being a detective isn't something that—'

'*Listen* to me, Kamil. The difference between you and Tahir is you *care*. About the victim. About people around them. Tahir will just want to solve the case and make his name. Someone has to be on Salma's side. This was the last place she came to before she died – we owe it to her. If you hadn't been there for us last year, I don't know how we would have coped.'

'You'd have coped just fine.'

Her face clouded over and I dialled it down.

'I'm sorry, Anjoli. It's been a shock. I'm done for. You should go to sleep too – it's late.'

Without waiting for a response, I went up the stairs, slammed the door behind me and threw myself onto my bed, embracing the darkness.

Why was I so angry?

Anjoli was being her usual caring self, and I'd behaved like a sulky teenager. Why had I downplayed my feelings for Naila? What *were* my feelings for Naila? Other than desire?

Salma's body swam up to the forefront of my consciousness, the pink hijab against the black of her hair. Acid bile burned the back of my throat.

I grabbed the glass by my bed, downed the water and lay staring at the ceiling, my throat raw with stabbing daggers.

I was a chef now. I liked it. *Was* there something in what Anjoli had said? She was right: I'd always been a romantic, looking for that perfect connection. The intimacy she and I had formed when unravelling the intricate mess of the murder had dissipated after we solved the crime and refocused ourselves on the reality of our grey lives, bursting the bubble we had created. I was finding it hard to come to terms with the physical familiarity of sharing a flat with her while the psychic intimacy had vanished. I wasn't sure what we were left with. We were not in a relationship – not family, not quite flatmates, not lodger and landlord – but in something else . . . a liminal in-between space neither of us could define. Sharing a bathroom, having breakfasts and occasional dinners together, working cheek by jowl had all bred a closeness I would have liked to pursue, but she had told me, without quite telling me, that it wasn't something that was right for her.

I missed having a partner. I'd been with Maliha for years and been happy. And now it seemed I had a chance with Naila. I *had* to take it. But who was this Imran? Naila wasn't happy to hear from him. Why was he calling her when it was so late in Pakistan?

Sleep. Try to sleep.

I couldn't.

Salma eating her dinner. The bell rings. Is she expecting someone? Puts the hijab over her head. Lets the killer in. He follows her into the living room. They argue. He grabs the scarf, and before she knows what he's doing, he's behind her, hijab knotted around her neck, pulling it tight, knee in her back for leverage. She's choking. What's happening? She kicks. Knocks the crate over, hairpins scattering on the carpet. The shock of it. The pain of it. Does she know she's going to die? Does she know why? Her last moments on the planet, and she sees the grim walls of her flat through watering eyes, hears the grunts of the killer behind her as he exerts ever more force. Then blackness. She goes limp and drops to the floor as he flees.

I sat up and retched, but nothing came out.

Enough! This was none of my business. I had left all of this behind me. Murder investigations took too much. Left you calloused. Numb. Caring was *not* an asset in a detective.

And yet.

Had the person in the yellow hoodie been wearing gloves? I couldn't remember. He would have left DNA on the hijab if he hadn't.

I buried my head under my pillow, trying to deafen myself against my thoughts.

A knock.

'I'm sorry, Kamil. Are you okay? Can I get you anything?'

I took the pillow off my head and took a deep breath. 'Come in, Anj.'

She opened the door, looking worried.

'*I'm* sorry. I lost it,' I said.

She sat at the end of my bed as I switched on my lamp, the glow lighting up one side of her face. I tried to find the words.

'See, I've put all that behind me. And I'm happy. I'm sorry. I didn't mean to shout.'

'You don't have to let go of your dreams, Kamil. You worked so hard to make it in the police and now—'

'Yes, but I *have* let go. It *wasn't* hard to leave everything behind. Look, the murder last year was a massive shock. To all of us. I'm more worried about you, to be honest. You never wanted to talk about what happened.'

'It *was* a shock, and it was horrible, and I was trying to move on too, Kamil. That's why I didn't want to discuss it with you. I was just scared of dredging it all up again. Like you said, life has changed so much over the last six months I'm not sure where my head is at. First Rakesh Uncle died, leaving Dad devastated, then my best friend arrested for murder. It was a horrible time and I'm not over it. And after Ma and Baba went to India, I felt like I had no choice – after all the sacrifices they had made for me, I *had* to step in to help with the restaurant. But I hated giving up my research job. Do you remember how happy I was when I got it? How many people get to use their degrees doing something they enjoy? I don't want to manage a restaurant for the rest of my life. I don't want to be cooking and cleaning and serving and totting up receipts and managing cash-and-carry merchants and butchers and fishmongers and . . .' Her voice trailed away. 'I want to do more. You know I started working in the restaurant when I was twelve, washing dishes after school and trying to squeeze my homework in afterwards.'

'Child labour!'

'I know, right? *Unpaid* child labour. I grew up sneaking sips of Lambrini and watching the restaurant grind my parents into the ground. I swore it would be different for me. And now here I am watching my life ebb away in a parade of chicken tikka masalas and onion bhajis. It's literally killing me! But you, you don't *have* to do this, and . . .'

I tried to interrupt, but she carried on: 'You have a calling. I envy that because I don't think I do. And you *are* a good detective. I've seen it first hand. You shouldn't waste your talents. So, if there's a chance to show it . . . And when you said Tahir was there, I just thought . . .'

She was struggling, but I understood what she was trying to say, in her own Anjolic way, and it made me feel warm.

'What's that face for?' she said, breaking into a smile – she could never stay down for long.

'Just that you're . . . amazing.' The bedsprings creaked as I shifted position. 'I'm sorry I was short with you; maybe I just didn't want to hear it. You say you envy my calling – that's because the cows are always fatter in someone else's field! Believe me, Anjoli, you have so many callings you can't hear them! You're brilliant at everything you try! You've transformed the restaurant in six months, more than your parents did in thirty years. You can do anything you put your mind to. This is just a detour. Once Saibal-da and Maya-di are back, they'll take over again and you can be on your merry way. You'll answer your calling. I know you will.'

She looked at me steadily.

'You wanna know something?'

'What?'

'I don't have a clue what I'm doing with the restaurant. I'm scared shitless, all the time. I took out a big loan to make all these changes – *after* you helped get Baba out of debt last year. And I'm trying to create . . . I don't know, a Kensington restaurant in Brick Lane? What if I screw it all up? What if it fails? What if I've literally ruined my parents?'

I shuffled forward till our foreheads were inches away and looked her straight in the eye, her breath warm on my cheek.

45

'Trust your instincts, Anjoli. You have the best intuition I've ever known. And it's working! Takings are up, and look at the reviews we're getting. Not just the one in the newspaper, even Tripadvisor. I believe in you. You just need to believe in yourself.'

'I guess.' She squeezed my arm and pulled away. 'My biggest fan, aren't you? I know you miss your life in Kolkata, but I'm glad you're here. I couldn't do this without you. And if you hadn't been here last year, then . . .'

The spectre of Neha, crying in a jail cell, floated between us.

'I don't miss Kolkata; I love it here. And I love working with you and I'm a pretty excellent chef.'

'I wouldn't go that far. Adequate at best.'

'Listen, I'm the Atul Kochhar of the East End. Just waiting for my invite onto *Saturday Kitchen – Cooking with Kamil.*'

She rolled her eyes. 'Kamil the Kook, you mean?'

I smiled. 'Okay, let me sleep now.'

'But you'll think about what I said, yes? *And* investigating will give you a chance to hang out with Naila. Think of that perk.'

I gazed at her framed in the lamplight as we both went quiet. There was an undefined, inviting danger in our silence.

'What about you? Don't *you* want someone in your life?'

She looked away. 'No, I don't. Not right now, anyway. I just want to make the restaurant a success. I don't have the time or head space for anything else.'

I felt a sense of desolation I didn't understand. Her message was clear. But I pushed.

'You know, last year, I thought . . . I thought maybe the two of us had a chance. I felt . . .'

She looked at me, softness in her eyes, then put her hand on mine. 'I know. I felt it too. But it was a hard time. And you had just broken up with Maliha. It's never good doing things on the rebound.'

Maliha. Just hearing the name of my long-term fiancée still

had the power to cause my insides to shrivel. She continued, 'Anyway, that time has passed. You have Naila and she's great for you. I think you need to be in a relationship more than I do. *And* get back to detecting, it's what you love. And if you are feeling guilty about Salma, that is your way to help her.'

'I don't think I'd want to do it without you as my sidekook.'

She rolled her eyes and I gave a weak grin at my joke.

'Think about it,' she said. 'Spending time with Naila will at least let you figure out if she's the one.'

My eyelids felt like they were weighted with dumb-bells as a wave of fatigue rolled over me. My head was throbbing, throat sore. I nodded. 'I'll think about it.'

'That's all I ask.'

She smiled and left, shutting the door behind her, leaving me feeling like I'd lost something I'd never had.

Chapter 7

Wednesday.

Anjoli banged on my door the next morning. 'Naila's here.'
I tore myself out of a dead man's sleep.

'Coming.'

I lay in bed for a few moments, looking at the sun making hesitant patterns on the ceiling, then levered myself out of bed and rushed myself ready. In the kitchen I found Anjoli looking far too awake, favourite deep blue cup in one hand, shortbread in the other, spilling crumbs on her *Insert whatever slogan will annoy you here* T-shirt. Naila sat next to her in ripped jeans and a red top, eating a slice of toast and jam. She looked wired, excitement thrumming off her. This wasn't a woman traumatised by seeing a dead body – she was locked and loaded, ready to fire off in all directions, very different from the almost catatonic person who had dropped me home the previous night. I hoped she wasn't suffering from PTSD.

I pecked her on the cheek, avoiding Anjoli's eye. 'You all right, Naila? No bad dreams?'

'I didn't sleep too well, to be honest. I kept seeing Salma's body. Lying there. Kamil, it made me so furious! She didn't deserve that! Nobody does. Having her life finished for no reason. This is my third cup of coffee this morning. I don't know how I'm going to make it through the day. I had to spend breakfast convincing Salim Uncle I didn't need to return to Pakistan and was not about to get murdered myself. How about you? Did you sleep?'

'Please be careful, Naila. Shock can hit you when you least expect it. Salma was your classmate and the way she died was . . . well, you know.'

'I know. I'm going to try not to think about it. Don't worry, I'm better now. Over the shock. I wanted to check if *you* were all right?'

'I'm okay. Didn't sleep great either, but I'm fine.'

'Okay, good.' She finished her toast and rinsed off the plate. 'I'll make a move. Get to college early and decompress in the canteen. Lectures all day today, no stroppy patients to deal with. In my current mood, I might have given them a tight slap if they didn't listen to me and got myself expelled. See you this evening?'

Anjoli snapped a glance at me.

I stared back at her and came to a decision.

'Hang on a sec, Naila,' I said

She looked at me.

'Anjoli had an idea last night.' I was finding it hard to get the words out. 'She thought it might be good if we – you and I – poked around a little at your school to figure out what happened to Salma. People may be more willing to talk to us than the police. Anjoli could help as well since she's friends with Tahir – the cop on the case. What do you think?'

'Oh?' Naila turned to look at Anjoli. 'Will the police be okay with that? Shouldn't we leave it to them?'

'We won't get in the way,' said Anjoli. 'We may find out more because we're *not* the police. And Kamil's an excellent investigator. Do you want to?'

Naila thought for a second then said, 'I know nothing about anything. But if you think I can help, of course I will. It was awful seeing Salma like that.'

'Okay,' I said. 'If you've got a few minutes, Naila, let's sit down and go through what we know. Our own little East End detective squad.'

'The three duskyteers,' Anjoli deadpanned.

Naila snorted a laugh, 'All for none and none for all. Although you two are duskier than I am.' She sat next to Anjoli and put an arm beside hers, underlining the Pakistani/Bangla comparison.

Revived by coffee and jammy toast, I pulled out my phone. 'All right, let's begin with a timeline. What time did Salma come into the restaurant last night?'

Anjoli said, 'After ten. The three of us were sitting together, remember?'

I typed in, *2205: Salma comes to TK to pick up food.*

'Then she phoned at 10.47 – I remember seeing the time on her phone – and I found her dead at 11.35 or so.' I added to my notes.

'How exact,' said Anjoli. 'Shame you don't have that level of precision when you're seasoning your dishes.'

Naila laughed. 'Or when we're supposed to meet for a film.'

So, this was what Tandoori Knights duskyteering was going to be like. Well, if being the butt of their jokes was what it took to keep them happy, that was easy enough. I looked at what I had put down. Not a lot, but a start. I passed the phone around.

2205: Salma comes to TK to pick up food, leaves around ten minutes later
2247: Phones to say she left her mobile behind
2300: Naila and I leave to drop phone off
2320: Arrive at Salma's place
2332: Person pushes past me at the entrance to her block of flats
2335: I find the body

'She had just started her dinner,' I said, hoping Anjoli hadn't noticed the twelve-minute gap between us arriving at Salma's and my heading up. 'So, if we assume she began eating after she called here, the killer must have come into her flat just after eleven. We can assume she knew him because she let him in and was found in the living room. If it had been a stranger, he would probably have killed her in the hall.'

'He?' said Naila. 'It was a man?'

'The neighbour heard a man's voice arguing with Salma. I couldn't say for sure whether the figure who pushed past me was a man or a woman. Anyway, let's assume a man for now.'

'The neighbour also said a young man visited her,' said Naila. 'We need to find out who that was. Maybe a boyfriend?'

'Yes, we do. So the murderer could have been there for around half an hour before we came. It's difficult to strangle someone; it takes a while for them to die. And he must have attacked her pretty soon after arriving, pulled off her hijab and choked her to death. He didn't bring his own weapon, so it must have been a spur-of-the-moment thing. He went there for some other reason. Something happened. They argued, and he took his chance. I wish I could see the forensics. It might let us know if it was premeditated or unplanned.'

'Does that matter?' said Naila.

'Maybe. If it was premeditated, we need to work out his plan and see what mistakes he might have made *before* the murder. If it was a spur-of-the-moment killing, we have to find out what he did *after* the murder as he tried to cover it up.'

'Makes sense,' said Anjoli. 'Any idea who the young guy might be, Naila? Was Salma friendly with anyone in class?'

Naila wrinkled her forehead. 'There *is* a young Bangladeshi fellow in our batch. Ziad something. I don't know if Salma knew him well though.'

'When her phone rang in the restaurant, it said Z,' I said. 'That could be Ziad. We can begin with him then talk to other friends she had.'

'What about her parents?' said Anjoli. 'We should interview them too.'

'If we can. The police should have informed them by now. Can you find out their details from the college, Naila?'

'I can try. So . . . we have a potential boyfriend, parents. Who else? Neighbour? Hey, I'm getting the hang of this investigation business!'

'Maybe. I can contact the woman we spoke to last night and see if she knows anything else.'

'Could it be a racist thing? The killer used her hijab to strangle Salma. Could that be a message?'

'Who knows. Can't discount any possibilities at this early stage of the investigation.'

'Investigation!' Naila gave a thrilled shiver. 'Okay, I have got to go now, or I'll be late for class. Do you want to come to college at lunchtime and we can talk to Ziad?'

Lunch was a busy time at the restaurant with office workers taking advantage of the midweek special £8.99 'biryani bonanza' that Anjoli had worked out.

'Can we try just after lunch? When the rush dies down here?'

Naila checked her phone. 'I don't have any classes after lunch till 3.30; shall we say two? I don't know if Ziad will be free though.'

'Let's take that risk.' I looked at my boss for permission to abandon her and got a nod back. Naila grabbed her coat, and I heard her running down the stairs as Anjoli said, 'Well, she's mercurial, your green-eyed goddess. Things have progressed so much you have to see each other at the end *and* the beginning of each day? And you sat in the car for ten minutes before going up to Salma's. Cho chweet! Did you spend all night on the phone asking the other to hang up first as well?'

'Hilarious,' I said, regretting the broken intimacy of the night before. 'It's nothing like that. Sorry about going off at lunchtime – are you sure it's okay?'

'We'll cope.'

I handed her the jam from the table. As she put it away in the fridge, she took out a plastic box of leftovers. 'Oh I forgot to take this to Yasir last night, with all the excitement. I better go now and give it to him before the mosque gets crowded.'

'I saw him on the way to Salma's. Gave him money. Hang on, I'll come with you. I could do with fresh air before I get buried in biryani prep.'

I felt energised, my heaviness of the previous night melted away. Much as I hated to admit it, Anjoli might have been right. Maybe this murder *was* the tonic I hadn't realised I'd needed.

Chapter 8

Wednesday.

I dressed, and we walked out into the crisp morning. It was a beautiful day, a few feathery clouds visible in the pale strip of blue sky between the buildings on either side of the narrow street. A good day to be alive. A shadow came over me as I realised Salma would never again see the city shaking off its sleep and waking.

We strode down Brick Lane – I knew every store in order now and nodded to the shopkeepers as I passed. It was still early, so the tourists were not out yet, but shops were opening, owners unlocking shutters, rolling down awnings and hosing down the pavement in front of their establishments; restaurateurs buying their daily food from the cash and carries and lorries blocking the street as binmen collected the rubbish, mechanical tippers groaning like ancient robots as they lifted and put down the bins.

Yasir was asleep under his blanket in his usual spot in the entrance to the mosque. 'Don't wake him,' I said. 'Just leave the food.'

'Someone might nick it.' Anjoli bent over him. 'Yasir. Wakey, wakey. Room service. We've brought your breakfast.'

There was no response.

She put out a hand and shook him. Still nothing. She turned to me, a worried look in her eyes. 'Kamil . . .'

I walked over and nudged him. Lifted off the blanket to reveal his face, eyes open. Peaceful. I knew death. Especially when it was the second body I'd seen in less than ten hours.

'Shit,' I felt for a pulse in his neck. 'Anjoli, he is no more.'

'What? No!' She looked at Yasir's dead face then turned away, white knuckles clutching her bag of food.

A shaft of sunlight hit his face, giving it an unearthly glow. Seeing his eyes staring straight into the sun made him seem even more dead than he was. I covered his face. He deserved dignity.

'I'm so sorry, Anjoli.' I put an arm around her. 'He was old. It's hard on the street – it was inevitable.'

'But you said you saw him last night?' Her voice was muffled against my chest. 'Did he look sick or anything? He always seemed so healthy.'

'He had a tough life.'

She pulled away. 'You'd better call the police. I suppose the imam isn't in yet.'

I dialled 999. Again. I could feel my heart beating underneath my shirt, damp with Anjoli's tears. All it took was for that one organ to stop and . . . that was it. We waited for the police, keeping guard over our friend who could not have known that a heart that had begun to beat in Aleppo decades ago would have given up under a blue suit under a worn blanket under the arched doorway of an east London mosque. Across the road, another homeless man stared at me as he rolled up his sleeping bag. I nodded at him, but he looked away. A bus moved between us and he was gone.

Ten minutes later a car arrived and to my surprise it contained the same two cops as the night before – Rogers and Tahir. They looked as startled to see me.

'Kamil, you again? Anjoli, hi. She's a friend, works at the restaurant too,' Tahir said to Rogers.

'Making a habit of discovering dead bodies, are we, sir?' said Rogers, an edge to his voice as Tahir performed CPR on Yasir then shook his head.

'You all right, Anjoli?' said Tahir, seeing the stricken look on her face.

'Oh Tahir,' she said, and to his boss's evident surprise, he put an arm around her shoulders and squeezed. A fleeting shard of jealousy pricked me. Had they ever dated? They always seemed very familiar.

'Maybe we could have saved him if we hadn't nattered with Naila?' Anjoli said to me.

'I don't think so, Anjoli,' said Tahir, removing his arm. 'It was his time. He may have been an alcoholic or a drug user. A lot of rough sleepers are.'

'He doesn't – didn't – drink,' said Anjoli.

'Are you sure?' Tahir held up a half-bottle of gardenia gin. 'He had this next to him.'

'He told us he didn't,' I said. 'He never accepted a beer when we offered him one in the restaurant.'

Tahir leaned over and smelled Yasir's mouth. 'I can't smell anything. Oh, and the bottle's unopened. Maybe you're right.'

'Wonder why he had that,' said Anjoli.

'Who knows. Now tell us what happened.'

I explained how we had found Yasir as Rogers listened without expression as Tahir questioned Anjoli off to the side.

'We already have your details,' said Rogers after I had finished. 'You can leave now, and we'll come back to you if we need anything else. You can give your statement on this as well when you come to the station.'

'Did SOCO discover anything at Salma's place?'

He looked at me. 'Oh, that's right, Sergeant Ismail said you used to be a detective, didn't he? Well, you're not in India now. You just let us get on with our jobs, sir. You needn't concern yourself.'

Was I a person of interest in Salma's death? The individual who found the body often was. If I were in Rogers' position, *I'd* suspect me. Maybe another reason for me to find out what had happened in case I was put under investigation. I looked at Tahir, bent over Yasir's body, bagging up the gin bottle and murmuring a prayer. A decent, respectful guy. I hadn't picked up on that aspect of his personality during our chats at the restaurant.

There was no staring crowd today as there had been the previous night. Police questioning brown people in east London was too common an occurrence, and the passers-by in their suits, thobes and hijabs kept their heads down as they walked by on their way to work, thankful it wasn't them. Bengalis had learned to stay out of other people's business, especially when a cop was doing the questioning.

We left Tahir and Rogers waiting for the ambulance and walked away from the mosque. Anjoli looked at the food in the bag. 'I suppose I may as well drop this off at the Whitechapel Mission. Coming?'

'Sure.'

We walked down Whitechapel Road, passing the Royal London Hospital, the clock above the door telling us it was 08:50. Anjoli looked at its grand, arched entrance and said, 'I don't understand London any more. How can someone just die on the streets, two minutes away from a hospital and five away from a homeless shelter? This fucking government . . .' She lapsed into silence.

Growing up in Kolkata had inured me to poverty. It was a fact of life and, if you didn't build a carapace to keep it out, it could consume you. It was everywhere, always present wherever you went in the city. You used your mobile as a shield to avoid looking at the beggars in the streets; the children who leaped out at traffic lights, enormous eyes in small faces looking at you, beseeching palms outstretched; the men with no legs who scooted themselves along the ground on their makeshift trolleys. Some even convinced themselves it was all a gigantic scam. 'These people make so much money from begging, if you give them anything it all goes to the criminals' was Ma's philosophy.

As Naila had said, it was shocking to see homelessness in London. In India you expected it – it was part of life in the developing world, part of its . . . ethos? But here? In one of the richest cities in the world?

We arrived at the mission, a small brick building on Maple Street. There were two men asleep outside the door, and we had to step over them to get inside as a stray dog watched us from the other side of the road. Why on earth would they sleep in the doorway to a shelter when ten feet inside they could have a bed?

We walked up a flight of stairs to a small hall leading into three large open areas. The layout of the mission was simple. There was a sleeping section with two rows of beds stretching away into the darkness, all occupied as far as I could see. A second door led to the dining area – a basic kitchen with more rows, this time of trestle tables and folding chairs. The third door opened into a smaller recreation room with a table-tennis table and four threadbare sofas. It was all clean and well cared for and, it being early, the normal bustle hadn't started yet, although two men were playing a desultory game of ping-pong as they waited for breakfast to be served, the *pock pock pock* of the balls echoing in the space.

Tapan, one of the centre workers, a young Bengali man in faded jeans and a bright red shirt with rolled-up sleeves, was washing plates in the kitchen under a sign that read BRINGING HOPE WHERE THERE IS DESPAIR. Hopefully there was enough hope to go around.

'Hi, Tapan.' Anjoli placed her bag of food on the hob, took a dish from him and started drying it.

'Hello, Anjoli. Haven't seen you in a while. Is that for us? Thanks very much.'

'Yeah, only a little today. I have sad news. Do you know Yasir, the Syrian man who sits outside the mosque?'

'Sure.' Tapan handed her another plate.

'We just found him dead. Right next to the hospital. It was awful.' She added the plate to a wobbly pile next to the sink.

Tapan shut his eyes for a second, then shook his head. 'Oh no! He was a nice man, just had so much bad luck. I'm sorry we couldn't help him. At times like this you wonder why we bother.'

'I know. Tragic. Anyway, I'll bring more food later tonight.'

She finished drying the last plate as Tapan put the food into the fridge, saying over his shoulder, 'He's the fourth in three months.'

'What do you mean?' I said.

'Fourth death on the streets in the last three months in this area.'

'Is that normal?'

'Not at all. I mean in winter sometimes we may have one or two people dying in a month, but four?' He shook his head. 'Especially in this warm weather? But then there are more people sleeping rough now so maybe it was bound to happen.'

'What happens when the police find someone dead?' said Anjoli.

'Nothing. They inform the local authority who organise a pauper's funeral.'

She shivered. 'Pauper's funeral. Is that what they call them?'

'Yes. If someone dies here, we do the same thing. But we try to make it nice. They should have a little dignity in death, no?'

I was still mulling over what he had said earlier. 'Do they perform autopsies?'

'I don't think so. I mean why would they? It's natural causes, innit? It's a hard life on the streets.'

'I suppose so. We had to step over two men asleep in your doorway – are you always this full?'

He sighed. 'Pretty much. We can't exceed the limits, or we'll be shut down. Health and safety. And you know what, sometimes people don't want to sleep surrounded by others. It's difficult. Everyone has their demons, whether drink or drugs or mental health issues.'

As we walked back to the restaurant, Anjoli said, 'Why did you ask about autopsies?'

'No reason. Unusual deaths sometimes just ring a little bell in my head.'

It was strange to think that close to where I was, people had been dying while I was going about my daily business. The two dead bodies I had seen, both had been living people I'd known. Well, Yasir better than Salma, but still. My visions from the night before resurfaced: Salma gasping for breath, dying in agony as the killer pulled her headscarf tight. And now Yasir, dying peacefully in his sleep.

But then this stuff happens all the time, every moment of every day. I was just not aware of people being born, going to school, getting married, laughing, fighting, crying, dying all around me. I floated along in my little bubble while life and death went on in this little corner of Brick Lane in the East End of London.

Bringing Hope Where There Is Despair.

There were worse things one could do.

Chapter 9

Wednesday.

Thick clouds rolled in to devour the morning's blue sky and a steady drizzle put off tourists, so we only had a dozen covers for lunch. One good thing about lunches was people ate the standards – kababs, samosas, rogan josh and, of course, our biryani bonanza (Anjoli made sure there were only six pieces of chicken in each portion so we could afford the cheap price). This meant I could cook the few dishes ordered on autopilot as I considered what I might have got myself into by agreeing to Anjoli's plan. Was I setting myself up for failure? And a very public one too, in front of Naila? I was already at a disadvantage as I wasn't a cop, so no one *had* to answer anything I asked them or even speak to me. And Anjoli had even got Naila excited about the idea of being a detective. Plus, she was struggling to make sure the restaurant was profitable, and my gallivanting around to solve this murder wouldn't help, even though it was her idea. But I didn't want to let the duskyteers down, so it was probably best if I visited Salma's college, poked around for a bit, then bowed out if no clues were forthcoming, having spent time getting closer to Naila.

In the kitchen Anjoli was sombre.

'Anjoli, would you like me to stay? I don't have to go out. I can finish the lunch service and we can talk about Yasir,' I said as she handed me a chit with an order for chicken tikka masala on it.

'No, I'll be fine. Although I was thinking maybe we should find a way for the restaurant to help rough sleepers? As a tribute to Yasir. Perhaps we can put aside an hour a week outside our main opening times where we can offer free food if they pitch up? What do you think?'

I stirred the chicken cubes into the masala sauce I'd whipped up, plated it and handed it to Salim Mian.

'Lovely idea. We all liked Yasir. I'll do the cooking.'

'Great, thanks. Maybe I'll start this afternoon. I'll tell Tapan to send people our way for the leftover biryani, and word will get around. Now go change, or you'll be late. Go find Salma's killer.'

Naila's classes were held in the James Clerk Maxwell building, opposite the circular IMAX cinema on the south side of Waterloo bridge. I texted her one-handed as I walked from the station, shivering under my umbrella and watching the headlights create patterns in the puddles, feeling the damp seep into my trainers.

She signed me in at the reception and said, 'I just saw Ziad in the canteen. I didn't speak to him, but we're on a break so let's ambush him. How do you want to do it?'

'Well, I'm thinking subtler than an ambush. Like, why don't you introduce me as a detective friend of yours? After that, we'll play it by ear.'

She looked dubious for a moment, then nodded.

The inside of Naila's college was like any academic institution around the world – somewhat dingy, students milling around, a slight smell of damp mixed with boredom. The authorities had tried to brighten things up with a selection of inspirational quotes and pictures of Florence Nightingale around every corner, but it only made it seem like they were trying a little too hard. How on earth had Florence found the time for nursing when she seemed to have spent her life thinking up epigrams?

I think one's feelings waste themselves in words; they ought all to be distilled into actions which bring results.

I stand at the altar of the murdered men, and, while I live, I fight their cause.

'I can identify with those two,' I said as we passed yet another picture of the lady with her ubiquitous lamp. 'She'd have made a good detective.'

'I know you're joking. But I realised when we were talking this morning that being a nurse *is* like being a sleuth. We must observe, gather evidence, sort through facts, come to conclusions – pretty much what you police wallahs do. *And* we save people. From pain and torment and a terrible life. Some of the people I see—'

'Fair enough,' I said, distracted by yet another quote: *Remember my name – you'll be screaming it later.* 'That's dark.'

'The Crimean War was not all ice cream and falooda, Kamil.'

We arrived at a pleasant canteen: yellow and white walls, a few large rectangular wooden tables and benches interspersed with smaller round tables and blue plastic chairs, all enveloped in a studenty buzz. Naila looked around and none too subtly pointed out a young Asian guy a few metres away picking at a sandwich, engrossed in his phone. A dark blue polo shirt hung off his thin frame as if it was on a hanger, and his face had the scars of old acne covered by a patchy stubble that seemed to be de rigueur for the male students, who were outnumbered about four to one by women.

'Can you get a couple of coffees, so we don't seem out of place,' I said to Naila and slid onto the bench opposite Ziad. He glanced up from his mobile and ignored my friendly nod, eyes skittering back to his phone.

I felt rusty. I hadn't questioned a potential suspect for a long time. I assumed the news of Salma's death hadn't got out yet and didn't relish breaking the news to Ziad that someone had strangled his girlfriend the night before. If she *was* his girlfriend

63

of course – we hadn't established that yet. And assuming he wasn't her murderer. Already too many variables.

Naila returned with the coffees. She sat next to me and kicked off proceedings with a cheery 'Hello, Ziad, how is it going?'

'Okay,' he said, looking over her shoulder. 'How are you, Naila?'

'Good.' She got down to business. 'This is a friend of mine, Kamil Rahman. He's a detective. Kamil, this is Ziad.'

That got his attention. He gave me a sharp glance, then looked back down at his phone. Was he naturally nervy or was there something else here?

I pumped his hand and held it. 'Nice to meet you, Ziad. I was wondering if I might ask you a few questions?'

He looked up but failed to meet my eyes, focusing just below my chin when he spoke.

'Me? What do you need to ask me?'

'About you and Salma Ali?'

A hint of panic crossed his face and his breathing quickened. He pulled his hand away.

'Salma? She's in our class. What about her?'

'I'm afraid I have bad news. She died last night.'

He looked at me as if I had broken into Swahili.

'What?'

'I'm afraid it's true.'

His next reaction startled me. He shook his head, barked a short laugh and rolled his eyes.

'Yeah, right. Hilarious. I'm not sure what kind of joke this is, Naila, but it's not very funny.'

He got up to leave, but Naila reached across, grabbed his hand and tried to pull him back down onto the bench. He jerked himself away, glaring at her.

'Ziad, it's not a joke. I swear, ma ki kasam. It's true. Kamil and I found her expired in her flat in Bethnal Green last night. It was –' her voice shook '– horrible.'

He lowered himself back to the bench in slow motion. His mouth opened and closed, no words emerging. Then he breathed, 'What . . . what are you saying?' Without waiting for a response, he pulled out his mobile and punched a name, fingers shaking. He waited a few seconds and whispered, 'No reply.' Then, to himself, 'She wasn't in today.'

He tried to compose himself, hands trembling.

'Was it suicide? Did she kill herself?'

This was unusual. Most people's reaction on hearing someone had died unexpectedly was to assume accident, not suicide.

'Not suicide,' I said. 'Murder.'

'What?' He shook his head. 'No, that can't be right. Why would anyone . . . ?'

I gave him an abbreviated version of the events of the night before, watching his reaction as he took it in. The pain on his face grew with every word I uttered, and by the time I had finished, his mouth had fallen open.

He rubbed his eyes with his sleeve. 'Strangled?' he said in a whisper, licking dry lips.

I nodded.

'Who would do that to Salma?'

'You knew her well, then?'

'Yes. There's no point hiding it now, is there? She's my . . . I'm her . . . We're . . . together. Dead? I don't . . . She's dead? Salma?' His voice broke, and a few of the students at the next table gave us side glances.

'Let's get out of here. Maybe you can help us find who did this.'

'I have a class . . .' he began, then followed us in a daze.

If this guy was an actor, he was a damn good one.

Chapter 10

Wednesday.

O utside the college the rain had vanished, and it had turned into a beautiful spring afternoon. The sun shone from a pale blue sky and a cool breeze played its way through the drivers and harried cyclists trying to navigate the IMAX roundabout. We reached the South Bank and stood staring at the light dancing on the Thames and the wet Embankment, its shimmers at odds with the palpable gloom that blanketed us.

I took a breath, centring myself as Naila buttoned up her coat. This was one of my favourite parts of London – the buildings a higgledy-piggledy mess of incongruous architectural styles. Upriver, Gothic Big Ben trussed up in scaffolding, visible through the spokes of the London Eye. Downriver, the classical dome of St Paul's dwarfed by strangely shaped skyscrapers with even stranger names – the Cheese Grater, the Walkie Talkie, the Gherkin.

We found an unoccupied bench, and after sweeping off the rainwater with our palms, Naila and I sat, flanking Ziad.

'We need to learn all we can about Salma,' I said. 'The first rule in finding the killer is to know as much as we can about the vic—the deceased. Something she said or did or saw would have caused her demise and we need to find out what that was.'

Ziad nodded.

'How long had the two of you been seeing each other?'

'Almost a year.' He stared at the buildings on the other side of the river. 'We had to keep it a secret – her parents are very strict and wouldn't have approved.'

'When did you last see her?'

'Yesterday. At college. She had a shift in the hospital after lunch.'

'How did she seem?'

'Normal. Maybe a little quiet. We didn't talk much. She had been back to visit her family in Leeds over the weekend and she always found that difficult.'

'Why?'

'She didn't get on with her father.'

'Why did she go in term time?'

'She wanted a break from college. I didn't speak to her over the weekend though; she left her phone behind in London by mistake. I missed her.'

'She left it in the restaurant too. Was she in the habit of doing that?'

A shrug. 'Salma could be scatty – not at work though. Just with her own stuff.'

'Do you have her parents' details?'

'No, they don't know about me.'

'Do you know who might have wanted to harm her?' said Naila.

His face twisted. 'Nobody. Who would hurt Salma? You knew her, Naila. You tell me. Okay, sometimes she could get a little passionate about her causes. But she always meant well. She was just . . .'

'She was. Just.'

'What types of causes?' I said.

'The usual. Women's rights. Green issues. Nothing that could offend anyone.'

'And how had she been for the last few days? Normal? Anything out of the ordinary?'

His gaze dropped to his lap. 'She was fine.'

'Talk to me, Ziad.'

'She was . . .'

'Yes?'

His breathing sped up.

'Nothing. She was fine.'

He was lying.

'Why did you ask if she committed suicide? Was she suicidal?'

'Of course not. I just thought that maybe . . .' His voice broke.

Naila put a hand on his shoulder and gave it a squeeze. He flinched, but she kept him in her grip. 'Talk to us; we want to help.'

She stroked his head, and he collapsed into her.

'Nothing,' His voice was muffled in her shoulder. 'She had things on her mind and . . . I don't know what I'm saying. I'm in shock.'

'What things?' I said. 'Ziad, you must tell me. We'll find out, anyway. What did she have on her mind?'

He pulled away from Naila and composed himself.

'She made an appointment to see the dean this morning.'

'The dean,' said Naila. 'Why did she want to see him?'

'I don't know.'

'You must have *some* idea,' I said.

'I thought it must have been family issues; her father was quite controlling. Or something she had come across in college. She had been preoccupied for a few weeks.'

'Preoccupied with what?'

'I asked, but she wouldn't tell me. She could poke her nose into other people's business, but she meant nothing bad. And then it didn't matter because . . . because she . . .'

'Because she what?'

'NOTHING! She is the only girl I have ever loved.'

Tears drifted down his cheeks.

I looked at Naila over his bowed head. There was something here, but I couldn't prise it out. I'd have to wait till the time was right.

I remembered the Holy Koran on her bedside table and tried another tack. 'Was she religious?'

'Religious? Yes, she is – was. I mean, she didn't pray five times a day or anything, but she went to the East London Mosque. I went with her sometimes; she was friendly with the imam. She was a very moral person. Believed in right and wrong. Believed in her causes. She was fasting for Ramadan.'

That explained the late meal the night before.

'And were you . . . intimate?'

He paused.

'We loved each other! We were going to get married.'

'So, you were?'

He nodded, shamefaced.

'You used to visit her flat?'

'Yes. I live with my parents, so we had to go to hers. My parents don't know about us either.'

I felt sorry for the two of them. Two young people living in London but having to skulk around keeping their feelings for each other secret as if they were in a Bangladeshi village. Life in Kolkata, or even Lahore from what Naila had told me, was more modern and accepting for educated young people than it was for second-generation Bangladeshis.

'Was there anyone else in college she was good friends with? Or who she might have had issues with? Think hard, Ziad – anything could help catch her killer,' said Naila.

He shook his head. 'I can't think of anyone. She would come to classes, and I was the only person she was close to. Maybe someone in St Thomas'? You're placed with her in the hospital, no?'

Naila nodded. 'I haven't seen her talk much to anyone at Tommy's.'

This was getting nowhere. I looked at the young man, now turning his phone between his hands like a talisman that could keep him from harm.

'How come you're doing nursing? You don't see a lot of young Bengali men in this profession.'

Irritation crossed his face. 'Why do people keep asking me that? They always assume it's because I couldn't make it as a doctor. They *have* male nurses, you know. It's a good vocation and I enjoy it. My father is happy I'm doing it. So what business is it of yours?'

'I'm sorry. I didn't mean to offend. It's a tough job. Did Salma enjoy it too?'

'She loved it. She was a fantastic nurse, and her patients adored her. She was so good at her studies – had an amazing memory, could remember everything – facts, dates, phone numbers – just had to see something once and she'd remember it. She had a hard life – she was an only child. Her parents were strict. She had to be tough herself, annoyed some people, I guess. But she was so soft and gentle underneath it.' He smiled at a memory. 'I once told her she was like a lychee. Spiky on the outside, sweet on the inside.'

Tears leaked from his eyes again, and this time he didn't brush them away.

'How about her teachers? Was she friendly with any of them?'

'I don't think so. Her personal tutor was Dr Mackenzie. He tutors a few of us.'

'He's my tutor too,' said Naila.

'You think she talked to him about what was bothering her?'

'I don't *know!*' Ziad was getting more distressed. 'I don't know what you want from me!'

'It's fine, Ziad. It's fine,' said Naila.

'You've been very helpful,' I said. 'Naila, maybe we can see Dr Mackenzie next?'

'Sure. We can go back and see if he is free. I think he has office hours now.'

Ziad looked down at the ground. 'She's gone, then?'

'I am sorry, Ziad. Sounds like she was a lovely person. I'm sure you made her very happy,' I said.

He nodded. Then stood. 'Thanks for telling me, I have to go now.'

'One more question. Where were you last night between 11 and 11.30?'

'That's when it happened?'

'Yes.'

'I was at home.'

'Can anyone vouch for that?'

'My parents were there.'

'They were awake?'

'No. They were asleep. I went to bed early, just after ten.'

'So, no one can vouch for you?'

'I suppose not. 'He cleared his throat. 'But I loved her. I would never harm her.'

'Where do you live?'

'Cambridge Heath.'

'That's close to Salma's?'

'Yes.'

'You said you used to go over there at night. Was it after your parents were asleep? Her neighbours saw you.'

He looked away from me. 'Sometimes.'

'But not last night? Didn't you want to? Since you hadn't seen her all weekend?'

'She didn't . . . want me to come last night.'

'Why not? Was she expecting someone?'

'No. We . . . had a fight.'

'What about?'

He went quiet. Then, 'Nothing special. People argue.'

71

Naila said, 'But something must have brought it on?'

'It was nothing.' A thought struck him, and his face contorted. 'You mean if I *had* gone over, then maybe she would have . . . I could have . . . I have to go home now.'

'Give me your number,' I said, 'in case I have any more questions. And here's mine. You can call me if you think of anything.'

We exchanged numbers and then he walked away. Naila looked troubled, and I took her hand, drew her to me and kissed her, her lips soft under mine.

She kissed me back, then pulled away, looked around, smiled and wiped her lipstick off my lips with her finger. 'What was that for?'

'I'm just glad you're here.'

'Me too. It was cool seeing you in action. You were very good, the way you got him to talk.'

'I was worried, to be honest. It's been a while. But we made an excellent team.'

'Did we? I'm glad I could help. It was horrible seeing him so upset. Did you believe him?'

'He *seemed* genuine, but he's hiding something. The fight they had. And that suicide comment was odd. What did you think?'

'I don't know,' she said. 'He wasn't sure about his alibi? Could he have been the person you saw last night?'

'It's possible. I just don't know; the person was maybe a little bigger? But it was dark, and he ran by so fast. Did you get anywhere with finding out about Salma's parents?'

'Not yet. I was going to get to it later.'

'The college won't just *give* you their details.'

'No, but I have an idea.'

'What?'

'Come, I'll show you.'

'All right, D'Artagnan. Also, we need to find out why Salma wanted to see the dean; that could be significant. And you can introduce me to your tutor so I can find out if you're as clever as you claim to be.'

'You don't need to see my grades to know that. What are you going to do when Ziad finds out you aren't on this case in any official capacity?'

'I'll cross that bridge when I come to it. I guess your tutor won't believe me if you tell him I'm a detective?'

'It's not a good idea to lie to Sir; he may fail me if he finds out. Better to tell him the truth – that you're investigating the murder and used to be a detective. Leave out the bit about being a cook.'

We walked back to the college. I had enjoyed feeling the old cogs whirring again – one question leading to another, delicately tacking to where the suspect took us.

Naila took me to the administrative offices in the basement and walked up to a bored-looking woman peeling a tangerine behind the front desk. 'Hi. I'm Salma Ali. My contact details have changed, and I just wanted to check you had the right ones?'

The woman said, 'Sure,' and clicked around on her screen. 'What has changed?'

'My father's mobile number. What number do you have for him?'

She pecked around a bit more, then read out a number I noted down.

'Oh,' said Naila. 'That *is* the right number. I must have changed it already. Sorry to have bothered you.'

The woman nodded and went back to chewing her tangerine.

'That was clever,' I said as we walked out. 'What will you do when they find out Salma Ali's ghost visited the admin office?'

'I'll cross *that* bridge when I come to it.' She grinned. 'Anyway, all brown women look the same to them.'

'You are way more beautiful than Salma.'

'You can't say that about the deceased! But I am flattered. Anyway, will you phone her father?'

'Yes, I'll do it now.'

I dialled the number. After a few rings a man's voice answered, 'Hello.' I could hear the rattling of a train in the background.

'Hello. Is that Mr Ali?'

'Yes, who is this?' He had a strong Bengali accent.

I switched to Bengali. 'Hello, sir. I am a friend of Salma's. I'm so sorry about the news.'

There was a silence and then, 'It is terrible. We are on our way to London now. Who are you?'

'My name is Kamil Rahman. I was the one who found her last night and I wanted to give you my deepest condolences.'

'Thank you. I cannot talk now, but thank you.'

Before he could hang up, I said, 'Would it be possible to meet while you are in London?'

'Why?'

'I would like to find out who did this terrible thing to your daughter. I think I can help. If you and your wife could find time to meet with me, I would appreciate it.' Remembering Salma's visits to the mosque, I added, 'Sheikh Masroor at the East London Mosque can vouch for me.'

Silence, save for the tinny *clackety clack* of the train. Then he said, 'All right. You have my number. We are staying at the Ibis hotel next to the mosque. Phone me tomorrow.'

'Dhonnobad. Thank you.' I disconnected.

'Well?' said Naila.

'All sorted. I'll meet him tomorrow in London. Now let's see what your Dr Mackenzie has to say about Salma.'

'He's free in fifteen minutes, I just checked with the departmental assistant. Let's get a coffee while we wait.'

We made our way back to the canteen. It still smelled of chips but was now empty save for a woman wiping down the tables. We got another couple of coffees and I said, 'So tell me about this Dr Mackenzie.'

'Not a lot to tell.' She blew across her coffee to cool it. 'He runs tutorials and gives lectures. He's good.'

'No rumours? Teacher–student hassles?'

'With Dr Mackenzie?' She laughed. 'Not a chance. Anyway, with all the #MeToo stuff, I don't think anyone would dare.'

We sipped our coffees, then she said, 'I've been thinking about what you said. Us going away?'

My heart felt like a defibrillator had sparked it. Had she changed her mind? 'Yes?'

'We should. When were you thinking?'

'I don't know. How about this weekend?'

'All right. Just let me check my schedule at the hospital.'

'What will you tell Salim Mian?'

'That I'm going on a weekend break with one of my college friends. What will you tell Anjoli?'

What *would* I tell Anjoli? For all Anjoli's teasing about Naila and me, I didn't know what she felt about us even though she seemed to encourage our relationship. And why should I care? She had made her position clear the previous night. But I did care. And the thought of telling her I was going away with Naila for a weekend felt wrong for reasons I couldn't comprehend. My strange ambivalence resurfaced.

Naila didn't wait for an answer, announced, 'It's time, come on,' and tossed her empty coffee cup into a bin. I followed her out of the canteen.

Time for rational analysis not emotional turmoil.

Chapter 11

Wednesday.

Another maze of inspirationally messaged corridors and I said to Naila, 'I had no idea Florence Nightingale was born in Florence. Lucky she wasn't born in Bengal – Kolkata Nightingale, the lady with the diya, doesn't have quite the same ring!'

A theatrical grimace. 'Kamil, you oscillate between toddler jokes and grandad jokes. Do you have a book you get them from?'

Before I could think of a snappy grandad comeback, we were in an office with an assistant at a desk who smiled and said, 'Hi, Naila, nice to see you again.'

'Is he in?'

'Sure, go right in.'

Naila knocked on the door with a nameplate that said *Dr L. Mackenzie, Senior Lecturer in Adult Nursing* and entered, me following.

Mackenzie was reading a document, sprawled in a comfortable-looking chair, feet up on a desk littered with books on which a laptop balanced precariously. He held up a finger as we entered. 'One minute.'

Well built, late thirties, thinning hair tormented by a bad combover, he had laughter lines around friendly eyes in a red, beefy face and was wearing a blazer over chinos. Two metal folding chairs sat expectantly in front of his desk, and bookshelves ringed the room. Hundreds of books lay stacked on the shelves, some pushed aside to make room for smiling photos of Mackenzie at work (receiving some award from a grim man in a three-piece suit), Mackenzie at home (the obligatory smiling picture with his wife and two young children) and Mackenzie at play (toasting the camera with a pint of Guinness in a pub).

He tossed the document aside, swung his feet off the desk and rose from his chair, eyes darting from Naila to me, then back again. 'Naila. How can I help you?' he said in a strong Irish accent.

'Hello, sir. How are you?'

'Grand, I'm grand. You?'

'Sorry for coming without an appointment, but I wondered if we might talk to you? Do you have a few minutes?'

'For you, always, Naila. Have a pew. And who do we have here?'

I assessed him as he squeezed my hand in an iron grip that made me wince. One of *those*.

'This is Kamil Rahman, a friend of mine.' The chairs squeaked as we sat. 'We have bad news, I'm afraid.'

'Bad news, is it? I hope you're not going to tell me you need an extension on your work again. This will be the third time!' He gave her a wry smile and leant back in his chair, fingers spinning a pencil.

There was something about this guy I wasn't sure of. An unspoken tension seemed to permeate the room. His casual, smiling banter seemed at odds with a wariness in his eyes, which constantly flicked between Naila and me, and he seemed to be breathing a little too fast. Or maybe I was just pissed off he had seen me react to his bone-crushing handshake.

Naila smiled back at him. 'No, I'm on top of that, sir. It's about Salma Ali.'

'Salma? Ah now, what about her? She missed her tutorial with me earlier today. Is she okay?'

Naila looked down at her lap. 'No, she's not. Kamil, would you . . .'

'Dr Mackenzie, I'm afraid Naila and I found Salma dead last night.'

The pencil in his hand went still. 'Dead?'

'I'm afraid so.'

'Jesus! What happened? Did she have an accident?'

'No, I'm afraid she was killed. By person or persons unknown.' I wasn't sure why I added the last bit.

'Strangled,' said Naila. 'With her own headscarf.'

He stared at her.

'No! That's terrible. Her poor parents. I'm so sorry to hear that. She was lovely. Who would want to harm her? Was it a . . . hate crime? Because she was . . . you know . . .'

He went even redder with the delicacy of white people when they try to avoid saying the word. I helped him out, 'A Muslim. Maybe. That's what we want to find out.'

'My God. I can't believe it. You said the two of you found her? Where? How?'

'At her flat,' said Naila.

'I see.'

He fell silent.

'Kamil used to be a detective, and we're trying to help her parents find out who might have done this terrible thing.'

His sharp eyes reassessed me. 'Ah.'

'You tutored her,' I said. 'I heard you were close. Did she say anything to you? Was her behaviour unusual over the last few days? Did you notice anything?'

He considered this, then stood and stared out of the window, which overlooked a courtyard within the college buildings. I turned on the recorder on my phone as he swivelled and said, 'Close? Who told you that? We weren't close. She stopped coming for her tutorials for the last couple of weeks. I emailed her, but she didn't reply. Her work had been slipping for a while.'

'For how long?'

He wrinkled his brow. 'A few months maybe? To be honest if she hadn't bucked up, she was in danger of failing. Which would have been a pity. She might have made a good nurse. She was desperate enough.'

'Did you speak to her about it?'·

'Of course. I wouldn't want one of our students to drop out. We need nurses.'

His voice was sorrowful and it took me a second to realise how subtly he had been tearing Salma down. He must have seen something in my face because he tried to walk it back. 'Don't get me wrong, I'm sure she would have made it. Hopefully this was a temporary blip.'

I nodded. Stopped her tutorials. Was failing classes. Had a fight with Ziad. The edginess I had seen in her the night before. *What was bothering you, Salma?*

'Was there anyone she was close to in class?'

He thought again for a moment.

'She always sat in the same place in my lectures, near the back. Next to Ziad Aziz. Talk to him. See if he knows anything.'

'We already have,' said Naila. 'He was her boyfriend.'

'Was he, now? I'm not too surprised, I suppose. They were always together in class.'

'Sorry to ask this, Dr Mackenzie,' I said, 'but where were you last night? Between 10.30 and 11.30.'

He looked at me in surprise, then gave a short laugh. 'Am I a suspect? I was at a faculty dinner, then went home and straight to bed.'

'Thanks. Where was the dinner and where do you live?'

'Dinner was here at college and I live in Bermondsey. Are *you* okay, Naila?'

'I'm fine, yes, thank you, sir. It was a shock seeing her last night, but I'm all right now.'

'Do you want to see the college counsellor?'

'No, I'm okay.'

I wasn't done yet. This guy was a little too smooth. 'And you're *certain* you were at the dinner between those times?'

'Yes. I left at a quarter past ten and was home by half ten.'

'And can anyone vouch for you?'

Irritation entered his voice. 'My wife, of course. Although I'm not sure why I need vouching for. I was just Salma's tutor.'

'Ziad said Salma had an appointment with the dean this morning. Any idea what that might have been about?'

'The dean?' He looked perplexed. 'Maybe about her grades? You better ask him.'

My phone pinged. Anjoli. *Police here looking for you. What should I tell them?*

'I need to go.' I switched off the recorder and tapped a quick reply. 'Thank you, Dr Mackenzie, you've been very helpful.'

'Have I? I'm not sure about that. Terrible news.'

'Thank you, sir. I'll hand in that work tomorrow,' said Naila.

He came around the desk and grabbed my hand. I was prepared this time and squeezed back but was no match for his steely grasp so went limp instead. He gave me a smile then put an arm around Naila, squeezed her shoulders and said, 'It must have been a real shock to you, Naila. If you need extra time on the work, don't worry about it. Dreadful thing to happen. Does the dean know? We must tell her classmates. Oh Lord, this will be a tremendous shock to everyone in the college.'

He showed us out and said to the young blonde woman waiting outside his office, 'Emily, I'm sorry, but can we reschedule your tutorial? Something has come up.'

Some instinct inside me put Dr L. Mackenzie, Senior Lecturer in Adult Nursing, high on my list of suspects. I hated it when things didn't feel right, and I couldn't put my finger on why they didn't. Well, I would have to find out.

Chapter 12

Wednesday.

Naila signed me out at reception. 'What did you think?'

'I don't know. Likes to show off his strength, doesn't he?' I rubbed my hand. 'There was something about him . . . Felt like a performance. I don't know. He seemed to be watching to see what effect his words were having. I could be wrong. Sometimes my instincts hit the spot but at others they've been way off. We'll see. Walk me to the station?'

She pondered as we headed towards Waterloo. 'Why did you feel he was acting?'

'I don't know, just a feeling that something else was going on. His comments about her grades – Ziad said she was a very good student. How exact he was about his movements last night.'

'If I can find out who else was at the dinner, I can check when he left.'

'Good idea. That she missed her tutorials was interesting too. *Was* she a good student?'

'*I* thought so. Always had her hand up in class. Of course, I didn't see her essays and stuff.'

'And if you can find out what Salma wanted with the dean, that would be helpful too.'

'Hmm, not sure I'd know how to do that.'

'You're smart, you'll figure something out.'

'Something was going on with her. I think Ziad knows a lot more than he is saying.'

'Yes, I thought that too. We must push him harder. Oh, I forgot to tell you,' I said as she bought a *Big Issue* from a man squatting outside the station. 'More bad news. Believe it or not, I found another dead body today.'

'What?'

'You know the guy we saw last night outside the mosque? Yasir?'

'The homeless man?'

'Yes. Anjoli and I found him dead this morning. She's very upset.'

Naila's eyes widened. '*You* found him? Oh no! What happened?'

'We went to give him food after you left and he was just lying there, eyes open, under his blanket. We called the police, and it was the same two cops from last night. They were pretty surprised to see me again. Anjoli just texted me – they are waiting for me at the restaurant to interview me.'

'Y'Allah! How did he die?'

'Natural causes, the police said.'

'That's horrible. Poor Anjoli. I must call her up. I can't believe you were the one who found him. After Salma last night.'

'Yes, call her. She'd like that. It wasn't fun. I'm not used to seeing dead bodies every day. Especially of friends.'

'Poor Kamil.' She took my hand. 'Do you want me to come to the restaurant with you?'

'No, I'll be fine. Go to class.'

She looked at her watch. 'Yes, I'm late. Take care.'

She pecked me on the cheek and ran off. I looked after her, the kiss on the Embankment still soft on my lips.

Anjoli was right: doing this with Naila was fun. Maybe I'd give it another couple of days.

*

It was after four when I got to the restaurant to find Rogers and Tahir sitting in a booth interviewing Anjoli and Salim Mian, cups of tea in front of them.

The restaurant was normally empty at this time, but to my surprise one of the larger tables was occupied with six people digging in. They didn't look like our normal clientele, and I guessed Anjoli had kept her word and was feeding homeless folk.

'Kamil,' she said as I walked to the booth. 'Tahir was just asking me and Salim Mian about Salma. I told them about her coming in last night for her takeaway and how she left her phone. They've also taken my statement about how we found Yasir.'

I squeezed in next to her and Salim Mian, his bulk leaving me hanging over the edge of the seat.

'And she had come here before?' said Rogers.

'Yes, she'd come and get takeaway, now and then,' said Anjoli. 'But I don't think she'd ever eaten in. Had she, Salim Mian?'

He shook his head, chins wobbling over his collar.

'I think the restaurant must have been on her way home or something,' said Anjoli.

Rogers nodded. 'Thanks, you've been very helpful. Now we'd like to speak to Mr Rahman alone, if that's all right, Ms Chatterjee.'

'Oh.' Anjoli looked disappointed that she wouldn't hear me being interrogated. 'Okay, I'll be in the kitchen if you need anything. You sure you don't want another cup of tea?'

'No thank you, miss.'

'Bye, Tahir.'

I let Anjoli and Salim Mian out of the booth and sat back down with the cops.

Rogers gave me a stern look. 'Impersonating a police officer is a serious crime, Mr Rahman. Tell me why I shouldn't arrest you right now.'

Shit. Had they spoken to Ziad? That was fast work on their part.

'I'm sorry, what do you mean, DI Rogers?'

'We spoke to Mrs Longfellow, Miss Ali's neighbour, and she said you told her you were a police inspector?'

'Well, I am. Or I was. In the Kolkata Police, you knew that.' Riding it out was my only option.

'Well, you're not a police officer over here, so please don't go around lying to witnesses. We can't have anyone interfering with our investigation.'

'I understand. Sorry,' I said as Tahir gave me an amused look.

He nodded. 'Now, we need to get your written statement about last night and this morning.'

Tahir took me through the events of the previous night again, pushing me hard to describe the man who had shoved past me. But there wasn't much I could say other than my impression it *had* been a man. After I'd finished, he got me to read and sign the statement he had taken.

Rogers said, 'Thank you. We'll need the clothes you were wearing last night. And your fingerprints and DNA for elimination purposes. You'll need to come into the station for that. And your friend who was with you – Miss Alvi?'

'My things are upstairs.'

Tahir accompanied me up to my room in the flat. As I rummaged through the laundry basket, I said, 'Was there any CCTV from last night, Tahir?'

'Nothing we could see.' He leafed through the Q magazine on my bedside table. 'Why the interest, Kamil?'

Tahir could be my way in. We'd always got on, and he and Anjoli were good friends. I knew from our chats he was ambitious and keen to impress his boss.

'Well, not often I find a dead body. And was curious about how you guys work compared to what I did in Kolkata. It's strange being an outsider.'

'Yeah, I get that. But I can't share anything with you, mate. You know that.'

I handed him the jeans and T-shirt I'd been wearing the night before, and he deposited them in separate evidence bags. 'Thanks, we'll get this back to you soon. And, Kamil, you're certain you had never met Salma Ali before last night? Anjoli said she used to come here.'

'We get so many customers, but I'm pretty sure that was the first time I'd seen her. I met Naila for lunch today and we found out Salma had a boyfriend. A guy named Ziad Aziz at her college. He used to visit her in the flat. I just saw him, and we had a chat.' I gave him the gist of what Naila and I had learned from Ziad, including the fact Salma had had a fight with him the day before and she had an appointment with the dean. As a bonus, I gave him Ziad's number.

He noted it down. 'Thanks, Kamil, that *is* helpful. I'll speak to him. But man, *please* don't do a Poirot and go around questioning witnesses. Rogers will have a fit. And it could jeopardise the entire investigation, not to mention get me in trouble because we know each other. We can hook our own fish – we don't need the Kolkata Police to lay the bait down for us.'

'I wasn't questioning him. Naila and I just met him in the canteen and got to talking. I thought I should tell you. We met Salma's tutor too and told him about her death.'

'Did you tweet it to the entire world as well?' He raised a hand. 'Forget it, don't answer. Just leave it to us. By the way, how *did* you land a gorgeous woman like that? You must have hidden depths. In addition to being a master cuddler.'

I grimaced. That word was going to haunt me for a while.

'Well, you're the master baiter.'

He guffawed and clapped me on the back. 'Hang on to her, she's a good one.'

When we got back downstairs, Rogers said, 'Now we need to discuss the second body you stumbled upon this morning.'

'I saw Yasir alive last night on my way to Salma's and then dead this morning when Anjoli and I went to give him food. How did he die?'

'Natural causes, as I guessed. He was old,' said Tahir.

'Did you test the gin bottle, by any chance?'

Tahir looked at Rogers, then back at me. 'You think someone tampered with it?'

'I don't know. I'd just never seen him with alcohol before. I don't think he drank.'

'We haven't tested it yet. It was full and sealed.'

I gave them another statement and signed it. It was a quarter to five by the time they left, the bell tinkling as the door closed behind them.

The restaurant had emptied, and Anjoli was sitting opposite a man who was dawdling over his meal.

'That's horrible, Louis,' she was saying as I joined them. 'Kamil, this is Louis. Tapan sent him and some others over from the shelter.'

Louis was a wall of a man, Black, in his sixties with close-cut grey hair, arms covered with bluish tattoos.

'What's horrible?'

Louis looked at me, suspicion in his eyes.

'Louis was in Waterloo a few weeks ago and came upon a dead homeless person in an alley with another rough sleeper using his body as a pillow.'

'Oh my God,' I said. 'That's so sad. What did you do?'

He shrugged, dropping four sugar cubes into his milky tea. 'Didn't want to get involved, mon.' He spoke with a Jamaican lilt.

We sat in silence for a while then I said, 'If you don't mind me asking, what's your background? I mean, how did you end up . . .' I struggled to find the right words – I didn't want to offend him. 'Like . . . this?'

He stirred his tea with slow deliberate movements and took a dainty sip, the cup tiny in his hand.

'Army. PTSD. Drank. Lived in a squat which got demolished. Nowhere else to go. Council said I wasn't at risk, so couldn't get priority housing. Veterans' housing was no help. Son doesn't want to know.'

'Where do you sleep?'

'Wherever. Last winter was cold. Tried to sleep on night buses. For the whole route. On the seats in the back. Difficult. Stopping. Starting. Announcements. Driver braked hard, and I fell off the seat. Hurt my shoulder.'

I just couldn't imagine this gigantic man – he must have been six foot six and at least 140 kilos – lying down, squeezed onto a row of seats in a bus.

'What do you do now?' said Anjoli, her voice wobbling.

'Walk around during the day. I like to walk. See the city. Find somewhere dry at night.'

'You don't use the shelters?' I said.

He shook his head. 'People.'

'How do you . . . stay fresh?'

'Public toilets. Got everything I need here.' He gestured at a bulging rucksack at his feet.

Anjoli reached a hand across the table and put it in his palm, her fingers like a child's in his bear paw.

'Please come and eat here whenever you like. In fact –' she jumped up and grabbed a TK card from the bar and scribbled on it '– here's my mobile. If you need anything, . . if I can help at all, let me know.'

He drained his tea, pocketed the card and a handful of sugar cubes, shrugged his rucksack onto his back and got up to leave.

'Thank you,' he said, in a gruff voice, his sharp, acidic smell wafting past me. Before he reached the door, he turned back to look at Anjoli.'Thank you for . . . seeing me,' and left.

Anjoli's self-control gave way and the tears that had been threatening since we had found Yasir brimmed over and slipped down her cheeks. She brushed at them with her fist and said, her voice thick, 'Did you know, they put volunteers in an MRI machine to see which bits of their brains lit up when they were shown various pictures. They showed them kids, parents, businessmen, homeless people and household objects. And . . . the subjects' brains reacted to homeless people the same as they did with the *objects*. They saw them as *things*, not people. Can you believe it? They dehumanised them. It's what the Nazis did in the camps.'

I couldn't do anything except listen because, to my shame, I understood that reaction. I had been conditioned to feel much the same way about the poor in Kolkata. I wasn't proud of myself, but if you empathised with all the poverty-stricken people you saw every single day, it would destroy you. There'd be no feeling left. For anything. You had to block it out just to survive.

Anjoli cleared her throat and jabbed at her fierce tears with a napkin. 'We have to do something, Kamil. This is unacceptable.'

'You're already doing something, Anjoli. Much more than most people do. Feeding them has an impact.'

'It's not enough. It's never enough. Dying alone on the streets. No, it's unacceptable.'

'I know. You're right, but what can we do?'

'I don't know.' The tears came again, and I sat there helpless. 'I'm sorry. I don't know what's wrong with me. I've been feeling so raw . . .'

'Of course you are, what with Yasir and Salma—'

'It's not just that. All the stuff last year, and then Ma and Baba going to India and the restaurant, and our conversation last night . . . it's all too much.'

'Anjoli, I'm so sorry. What can I do? Just tell me and I'll do it. How can I help you?'

She shook her head. 'No, I'll get over it. I just need to pull myself together.' She wiped her face and started clearing the plates. 'So, what did the police say?'

'Leave it for tonight, Anjoli. You're upset.'

'I asked what Tahir and the other detective said?'

I gave up. Anjoli would just not accept anyone's help. That was her superpower and her superweakness. 'Not much. I told them about the conversations I had at Naila's college. They gave nothing away. Took my clothes to eliminate me from their enquiries.'

'You're a suspect?' A thin smile. 'Will I have to visit you in jail and smuggle a nail file inside a kulfi?'

'Yes, so I can have a nice manicure while I wait for my life sentence. No, just solve the crime and get me out.'

'I thought you had Ms Green Eyes for that.'

'I'm not sure if she has green eyes or if you do, the way you keep talking about her.'

She gave a short laugh. 'You actually think I'm jealous of Naila? Over you?'

I felt my face turn hot.

'Of course not. Why would you be?'

'She can have you with my compliments.'

I was beginning to get annoyed and it must have showed in my face because she said, 'Sorry, Kamil. I'm all over the shop today. What did the two of you find out?'

I controlled myself and told her about our conversations with Salma's boyfriend and her tutor.

'It sounds like something's going on with that Ziad dude. We should get him in here and interrogate him, with snacks.'

'Yes, Naila thought there was something dodgy about him too. I felt there was something off about Mackenzie as well. And

I'm seeing Salma's parents tomorrow. They may tell us something. Okay, I better get ready and start prepping the meat. You sure you're all right?'

'Yeah. I'm a soldier. Come on, let's sort things out for dinner. I said you'd enjoy ferreting around, didn't I? I know you better than you know yourself, Mr Detective! You literally can't function without me.'

'Literally.'

'Well, I am the psychologist; you're just PC Plod. In fact, just Plod.'

'Plod it is. All right, it *was* fun. Now stop gloating.'

I went up and changed into my chef's whites. Well, off-whites; I'd forgotten to do my laundry over the weekend. I wandered into the kitchen, where our second chef was chopping onions and tomatoes. I joined him as Salim Mian lumbered over.

'How is Naila, Kamil? She would not talk to me after that terrible thing last night.'

'I think she's okay, Salim Mian. She's pretty tough.'

'I don't know what to tell her father. He will think I am not looking after her.'

'I'll make sure she is okay, don't worry. By the way, who is Imran?'

'Imran?' His eyes were suddenly alert. 'Why?'

'He phoned Naila last night, and she seemed a little hassled by the call.'

'She is fine. Don't worry about Imran. That girl should concentrate on her studies.'

The mystery continued. Best not to tell Salim Mian that Naila had agreed to be D'Artagnan to my Aramis. Her family would yank her back to Lahore if they thought she was dabbling in unseemly matters – they might even marry her off. Studying nursing was one thing, helping me investigate a murder was another. No, as far as the outside world was concerned, we were a nurse and a cook, tending to the health and hunger of the public. It was only under cover of night we would rip off the trainee nurse's uniform and stained chef's outfit to reveal the valiant crime fighters underneath.

For now, there were curries to cook and naans to flame.

Chapter 13

Thursday.

S alma's father was due at the restaurant at eleven in the morning. Tandoori Knights was more private than a hotel lobby, and with Naila free of lectures and Anjoli wanting to do her bit, all members of the super-sleuthing triumvirate – the cook, the nurse and the restaurateur – were present and correct to interrogate the grieving dad.

But first I had my regular chores to get through. I traipsed over to our butcher on Hessel Street to buy the industrial quantities of chicken, goat and lamb we went through every day. Over the last three months my biceps had transformed from Sanjeev Bhaskar arms to Salman Khan guns. No one but me had to know these had appeared because of my lugging twenty to thirty kilos of meat back to TK daily from Hamdullah Halal, and not from regular bench-presses or pull-ups or whatever most people do to achieve them. One of the side benefits of my job.

After depositing the meat in the fridge, it was over to the Bangladeshi grocer for spinach, carrots, potatoes and other staples, then the grind of peeling and chopping the onions, ginger, garlic and tomatoes that form the basis of most dishes in Indian cuisine. Even though we precooked the fresh meat daily with dry spices, the sauces, rotis and naans were made to order from scratch. This was the best way to feed dozens of covers every night with speed, efficiency and optimum flavour. Rolling, cooking and serving the breads hot and fresh was a precise military exercise. Falling out of sync meant hot food and cold rotis, or cold food and hot rotis, both of which were a recipe for reduced tips and poor Tripadvisor reviews. We couldn't afford that, given the intense competition in Brick Lane and the precarious state of the restaurant after Anjoli's expenditure on going upmarket.

Naila came in just before eleven and stood in the doorway of the tiny kitchen, watching as I wiped peelings into the bin. 'So strange, Kamil. At home these are all menial tasks done by the khan sama. Never imagined I might date a cook.'

That stung. Tired from the stress of the day so far and expecting more, I said, 'Must distress you to drop your standards so low.'

'Don't be like that. I didn't mean it that way. You know what *I* do in hospital. I was just . . . Anyway, let me help.'

Naila had inadvertently poked at a sensitive spot. Deep down, was I ashamed of being a cook? Had that been behind my exploding at Anjoli the other night? Did I think I wasn't good enough for Naila?

Stop. This wasn't the time to start a bout of self-pitying navel gazing.

I took a breath.

'No, *I'm* sorry, Naila. I didn't get much sleep. It's true, I can't compete with the bodily fluids you have to deal with.'

'Not to mention solids.' She mock-retched, and I grinned, glad for the release in tension.

She washed her hands and pitched in with gusto, crushing clove upon clove of garlic under my biggest knife as she updated me on what she had discovered.

'I checked with a server at Sir's dinner. She said he left when he said he did, soon after ten; it all started winding down, and he tipped her, which most of the others don't.'

'Nice work. Any luck with the dean?'

'No, still don't know how to find out why Salma wanted to see him. Maybe the police will have more luck there.'

'Perhaps. Let's see what her parents say.' I knotted a rubbish bag. 'Here, would you mind chucking this out the back? The bins are in the alley behind the restaurant. I need to get things ready in the front.'

I watched her stagger out, washed my hands and walked into the restaurant, chairs still upside down on the tables. I swept the floor, and Naila returned to help me and the waiters set the chairs down on the now pristine wooden floor, Salim Mian looking on as he polished the glasses.

'You really need to multi-task in this job,' said Naila, putting down the last chair.

'Order from chaos, that's what I create, Naila.' I laid out the silverware. 'Whether it's solving a crime from random clues, cooking a delicious dish with spinach, paneer and onions or setting the table, my calling is to create clarity and fight the forces of chaos.'

'Goodness. And I thought you were just scraping last night's lamb dhansak from the floor.'

Salim Mian guffawed. 'You created only chaos in the kitchen when you first started cooking, Kamil. Too much salt, too little chilli, onions underdone – I had to teach you everything. Even as a waiter, you spent more time watching our guests instead of waiting on them.'

He wasn't wrong, but I'd learned fast since arriving here. I'd enjoyed honing my observational skills on our diners. While I hadn't reached the mythical Holmesian standard – discovering one of our punters had recently returned from Shanghai, where he had been at a conference on building materials with a woman who was not his wife – I'd become pretty good at clocking interactions between people and making educated guesses about their relationships. It was all in the eyes. How one person looked at the other when they were speaking; how they looked when

94

they thought they weren't being observed; how the eyes glazed over when their companion launched into a story they'd heard a dozen times before. Anjoli and I would have whispered competitions to work out which date a couple might be on. The skittish solicitousness of the first, the expectant electricity of the third or the wary watchfulness that presaged a break-up. It passed the time on slow nights.

Just as we got the restaurant back to its perfect pre-lunch state, there was a tapping on the door.

'There they are.' I opened it and stood aside as a small, thin man in his early forties wearing rimless glasses and a dark blue skullcap on his head entered, followed by a larger white woman of about the same age, very pale, dressed in a dark skirt and white top, pulling a small black wheelie bag.

'Mr Ali? I'm Kamil Rahman, thanks for coming.' I extended a hand to shake.

The man slammed me against the wall of the restaurant, my head jerking back and connecting with the brickwork with a *thwack*. Before I could react, an arm was across my neck, his face an inch away from mine, hot cigarette breath invading my nostrils. I scrabbled to remove his arm, but he was unexpectedly strong, given his compact frame.

'YOU BASTARD! What did you do to my daughter? What did you do to her?'

Naila and the woman looked on in shock as I grabbed his wrist with both hands, trying to pull him off, but he pressed harder, choking me. I gagged, eyes tearing up, and dug my nails into his tendon, but it had no effect. My sight darkened as the restaurant swam around me. I gathered what strength I could and slammed the toe of my shoe into his instep, causing him to lose his balance and stumble back into his wife's arms.

'What are you do—' I gasped, bending over as he pulled himself upright.

'I have told the police about you! You won't get away with it. Wait and see.'

I pulled myself up and rubbed my throat, struggling to get words out. 'What . . . Why did you do that?'

'I know. You did this to Salma. I know everything.'

My voice rasped out: 'I don't know . . . what you think, Mr . . . Ali, but I had *nothing* to do with Salma's death . . . I just want to . . . help.'

'You have helped enough.' He turned to his wife. 'I told you. I told you this would happen, but you insisted. Let her go to London, you said. This is your fault.'

Anjoli had run out from the kitchen to see what the commotion was and heard Naila say, 'Woh sach bol raha hai – he is telling the truth, Uncle. I am Naila, Salma's friend from college. Kamil doesn't know her. Please. Sit and have a cup of tea and we will explain everything.'

The woman looked at me in distress. 'I'm sorry, Mr Rahman. Please forgive him, he is very upset. I'm Sandra, Salma's mother. Sit, Yusuf, it's all right.'

My breathing returned to normal, although it still felt like someone had scraped the inside of my throat with sandpaper. I ignored it and focused on Salma's father. Who did he think I was? What could have prompted this reaction? I hadn't realised Salma was of mixed heritage. Did that mean anything? Her mother didn't wear a hijab, blonde hair uncovered for the world to see.

To calm things down, Anjoli brought in a tray of tea and Bombay mix. The five of us sat in awkward silence around the table as she poured the tea and proffered cups to Salma's parents. They shook their heads and Sandra said, voice cracking, 'Ramadan,' which just increased the embarrassment. I needed the tea for my throat, and took a sip, grateful for its soothing warmth. Sandra continued, 'We've just returned from seeing the police. We had to . . . had to identify . . . our daughter. In the morgue. It was very shocking. My poor girl. Her face . . . They told us you had found her body and because you phoned him, he thought . . .'

'You are not Salma's boyfriend?' said Mr Ali.

'Uncle, I only met her for the first time two days ago. She left her phone at the restaurant. Naila and I went to return it to save her the trouble of travelling late on public transport and we found her. I am very sorry for your loss.'

'You knew she had a boyfriend?' said Naila.

'NO! The police told us. I don't know how she could . . .'

'They told us she was pregnant,' said Sandra.

Pregnant. The word hung in the air, as though she had given it a physical form. The religious, opinionated nurse had secrets. This explained her father's reaction. And Ziad! Did he know?

'Salma was carrying?' Naila said, shock apparent on her face.

Mr Ali looked down and nodded. 'I am sorry. I thought you were the bastard who . . .'

'It's okay, Uncle. I understand. And Salma *never* told you about anyone she was seeing?'

'No,' said Sandra, tears dropping from her eyes. 'She feared . . . him.' She pointed to her husband. 'He would have dragged her back to Leeds if he'd known.'

'I *should* have done that.' His voice broke: 'My girl.'

'Did the police say anything else?'

'Nothing,' said Sandra. 'They told us they had a few leads they were following up. We have to empty her flat and take her things back. She was a good girl, you know.'

'Did she have anyone at home she might have confided in? Siblings, close friends?'

'She had friends, of course. We don't have any other children. She was our pearl.' She broke down again, her husband patting her hand. Naila put an arm around her. 'We are so sorry, Mrs Ali. I knew her, she was lovely.'

97

'The imam,' said Mr Ali.

'I'm sorry?'

'She might have spoken to the sheikh. At the mosque. She used to go. She told us.'

Ziad had said the same thing.

'Thanks. When are you heading back to Leeds?'

'Soon,' said Sandra. 'We can't afford to stay here another night, and the police have not said when they can . . . release her to us. We can't even have a funeral yet.'

Had Yusuf Ali known about Salma's pregnancy before the police told him? If he had, given his anger and the fact she was frightened of him, it was possible that . . . I had to be careful.

'The police told you about Salma's death yesterday?'

'Yes, they phoned us in the morning. Woke us up. They found my number in Salma's phone. We had to close the shop and come as soon as we could. And this morning . . . seeing her lying there like that . . . all cold and . . .'

Naila handed her a napkin. She dabbed at her tears, then blew her nose.

'You said they woke you, were you up late the night before?'

'I went to bed early, but he had gone—'

'I was at my snooker club then home all evening. With her,' said Mr Ali, as Sandra compressed her lips and looked down at her hands, folded in her lap. 'All evening. But what business is this of yours? Why are we here? Why are you asking these questions?'

'I used to be a police officer in Kolkata,' I said in Bengali. 'I would like to help find her killer.'

'What did he say?' said Sandra. Yusuf told her and she said, 'Oh, that would be wonderful! Yes, please look into it. I'm not sure the police care.'

'Yes,' said Mr Ali. 'If you can help, help. Now we have to catch our train. Come, Sandra.'

'If there is anything we can do, Aunty, Uncle, please let us know. Okay?' said Naila.

They nodded and left, wheelie bag trailing in their wake.

Chapter 14

Thursday.

The three of us looked at each other as the restaurant door shut behind them. 'Well,' said Anjoli, clearing up the tea things, grimacing as she spilled a drop on her *Bengali Queens Have the Best Dramas* T-shirt. 'That was heavy. Are you okay, Kamil?'

'I'm fine. He was bloody strong, though.'

'Did you notice Sandra's face when he said he was out the night before?' said Naila.

'I did. There was something there.'

'Do you think he might have come down to see Salma that night?' said Anjoli.

'It's possible. She would have let him into her flat, and he could have lost his temper and killed her if he found out she was pregnant.'

'Honour killing, you mean? I saw a documentary about that.'

'He went for your throat. Maybe a pattern? Could it have been him you saw leaving?' said Naila.

I shrugged. Mr Ali seemed a little smaller, but the person I'd seen was growing hazier in my mind. It could have been anyone.

'*You* didn't see anyone leave, did you, Naila? When you were in the car?'

'No, I had my back to the front door of the block.'

'Did you hear a car or anything? Just after I left?'

She shook her head. 'Nothing. I was watching Tik-Toks.'

How had the killer left the area? I needed to find out somehow. I was working blind without the tools of my trade – CCTV, fingerprints, photos of the crime scene, blood spatter analysis, results of door-to-doors. I needed to get Tahir Ismail on side.

But in the meantime there was a more immediate avenue to follow. 'Listen, I want to pop over to the mosque and see the imam about Salma,' I said. 'Can you manage without me for a bit, Anjoli? All the prep's done.'

She looked at her watch, then at the empty restaurant. 'Should be okay. Come back soon.'

Naila and I walked down Whitechapel Road to the East London Mosque, where she went in through the women's entrance and I entered through the men's. I paused in the doorway, seeing the empty spot where Yasir had lain under his blanket just a day ago. I felt something stir in my gut. Two corpses in two days.

I caught up with Naila inside and we made our way to the imam's office. His assistant looked up from his desk. 'Hi, Kamil, come to see the sheikh?'

'If he's free?'

'He's on the phone, I think. Wait outside his room till he's done.'

We could hear the imam inside. 'But what *else* can we do, Father Spence? There are so many more of them now. You and I have done what we can, but it's not enough. We have to rethink our strategy, work together even more to clear this terrible scourge . . . Yes, that's a good idea. Come and see me . . . How about Tuesday morning? Okay, thank you. Salaam aleikum.'

We knocked and entered the small room where Imam Faisal Masroor was sitting behind a desk, peering at a form. A smile covered his face as we came in. 'Come in, Kamil, you have saved me from a very boring piece of paperwork. Sit. You know, when I became imam of the mosque, I thought I would spend my time looking after the spiritual path of my fellow Muslims, not worrying about whether the facilities and services manager is doing a good job.' He came around his desk, shook my hand and gave me a brief hug, his grey bushy beard with its familiar rosewater scent tickling my face. Wearing his usual brown pin-striped jacket over a white thobe, an even whiter topi almost sparkling in the dingy room, his unlined face made him look a lot younger than his sixty years. At Anjoli's behest I'd started using moisturiser – what I thought were sexy laughter lines she said were signs of premature ageing – but judging by the imam's appearance, what I needed was less devotion to Loreal and more to Allah.

'This is my friend Naila – she's from Pakistan. Are you well, Sheikh?'

He put a hand to his chest and bid her salaam aleikum as we took a seat across the desk from him; he sat back under the pictures of Mecca and Medina, the only decoration in his spartan office.

'Alhamdulillah. How can I help you today, my friend? Have you come to debate morality again?'

The imam and I had been meeting to discuss things on my mind, and I now counted him among my few friends in London. It was cheaper than therapy, and I liked the fact he was pragmatic, trying to promulgate a more progressive Islam that maintained its core values while easing Muslim integration, something we needed in an age of fire and jihad preachers and police infiltrating mosques to identify and weed out potential radicals. 'Islam has always been relevant to the times,' he would say. 'But nothing is set except the love of Allah.'

'Not today, Sheikh. Today we wanted to talk to you about Salma Ali.'

His face fell. 'Poor girl, I heard what happened – a terrible thing. Her parents were here for morning prayers and they told me. Very sad occurrence. For one to die so young . . .'

'I know. Naila and I found her.'

His eyes widened. '*That* I did not know. It must have been an enormous shock. What happened?'

Once again I rehashed the circumstances of Salma's death, ending with '. . . and she was religious, I believe? She used to come here?'

'She came here, yes. You don't see many young girls coming nowadays.'

'Did she confide in you?'

'Confide?' He waggled his head from side to side, beard swaying. 'We would talk now and then.'

'Did you know she was carrying?' said Naila.

Once again, the imam's eyes opened in shock. 'No, I did not.' He went silent for a moment, mulling over what he had heard. Then, 'Poor child. She did not take her own life, did she?'

'No,' I said. 'It was murder. Did she mention she had a boyfriend?'

'No. She came and saw me two weeks ago because she was worried and wanted my advice. But it was not about this thing.'

'What was it?'

He went silent again. 'I cannot break her confidences . . .'

'It is important, Sheikh. I'm trying to investigate what happened and bring her justice. Anything you can tell me would help.'

He smiled. 'Ah, Kamil, you are finding your way back to your purpose. I told you the jihad never stops, didn't I?'

'I am. You did. You saw something in me I hadn't seen myself.'

He tented his arms under his chin and looked at us, looking for all the world like the ancient stone sculpture of an Assyrian king I had seen with Anjoli at the British Museum. His eyes seemed to be full of compassion and a wisdom I would never attain. The beard helped. Only religious leaders and Shoreditch baristas could pull it off.

'All right. I will tell you, if it helps catch her killer. She saw me two weeks ago and was quite upset. She said someone had made a fool of her in the college.'

My pulse quickened.

'Who made a fool of her? Could it be about her pregnancy, do you think?' said Naila.

He shook his head. 'I don't think so. She did not give me any details. She told me something bad was happening at her college and she didn't know what to do about it. Something had occurred around six weeks ago, but she thought she had resolved it. But it had now happened again, and someone had lied to her. She didn't know if she should tell the truth and expose what she knew. But that could destroy many lives. Or should she stay quiet? But if she did not speak out, she would be complicit in what was going on. And she was not certain she could live with that. She had a powerful sense of right and wrong.'

'Did she tell you what was happening in the college?' said Naila, excitement in her voice.

'No, she didn't. She said it was very serious and she should go to the dean and tell him. Maybe it was something to do with bullying?'

'Why do you say that?' I said.

He shrugged. 'Just an impression?'

'And what did you advise?' I knew full well what the imam's advice would have been. This was not a man who cared for dissembling.

'I told her to tell the truth. The Surah al-Baqarah says "Confound not the truth with falsehood nor conceal it knowingly." And that is what she should do. The consequences will fall on the evildoers, not on her. Her conscience would be clean.'

'And did she?'

'I don't know. I told her to confront the person who she thought might be responsible, but she worried about hurting innocent people.'

This opened up a whole new line of enquiry. It also explained her meeting with the dean. What had Salma uncovered in the college? How could I find out?

'So, there was a *specific* person she mentioned?' I said. Who could that be? Who was the innocent person who would get hurt? It didn't sound like Ziad.

The imam scratched his head under his topi. 'There was a man she said she had to speak to. I told her to do that. It is always best to tackle these things upfront.'

'You're definite she mentioned a man?'

'Yes.' He hesitated. 'But you should know something.'

'What?'

'I don't want to speak ill of the dead, but this was not the first time Salma had come to me. There was always something upsetting her. Sometimes her idea of right and wrong was maybe too . . . extreme.'

'What do you mean?'

He looked uncomfortable.

'Occasionally I wondered if she was making things up. She liked to feel important, I think. To be the centre of attention. I was not sure whether I should believe her. It was always something different. She had found someone cheating on exams; should she complain? She had seen one of our faithful from the mosque drinking beer; should she tell him to stop? Things like that. I always told her to be truthful, but maybe occasionally she was not. I hate to say it, but she could be a bit of a busybody.' He looked at his watch. 'It is almost time for zuhr namaz. I must prepare. Is there anything else I can help you with, Kamil? Will you stay for prayers?'

'No, thank you, Sheikh. You have been very helpful. I wish I could stay, but I have to get back to the restaurant. Did you hear about Yasir?'

His face saddened. 'Yes. Very sad. He was a good man. I will miss him.'

'Did you ever see him drinking?'

'Drinking?' He looked puzzled. 'I don't think so. What little money he had, he spent on cigarettes and food. When you and your Anjoli didn't feed him, of course. He was not an alcoholic. Why?'

'No, reason. I was just wondering.'

'Khuda hafiz,' said Naila, and we left.

We walked out of the mosque and crossed the road, dodging the people coming in for prayers and a bus that lumbered towards us.

'Well,' I said to Naila, 'that opens everything up. What do you think Salma was talking about?'

'I don't know.'

'Had you heard rumours about any scandal in the college?'

She thought for a moment, then shook her head. 'I can't think what it might be. I've read about cheating and bribery at other unis but nothing at King's.'

'Or sexual harassment, that's another possibility.'

'Yes, that's true. Do you think someone was harassing Salma? But the imam also said she made things up.'

'I don't know what to think. I wonder if she told Ziad. We have to speak to him again. *He* also mentioned she seemed preoccupied.'

'It could have been the pregnancy. Salma may have made up stuff, but she didn't make *that* up. Looks like Ziad is at the centre of all this, no? I mean, she was pregnant; she was scared of her dad; they had fought . . .'

'Let me leave Ziad a message.' I dialled and to my surprise he answered. 'Ziad? Hi, this is Kamil Rahman – we met yesterday. I was—'

His voice exploded through the phone, almost tearing my ear off. 'You lied to me! You're not a policeman – you're a bloody cook! The police told me. What the fuck was it to you to come and tell me about Salma like that?'

I had been expecting this and tried to calm him down. 'I didn't lie to you, Ziad. I *was* a detective. In fact, I helped solve the Rakesh Sharma killing last year. Salma's parents have asked me to investigate her death, so we had to speak to you. You want to help find her killer, don't you?'

There was silence, then he said, 'You're a bullshit artist. Fuck off!' and hung up.

'Damn.' I looked at Naila. 'Now what?'

'Let me try.' She pulled out her phone, composed a WhatsApp message and showed it to me.

Ziad, this is Naila. We're sorry for the misunderstanding. But we have information from the imam, and it could help get us closer to the truth. PLEASE meet us tonight at the Tandoori Knights restaurant in Brick Lane. Dinner on us.

I nodded, and she pressed Send.

We walked to the restaurant in silence, then her phone pinged.

'It's Ziad. He wants us to go to 13 Middleton Street. Nine tonight.'

Damn. I'd have to figure something out with Anjoli. Nine was peak time at TK.

'There you go,' said Naila. 'We have lots of suspects now – Ziad, Salma's father . . .'

'Well done. I wonder if the person Salma was talking about to the imam was Dr Mackenzie; there was something about him I didn't like.'

'I'll poke around and see if I can pick up anything. See you there at nine.'

She turned and made her way towards Whitechapel station,

her blue backpack heavy with books bouncing against her back. I watched her marching down the road till her trim figure was lost among the other pedestrians, then turned in the opposite direction to return to my chef's duties at TK and figure out how to tell Anjoli I would need to abandon her again this evening.

Chapter 15

Thursday.

Lunch was a nightmare. Two burners on the hob gave up the ghost, and an unexpected influx of dozens of diners (influenced by Anjoli's curated Instagram posts of salmon in coconut sauce and lamb chops with coriander) caused chaos in the kitchen. I ran around like a monkey with its tail on fire, chopping, frying, boiling, seasoning and whipping pans on and off the working burners while trying not to barge into the waiters rushing in and out of the kitchen shouting orders. A stroppy diner demanded I be summoned to personally explain to him why the butter chicken was not up to his expectations. I stood, an ingratiating smile stuck on my face, as he informed me his dish had too much fat in it and wasn't 'the way butter chicken should really be cooked. I have been to the Poon-jab so know what is authentic.' It was only the apologetic look on his girl-friend's face that stopped me from replying 'I'll jab your poon in a minute' and pouring the remaining sauce over his self-satisfied, florid face. This kind of bullshit happened every so often and I just had to suck it up, knowing that – besides the humiliation in front of the other diners – there would be no tip. I finally kowtowed my way back to the kitchen and, to put the ghee on the naan, splashed hot oil on my arm while swapping a pan off the hob, so stood cursing, running cold water over it as our other chef finished the lamb bhuna. My legs felt like lead by

3.30 when I turned the sign on the restaurant door to CLOSED and stumbled up to the flat to have a well-earned lie-down.

An hour later, after a fitful sleep, arm stinging, I was still fatigued, but had to go down to start the evening shift. Anjoli was studying OpenTable on her laptop and said, 'It's busy tonight. A batch of late reservations just came in online. Also, we may get a bunch of Deliveroo orders.'

Shit. I'd hoped it would be a slow night. I needed to see Ziad with Naila at nine. How was I going to tell Anjoli?

I got to work as her full-house forecast was communicated to the kitchen. As predicted, it was a hectic evening, exacerbated by the defective hob, plus my burnt arm felt like a skewered seekh kabab.

I got antsy looking at my watch every few minutes as I prepared the orders that kept coming. According to Google Maps, it would take around twenty minutes to get to Middleton Street. I didn't want to cancel the meeting as I wasn't sure if Ziad would agree to talk to me again, but neither could I leave Anjoli in the lurch. Working as a cook wasn't conducive to investigating murders. Or anything else. Maybe it was time to give up the investigation. I hadn't wanted to do it in the first place, and it was becoming too much hassle. However, since Naila had said she'd meet me there, I'd see Ziad and then call time on the case. At 8.30 I bit the bullet and asked Anjoli if I could have a word.

'What?' she said, pushing her hair out of her eyes as she calculated the bill for a customer.

'Listen, I know it's a terrible time, but I need to interview Ziad. This is the only time he could do. I'm sorry.'

'You're kidding, right?'

'No.'

She looked up. Stupefied.

'Kamil, no! We're full. How the hell are we going to cope?'

'I know, I know,' I said. 'I didn't think we would be so busy, otherwise I wouldn't have . . .'

'Thursdays are always busy. You know that!'

'And my arm's worse . . .'

'Oh, come on! It's a minor burn, it goes with the job!'

'You're right – that was a stupid thing to say. I'm so sorry, Anjoli, but Ziad may not talk to me again, and . . .'

I could hear myself whining and didn't like it.

'Fuck it. Okay, go. But I'm paying you to cook, not be a detective. Jesus! Salim Mian, can you please take over at the cooker from Kamil, he has to step out, I'll cover for you inside the restaurant.'

Now I was irked. She was the one who had pushed me to investigate the murder to begin with. I bit back my annoyance, said, 'Thanks. I'll make it up to you. This will be the last time,' threw off my chef's coat and ran out.

I jumped off the bus fifteen minutes later and raced to Ziad's house, arriving at five past nine, out of breath, to find Naila waiting for me outside, sitting on a low wall. 'Shall we go in?' I gasped.

'He texted to say he was running half an hour late.'

'And you didn't think to tell me? I almost gave myself a heart attack racing here. *And* I pissed Anjoli off.'

'Sorry, darling. I thought you would be happy to spend some extra time together.'

'Right.' I tried to control my panting. 'Sorry. Busy night, that's all. Need to catch my breath. Let's wait over there.'

We walked into Bethnal Green Nature Reserve opposite Ziad's house and found a bench, where we sat surrounded by medicinal plants. My heart rate slowed as I breathed in the scent of chicory and wild garlic. I looked around at potted trees with signs asking people to take and plant them at home and a strange black totem pole sculpture that appeared to have bats hanging from it. It was a peaceful moment after a frenetic day, and I felt the tension ooze out of me and drop onto the grass under the bench.

I took Naila's hand and after sitting for a few minutes in comfortable silence, her head on my shoulder, I turned my attention back to the case. 'Any luck in college? Did you get a sense of anything going on?'

'No.' She lifted her head to look at me, her earnest green eyes taking on a dusky tinge that matched the twilight mood. 'Everyone is shocked by Salma's death. Nobody can believe it. Especially that it happened to her of all people. She was vocal about things she didn't like, complaining about things that weren't up to her standards, but no one can think of anything specific upsetting her in recent weeks. The police came and checked out her locker and everything. Interviewed her classmates. I had to give a written statement of how we found her. They want my clothes from that night for fibres because I told them I gave her CPR.'

'Yes, they took mine too. So, no one knew anything? Did their reactions seem genuine?'

'It was a little difficult for me to ask people for information, Kamil. I mean, we don't know what Salma was talking to the imam about – I wasn't sure who to ask. It felt like I was playing cricket in the dark. I talked to my batchmates to see if they had heard of anything strange going on. One of them mentioned a rumour about hospital medicines being sold to drug dealers but had nothing to substantiate it. Ziad seems to be our best bet.'

'What types of medicines?'

'He didn't know – opiates, I suppose.'

That would make sense. From what I'd heard of her, I could imagine Salma, her hijab afloat like a cape, apprehending a drug thief.

'Aren't they kept under lock and key?'

'They are. Although if you work in the pharmacy, you have access.'

'Maybe we should interview the people who work there?'

'Good idea. I can set that up.'

'Thanks. I know this is a pain, in between doing your classes and hospital shifts.'

'It's fun, I'm learning a lot.' She slid down the bench to lie with her head in my lap. 'And I feel like I owe it to Salma.'

'How about Dr Mackenzie?' I looked down at her delicate-featured face. 'Maybe you can ask him?'

'Ask him what?'

'About these rumours of medicines going missing?'

'I'll check with Sir next time I have a tutorial.' Her eyes were closed. 'What about you? How was your day?'

'Tiring, usual nightmare in the kitchen.'

I stretched my legs out, clocking a sign saying volunteers used medicinal plans from the garden in a mobile apothecary, distributing creams and balms to the homeless. I sneaked a look at Naila, face peaceful in my lap. I needed to organise our trip away. The weekend was just two days away and I hadn't yet asked Anjoli for the time off or found a place to go. She would be even more annoyed with me. Fuck it. I needed this. The more time I spent with Naila, the more I liked her. Her spunk, the spark in her eye, the subcontinental connection we had. Yes, there *was* something real here.

As if she had read my mind, she opened her eyes. 'What?'

'Nothing. Just planning our weekend.'

'Mmm. Have you sorted it yet?'

'I will. But I was wondering . . . I mean . . . what's happening here?'

She sat up. 'What do you mean?'

'Us. I mean, I . . . l-like you, Naila,' I said, stumbling over my words. I was not very good at analysing or expressing these types of emotions.

'And I . . . like you, Kamil,' she mimicked, a smile hovering on her lips as she batted her eyes at me.

I felt like an idiot. 'Shut up.'

'Okay,' she said and kissed me. My fingers in her hair, her

113

soft body pressed to mine, the surrounding birdsong, the smell of fresh herbs and the warm breeze – all made me feel like I was in a Disney movie. My breathing got faster as the kiss continued; hers did too and soon it felt like our inhalations and exhalations were perfectly synchronised and we were in our own bubble in some other dimension. When my head began to swim, I pulled away and said, 'My God!'

'Goddess,' she said, eyes closed, the tip of her tongue licking her lips.

'What *is* happening here, Naila?'

She opened her eyes. 'Why do we have to label it? Let it evolve.'

'Do we *have* to keep sneaking around? Why not tell your uncle? He likes me.'

'It's . . . complicated,' she said after a long silence.

'Why?'

'Because . . .' She looked at her watch. 'Oh, we're late. Come on, we have to go.'

At that moment I'd have given up on Ziad and the murder and stayed with Naila all evening.

'Tell me what you mean. Why is it complicated?'

'I'll tell you later. On our weekend away.'

'Ohhh. Okay. A few more minutes, please. Kiss me again.'

She grinned. 'That's just the dopamine talking, Mr Rahman. Come on, we have a job to do.' As we crossed the road, she said, 'You know all this love-shove is just chemicals in the brain. Dopamine, oxytocin, serotonin – they all give you a natural high. Love is a drug. But it wears off. You shouldn't rely on it.'

'Chemicals or not, it feels real to me. Doesn't it to you?'

'I'm the scientist, you're a cook-cum-detective.'

And I had to be satisfied with that.

As the song went, love was the drug, and I needed to score.

Chapter 16

Thursday.

Naila and I walked through the small, well-tended front garden and I rapped on the door to the compact house with the brass nameplate saying, *Aziz*.

As we waited, I composed myself and said, 'I might need to talk to Ziad alone. I'll signal if it goes that way.'

Before I could tell her what the signal would be, a man in his early forties, dressed in trousers and a striped shirt opened the door. 'Yes, can I help you?'

'Mr Aziz! Hello, sir,' said Naila, clearly surprised.

'Hello, Naila,' said the man. 'What are you doing here?'

'You're Ziad's dad? I didn't know.'

'Of course I am.' He called over his shoulder. 'Ziad, Naila is here to see you.'

Ziad clattered down the stairs and glanced at us. 'Thanks, Daddy. Come on in. You can leave your stuff there.'

He gestured at a coat stand at the foot of the stairs as the sound of canned laughter from a television in the living room curled its way into the hall. Naila shrugged off her raincoat and hung it up, throwing her rucksack under it, and Ziad led us into a pretty, yellow kitchen, followed by his father.

'Terrible news about Salma Ali. Naila, she was in your class, wasn't she?' said Mr Aziz.

Ziad looked at the floor as Naila said, 'Yes, horrible. We found her. This is Kamil, a friend of mine.'

I shook his hand.

'Terrible,' repeated Mr Aziz, his hand limp in mine. 'Don't be too long, Ziad, it's late. Goodbye, Naila.'

Ziad shut the kitchen door, and we sat around the small table. The smell of fried onions lingered in the air. I wondered what they had eaten for dinner.

Naila spoke first. 'I didn't know you were Mr Aziz's son.' She turned to me. 'He's the pharmacist in the hospital.'

Ziad shrugged, 'Tea?'

We shook our heads, and I said, 'Thanks for seeing us again.'

He looked at us, face blank. His eyes were red and swollen – he'd been crying. 'Why have Salma's parents asked *you* to investigate? What's wrong with the police? What did they tell you? They questioned me for hours. It was terrible.'

'I'm an experienced detective, and I think they feel more comfortable having someone from the community look into it.'

He looked at me but said nothing.

'As I said on the phone, I'm sure you want justice for Salma as much as they do. I need help to find her killer. So, can I ask a few more questions?'

'I've answered all the police's questions.'

'On your advice, we spoke to the imam at the mosque, and he said Salma was worried about something she had seen at the college. Did she say anything to you about this?'

He shook his head, then paused mid-shake. 'Maybe. We were talking on the phone one night five or six weeks ago and she said she *had* seen something that bothered her. I asked her what it was, but she wouldn't tell me. She said it didn't involve me but concerned other people and the secret wasn't hers to tell.'

'Where did she see this?'

'I don't know. Maybe the college? Or the hospital? Or on her way home?'

This was about as helpful as a lion's cage made of mosquito netting.

'Was this linked to what you said she was worried about before?'

'Maybe.'

'Why didn't you tell us this then?'

'I didn't remember to be honest. Salma was always seeing things that bothered her.'

'Like what?'

'I don't know. Someone might be cheating in their exams or wasn't pulling their weight in the hospital . . . There was always something.'

'Stealing from the pharmacy?' said Naila.

'Is that what it was? Someone stealing drugs? Is that why they killed her?'

'We don't know,' I said. The last thing I wanted was a rumour spreading across campus that would muddy the waters.

'What did her parents tell you?'

I glanced at Naila. 'They told us Salma was pregnant. Did you know?'

His eyes darted to the kitchen door.

Got him! He knew all right.

He turned back to me and chewed his lip – was he weighing up his response? I gave him a pointed look to tell him I knew he had known. Naila noticed and ran with it.

'You knew, didn't you? That she was carrying. Was it your baby?'

'Talk softer.' A desperate whisper. Then his face twisted. 'Yes, I knew. She found out last week.'

'And what were you planning to do?' I said.

'I wanted to *marry* her. I *loved* her. But she said her parents would never agree, and if they found out she was pregnant, they would stop paying for her accommodation. And she wouldn't be able to finish her degree. She couldn't live here; my parents would never allow that. She wanted more than anything else to be a nurse. We argued. She was so upset; I didn't know what to do.'

'Is that what you fought about that night?'

He nodded, face in pain.

'Yes. She . . . she wanted to . . . she said she would . . .'

'Have a termination,' Naila finished the sentence for him, and he nodded miserably.

I had my motive.

'She was going to get some pills. I kept trying to talk her out of it, but she wouldn't listen. She was torn up inside. She was so religious, you see. I tried to tell her abortion was haram, but she convinced herself Islam permitted it if the mother's life was in danger, and *her* life would have been in danger from her father if he had found out.'

This was some convoluted reasoning, I wasn't sure Imam Masroor would have condoned Salma's logic.

'Why, what would her father have done?'

'She said she feared him. I don't know what he would have done; I never met him.'

'Did he hit her?'

'I think so. Maybe. Sometimes.'

We went silent as I saw Salma, alone in her flat, wrestling with the biggest decision she had ever had to make in her brief life, the two most important men in her life at loggerheads about it. One begging her to keep the baby and the other a threat if she agreed to do so.

'Was this all she was worried about, or was there something more?'

'I told you, there was something else, but I don't know what.'

It was time to apply more pressure. I needed him alone.

118

I looked at Naila and inclined my head to the door. Without acknowledging me, she said, 'Can I use your bathroom?'

Ziad nodded. 'Up the stairs to the left.'

She left and shut the kitchen door behind her.

'Salma's death has upset her. She thinks you had something to do with it.' I leaned back in my chair. 'I believe you, Ziad. From my time as an inspector in Kolkata, I know how the police think. They will look at the obvious things. And Ziad, it doesn't look good. You were her boyfriend. She was pregnant. They have a witness who knows you used to visit her at her flat. You had a fight. The neighbour heard shouting. You have no alibi for the night she died . . .' He tried to interrupt, but I steamrollered on. 'The police will find your fingerprints in the flat. So, that gives them motive, means and opportunity. That's all they need to arrest you.'

'Arrest me!' His voice rose in panic. 'But I didn't do it. I loved her.'

'I know you did. I believe you. But here's the thing, Ziad. I saw the killer leave that night.'

He froze. 'What do you mean you saw him leave? Who did you see?'

'I didn't see his face. But he was about your build, and I couldn't swear it wasn't you if the police asked me.'

He looked at me like a little boy caught stealing sweets from a shop.

'What should I do? What will the police do?'

'Let me help you, Ziad. I think you *were* there the night she died. I don't think you killed her. You loved her; I can see that. But I believe you met her that evening; maybe you fought, then left. Or perhaps you found her dead, and it *was* you I saw leaving. The neighbours said they saw you.' Well, Mrs Longfellow *had* said she'd seen Ziad, just not that night. 'If you tell me the truth, I can help you deal with the police. Nobody will need to know. I won't tell Naila. I only want to find the killer. And we both know you would never harm Salma.'

He looked at me, mouth open, processing what I had just said. Was he weighing up the benefits of confessing he had been there? This was the most delicious moment of being a cop, the second before the confession.

Then it was gone. His face closed like a door slamming shut.

'You're trying to trap me, like the police were. I wasn't there. I told you the truth. Yes, I *was* upset about Salma not wanting to keep the baby, but I was right here with my parents all night. You can ask them. I don't need your help. I think you'd better go now.'

I had been gambling with a six high and he had called my bluff. I looked into the steely eyes that stared back into mine. Did he have anything to do with it? While laying out the case against him I'd almost convinced myself he was the killer. But looking at that furious face, I wasn't sure any more. This was the problem with being a detective – you always had to assume the person you were talking to was lying. If you later found they were telling the truth, fine, no major harm done. But if you assumed they were truthful, and they weren't, that's when things went to hell.

'Okay, if you want to play it that way, here's my advice for free. Be careful, Ziad. I had a lot of experience with the Met Police last year, and they are busy, overworked and can be racist. They will often go with the most convenient culprit just to close the case. And that's you. If you decide you want to talk, or if you remember something, call me. I'm the only person who's on your side.'

He didn't respond, and we walked out of the kitchen. I heard Naila's voice in the living room and poked my head in to find her chatting with Ziad's parents. She looked up and said, 'All done? I was just catching up with Mr and Mrs Aziz.'

I nodded.

'Well lovely to see you. Nice to meet you, Aunty.' She came out and grabbed her stuff. 'Bye, Ziad.'

Ziad said nothing, just opened the door, stood to one side to let us out, then shut it behind us.

As we walked to her car, Naila said, 'Well? Did your plan work?'

'No, it didn't.' I told her what had transpired.

'Do you think he did it? What you said sounds compelling. His parents went to sleep early that night, I checked.'

'Nicely done,' I said as she looked pleased with herself. 'I don't know if he did it or not, but he's an obvious suspect. The police will be all over him, and we need to know if they find out anything. I'll try to speak to Tahir, see if I can wheedle anything out of him.'

'How will you do that?'

'He's a friend of Anjoli's from school.'

'Oh, I wondered what the connection was between the three of you. What did you think about what Ziad said about Salma's father hitting her? He seemed violent, the way he attacked you in the restaurant.'

'Yes, that struck me too. And there was something off about his wife's reaction when he said he was at home the night Salma was killed. I need to follow up on that.'

'Maybe he found out about the pregnancy and killed Salma rather than bear the shame of it. You read about that kind of thing all the time.'

'That's what Anjoli said – honour killing. Maybe. Although given the way he attacked me, he seems more likely to kill the guy who made her pregnant. But you're right, he is a suspect. The key must lie in what she found out in college. It was important enough for her to talk to the dean.'

'All right. You handle her parents, I'll keep investigating in the college. Between us, I'm sure we'll get somewhere.' Her face fell. 'I keep forgetting this is about an actual person I knew and not a puzzle to be solved. She's no more. How do you not go crazy, Kamil, with all this darkness and death?'

'Distance yourself. But not too much. You've got to care and not let it become just another job.'

But I knew what she meant. It was too easy to get caught up in the chase and enjoy the rush when things fell into place. I had to keep remembering this was about Salma. I had nothing to prove and no one to prove it to any more.

But my mind kept going back to that moment when I'd felt Ziad was going to confess – I'd felt an adrenalin rush that beat dopamine into the ground. It was as if a spotlight was illuminating my way ahead, and the evening had given me clarity about three things.

I would not give up the investigation.

I would make a future with Naila.

I was a cop not a cook.

Chapter 17

Friday.

The first call came at 10.30 in the morning.

'Can you come and see us at Bethnal Green station today, Kamil? We'd like your help with something.'

'What's it about, Tahir?'

'I can't discuss it over the phone – can you come around four?'

'That's after the lunch service, it should be all right.'

Very mysterious. I'd told them I'd touched the body, but the thought that they'd found something on my clothes was making me sweat. If I was a suspect in a murder in a foreign country, the authorities had the power to send me back home with the stroke of a pen, even if I was innocent. I've always had an ambiguous relationship with authority; being questioned or told what to do by anyone has never sat well with me.

The second call was half an hour later on Anjoli's phone.

'Hello . . . Yes, this is Anjoli Chatterjee. Who?' Horror entered her voice, and she whispered, 'No, that can't be right . . . Oh no! I can't believe it. He was just . . . Can I come and see you . . . Damn. No, I can't now, how about around three . . . Thanks very much, I'll see you then.'

She hung up and looked at me, face crumpled, as she sat down with a bump.

'What's the matter, Anjoli? What happened?'

'That was the Webber Street Mission. A homeless shelter in Waterloo. They ... they just found Louis dead. Outside their shelter.'

'Louis?'

'The Black guy who ate here the other day. Oh my God, Kamil. What's happening? How can this be?'

'Shit!' I said, remembering the burly veteran. 'Did they say what happened? He didn't look sick or anything.'

She shook her head. 'No, he seemed fine. I'm going to talk to them after lunch. Will you come?'

'Of course. I need to see Tahir at four, but I'll come with you first.'

She looked at me gratefully and I decided to take my chance. I'd found a romantic Airbnb in Brighton that was available for my weekend with Naila – all I needed was Anjoli's go ahead.

'Listen, this may not be the best time to raise it, but could I have Saturday and Sunday off?'

'Why?'

'Umm – Naila and I wanted to go away for the weekend.'

Her face gave nothing away as she said, 'It would have been good to get more notice.'

'I know – it just happened. I'd really appreciate it.'

She let out a sigh. 'Well fine, I'll get one of the others to cover and ... hang on, Saturday is Yasir's funeral – don't you want to come for that?'

Damn! I'd completely forgotten the imam had rung to tell us. I *couldn't* miss that.

'You're right. I did forget. How about next weekend? I can check if Naila is free?'

'Sure.'

Just then my phone pinged with a text. I felt a lift when I saw it was Naila.

On earlies at Tommy's meet after lunch?

Need to go webber st mission in W'loo at 3, meet there? Then Tahir at 4

Why webber?

Tell you when we meet

OK. have my clothes from night we found Salma for Tahir x

BTW can't do this weekend away – have funeral. How about next?

A pause as my tension rose.

Then: *OK, I'll rearrange my shift xx*

Great! I'll fix xxx

I could wait a week. The anticipation was half the fun. Well, maybe not half.

Anjoli was preoccupied during the lunch service. We turned the sign to CLOSED at 2.30, and a bus and a train later were at the mission at three to see Naila waiting outside a red-brick building with large, arched windows, a CCTV camera above her, pointing at the street. We walked in past two people engrossed over a chessboard, and Anjoli asked for Masika at reception.

'What are we doing here?' said Naila as we waited.

'They found another homeless person we knew dead this morning,' I whispered.

Before Naila could say anything, Masika, a large Black woman dressed in a colourful dashiki, came out and we introduced ourselves.

'One of our volunteers found him this morning. He was sleeping on the street outside. She tried to wake him to see if he wanted breakfast, but he was dead. He had no identification, but we found your card in his pocket, so I rang you on the off chance.'

'His name was Louis,' said Anjoli, as Masika led us to a room. 'What time was he found?'

'Around ten.'

'What did you do?'

'We called 999, and the police came. They took the body to the hospital. We reported it to the local authority in case they want to do an SAR review. Did you know him?'

'Yes. Well, no, not really. He ate at our restaurant two days ago. What's SAR?'

'SAR? Safeguarding Adult Review. It's done to see what lessons we can learn from homeless deaths. But this looked quite natural. We have his things here, if you want to see them.' Masika pointed at a box.

Anjoli and I looked through Louis' few possessions – his rucksack, a worn sweater, two grubby fishing magazines, a bag of sugar cubes.

'He liked sugar, didn't he – he took some from us too and . . . that's funny,' said Anjoli, taking out an empty bottle of gin.

'What's that?' said Naila.

'It's the same size and brand of gin as the bottle we saw next to Yasir.'

'What does that mean?'

'Dunno. This one's empty, though. Louis must have drunk it.'

I took the bottle from Anjoli, looked at it for a few seconds, then said, 'I noticed a CCTV camera outside – is it working?'

'Yes, of course,' said Masika. 'Why?'

Anjoli looked at me, brow furrowed in a question, as I said, 'Just curious about something. Could we look at the video from last night?'

Masika shrugged. 'Follow me.'

I pocketed the gin bottle, and we followed her into a small office where she booted up a computer and scrolled through the black and white footage, Anjoli and Naila tense next to me.

Louis shuffled up at 6.21 p.m., laid out a large piece of cardboard on the street in front of the mission and sat on it. He arranged another piece on top of himself.

'He doesn't even have a blanket; he's just using cardboard,' said Naila, shocked. 'Why on earth doesn't he come into the shelter? He could have got a bed in here, no? I don't understand this at all. Why did he want to suffer outside?'

Anjoli said nothing, just stared mute at the screen, her eyes willing Louis to be well.

'I don't know,' said Masika. 'We had room last night. Sometimes people don't like to be with others.'

'He said he didn't,' said Anjoli, under her breath.

Louis lay under his cardboard blanket, thumbing through a magazine in the evening light, people ignoring him as they passed. Anjoli kept scrolling, then stopped. At 7.18 p.m. a man in a dark suit wearing a baseball cap approached Louis and bent over him. He said a few words, then reached into the pocket of his coat. The video captured the glint of glass as he handed a bottle to our man, then left as Louis opened it, took a swig and looked blankly at the camera.

The atmosphere in the room was electric as his eyes stared at us. The hair on the back of my neck rose, I could sense Naila holding her breath next to me and Anjoli staring fixedly at the screen.

'Oh God, Kamil,' said Anjoli. 'I can't believe he'll be dead in a few hours. He looks fine. I wonder who that man was.'

'Someone thinking he was helping, probably,' said Masika, freezing the CCTV on the hand holding the bottle. 'Although giving them alcohol isn't a good idea.'

'Do you think there might have been something wrong with the gin? Maybe that's why Louis died. Funny that Yasir had the same bottle.'

'Tahir said Yasir's bottle hadn't been opened, though,' I said.

'Tahir!' said Naila. 'Didn't you say you had to see him at four, Kamil? You're going to be late.'

I looked at my watch: 3:35. 'Shit, you're right. We'd better go, Anjoli.'

'Wait. Masika, have homeless deaths gone up around here? Do you know?'

Masika paused for a few seconds, then nodded. 'Now that you mention it, you may be right. It's hard to tell, but a few other shelters in the area have seen a few. It's been warm, so there's no reason for it.'

Anjoli sat, deep in thought, then looked up. 'Can I just take a video of that footage, Masika?' As she filmed it on her phone, she said, 'I'm coming with you to see Tahir, Kamil. Thanks so much, Masika. I'll let you know what happens.'

'Why did you ask that, Anjoli?' said Naila as we walked to the Underground.

'Tapan, the guy in the shelter near us, said an unusual number of rough sleepers had died in our area in the last month.'

'And?'

'I don't know. It's just odd, no?'

'It's sad, Anjoli, but what are you saying? I mean, what's a normal amount of deaths? There must be all kinds of reasons for this?'

'I know, I know. But first Yasir and then Louis . . .'

'It must be a coincidence. I think Yasir's death has affected both of us, Anjoli,' I said. 'I know we liked him, and you feel strongly about this, but sometimes awful stuff just happens.'

'You're the one who wanted to look at the CCTV, Kamil,' said Anjoli, frustration in her voice. 'How *can* it be normal? Two homeless people we know both die within a few days of each other? Especially at this time of the year when it's warm. Both the centres said it was odd. *And* the same gin bottle at both locations? That's weird. That guy on the CCTV. I just . . . just feel something's wrong.'

'I admit I was a little curious about Louis having that bottle as well. But do you think this guy is *killing* homeless people?'

'I didn't say that.'

This was a giant leap, even for Anjoli. Coincidences happen. I knew she had a strong social conscience and went through causes like a hurricane through a town, but a suited baseball-capped serial killer stalking the homeless was a stretch. Her passion was admirable, but I doubted very much that her theory had any basis in reality. It was an increasing fact of life that people were dying on the streets, and an extra dozen could just be a statistical blip. But there was no stopping Anjoli when she was on a crusade.

'Why would anyone want to kill Yasir? Or Louis? They were both harmless.'

'I don't know, Kamil, but let's see what Tahir says.'

'I agree with Kamil, Anjoli,' said Naila. 'These people are old, drug addicts, alcoholics, runaways, they have mental problems. It's tough on the streets. It's not surprising they don't survive.'

'Exactly,' I said, glad I had an ally. 'You can mourn Yasir and Louis, but not by haring off on—'

'All right,' she said as we got to the Tube. 'Leave it. You're right. I'm stupid. I just won't say anything ever again!'

I didn't want her annoyed with me; I still needed her support and time off to investigate Salma's death and go on my weekend. I looked at Naila and said, 'Okay, let's see what Tahir says.'

'Leave it.'

The rest of the journey was in silence.

Chapter 18

Friday.

Bethnal Green police station was an unprepossessing red-brick building, a far cry from the cool, colonial elegance of Lalbazar police headquarters in Kolkata where I had worked for so many years. A shaft of regret ran through me as I recalled the daily rhythms of my former life, walking into the squad room every day, being greeted by my sergeant, assembling my team in the incident room – missed opportunities in a different life. Maybe I could get a second chance; the last few days had awakened desires I thought were buried.

We entered the station under the anachronistic blue Metropolitan Police lantern, asked for Sergeant Ismail at the front desk and settled down to wait on a bench in front of the Plexiglass-screened reception. Naila scanned the notices on the board, a combination of the usual health and safety bulletins interspersed with appeals to the public for help with crimes in the area, as Anjoli pored over the CCTV footage she had recorded at Webber and I took in the place and people. It was a total contrast to the bustling Lalbazar with its never-ending queues of complainants and desperate relatives waiting to see the duty officer. This station, with its strained silence, stained walls and uncomfortable seating had the air of having given up all hope years ago. Maybe they kept it this way so the criminals would confess just to get out of this waiting room. My phone beeped: *Please call me asap. Ziad.* Just as I raised a finger to reply, a harried-looking Tahir came out, plastic bag in hand.

He paused when he saw us all, 'Oh, you're all here. We just needed Kamil.'

'We had a couple of things to discuss, Tahir,' said Anjoli. 'I hope it's okay.'

He hesitated and looked at his watch. 'All right, thanks for coming. Sorry to keep you waiting. Follow me, guys.'

He waved at the officer behind the screen, who buzzed us through, and we followed him into a corridor painted a maudlin mauve. Stopping at a small kitchenette, we helped ourselves to institutional coffee and milk pods, then continued to a door marked, helpfully, *Interview Room.*

'Terrible coffee. I apologise, but it's all we've got. Here we are, have a seat. Classy shirt, Anjoli,' he said glancing at Anjoli's *Ceci n'est pas une t-shirt* T-shirt.

'You know me so well, Tahir.'

I looked around at the space, a far cry from the dingy, stained rooms with barred windows, hard plastic chairs and scratched tables we used in Lalbazar. This room boasted a carpet, padded chairs, a bright curtain over the window and video cameras in two corners of the ceiling. In Kolkata the outside was pristine and the inside rotten, here it was the other way around. I preferred this – show over substance was never my bag. It did, however, smell of stale sweat and was uncomfortably hot, as if the heating was on full in the middle of spring. Maybe they kept it this way to discomfit the interviewees.

The three of us sat on one side of a table in the centre of the room, Tahir on the other – as if he was the candidate for a panel interview instead of the other way around. After a minute DI Rogers joined us and sat next to him, restoring balance to the proceedings.

'All of you?' he said.

'They had something to tell us,' said Tahir.

The tape recorder on the wall next to me remained switched off, so perhaps it was just a chat as opposed to a formal interview.

'Thanks for coming in, sir, madam, madam,' said Rogers. 'It's about the person you saw leaving the flat of the murder victim the other night, Mr Rahman. What did you say he was wearing?'

'I didn't say it was a man. *They* were wearing a yellow hoodie and dark jeans, I think.'

'It was a warm night, wasn't it? Wasn't it odd they had a hoodie on?'

'Doesn't everyone wear hoodies these days?' Did they think I'd made it up? Would he switch the tape on now?

But he laughed, said, 'That's true,' and nodded to Tahir, who pulled out an evidence bag which he held up in front of me. It contained a yellow garment.

'Do you think this could be the hoodie you saw?' said Tahir.

I peered at it. 'Can I take it out?'

'I'm afraid not.'

I took the bag from him and held it up, turning it from side to side, Naila and Anjoli looking on with fascination.

'I only got a quick glimpse, but it looks like it *could* be. Who does it belong to?'

Rogers nodded, seeming satisfied. 'I'm not at liberty to say, I'm afraid. But thank you. What did you want to tell us?'

Anjoli said, 'It's about Yasir. The homeless man we found dead the other day. Remember?'

'Yes, of course,' said Tahir.

'So, we just found out *another* homeless man we know – Louis – died in Waterloo this morning. And the same brand of gin was next to him. And we have CCTV of someone giving him the gin. Look.'

She showed Rogers and Tahir the footage on her phone and

I gave them the gin bottle I had pocketed, holding it by the screw top.

'I see,' said Rogers. 'And . . .'

'Look, I know it sounds silly, but both the shelter near us and Waterloo said they had seen an unusual number of homeless deaths. Suppose someone is intent on doing homeless people harm?'

There was a long silence. Then Tahir cleared his throat and said, 'That's quite a supposition, Anjoli. Did anyone you spoke to say they had any suspicions of foul play?'

'No, but—'

'They tested the bottle of gin found near Yasir. There was nothing wrong with the booze and the bottle was unopened and not tampered with. They did a tox screen on the body – it came up clean. No drugs, no poison, no alcohol. Unusual for a rough sleeper. The pathologist said he died of natural causes.'

'They found nothing at all?' said Anjoli, disappointed.

'No.'

'Can you test *this* bottle? And do another screen on Louis? Maybe check it for fingerprints as well?'

Tahir picked up the bottle and looked at Rogers, who nodded.

'Thanks,' said Rogers. 'But it's probably just a coincidence. Unfortunately, rough sleepers die all the time. There are a lot more around year on year so you would expect the numbers of deaths to go up.'

'But this may be beyond normal statistical bounds.'

'I can't comment on that, miss. But listen, we will check this out and let you know. Thank you for bringing it to our attention – we want the public to be vigilant. Sergeant Ismail will show you out.'

'Oh wait,' said Naila. 'Here are my clothes from the other night.' She reached into her backpack and gave Rogers a Tesco carrier bag.

'Thanks.' He took them and left.

As Tahir rose to lead us out, I said, 'Coming back to Salma for a minute, Tahir, have you interviewed Ziad? Her boyfriend? There were a few oddities in what he told us.'

'Yes, he told us you had spoken to him. And you told him you were with the police. Come on, Kamil, you've got to stop this.'

I brushed that aside. 'The girl's parents asked if I could help. Ziad knew about her pregnancy and wanted her to keep the baby. She wanted to get rid of it and they had a fight about it. And he used to visit her flat regularly. He has no alibi for the night.'

'Yes, we know about his visits to the flat and his movements on the night in question. But I didn't know about his fight with Salma. Tell me more.'

'Not a lot more to tell. Her phone, forensics and CCTV may provide more information. Has it?'

'I *can't* tell you that, Kamil.'

'Here's the thing. Tahir. I think I can win Ziad's trust and see if he knows anything – he just texted me, look. I also spoke to Salma's father – *he* has quite a temper. He attacked me, thinking I was her boyfriend. And I'm not sure he was home when he said he was.'

I didn't tell him what the imam had said about Salma finding out something in her college – he could discover that himself, and if I didn't have access to their resources, I needed an edge in this investigation.

I waited, seeing his eyes narrowing. Tahir was ambitious. If he could bring in the killer it would be a tremendous fillip for his career. And I needed to show him I was the guy who could help make that happen.

Anjoli chipped in, 'We could be a lot of help to you on the ground, Tahir. Like you, I've lived here all my life. I'm from the community; people know me from the restaurant. Ziad and Salma's parents trust Kamil.'

Naila piped up, 'And I'm at the college and can be your eyes and ears there.'

I summed up: 'So we have perfect coverage between us, and we can get information you may not be able to, because . . . you know what people think of the police around here. And of course, you'd get the credit.'

'What are you, the Famous Five?' he said, but I could see he was considering it. Then he sighed. 'I suppose I can't stop the three of you asking questions. If you find anything, let me know. But be careful, Anjoli, this isn't a game.'

'We will,' I said. 'I appreciate this Tahir. We both want to find out who did it, right? That will be our top priority.'

Anjoli chimed in, 'And the homeless deaths.'

He grunted, and I said, 'So, Tahir, where did you find the hoodie?'

This was the crunch point to see what he would share. It almost felt as if the room was holding its breath, then I realised I was.

'I can't tell you,' he said. As I exhaled, deflated, he added, 'But the points you made about Ziad weren't wrong. We went to visit him this morning and searched his house.'

I had my answer.

'Thanks. I'll tell you what I learn from him. Anything from SOCO? Her phone?'

'Don't push it, Columbo! We're testing the hoodie for DNA and fibres.'

'If the hoodie was Ziad's I guess his DNA on it together with Salma's wouldn't be unexpected? He *was* her boyfriend.'

'If the hoodie don't fit, you must acquit,' said Anjoli.

'Ha ha. Let me know what you learn. There are other people we are looking into. I'll let you know if we need anything else from you. I'll also check out the homeless deaths, Anjoli. Okay, Naila and Kamil, we need to take your prints and DNA to eliminate you from Salma's crime scene. Can you come with me, please? Anjoli, you can wait in reception.'

He took us to another room where he took fingerprints and hair samples. After he had finished, Naila said brightly, 'Can I get a pic of you doing my fingerprints for my Insta?'

Tahir rolled his eyes and I said to Naila, 'Shows how bad-ass you are,' feeling somewhat strange at having had to go through the process I had performed on dozens of suspects myself.

'That I am,' she said.

I had my source inside the police. Now I just had to beat them to finding the killer.

Chapter 19

Friday.

Naila and I collected Anjoli, walked out onto the busy Bethnal Green Road and headed back towards the restaurant.

'Well, that was successful,' said Naila. 'Nice work, Kamil, I think he'll help now.'

'Yes, I figured if we could make him a hero, he'd be open to it,' I said, enjoying her approbation.

'He said he was looking into other people,' said Anjoli. 'Who do you think they could be?'

'I don't know,' I said. 'Her dad, maybe? Someone else in college? Neighbours?'

'We should try to find out,' said Naila.

'Naila, can you kill someone and make it look natural?' said Anjoli.

'Is this about Louis again?' I said. 'This isn't an Agatha Christie mystery, Anjoli. You shouldn't have brought up the homeless deaths with Tahir. It's very far-fetched. It made us look silly.'

Anjoli gave me a glare and turned back to Naila. 'You know a bit about drugs. Do you think untraceable poisons exist?'

'I don't know of any – we don't have a module on undetectable poisons in our course.' A smile. 'I think they are pretty much fictional. If the police do a post-mortem, they should be able to find any toxins – like the Novichok those Russians used in Salisbury, they are all traceable. Also, didn't Tahir say the gin bottle had nothing wrong with it? Let's see if they find anything on the one you gave him today and on the post-mortem on Louis.'

'Do you think Russian agents are trying to clean up London's streets so that oligarchs don't have to step over homeless people when getting out of their Bentleys?' I laughed.

'What the fuck's wrong with you, Kamil?' said Anjoli. 'I am worried about these people, and you're standing around making stupid jokes.'

'Sorry,' I said, taken aback. But she wasn't done yet.

'You may be obsessed with yourself and how demeaning your cook's job is, and—'

'I'm not—'

'And what a turn for the worse your life has taken, but these people have literally NOTHING. They sleep on the fucking streets, eat out of bins, cover themselves with fucking cardboard for fuck's sake, and okay maybe there isn't a killer trying to murder them but show compassion at least.'

She ran out of breath and strode off.

'Anjoli, wait!' Naila ran after her and I followed. 'Anjoli, Kamil's being horrible. Apologise, Kamil.'

'I'm sorry, Anjoli,' I said to her back as she marched in front of me. 'I do care. I do understand. It's . . . it's my way of coping.'

When we reached the restaurant, she went in, then wheeled around, eyes still blazing.

'You were being a complete arsehole.'

She vanished into the kitchen as Naila caught up with me.

'That was *not* nice, Kamil.'

Shame washed over me. 'I know, it was stupid—'

My phone rang, and I answered, heart rat-a-tatting because of the argument that had erupted. Anjoli had never dressed me down like that before, and I didn't like it.

'Kamil?' said a voice I didn't recognise.

'Yes?'

'This is Sandra Ali. Salma's mum.'

'Oh. Hello, Mrs Ali.' I calmed myself. 'What can I do for you?'

'I'm in London to move Salma's things out of her flat. I was wondering if we could meet if you found out anything?'

I hadn't anything of value I could tell her, but it could be useful to talk to her without Mr Ali watching over her.

'I did.'

'Can you come now? I'm at Salma's flat.'

Did I need to calm Anjoli down? *Fuck it.* 'Yes, I'll be there soon.'

As soon as I disconnected, the phone rang again.

'Hello, Kamil, this is Ziad. I texted.'

'Hi. Yes, sorry, I've been busy.'

'You said you would help me?'

'I can try.'

'The police came to see me first thing this morning. They searched my house.'

'What did they find?'

'They took away a bag of my clothes. But one piece of clothing wasn't mine.'

'What do you mean?'

'They found a yellow hoodie scrunched up in the bottom of my wardrobe. It wasn't mine.'

'Whose was it?'

'I don't know, I've never seen it.'

'But it was in your wardrobe? Who else has access to it?'

'Just my parents. That's what I don't understand.'

What was Ziad trying to do here? The obvious answer was the police had found a vital piece of evidence that would place him at the scene of the crime. But denying all knowledge of it seemed odd, given they had found it in his room. And there could be an innocent explanation for any fibres. Or was his father involved in some complicated way? Was *he* another of Tahir's suspects?

He was a pharmacist and, based on what Naila had said, the murder might involve drugs. But would a father frame his son?

'Were your parents there when the police searched the house?'

'Yes. They are upset and furious with me. You said you were on my side. Can you help?'

'Help you do what, Ziad?'

'I don't know. Tell the police the hoodie isn't mine. You said you saw the man. You can tell them that's not what he was wearing.'

'I can't lie to the police, Ziad,' I said, not mentioning I had already tentatively identified the garment. 'But let me think on it. Did the police make you try the hoodie on?'

'No. It looked big for me. But most clothes are big for me.' His voice sounded forlorn as he repeated, 'It isn't mine,' and hung up.

Naila pointed to the kitchen.

'I know, I know!' I said and went in. Anjoli was clattering dishes, getting ready for the evening shift.

'I'm sorry,' I said. 'Please forgive me.'

'Whatever.'

'Anjoli, sorry again. I was being insensitive.'

'You weren't insensitive. You were a dickhead.'

'I know. I'll make it up to you.'

She grunted and went back to pulling crockery out of the cupboards.

'But . . . I'm sorry, and I know I'm leaving you in the lurch again, but I must see Mrs Ali at Salma's flat. I'll be back by six. Is that okay?'

She shut her eyes tight and took a deep breath but said nothing. I took that as agreement, mumbled another apology and left her to her clashing pans.

Naila gave me a questioning look as I came out of the kitchen.

I shrugged and said, 'I tried. Look, please come with me to Mrs Ali's, Naila. I need you. The number 8 goes straight there, and I'll tell you what Ziad said on the way.'

She grimaced. 'I'm not sure how to comfort a grieving mother, but okay.'

We walked out of the restaurant – I'd have to figure out how to make up with Anjoli later.

Chapter 20

Friday.

S alma's block of flats looked different in the evening sunshine. Three nights ago it had seemed derelict, dangerous and desolate, but now it just seemed . . . sad. Yet another East End building with discoloured brickwork, damp walkways, dumped mattresses and decades of depression. Forbidding signs barked warnings from every corner: NO DUMPING. DO NOT FEED THE PIGEONS. NO BALL GAMES. Three kids were kicking a football half-heartedly around a small patch of grass ground down and faded to the same colour as the building.

We paused in front of the entrance and I tried to recall in my mind's eye the figure in the yellow hoodie pushing past me on the night of the murder. Try as I might, nothing else came to mind. Maybe I should try hypnosis.

Mrs Ali buzzed us in, and Naila and I made our way up the stairs to Salma's flat. Her mother was sitting, dressed in jeans and a top, blonde hair tied back, sipping a cup of tea at the table, surrounded by empty boxes. The flat already looked abandoned with the signs and smells of forensics everywhere – furniture moved to one side, fingerprint powder, Luminol . . . Cops didn't believe in returning crime scenes to their original condition. Somehow, I didn't think the Alis were getting their deposit back on this residence.

'Thank you for coming,' she said. 'Would you like tea?'

'I'll make it,' said Naila, and busied herself in the kitchenette as I took a seat at the table with Sandra Ali.

'How have you been?' I knew as soon as the words came out of my mouth that it was a stupid question.

'How do you think?' Her eyes were red, and she looked exhausted, face and body tight with grief. 'It's been . . . hard. Yusuf has taken it badly. Just sits and stares at the TV. I needed to get away from him so came down to get Salma's things. But,' she gestured at the remnants of her daughter's life, 'maybe it wasn't a good idea.'

I nodded in sympathy. Death was always hard for survivors, but accident or illness could be rationalised as an act of God or, if you weren't a believer, a random occurrence in an unfeeling universe. Suicide or murder was different. Loved ones always blamed themselves, as if they could have prevented it. *If only* they had been in the right place at the right time, to offer support or to defend the victim from the attack that took their life. The loss plus the guilt made it unbearable.

'So what have you found?' said Sandra.

'I have a few leads I'm following up. Here, let us help you pack.'

'Thanks, I've done her bedroom. Her sheets still smell of her. I don't think I'll ever wash them.'

Tears leaked from her eyes. She brushed them away and gestured around her. 'I just need to do this stuff now. The furniture all came with the flat. I have a van downstairs.'

Naila and I packed away Salma's things, sipping our tea as we worked. Naila was far more careful than me, wrapping breakables in the bubble wrap Sandra had brought with her, labelling the boxes, taping the tops and bottoms so they wouldn't fall open while being transported. There was an ineffable sadness about handling the objects that had been part of the weave of Salma's life – some everyday, like the plates and cups and pans, others that had meant something to Salma, but now their mean-ing was lost along with her, never to be remembered again: a tiny boat made of blue glass, a ceramic ashtray with *Barcelona* written on it, a wooden apple. On a small bookshelf in the room were nursing textbooks, a couple of books on climate change and autobiographies of Malala Yousafzai and Michelle Obama. The remnants of a life, boxed up to be given to a charity shop, where they would form new memories for a stranger or sit on a shelf, gathering dust, unwanted, till they were thrown in a land-fill, buried like their original owner.

We finished the kitchen and living room in silence over the next half-hour and I sat on the sofa, avoiding looking at the spot on the floor where I had found Salma's body. I don't believe in ghosts and stuff like that, but a few nights ago a killer had choked a woman to death here – surely something of her essence must remain in the air? She was present in the objects I had just packed; was it so fanciful to feel that part of her spirit might remain in the room like the long keening fade of the final chord of a song? 'A Day In The Life' – the never-ending build followed by that last crashing note that just rang and rang and rang around your head.

I shook off my melancholy; enough of this ectoplasmic bullshit. Salma was no longer here. But her mother was.

Naila made us another cup of tea and I said, 'Tell me about Salma, Mrs Ali. What was she like?' I had to break through the guilt Sandra was feeling and get her talking without the con-stant undertow of *What could I have done differently?*

Her face twisted. 'She was the most wonderful thing in my life. Marriage to Yusuf isn't easy, but she made everything worth it.'

'Did she have a lot of friends?'

'The usual school friends. A few she was close to, others not so much.'

'No boyfriends?'

144

'No, her father would never have allowed it, she knew that. It was a battle when she wanted to study in London. But it's such a good college we couldn't refuse. Causes attracted her and nursing was her way of giving back. But she wanted to help with climate change, alleviate poverty, march for women's rights – all kinds of things.' Her eyes softened. 'She came back from this climate rally once with a T-shirt with that girl on it – what's her name? Greta Thunberg, that's it. She's my hero, Salma said. *She speaks truth to power*. And Malala – Salma was inspired by *her* bravery. And Malala was a Muslim! "I wish I could be more like her, Mummy," she would say.' Her face clouded over again. 'And now she'll never have the chance.'

Naila took her hand. 'I'm so sorry, Mrs Ali. Salma was a lovely girl. Everyone in college is upset at this tragedy.'

'She was such an upright girl. Moral.'

Moral, that word again. Ziad had used it too. I needed to get some facts before the memories of the daughter overwhelmed her grieving mother.

'I believe Salma came home last weekend?' I said. 'Was that normal? In the middle of term? Did she have any reason for coming up to Leeds?'

'I wouldn't say it was normal. She said she needed a break and wanted to come home for a bit. Looking at this place –' she gestured around her '– I'm not surprised.'

'Did she say anything while she was at home? See anyone?'

'Something had been worrying her. Something in college.'

I sat up, alert, but Naila beat me to it. 'Did she say what?'

'We were watching a programme on TV on Saturday night. Her father had gone to bed. The programme was about the Weinstein case and the women who had come forward. Salma said, out of the blue, she was worried about sexual harassment in college. I asked her if anything had happened to her, but she didn't answer. Just said she would deal with it. That was her.

145

Private. If she didn't want to tell you something she would clam up. She'd always been like that, ever since she was a child.'

I chose my words. 'The imam mentioned she sometimes made things up? To feel important.'

Sandra gave a short laugh. 'She did that, yes. Drama Salma I used to call her. But I don't know . . . this seemed different. Then when the police told us about her . . . being pregnant. Do you think something happened to her? That sexual harassment comment, that's what's been consuming me. That someone . . . hurt her. Against her will.'

An ugly word hung in the air, unsaid, but all three of us were thinking it.

Sandra continued: 'If only she had spoken to me about it. Then I might have—'

'I don't think anything like that happened to her,' I said. 'We spoke to her boyfriend. He's pretty sure the baby is his.'

'I don't want to know anything about him. If Yusuf finds out who it is, I don't know what he'll do.'

'Mrs Ali, the night it happened. Your husband wasn't at home, was he?'

She looked at me, tight-lipped. 'What are you implying? That has nothing to do with what happened here. Yusuf can be emotional, but he would never harm Salma.'

'But he *was* out late, wasn't he? Even though he said he was home.'

'Sex is at the bottom of everything,' she said softly.

'What do you mean?' said Naila.

'I don't know why I stay with him sometimes. I told myself it was for Salma. But now there's no reason. Maybe the time has come.'

She was almost talking to herself. Working things out in her mind as though we weren't there. She looked around the room. 'Is this where I'm going to end up? A tiny bedsit somewhere?

Alone? At my age? What will I have to show for my life? No daughter, no husband, no savings. Nothing to remember me by . . . when I go.'

'I'm sure there will be many people who will remember you. And it's not going to be for a long time,' said Naila. 'It must be hard being married to Yusuf. You didn't convert, did you?'

'I refused. But he insisted on bringing up Salma in the faith. And I let him. It wasn't worth the fight. He was so dashing when I met him. Such a natty dresser. And when Salma left home, he decided he could do what he wanted.'

'What do you mean?' I said.

'He wasn't home till two in the morning that night. He was with her.'

'With Salma?'

'Don't be stupid. With *her*! Her! His woman on the side. His mistress. His piece of fluff. Once every two weeks when he pretends he's meeting friends at the snooker club, he's with her. He was with her that night. I can always tell. The hypocrite, for all his praying five times a day. It's always sex. The hell with him. I don't need to take it any more. I won't.'

She stood and strode into Salma's bedroom as Naila and I glanced at each other.

'Wow,' she said. 'I didn't see *that* coming.'

'No, me neither. Guess he didn't have the time to come to London and be back for 2 a.m. Poor woman.'

Sandra came back, having washed her face. She looked around. 'I think we're done here. Thank you for all your help. Can you give me a hand carrying this stuff to the van? I'm driving back to Leeds.'

'Of course,' I said. 'One more thing: did Salma speak to anyone or see anyone while she was home at the weekend? Any friends?'

'No, she just sat at home. Slept.'

'Didn't call anyone?'

'She'd left her phone in London. She was late for her train and rushed off without it. She was annoyed with herself for forgetting it.'

'Do you have her phone?'

'No, the police have it. They needed it for evidence, they said.'

This was disappointing. I couldn't see Tahir giving me access to it, however much he was prepared to help.

Sandra continued: 'She used *my* phone to make a call, but I don't think she got through. She borrowed it a few times.'

Now this was something. Ziad said he hadn't spoken to Salma that weekend.

'Do you have your phone? May I see it?'

She looked around for her handbag among the boxes, found it, delved inside, unlocked and handed me an iPhone in an orange case.

'When did she call? Do you remember?'

'Sunday morning, I think. Yes, that's right, it was after breakfast. She asked if she could borrow it and disappeared into her room.'

Naila looked over my shoulder as I scrolled back to calls five days before. The same number had been dialled three times at half-hour intervals, on the Sunday after ten. Just a few seconds for the first two calls, which must have been unanswered. The third call *had* been answered and Salma had spoken for five minutes and twenty-seven seconds. It wasn't Ziad's number. I tapped the number into my phone and gave Sandra's back to her.

'Thanks, that was helpful. Did you tell the police this?'

'No, I forgot. Shall I?'

'It's fine, I'll tell them. Leave it with me.'

We helped Sandra load the boxes into the van and watched as she drove off. It was almost time to return to the restaurant, but I couldn't wait.

'I'm calling the number.'

'Put it on speaker,' said Naila.

I dialled, and it was answered immediately.

An Irish voice.

'Liam Mackenzie. Hello?'

Chapter 21

Friday.

Naila and I stood outside Salma's flat, staring at each other as I disconnected the call with a jab.

'Was that . . .'

I nodded.

'Wow. Why would Salma be calling Sir? At the weekend? From Leeds. It doesn't make sense.'

She wasn't wrong. What could be so urgent Salma needed to call her tutor on a Sunday? It *might* be innocent – her grades or maybe she was going to miss a tutorial or needed an extension or something – but three times? When she could have texted or emailed.

Dr Liam Mackenzie had questions to answer.

'She must have known him well to remember his number,' I said. 'I don't remember anyone's number. Not even my own. Are we sure the baby is Ziad's? Maybe Salma and Dr Mackenzie were having an affair.'

Naila laughed. 'Salma? An affair with a married man? While going out with Ziad? No way! She wasn't that kind of girl.'

'How do you know, Naila? It seems to me the more we learn about her, the less we know about who she really was. We need to speak to Mackenzie. And I have to tell Tahir. He should get a DNA test done on the baby.'

'That's a good idea. It's quite something watching you at work, Kamil. Impressive.'

I allowed myself a moment to let the enjoyment of that sink in. I picked up the phone to ring Tahir when it rang in my hand.

'Hello?'

'Howya. Who is this? You just called, and we got disconnected?'

Shit.

'Mackenzie,' I mouthed to Naila and put the phone on speaker.

'Oh, Dr Mackenzie,' I said, improvising as best I could. 'This is Kamil Rahman. I met you with Naila earlier in the week. Sorry, I have terrible reception here.'

'How did you get my number?'

'Naila gave it to me. Sorry to bother you so late, but I was wondering if I could come and see you tomorrow. I have information about Salma I'd like to discuss.'

He went silent for a moment, then said, 'It's the weekend, Mr Rahman. I can see you on Monday. At the college.'

'It's urgent. Can we meet somewhere tomorrow? Anywhere you like.'

Another pause.

'Look, it's not convenient . . .'

'It would be great if I could speak to you before I talk to the police.'

Silence. Then, picking up on my not so veiled threat, 'All right, come to my house. Three p.m. I'll text you the address.'

Yasir's funeral was in the morning, I could make that.

'Want to come and see how your Sir lives?' I said to Naila after he disconnected.

'Are you sure you want me there? Won't I get in the way?'

'No, it would help. Always better to have two people asking the questions.'

'Right – good cop, madcap. All right then, if you need my help. How do you want to play it?'

'We'll start with his affair with Salma and take it from there,' I dialled Tahir.

I told him what we had found out, omitting the fact I was going to interview my new prime suspect the next day. He surprised me by saying, 'Yes, we know that.'

'How could you?'

'Salma called him several times from her own phone. We've spoken to him and are looking into it. We're not *complete* idiots you know, Sherlock.'

'Did you do a DNA test on the baby?'

'It's underway. But it'll be a few days before we get the results.'

'Had she texted Dr Mackenzie as well as calling?'

'Twice. Just saying she needed to speak to him urgently, and could he call her.'

'What was the tone of the texts? Loving? Angry?'

'Neutral, I'd say.'

'When was the first contact made?'

'On a Sunday two weeks ago, I believe.'

On a weekend again!

'Hmm. Nothing before that? That doesn't sound like an affair?'

'We're on it, Kamil, *don't* interfere.'

'I won't.'

But my 500 mph racing mind and quickened heartbeat told a different story.

Chapter 22

Saturday.

A reluctant local authority agreed to pay for a Muslim funeral for Yasir as a result of forceful persuasion by Imam Masroor. ('If he dies on my property, I have to ensure he gets a proper Muslim burial, not a pauper's funeral.') Anjoli could not participate in the burial itself, but had received special dispensation to watch. Dressed in a white kurta and trousers, she laid one of the bouquets she was holding in the doorway where Yasir had died, and we got into the imam's car, heading for the Eternal Gardens Muslim cemetery. It was preying on my mind that Anjoli was still mad at me and I hadn't figured out how to make amends for my crassness the day before. I'd have to speak to her today and get her to forgive me.

'Why are we going all the way to Sidcup?' she said. 'Are there no Muslim burial grounds in Tower Hamlets?'

'We get a discount there,' said the imam, weaving his way through the traffic on the A2. 'The council didn't want to spend too much, but he was one of our own so I said I would perform the janazah after they did the kafn.'

We arrived to find an ambulance waiting for us in the cemetery car park. The imam and I helped the driver and the council representative carry the simple coffin from the ambulance into the burial grounds, a neat green area with evenly spaced mounds, each topped with a plaque, all facing in the direction of the qibla – towards Mecca. We opened the top of the coffin, lifted out Yasir's body, wrapped in a white kafn, and placed it on the ground next to the hole that had been dug. The ambulance driver left, and the imam asked Anjoli to stand a few metres back to respect Islamic custom. The rest of us stood around the body as the imam recited the janazah prayer. I glanced back to see tears falling from Anjoli's eyes.

The solemnity of the scene overwhelmed me as the reality of Yasir's death hit. Whether he'd died of natural causes or been killed, he'd achieved a dignity in death that had eluded him in his life in London. This homeless Syrian refugee who had opened my eyes to what millions of people were going through on the borders of one of the richest continents in the world deserved a funeral in Aleppo, at home, surrounded by people who loved him. Instead, he was being buried in south London in a simple white shroud as an imam recited a prayer, a council official sneaked a look at his watch and a young woman who had tried to help him wept.

I mumbled a few half-forgotten words of prayer along with the imam, but they caught in my throat. I couldn't bring myself to look at the small body any more but couldn't look away either, not wanting to disrespect Yasir in his last moments before the darkness of the grave.

'Not Rima. Not Jamal. Not Saad. Not Rima. Not Jamal. Not Saad.' I remembered his incantation. Now it was 'Not Rima. Not Jamal. Not Saad. Not Yasir.' Maybe he would join them in Jannah, and they could be Yasir with Rima with Jamal with Saad.

I walked over to Anjoli and whispered, barely able to get the words out, 'If someone did this to him, I'll help you catch him, Anjoli. We won't let them get away with it. I promise. Yasir's life meant something. I understand what you're feeling. I'm just an arsehole.'

She looked at me, then nodded and squeezed my hand as the

imam finished with 'Assalaamu alaykum warahmatullah,' and the body in its shroud was lowered into the grave.

Anjoli watched as I went back to the imam and followed his lead as he took three handfuls of soil and poured them into the grave reciting in Arabic, 'We created you from it, and return you into it, and from it we will raise you a second time.' This phrase I recognised from family funerals I had attended in Kolkata; I was glad of these few Arabic words that came to me in time to pay my last respects to Yasir. In the final reckoning, we were all just dust and ashes, living a few brief moments in which we could try to make our mark, love and be loved.

The gravediggers pushed the soil over the coffin as the imam recited his last prayers and we all bent and patted the earth into place, grey clouds threatening rain above us. Anjoli walked up and placed the second bouquet she had been clutching throughout the funeral at the head of the grave, and I put my arm around her. The council guy nodded at us and slipped away as the imam thanked the gravediggers and we walked in silence back to his car. There was nothing more to be said.

On the way back to Brick Lane, Anjoli, sitting in the front passenger seat next to the imam, stared out of the rain-streaked window at the passing cheerless, characterless cityscape of south London as I watched the stop-start traffic ahead of us past her profile. I hadn't been to this part of London before, which seemed a different world. This city was a collection of villages – from the swanky stuccoed terraces of Regent's Park, through the edgy Bohemia of Shoreditch, passing the Bangla familiarity of Whitechapel to this . . . anonymity. Even the people inhabiting the villages were different. The old English money and new Arabs, Indians and Russians of Knightsbridge; the bearded, artisanal coffee-swilling hipsters and techies of Hoxton; the salwar'd and sari'd aunties of Southall. And here . . . I wasn't sure who lived in these identikit houses we were speeding past on the A20. Just Londoners, I supposed. We were all Londoners now. The city sucked you in and, with Yasir, spat you out.

Anjoli broke the silence: 'Do you do a lot of funerals for the homeless, Imam Masroor?'

'Not so many. Sometimes.'

'Have you found there have been more funerals for rough sleepers over the last year?'

'I don't know, why?'

She glanced at me over her shoulder and I gave her an encouraging nod I didn't quite feel. She said, 'I have this theory.'

She told him her thoughts about the homeless deaths and waited for his reaction. He braked to avoid a cyclist who had swerved in front of him, jerking us all forward.

'But that is terrible.' He gunned the car again. 'Have you told the police this?'

'Yes. I don't think they believe me. Have you heard or seen anything that might tell us if it's true?'

'That someone is killing these poor souls? No. But I can ask if anyone else has seen anything. As you know, Anjoli, Prophet Muhammad, peace be upon him, said, "He who sleeps on a full stomach while his neighbour goes hungry is not one of us." Muslim Aid and Crisis are having a food drive for the homeless at the mosque after Friday prayers, and we will donate care packages. I'll check to see if anyone else has heard anything.'

Anjoli nodded her thanks and turned back to look out of the window, hands tightly clasped in her lap, neck rigid. She was convinced a killer was at work, but it seemed impossible to prove anything.

Chapter 23

Saturday.

After a busy Saturday lunch service, Naila picked me up, and we drove back south of the river to see Mackenzie in Bermondsey.

'I have to show you something,' she said after a long silence.

'Mm hmm?' I was focusing on her close-cut light pink nails resting on the steering wheel, which were sending an electric charge down my spine. Only a week to go.

Her hand snaked its way into the handbag next to her and emerged with her mobile. She glanced at it, tapped the screen and handed it to me.

'Read that. I got it this morning.'

A text. Number withheld. All caps. Ugly as hell.

ENOUGH IS ENOUGH. GET BACK TO PAKISTAN YOU BITCH OR GET WHAT SALMA GOT. LONDON IS NOT FOR YOU ANY MORE.

My first reaction was anger.

'Bloody hell, Naila!'

'I know, right?'

'Who could this be from? I didn't know you could send anonymous texts.'

'Apparently you can.'

'Are you okay?'

'Maloom nahin. I don't know.'

I looked at it again and my anger was replaced by apprehension. I had to keep Naila safe.

'Who do you think it's from? Has anyone been harassing you?'

She went quiet.

'Naila?'

'I have a suspicion. But I need to check.'

'Tell me.'

'Not now, Kamil. I will, I promise, but not yet.'

'Naila, not sharing this information will lead to you being hurt. Or worse. You've read the books and seen the films – believe me it happens in real life too. It happened to Salma.'

'Lucky this isn't a book then.'

'Is it anything to do with this Imran guy?'

'Why do you ask that?'

'If it was just random racist bullshit, they'd say, "Go back to Pakistan." "*Get* back to Pakistan" sounds like it might be someone from there.'

She looked at the text again. 'I hadn't noticed that. Leave it with me for now. Please, Kamil.'

'Who is he, Naila?'

A long pause.

She wasn't going to answer.

'This has to be connected to Salma's death. Are Muslim women on your course being harassed?'

Her hands tightened on the steering wheel till I could see the whites of her knuckles. 'I don't know, Kamil. It's scary.'

'I'm calling Tahir.'

He answered immediately. 'It's Jessica Fletcher! How are things in Cabot Cove?'

'Hilarious, Tahir. Sorry to trouble you at the weekend, I had a quick question. Did you see any racist or threatening texts on Salma's phone?'

'Racist? No. Why?'

'Naila's just been sent something.' I read it to him. 'It's anonymous. Can you trace it?'

He thought for a moment. 'I don't know. Let me ask my tech people and get back to you. When did she get it?'

I looked at the text. 'Ten thirty-seven this morning.'

'It wasn't Ziad then,' he said, almost to himself.

'What do you mean?'

'We arrested him at five this morning. He's been in custody ever since.'

'Wow, you must have been serious to grab him at stupid o'clock.'

'We've found his and Salma's DNA on the hoodie you identified, but he keeps insisting it isn't his. But we'll break him. I've got to go.'

He hung up, leaving me with my mouth hanging open.

'What happened?' Naila said.

'They've arrested Ziad. Watch out!' I said as she slammed on the brakes to avoid hitting an old lady on a pedestrian crossing.

'Shit! Really?'

'Apparently. I don't know if they've charged him. I think they can hold him for twenty-four hours.'

'What's stupid o'clock?'

'Just something we used to call early arrest in Kolkata. Get them dozy and off balance, hoping they give something away.'

'Oh. Is there any point seeing Dr Mac? Shall we go back?'

I considered this. Ziad was the obvious suspect – means, motive, opportunity. Yet . . . there had been something else, and what did the text to Naila mean? Was it just a random hate text? There were too many threads in this case – Salma's pregnancy, her worry about something in the college, the call to Mackenzie and now this message. How did Ziad fit into them all? Why wasn't Naila telling me who she was suspicious of? And who the hell was this Imran?

'We're here now, so we may as well see him. I want to understand Salma's relationship with him.'

Beatrice Road turned out to be a pretty street with plane trees on both sides, and number 15 was a red-roofed bungalow with a Volvo and a Golf parked outside.

'So nice and suburban,' Naila said, parking behind the Volvo. 'A two-car, two-child, two-parent household. I don't know why, but houses like these give me the creeps.'

'I quite like it. Compared to my room in Anjoli's and the one-bedroom flat I had in Kolkata police quarters, this is palatial.'

'That's true. Just reminds me too much of the bungalows where I grew up in the cantonment towns, I guess.'

'Be nice. I need information from this guy.'

She made a zipping motion over her mouth then giggled when the doorbell chimed a tinny 'Greensleeves'. A dog barked, a woman's voice shouted, 'The door, Siobhan!' and it was opened by a girl of about six in bare feet, wearing a pink dress and clutching a tattered Madeline doll. She stared at us with astounded blue eyes under a raggedy fringe, as though we were a pair of T-Rexes that had just materialised in front of her. I couldn't tell if her fascination was because we were strangers or because we were brown.

'Hello, Siobhan,' I said. 'Is your Daddy home?'

She shouted, 'Mammy!' not taking her eyes off us as a woman in her late thirties with pale freckled skin and a tangle of red hair came up behind her, wiping her hands on a tea cloth and shouting, 'Be quiet, Lulu!' to the little brown and white dog scampering around her feet and somehow wagging its entire body. 'Yes? Sorry about the racket.'

'We're sorry to disturb you,' I said. 'Is Dr Mackenzie home?'

'Oh yes, he said he was expecting someone. He's in the garden. Come on through. *Don't* let the dog out, Siobhan!'

With Siobhan and Lulu padding after us, we followed her through a living room filled with the warm smell of something stewy being cooked in the kitchen beyond. The room, scattered with books and Legos, had a homey feel, a television playing a cartoon. We went out through the French windows into the small garden. The sun had made an appearance and Mackenzie, dressed in shorts and a Rolling Stones T-shirt was fiddling with a lawn mower on the grass.

'Pass me the screwdriver, Donal,' he said.

A boy of about four rooted around in a black and yellow box, then ran over to his father and handed him a tool. Mackenzie tightened something, said, 'That should do it,' and walked over to us, tossing the screwdriver into the toolbox on the way.

'You made it then. Any problem finding the place? Oh. Hi, Naila, I wasn't expecting you,' he said with the awkwardness of a teacher seeing students outside their normal milieu.

'Nice place, sir,' she said.

'Ah, the house is more Roisin's taste than mine. Roisin,' he said to his wife, who was trying to pull their son away from a bee buzzing around a pot of primroses, 'this is Kamil and Naila. Naila is one of my students, and Kamil is her friend. They're here about that poor girl who –' he lowered his voice to avoid the children, who weren't paying him any attention, hearing '– died. And this gurrier is Donal, and Siobhan you seem to have met. Take the weight off your legs. Would you like a beer?'

I hesitated, but Naila said, 'Yes, that'd be great, thanks.'

'Grand,' he said. 'Roisin, would you mind? I think I've earned one after my exertions.'

Donal came up to us. 'I've lost a tooth. The fairy is coming tonight.' He grinned, showing us the evidence.

'I hope you kept it safe,' said Naila. 'It's precious.'

He nodded and scampered off as his mother re-emerged from the house with open bottles of Corona. The four of us sat on garden chairs in a circle around a table drinking our beers, the kids sitting on the ground next to Siobhan, staring at us. I pulled a face at Donal and he burst into laughter as Siobhan continued to give me her death stare.

'You need not stay, Roisin,' said Mackenzie.

'I need a break. Don't mind me.'

He gave her a look, then smiled at me. 'So, what can I help you with?'

His accent seemed to get more Irish in the presence of his wife. He also seemed nervous, although he was doing his best to hide it. I couldn't tell if it was because of us or Roisin. There was tension here.

'It's about Salma, as I said on the phone. We found out some information.'

'Oh yes?'

'Before we get into it, can you remind us where you were the night she died. Tuesday night?'

'Like I said, I was at a function at the college and got home at around half ten. Isn't that right, Ro?'

She sipped her beer and inclined her head a fraction. I'd seen more enthusiasm in a cow refusing to get out of the traffic in a busy Kolkata street.

'How did you know that was the time, Mrs Mackenzie?'

'I'd gone to bed early. I woke up when he came home.'

'The police have been through all this. What's this additional information you have?' Mackenzie interrupted.

'Ziad's been arrested for Salma's murder, sir,' said Naila.

Mackenzie let out a long breath. 'Oh my God, really? He killed her?'

'Looks like it,' she said.

'Who is Ziad?' said Roisin.

'Her boyfriend,' said Mackenzie. 'So if he's been arrested what do you want with me?'

The conversation was going in a direction that wasn't helpful.

I took control again. 'I believe Salma called you on the Sunday morning before her death?'

Roisin's head jerked towards her husband.

'She did,' said Mackenzie. 'The police asked me about that. She was worried about something going on in the college and wanted my advice.'

'Oh? What was so important she had to phone you at the weekend?'

'Huh? Oh sorry, I'm still processing the news. Ziad, a killer. I didn't see that. Right, Salma's call. I'm sorry I couldn't tell you last time we spoke because it was rather sensitive. But I have told the police and the dean, so I suppose there's no harm in you knowing now. She was concerned someone might be stealing drugs from the pharmacy and wanted to know who to speak to about it.'

'Drugs? Not her failing grades?'

'Not her grades, no. Although she had discussed them with me before. If this drug thing was true, it would be a major scandal.'

Was this what had preoccupied Salma? Drugs? I looked at him as he sipped his beer. I didn't trust this charming Irish guy as far as I could throw him.

'Did she say who was stealing the drugs?' said Naila.

'Look, I don't want to fling accusations around without proof. Especially in front of students. But *she* said it was Aziz. The guy who runs the pharmacy at the hospital. Ziad's father. Is that why he did it? Because she was going to expose his da?'

Maybe things were slotting into place now. Mackenzie could be right about Ziad protecting his father.

'And are you investigating the pharmacy accusation?'

'I've handed it over to the registrar in the hospital. I assume they'll look into it.'

I looked at his wife, who was now sitting on the grass playing pat-a-cake with Siobhan. Donal was blowing bubbles that Lulu was trying to catch, looking puzzled when they vanished. A perfect family on the skin of it. But flawless skin has guts and gore underneath.

'You never saw Salma outside college?'

'No, of course not. That would be inappropriate.' His wife gave a sharp snort. Mackenzie ignored her as I exchanged glances with Naila.

'And when was the first time she brought this pharmacy business to your attention? The police said she called you several times?'

He held his beer bottle up to the sun, watching the rays refract through the amber liquid. 'A couple of weeks ago, maybe?'

'But why did she keep calling you then? I mean, she had told you, and you were dealing with it? So why keep calling? And at the weekend?'

'Honestly, I thought she was making it up. She liked to be the centre of attention. Her grades were off, maybe she believed this would cause me to go easy on her. So, I did nothing about it. But she kept saying if I didn't, she would talk to the dean herself. I continued to fob her off; I didn't want this kind of stuff being spread around. It can harm the reputation of the college and the hospital. But when she called on Sunday, I promised I'd speak to the dean and that seemed to satisfy her.'

He was building a house of bullshit right in front of my eyes.

'Did you know she was pregnant?'

Silence and an immediate tension like a taut guitar string about to vibrate filled the garden. Lulu stopped lolloping around, ears pricked up. Even the kids felt it, looking at their parents, wondering what was wrong.

'Pregnant?' he said after a pause. 'Jaysus. No, I didn't.'

He was lying. I knew it, and so did his wife. I could tell by her eyes lasering through him, her skin flushing almost as red as her hair.

'Was it your man? Ziad?'

'We don't know. The police are testing the baby's DNA.'

'Poor lass. Such a tragedy when a young person dies, their entire life in front of them . . .' he trailed off and drained his beer. 'If there's nothing else . . .'

He definitely wasn't telling us everything. I'd sensed relief when he heard Ziad had been arrested. But why would he be relieved?

We rose and returned to the house. As we walked through the living room, we passed a side table with various framed photographs. I walked over to one of Dr Mackenzie standing in front of a tree in a field full of bluebells, Donal on his shoulders and Siobhan standing at his feet, all three grinning at the camera.

'Naila,' I said, and she came over with Mackenzie.

In the photo the good doctor was wearing a yellow hoodie, identical to the one found in Ziad's house.

'Something wrong?' said Mackenzie.

'This picture, when was it taken?'

'Last year. We'd driven to Ashridge to see the wildflowers. Why?'

'This hoodie you're wearing in the picture. Do you have it?'

'What is this? Of course, I have it. Listen, I'm—'

'May we see it please, sir?' said Naila.

'What the hell is all this about? Oh, all right! Wait here, I'll get the yoke.'

He disappeared into another room and emerged a few minutes later holding the hoodie, which he thrust into my hands. 'There. Happy now?'

I turned it around in my hands, then smelled it. There was something odd about it, but I couldn't quite place what. But here it was. The other one was in an evidence bag in the police station. This was a thumping great coincidence. And I don't like coincidences.

'Where did you get it from? I only ask because Ziad has the same one.'

'Does he now? That doesn't surprise me. They gave a few of them out at the away weekend we had with our students last summer. We went on a three-day intensive offsite near Oxford. Do you remember, Naila? July last year?'

She shook her head. 'I wasn't here. I'd gone back to Pakistan to visit my father when he was unwell.'

'Oh yes, I remember. Well, if it's all the same with you, I'll go back to enjoying my Saturday with my family. Thanks for coming by.'

He took his hoodie back and showed us out.

As we got into the car, I said, 'When do bluebells come out, Naila?'

'I don't know. Spring? March, April, I think.'

'I think so too. So how was he wearing the hoodie *before* he got it at his away weekend last summer?'

Chapter 24

Sunday.

P eople lie for many reasons. I'm no Sufi saint, having told my fair share of little white lies, bigger grey fabrications and a few massive red-flag waving whoppers over the years. *One* or both of the two things I'd heard relating to the yellow hoodie was a lie – either Ziad insisting the hoodie wasn't his when it had been found in his wardrobe at home with his and Salma's DNA on it, or Mackenzie's lie about when he had got *his* hoodie. Whichever was the lie, it seemed pointless but had to have *something* to do with the murder.

Naila and I tossed this ball back and forth on the way home from Mackenzie's. We couldn't think why the lecturer would have lied about his hoodie, and Naila pointed out that the police must have something more on Ziad to have arrested him.

'Something about Mackenzie's hoodie when I held it seemed off to me,' I said.

'What?'

'I don't know. I can't quite put my finger on it.'

'Maybe it'll come to you.'

'Maybe. I'll get Tahir over for lunch to find out what else he knows. A taste of my butter chicken and he'll be chaputty in my hands.'

I rang him and extended the invitation. He joked it was

unlikely to be seen as a bribe given the quality of the food, but agreed to join me at noon the next day.

Anjoli was not at all happy at this further dereliction of duty – Sunday lunches were busy, and things between us were still brittle after the way I'd behaved with her. I explained that, with Ziad under arrest, the case was coming to a close and this would be the last time.

'Yeah, that's what you keep saying, Kamil. You don't understand how much of a hassle this is for me.'

'I'll make it up, I promise.'

She wasn't having any of it. 'It's not about making it up to me, Kamil. It's about managing without you, which we can't. And you're using a table which two paying customers might fill on our busiest day of the week! Running a small business is hard. These things matter a great deal and are the difference between making the rent and paying staff. Paying *you*, I will point out. Look, I know I told you to do this investigation, but I thought you'd do it in your own time or go part time so I could hire someone else. I'm not trying to be nasty, just realistic. I have responsibilities.'

Of course, she was right. 'Okay, it will be the last time, I promise.'

'Don't make promises you can't keep.'

Naila had taken a weekend shift at the hospital to get the following weekend off, so it was just me and Tahir. It felt weird to be eating in the restaurant with an actual diner, being served by Salim Mian.

'Have the butter chicken; it's great today,' I said, and Tahir ordered it, together with a naan and baingan bharta. I opted for finger food so I could spend my time listening instead of eating – tandoori chicken and paneer tikka, accompanied by a naan.

'Well, Maigret, yesterday I bumped into the DI in charge of

your Bishops Avenue murder last year,' he said, clinking his glass of Cobra lager with mine and taking a large gulp. 'I mentioned you and how you wanted in on this one, and she said you had buggered up her crime scene. Inept was the word she used.'

I felt my cheeks flush. That hadn't been my finest moment. But it had worked out. From time to time, I still relived the shock and righteous glory of discovering how the murderer had committed the crime and knowing in my bones I was right. And how my future had changed with that revelation.

'Well,' I said, 'that bit might have been inept, but I got pretty ept by the end. I was the one who spotted the key clues your friend missed. I pointed her towards the actual murderer instead of the person they arrested.'

'Yes, she wasn't *un*complimentary about your efforts. But you and Anjoli should have called me; I'd have been on it like a shot. Don't need you amateur tecs mucking things up.'

'Yeah, right, Lestrade. Anjoli thought of getting in touch with you, but you were away on training.'

As I mentioned her name, Anjoli appeared, delivering the food herself.

'Hi, Anj,' said Tahir. 'Jonathan Creek here was just telling me how brilliant he was on the murder last year.'

'All right, Tahir?' She gave me a dirty look and slammed down a plate of naans.

'What's up with you?' he said.

'Nothing, sorry. Busy day and we're short staffed. Listen, did you get anything out of that gin bottle?'

'Oh yeah, my guvnor fast-tracked it. Nothing, Anj. It was clean. Just gin. *And* we had a post-mortem done on the body in Waterloo. Again nothing. Natural causes, they said. Nothing untoward they could find.'

'Damn, really?'

'Damn? I'm sorry you're disappointed there isn't a crazy

serial killer roaming the streets, killing rough sleepers. It's just the everyday tragedies of the homeless dying. Nothing to point to anything violent, or murder.'

'I'm glad, of course. But who was the guy in the video?'

'Some Good Samaritan? Thought he was helping?'

'It *can't* be a coincidence! Yasir had the same bottle!'

'What can I say, Anj! *Both* bottles were clean. But I will say this. I asked around and there is something a little odd: a few other homeless people who died also had gardenia gin next to their bodies. And these weren't alcohol-related deaths.'

'See! There is something here! Did you check the bottle for fingerprints?'

'Well . . . no. There was no reason to. There hasn't been a crime committed. Maybe the guy just likes to give rough sleepers booze to help them warm up at night? You can't arrest someone for that. Perhaps there was a promo on the brand and now it's become the tipple of choice for the homeless. Can't imagine them using that in their advertising though.' He laughed. ' "Gardenia gin keeps you snug on the streets." '

'I don't know . . . I was so sure . . .' Anjoli sighed and went back to work.

Tahir heaped spoonfuls of the creamy, spicy butter chicken onto his plate and mopped up the gravy with hot naan. I'd come up with an alternative way of smoking the curry using a glowing piece of charcoal and was happy to see how much Tahir was enjoying it – it felt like an implicit five-star review.

'She's obsessed with this homeless stuff,' I said. 'Grieving for her friend, I think.'

'Poor Anj, she was always the sensitive sort.'

I took the chance to slip in a question I had been wondering about. 'Did you guys ever go out?'

He winked. 'Let's say we know each other verrry well. But you know me, I'm not a one-woman kinda guy.'

That cut.

'Yeah, you're a regular James Bond. Carrying bags for Rogers. Yes sir, no sir, three bags full, sir.'

'Whatever, dude. So, listen, are you going to take my advice about applying to the force? Have you seen the new ads running in the Underground? Metropolitan Police looking for candidates from Black, Asian and minority ethnic backgrounds?'

'Minority ethnic. Sounds like the politically correct sequel to that Spielberg film starring Shahrukh Khan instead of Tom Cruise. I might be interested.'

'Get an application form, and I'll put in a word.' He chewed his naan while reaching over to spear one of my paneer tikkas. 'Although if the Met used the pre-crime techniques from that film, all us Muslims would be locked up.'

'Is there much racism in the force?' The bitter taste of the discrimination I had experienced being a Muslim detective in a Hindu force in India returning like a burned samosa.

'Nothing overt these days. Too much attention on it. Rogers is okay, allows me to do my thing. Bit of a stickler for the rules, but there are worse guvnors. You don't see too many black and brown faces in the senior ranks, though.'

'And you're going to change that?'

'Well, I didn't join to make the tea. I'm ambitious, I don't pretend otherwise. I'm a good copper, and if I can push my way to the top, why not? So, tell me,' he exuded a gentle burp and waved his glass at Salim Mian for another pint. 'What have you got for me?'

I told him about our visit to Mackenzie and what he had said about Salma and the drugs.

'Yeah, he told us the same thing. She had called him a few times, and we wondered why. And as you know, Ziad's father works in the pharmacy in St Thomas', so it seemed to hang together. She wanted to see the dean on Wednesday morning, to tell him her suspicions, I guess. She told his assistant it was a personal matter.'

'Yes, I know about that appointment. But would she turn in her boyfriend's father? I assume she'd speak to him first. It seems odd to me.'

'Gives Ziad another motive though, if she had told him.'

'Maybe. There was one other oddity.' I told him about Mackenzie's hoodie.

That gave him pause. 'He has one as well? Now that *is* interesting. And why would he lie? Maybe he got the dates wrong.'

'Did you find any evidence on Ziad's hoodie?'

Tahir dabbed masala off his chin. 'He keeps insisting it isn't his and we must have planted it. But it's his, all right. We found his hair inside the hood.'

'Any DNA to link it with the actual killing?'

'Scads of it. Fibres from the dress Salma wore that night. From her hijab. His prints all over her room. None of Mackenzie's prints, though.'

'Ziad *was* her boyfriend, so it could have been innocent.'

'You're not wrong. But why would he keep denying the hoodie's his? We grilled him hard, but he wouldn't budge from his story, so we had to let him go. All the evidence is still circumstantial, and CPS doesn't think we have enough to charge him and make it stick. But we're pushing on.'

'And we had the racist text to Naila. That's another oddity.'

'Yes, I looked into that. You *can* send anonymous texts from websites that are impossible to trace. No idea what to make of that. Why would the murderer send a text to your friend? She's not an investigator. I'd understand if they sent it to you, you being Hetty Wainthropp investigating and all. And why would one Muslim be racist to another?'

'I don't know. Hell of a coincidence though. Maybe someone is targeting Muslim women on that course? You said Ziad was in custody when it was sent. And I don't know why Mackenzie would send it. Is there anyone else in the frame?'

He shook his head.

'Ziad's father? Salma's father?'

'Salma's father has an alibi. He was with a woman that night, only not his wife. She corroborated it. Ziad's father . . . well, he says he was at home. Says he knows nothing about any drugs going missing or even that Ziad had a girlfriend.'

We were tying ourselves tighter and tighter in knots; pulling on a strand just made the tangle worse.

'No,' he said. 'The simplest solution is often the right one – she and Ziad fought about the pregnancy. He killed her. Maybe he got someone to send Naila that text to muddy the waters, knowing we were on to him. We just need to keep digging and we'll get him.'

'Salma's social media? Any clues there?'

'Naah. Lots of posts about minority oppression, climate change, that kind of thing. Followed the usual people on Twitter you'd expect from a girl her age into causes.'

'Internet searches?'

'Again, nothing special. She'd looked into terminations, but we already knew she didn't want to keep the baby.'

'Nothing about illegal drugs being sold? She might have researched that if she had found something?'

'Not a pixel.'

'Nothing else on her phone? Emails, texts, calls?'

'She texted Mackenzie a few times. Other than that, just Ziad and people in her class. No naked selfies, nothing lovey-dovey.'

'Maybe we need to focus on the date of her first text to Mackenzie? Everyone says her behaviour changed a couple of weeks ago. If we can find the exact date, we can track her movements that day and see what pops up.'

Tahir furrowed his brow, then nodded. 'That's worth looking into.'

'Anything from the neighbours?'

'Nope. Did a house-to-house. The woman next door heard an argument that night but nothing else.'

'There were kids downstairs when I arrived – did they see anything?'

'They were too busy getting rid of their drugs when we questioned them, so nada. They saw you arrive and Naila sitting in her car when you went up.'

Damn, this was a big rubbish bin of nothing.

'And no CCTV?'

'We checked the roads a mile around Salma's flat after eleven. Didn't see the hoodie person. Ziad doesn't have a car, and we also looked for Mackenzie's Volvo, Ziad's father's and even Salma's father's car. Didn't catch any of them on video or ANPR. No, Ziad remains our best bet. We will crack him, I'm sure of it. Just let us get the DNA test back on Salma's baby.' He mopped up the last of his butter chicken. 'Okay, enough talking shop. You shouldn't even be in the shop! Did you catch the cricket on TV? India are playing well.'

Our discussion moved on to a pleasant argument about the merits of Root versus Kohli until he stood and said, 'This has been fun, but I should dash; I'm meeting my girlfriend for a film.'

'Which one is this?' Tahir seemed to have a new woman with him every time I saw him. Anjoli and I were always amused by who he'd bring on dates to the restaurant. He was an equal opportunities boyfriend – they were all beautiful – English, French, American and, on one occasion, Korean. I needed to look at his Tinder profile to pick up tips.

Before he could answer, my phone rang. Naila. I answered it, 'Hi, I'm with—'

'Kamil . . .' A whisper.

She sounded scared. Naila never sounded scared. She was the one person I knew who was always cool, calm and composed.

'Naila, are you all right?'

Tahir caught the concern in my voice and sat back down.

'I had a call. From an unknown number.'

'Hang on, Tahir is here. Let me put you on speaker. Okay, go ahead.'

We leaned forward and could hear her jerky breaths.

'Hello, Sergeant. I just had a call. I don't know from whom. A man. His voice was muffled, as though he was disguising it. He said the cook and I had to stop hanging around and poking about in matters that didn't concern us. He was watching me, and if I didn't go back to Lahore, I would get what Salma got.'

'Can you describe the voice?' said Tahir.

'I don't know. Deepish.'

'Did he sound Asian? Could it have been Ziad?' I said.

'I think so, I don't know. I thought Ziad had been arrested?'

'They had to let him go as they didn't have enough to charge him.'

'Oh. Maybe it was him. But why would he threaten me? When did they let him go?'

'Last night,' said Tahir.

'Oh. So it could have been him.' She paused. 'But that's not all.'

'What?'

'I think . . . Look, this may sound stupid, but I think someone may have followed me to work this morning.'

'Why do you think that?' said Tahir.

'I don't know. I told you it was dumb. Just a feeling. To be honest, I'm a little scared.'

I knew better than to ignore those feelings. I wanted to ask if it could have been this Imran guy but didn't want to do so in front of Tahir.

I said, 'Naila, shall I come and get you from the hospital?'

'I can't leave early; they need me here. I finish at five. Will you come then, Kamil? I'd appreciate that.'

Oh God! I'd have to abandon the restaurant again in the evening. Maybe Anjoli would understand. Or not, given her current mood. Well, I'd cross that bridge later.

'I'll see you then. Just take care of yourself.'

'You okay?' said Tahir as I disconnected.

'Bit shook up, if I'm honest. I can't have anything happen to Naila. Why is she being targeted?'

'No idea, but I'll see what I can do.'

'Could it be Ziad?'

'I don't know. He doesn't strike me as the type of guy to issue threats. And what would his motive be? We've let him go. His best shot is to lie low and hope we find nothing else. And why would he follow her?'

'Who then? It's unlikely to be Mackenzie; she'd have recognised his accent.'

'Unless he was disguising it.'

'Hmm,' I said, unconvinced. 'It must be linked to whatever Salma found at the hospital. And the caller mentioned me. The two of us asking around must have spooked him. I think maybe we need to look deeper into this drugs business.'

'Okay. See if you find anything. Look, I have to run now. Don't worry about your girlfriend; I'm sure she'll be fine. Thanks for lunch.'

He left, and I took the dirty plates and dishes back to the kitchen, where I was greeted by Anjoli's scowl.

'Anjoli, you won't believe this, but Naila's just had a guy call and threaten her.'

'Shit! What happened? Is she okay?'

'She's terrified. Look,' I said, bracing myself for an argument, 'would it be okay if I went and picked her up from the hospital and took her home? I'll be back by six for the dinner service, I promise.'

Her voice softened. 'Go, go! She needs you. But please come back as soon as you can – we're booked up tonight and we won't be able to cope without you.'

'I will, I promise. Thanks, you're the best.'

I got on with prepping the food, just relieved she hadn't torn another strip off me.

Chapter 25

Sunday.

I left the flat at four and headed towards Aldgate East to grab the District Line, mind ricocheting with random thoughts. How could I keep Naila safe? I couldn't follow her around like a guard dog all day. She was tough. She would manage. But what if something happened to her ... No! Not on my watch. This had to be dealt with. Naila was my responsibility; I'd got her to work this case with me, and there was something growing between us I had to nurture.

I plugged in my headphones and cranked up Radiohead to calm myself as a 'Poem on the Underground' on the opposite side of the carriage caught my eye. The last lines pierced through me: *make small / The old star-eaten blanket of the sky, / That I may fold it round me and in comfort lie.* All the Yasirs and Louis reaching for that sky on the streets above my thundering Tube train, feeling the vibrations as I passed below. Tower Hill ... Monument ... Cannon Street ... Mansion House. The stations whizzed by as Thom Yorke informed me I would be the first against the wall when he was king. It wasn't just androids who were paranoid; it struck deep.

I arrived at Westminster and crossed the bridge to St Thomas'. Four forty. I was early. I texted Naila and wandered into the reception area. Wooden floors, abstract art on the walls, recessed lighting and curved sofas made the hospital look more like a luxury hotel than any kind of health facility I had ever been in. The contrast with the down-at-heel government institution I had visited in Kolkata when Abba was ill felt extreme – the difference between a Rolls-Royce and an old Indian Ambassador.

As I sat on a rather uncomfortable grey backless sofa, my phone pinged – *will be another 30 mins, soz xxx*. I groaned. I was going to be late for the dinner service, and Anjoli was going to kill me! I tapped back – *np*. As I was about to forget my worries in the atonal world of Radiohead and *Kid A*, I saw a sign – PHARMACY – with an arrow. 'Everything In Its Right Place' could wait; something more urgent beckoned.

I followed the arrow around the corner and came to a large steel and glass retail outlet which announced itself as OUT-PATIENT PHARMACY. If reception was the Ritz, this was Harrods. Naila kept telling me how under-funded the NHS was, but these fitments didn't suggest it was struggling. I walked into the stylish red and white store, shelves stacked with all manner of products needed by the sick looking to get well or the healthy looking to stay healthy. The contrast with the tiny, cramped chemists in Kolkata (always chemists, never pharmacies or dispensaries or, God forbid, apothecaries like the ones in Shoreditch) was extreme.

A young woman wearing a headscarf at the dispensing desk looked up and smiled as I approached. 'Can I help?'

'Is Mr Aziz here by any chance?'

She shouted over her shoulder, 'Mr Aziz, someone here for you.'

Ziad's father appeared from behind a rack of shelves, glasses pushed up on his forehead. 'Can I help?'

'Mr Aziz,' I plastered on my best smile and extended my hand. 'Kamil Rahman. We met at your house the other day when Naila and I came to see your son.'

His eyes flickered. 'Yes. What can I do for you?'

'I was wondering if I might have a private word. It's about Ziad.'

Worry crept over his face.

'Is he okay? I don't know what that boy is doing. Why the police are so interested in him. He is a good boy. They questioned him for hours. We have retained a solicitor.'

'I'm trying to help Ziad. Do you have a minute?'

He nodded. 'Khadija, I'm stepping out. James is at the back if you need him. Come with me please, Kamil. We can have a coffee.'

I glanced at my watch, ten to five. As we walked, I texted Naila, *having coffee with Ziad's dad.*

We walked past a WH Smith, a gift shop and a hairdresser (Creative Hair! Was this a hospital or a shopping mall?) then arrived at AMT Coffee.

'You want a drink?' he said.

'No, let me,' I paid for his chai tea latte and an Americano for myself.

We found a small table at the back. He sipped his tea, then looked up at me. 'So how can you help Ziad?'

'I don't know if he mentioned, but I used to be a detective in the Kolkata police. I'm looking into Salma's death for her parents. I believe your son is innocent, and if they pin it on him, the actual killer will still be out there. Would you be willing to help?'

Relief and gratitude filled his face. 'Of course. Anything.'

'Did you know Ziad was . . . friends with Salma?'

'No. I didn't know before all this happened.'

'But you knew Salma?'

'Yes. She works – worked – in this hospital as a student nurse. They were on the same course. She helped in the pharmacy sometimes.'

'Would it have bothered you if you had known they were friends?'

'Ziad needs to study. Should not be wasting his time with girls. Plenty of time for that later.'

'He was with you the night she died?'

'Yes. I told the police. All night.'

'Do you know if that yellow hoodie the police found in his room was his?'

The upset and anger he had been trying to control burst through. 'Coming and searching our house like that! Who do they think they are? Scaring my wife. Then coming early morning and banging on the door and taking Ziad away. What the neighbours must have thought. The police are terrible. They just want to persecute us and—'

I persevered: 'The yellow hoodie. Was it Ziad's?'

'I don't know. I had never seen it before. Nor had his mother. But I don't know what all his clothes are. Naila?'

I turned to look behind me.

'Hello,' said Naila and pulled up a chair to join us at the small table.

'Do you want anything?' I said, and she shook her head.

I continued my interrogation. 'Mr Aziz, Salma told her tutor she was worried someone was stealing drugs from the pharmacy. Have you heard anything about this?'

His voice rose. 'Yes, the police asked me about that bloody nonsense. I told them nobody could steal medicines. We have strict procedures. I would know. We keep all our controlled drugs under lock and key and track them in the drugs register.'

'What kind of controlled drugs?' said Naila, keen to return to her job as a detective's assistant after a hard day of emptying bedpans and ministering to the sick.

'Poisons, addictive drugs, painkillers – all types.'

'So, if someone was stealing drugs, how could they do it?' I said.

'They cannot,' said Mr Aziz. 'Unless they are an insider who has access to them. And even then, all our people are vetted, and we keep careful count of our stock.'

'So why would Salma say it was happening?' said Naila.

'Look, Naila. I am not saying it never happens. But I would *know*. We do a regular count of the medicines and compare it to the online register. I did one just last week and there were no discrepancies. I showed the police.'

'Is there any CCTV?' I said.

'Not in the pharmacy, no.'

'And are these drugs kept on the wards?'

'Of course. You can't come to the pharmacy every time you need something. Maybe they were stealing them from the wards? Salma would have been more likely to see someone take them from there than from the pharmacy.'

That made sense. Although Mackenzie said Salma had mentioned Mr Aziz. And given the comings and goings in the wards, it would be impossible to determine who Salma might have seen.

'Would you mind showing us?' I said.

He was getting irritated. 'Look, I don't know what the two of you are up to, but what has this got to do with Ziad? How will this help him?'

'We don't know,' said Naila, her soothing nurse's voice taking over from my staccato questioning. 'We need to explore every angle. See, if drugs were being stolen and Salma threatened to expose the culprit, and the thief killed her, then Ziad is innocent. And if we can point the police to who this thief is, then it will clear Ziad.'

'How about the woman in the pharmacy – Khadija?' I said. 'Does she have access to the controlled drugs?'

'Her? No, of course not. She is just an assistant. She can dispense them, but only after I or another on-call senior pharmacist has checked and released them for use.'

'How many other senior pharmacists are there?'

'Three others, but they have all been here for years. I'm sure it involves none of them. Now if you don't mind, I have to get back.'

'Can we stop by a ward on the way? I'd love to see how they store the drugs.'

'They are in the drug stock wards. I can show you later,' Naila said, but Mr Aziz marched us into Florence Ward – Ms Nightingale was everywhere!

I looked around at the depressed-looking patients in the beds and the efficient nurses wandering around. I hated hospitals – giving a stranger power over you who controlled what you ate, when you went to the toilet and analysed everything in between. I had my parents for that, I didn't need a doctor as well.

Mr Aziz showed us an unmarked cupboard. 'See, they are locked in here. There are no signs showing it has controlled drugs to prevent opportunistic thieves.'

'Where do you keep the register?'

'The Controlled Drugs Register and order books are locked in the CD cupboard with the drugs. That way no one can amend stock numbers and things like that.'

He produced a key, unlocked the cupboard, waved the registers at me. 'Here they are. Only senior nurses and registrars have access. Happy?' then locked it again.

We walked away and passed a refrigerator with a glass door packed with medicines, the key in the lock.

'What's this? The key is just there.'

'Those are the regularly used drugs, not anything anyone would bother to steal,' said Naila.

I peered inside at a series of meaningless names – Lamatan, Prednisolone, Lantus, Apidra, NovoRapid . . . Why didn't pharma companies give normal names to medicines?

'What are they?'

'Steroids, painkillers, antibiotics – just the usual stuff you need day to day.'

We thanked Mr Aziz and left the hospital.

'How are you feeling Naila?' I said.

'I'm okay. I'm sorry I dragged you all the way over here. It was stupid. I just freaked out a bit when I got that call and kept imagining someone was following me. I'm sure it was nothing.'

'Could it have been Ziad or his father on the phone?'

'I just don't know. I've been trying to remember if there was anything in the voice, but it keeps fading away.'

'Was it the person you suspected? The one you mentioned in the car. Imran? Tell me who he is now. If you're being threatened and followed, I need to know.'

A pause. Then, 'I will. At home.'

It was 5.20. I'd promised Anjoli I'd be back by six.

'I must get back to the restaurant to cook, Naila. Tell me on the way.'

'It's . . . complicated, Kamil. You go back, and we can talk about it another time.'

I was torn. I had to know what Naila knew – she might be in danger. But I couldn't let Anjoli down again. What the hell should I do? As I weighed up one against the other, we passed a statue of a woman in flowing robes against a large bronze circle with what looked like broken limbs etched on it.

Naila stopped to look at it. 'My heroine.'

'Who is she? Florence Nightingale?' I was itching to keep going – this was not the time for an art appreciation class.

'The Jamaican version – Mary Seacole. She nursed with Florence in the Crimean War. The government refused to let her go to Crimea because she was Black and had no formal training, but she went anyway and saved thousands of lives. Came back destitute, but the soldiers she had saved raised money for her.

Then she was forgotten. When they erected this statue, Florence Nightingale's supporters objected. Bloody ridiculous. Easing suffering is the primary responsibility of all nurses, and I can't believe these stupid rivalries and rules prevent us from doing our duty.'

I looked up at the grim face towering above me and the equally resolute face glowering below. I was falling hard for this woman. I took her hand and speed-walked her onto the Embankment, the Houses of Parliament on the opposite side of the Thames glowing a mysterious red as a few errant rays of the sun broke through the scudding clouds overhead.

Chapter 26

Sunday.

On the Underground Naila was taut as a cat; I was stressed out trying to calculate just how late I would be for the dinner shift and how I could deflect Anjoli's wrath.

'Listen, given that call you got, maybe it's not safe for you to be alone at home, Naila. Why don't you come back to TK with me and then go back with Salim Uncle?'

She paused for a second, then said, 'I can't live like that, Kamil. I've lived in fear before and I will not do it again. I'll deal with whatever comes.'

'What do you mean you've lived in fear?'

'Let's get home first. I'm just saying I can look after myself. But it's sweet of you to worry.'

'It's not a joke. A woman has already been killed. You may be a target.'

'I *know* that, Kamil. But how would it work? Are you going to be my constant bodyguard till they find the killer? No. It's better I stick to my routine, but I will make sure I am careful and will ensure you know where I am so you don't worry.'

And I had to be content with that.

The carriage was half empty, so we sat staring at the advertisements opposite as I tried to control my apprehension when the train stopped in the tunnel outside Liverpool Street for no apparent reason. Then, with a rattle, it jerked off again, and we arrived at Mile End just after six. We half-ran to Salim Mian's house on Brokesley Street.

'This is a nicer part of the East End,' I said, panting as we slowed down through the wide, tree-lined streets with signs of fresh development everywhere.

'Uncle is not thrilled with it,' said Naila, who didn't seem out of breath. 'He believes all these betting shops and burger bars will be replaced by artisanal coffee parlours, speakeasies and organic vegan cafes with beardy hipsters, and he won't be welcome here any more when house prices shoot up. He's taken to singing "Jaane Kahan Gaye Wo Din" in the shower every morning, much to Aunty Alaya's irritation.'

'Yeah, I wonder where those days went as well sometimes. And I've not lived here for five minutes.'

We reached Salim Mian's small house overlooking Tower Hamlets Cemetery Park at the end of the cul-de-sac. 'Come up, have chai and we'll talk. Or we can leave it for another time; I know you have to be back soon.'

Six fifteen. 'No, it's fine.' I shot off a WhatsApp to Anjoli: *running late, be there as soon as I can, sorry x*. Two blue ticks showed she had received and read it, but I got no response. Couldn't be helped. I had to sort out this Imran business and would deal with Anjoli later.

Naila led us into the kitchen to grab a couple of drinks, 'Salim Uncle is in the restaurant and Alaya Aunty is in the shop. Chai or Pepsi?'

I opted for Pepsi as it was quicker, and she opened the fridge, which had a sign stuck on it in her neat handwriting: *Don't forget your diabetes shots, Salim Uncle.*

'That's sweet,' I said as she handed me the can. 'You look after him well.'

'It's the least I can do; he keeps forgetting and eating the wrong things. Don't want him keeling over on me. You must make sure he eats proper food in the restaurant. And you should too; you eat too many sweet things. Here take this Vitamin D – south Asians are often deficient.'

She reached into a drawer, pulled out a bottle of Vitamin D tablets, tipped out a pill and handed it to me together with the bottle.

'Take this now, and then one every morning. Don't forget. Come.'

Touched and somewhat excited by her nurse persona, I swallowed the pill with a swig from the can and pocketed the bottle as she led me up the stairs to her room, which overlooked the cemetery – peaceful mossy graves with birds singing and flitting between the trees. Throwing her rucksack on the floor, she kicked off her sneakers, grabbed some clothes from the closet and vanished into the bathroom.

I looked around the room – she'd never let me into her life like this before. There was little to see: a few cosmetics arranged on the dressing table, four pairs of shoes in a line against the wall. It felt temporary, transient, and a total contrast to the manic clutter I was used to tripping over at Anjoli's. There was a book next to her bed – *Only a Factory Girl* by Rosie Banks. I opened it to a dog-eared page and skimmed it. Naila emerged five minutes later dressed in smart jeans and a pretty blue top.

'That's better, I'm a person again. What are you doing?'

'Shh. I've just got to the part where Sophie, against her better judgement, has gone to the Riviera with her boss on a business trip. I think he has a nefarious purpose in mind for this sweet, innocent factory girl.'

'Give me that,' she squealed and made a grab for the book.

I held it behind my back as she scrambled to get at it. 'Ms Naila Alvi, a Mills & Boon aficionado. Who would have guessed?'

'Yes, well!' She snatched the book from me and tossed it into the corner of the room. 'Let's just say a girl needs a dose of romance as well as Vitamin D from time to time. Come sit.'

She sat on the narrow bed, patting the space next to her. I took off my shoes, sat against the headboard and put an arm around her as she leaned into me, the scent of her shampoo tickling my nostrils. She shut her eyes as we sat sipping our drinks.

I squeezed her shoulders, feeling my breath quicken. This was the most intimate we had ever been. Anjoli could wait.

'How are you doing?'

'Not great, if I'm honest. That call freaked me out. But I'll be fine.'

'We have to get to the bottom of all this. I think we should speak to Mackenzie again – I need to find out about that hoodie. Can you arrange a meeting?'

'I'll try. Kamil, I wish we could get away from all this, it's becoming too much.'

I kissed her hair and said, 'I know, I'm so sorry.'

She snuggled into my arms. 'This is nice, I feel safe with you.'

My growing excitement made me feel guilty. Naila was going through a terrible time and here I was wondering whether to make a move.

But she may have been feeling the same thing as she said, 'So are we sorted for next weekend?'

My pulse raced. 'Yes. I've booked a lovely place in Brighton for one night. I thought we'd leave first thing Saturday morning and come back Sunday evening. We can drive or take the train. Don't worry, I'll bring the romance back into your life.'

I tried to kiss her, but she moved her face away and said, 'So you've done these types of weekends before?'

'Hardly!'

'Well, you've had more relationships than me.'

'Have I? I mean I had a couple of girlfriends in college, but my only serious relationship was with Maliha.'

'How long were you together?'

'Six years.'

'You were engaged, no?'

'Yes.' I didn't add I'd been the loneliest I'd ever been since she'd broken off the engagement ten months ago. And the most frustrated. 'But why are we talking about her? Tell me about you.'

'I'm glad we're going to the sea. I miss the sea.' A hint of sadness. 'When Daddy was based in Karachi, we used to go to a place called Churna Island. It was so beautiful and uninhabited. We would picnic on the beach and snorkel. I saw turtles and sea urchins and angel fish. It was one of the happiest memories of my childhood. I had Daddy and Mummy all to myself – they had no work, no parties. I felt so free.'

'Didn't you feel free in Lahore? Is that where this Imran met you? Was he your boyfriend?'

'I *wasn't* free. I mean, we had everything. But Daddy was always busy, and Mama was always at social occasions, so the maids brought me up. Because Daddy kept moving from cantonment to cantonment, I had no one place that was home. Or any real friends I kept up with. Just new towns, new schools, new friends. Groundhog Day. It was easier not to get too close to anyone because you just ended up leaving them.'

She looked into the distance somewhere, melancholy.

'So, what did you find comfort in?'

'I don't know. Films, music, books. Long walks.'

'Well, now I know what books you like. What types of films?'

'The usual. Bollywood movies. Romcoms. And I always had a sneaking love for film noir.'

'Your inner detective coming out! I used to love them too.'

'I guess so. It took me into a different world. Made me want to get the hell out of Pakistan.'

'What was so bad there? It sounds like you had an idyllic life.'

I could sense her shutting down again and squeezed her shoulders. 'Please talk to me, Naila. I won't judge.'

She looked at me for a long while. Then glanced away and said, 'Kamil, I have to tell you something.'

I waited. Finally.

'I was – *am* – married.'

The air turned to nettles, and the silence that followed was palpable. Even the birds outside appeared to be listening. Something inside me closed like a book.

'What?'

'It was a mistake,' she said, eyes going somewhere deep inside herself. 'A big mistake.'

'Imran is . . . your *husband?*'

'Yes. I met him at a party when I was seventeen. He was so handsome, smart, dashing . . . I fell for him. And he for me. Then he asked me to marry him.'

'What happened?' My heart was threatening to force its way through my ribs as a tumult of conflicting emotions shivered through me. I'd imagined every possibility about who Imran might be but never dreamed Naila was *married* to him.

'This is pathetic.' She sat up, moved away from me and started pacing around the room.

'I was young. Just finished school at eighteen. Who the hell gets married at eighteen these days? Daddy and Mummy were against the marriage, but I insisted. Fought for it. He said I could work after we got married, so I would be independent. I wasn't thinking about nursing then; I wanted to work for an NGO. Pakistan is such a mess, I could do some good. I even got an offer from Dar ul Sukun – they help mentally disabled children. But he made me turn it down. Said I didn't need to work, he was making enough money.'

'Was he . . . violent?'

'Not physically. But he was super-controlling.' She paused.

'You know, Kamil, there is a thin line between feeling safe and comforted in someone's arms and being suffocated. We all need to be soothed when we are in pain, but when it . . .' She shook her head. 'I could see myself slipping into the traditional Pakistani wife's role, from showpiece to housekeeper to mother. We'd both get frustrated. Then he would lash out and I'd push him more. We were trapped in this cycle we couldn't get out of. He oversaw every aspect of my life till I couldn't take it any more. So I said I needed to come to the UK for my degree, and here I am.'

'And you're still married?'

'Technically.'

'Why didn't you tell me?' I could feel anger rising inside me, replacing my previous intoxication.

Misery filled her eyes. 'I'm sorry, Kamil, I wanted to. But I like you and needed to know if we had anything between us that was real. I want to leave him, but I'm scared. I guess I thought if you and I had a future, then maybe I'd have the strength to do something about it. I am sorry. If you had known, would you have been interested?'

'Maybe not, if I'm honest. Salim Mian knows about Imran, I assume?'

'I knew you wouldn't be, and that's why I didn't tell you. Yes, of course Uncle and Aunty know and have been very supportive. If it wasn't for them, who knows where I'd be.'

'How did you escape to London? I mean, why did he let you come here?'

She stared at me. I felt as though she was sizing me up, wondering how much more she could share.

'In Pakistan, izzat – honour – is everything. Imran has a reputation in Lahore. He was respected and, you know, liked to portray himself as a modern man. So I applied in secret to King's, then when it was my birthday, with my parents and lots of guests around, I announced I was coming here and said it was his idea, his present to me. He loved the adulation of his family and friends – such a good husband, so caring about his wife, blah blah blah. He had no choice but to agree. But he didn't like it. He didn't like it at all.'

I could sort of understand where she was coming from; izzat was a serious motivator in India as well. But was that all? In my experience, controlling types always found a way. He could be engineering his revenge while we sat here.

'And he just let you go, without pushing back at all?'

'Oh, he pushed back as much as he could. I wanted to stay in halls, but he insisted I stay with Salim Uncle, so he'd know where I always was. Going back and forth between campus and here is a pain, but I have to. I need to call him once a week. Tell him everything I've been doing. Of course, he doesn't know about you. He keeps threatening to come to London to see how I am and to "look after" me. But khuda ka shuker so far, he hasn't. I live in constant fear that one day I'll open the door and there he'll be.'

'And you think he's the guy who sent you the text and called to threaten you?'

'I think he might be trying to scare me into returning. I'm worried he's here. I keep thinking he's following me. Maybe he's seen us together. Maybe that's what all this is about.'

'I don't see how, Naila. Someone killed Salma, and that can't have been Imran. Why would he? I assume he didn't know her. I mean, it's not like she was a close friend of yours?'

'I know, I know,' she burst out. 'When I think about it rationally, of course you're right, Kamil. But when I'm lying in bed at night, I wonder if it could have been a warning. I know I sound crazy and paranoid, but I'm feeling like I did in Pakistan and I *hate* it. I can't stand it. I don't know how he can do this to me. That's why I have to manage this on my own. You're nothing like him of course, but *he* always wanted to make sure I was –' she made air quotes '– "safe".'

I wasn't sure I liked being equated with a controlling monster, but I got off the bed, put my arms around her to stop her trembling and kissed her forehead. 'Did he just let you go, Naila? Or is there something you're not telling me?'

She shut her eyes for a long while and leaned into me.

'I . . . found out something. Something important to him. I told him he had to let me go or I would make sure it came out.'

'What was it you had on him?'

Another long silence. I waited her out. Then, in a rush, as if she had been waiting for years to share this with someone, 'Imran's built a successful business in Pakistan in the defence industry. Daddy helped him. But I'd always wondered how he won all the contracts because his company is quite young and there are many more reputable firms around. Then I found he had been bribing a lot of key officials.'

'How did you find out?'

'He'd written it all down in a ledger – dates, amounts, people the money went to. He must have thought it would give him leverage over them if he needed it. But I found the ledger, and it gave *me* the power I needed over him. If this comes out – if the press finds out about it – he'll be finished. The ministers and others he's bribed will survive – they are like cockroaches; they always do – but he could well be sent to jail as an example. And Daddy will have nothing to do with him – he's very upright.'

'So you blackmailed your own husband?'

'Sort of. I guess so. I told him I had the ledger, and if he didn't let me come to England, I'd make it public. He was furious, but there was nothing he could do.'

'And where's the ledger now?'

'I have it here. Look.'

She opened the suitcase under her bed and handed me a black wire-bound book with a hard cover. I opened it – lists of names, dates and amounts. I flipped through it and handed it back to her.

'Wow. That must have taken a lot of guts. You better keep it safe.'

She gave me a watery smile and put it away.

'I was terrified he would kill me, Kamil. That night . . . after my birthday . . . when I told him. It could have gone either way. I've never seen so much fury in anyone's eyes. We were in my bedroom and he had just told me there was no way he would ever let me come here, but I held my ground and said I was coming. I had to flatter him and tell him I was helping his business and got him to agree. But believe me, he didn't like it. When I go back, I do not know what he will do to me.'

'So, you think maybe this has been festering inside him and now he's trying to scare you into going back?'

'Maybe.'

'You could be right. I've seen this kind of stuff before in Kolkata. Guys like that, Naila, they don't just let go. If, as you said, somehow he saw you with me and freaked out, he *could* be trying to force you back. Listen, maybe Tahir could see if he has entered the country. There must be a record. What's his full name?'

A whisper, as if she had to force the name out. 'Imran Akram. If he's here, Kamil, if he has come after me, I don't know what I'll do. I can't go back to him. I just can't. And what if he harms me? I'm stuck.'

I didn't know what she should do either. She was in a terrible position.

'I'll look after you.'

'Thanks. But what can you do? No. If he is here, we need to find him and confront him. That's the only thing I can think of.'

'Have you tried to check if he's left Lahore?'

'I called his office. They said he was away on a business trip. In Europe.'

'Oh. So, he could be in England.'

My phone pinged: *Where the hell are you!!!!*

Six thirty-five. Shit! I'd forgotten all about Anjoli.

'I'm sorry, Naila. I *have* to go back to the restaurant. Anjoli is mad as hell. We'll talk later, I promise.'

'Go, go, don't make the boss angry. Alaya Aunty will be back soon, anyway. She'd be shocked to find you in my room.'

'Will you be okay?'

'I'm good. It was a relief to share. I'm glad you know now. It's good to have someone on my side. I feel . . . lighter.'

That was because she had transferred all the weight to me. I forced a smile. 'Always.'

'Thanks again.'

I tried once more. 'You're sure you don't want to come with me to TK? You can study there.'

'I'm certain.'

'Well . . . okay. Don't open the door to anyone.'

'I won't.'

She kissed me and shut the door as I sprinted to the Underground.

I got serious grief from Anjoli for the rest of the evening every time she passed me in the kitchen going from sarcastic: 'Kamil, if you want a part-time job let me know and I'll pay you part-time wages,' to direct: 'Mess around with your girlfriend on your own time, not on mine,' to passive-aggressive: 'It's so busy tonight and we're behind on the orders.'

I accepted her hits without responding – just took a deep breath and vented my frustration by pummelling the dough on the counter in front of me, the glowing naan oven reflecting my mood.

Chapter 27

Monday.

The restaurant was closed on Mondays so I could sleep in. But the curtains in my room didn't meet, and I hadn't got used to the shaft of early May sun streaming through the window, so I found myself awake just after five, unable to go back to sleep. I hadn't slept well, Anjoli's annoyance and Naila's confession churning around inside me. Could her husband be behind all of this? How could we find out? I'd spoken to Tahir the previous night, but he didn't believe Imran was a serious suspect and didn't hold up much hope of getting news from the immigration service soon. There were just too many potential suspects now – Ziad, Mr Aziz, Mackenzie and now Imran. I pulled the pillow over my face in frustration. Something was lurking in the corner of this case; I just wasn't seeing it. And what was I going to do about my nascent relationship with Naila? I hadn't called her back the previous night despite my promise. I needed to figure out where my head was first. Maybe the time had come to give up on it; where could it go? I suppose I could just be her friend and make sure she was safe.

But the sensation of her lips against mine, her eyes smiling at me . . . I drifted in and out of sleep for the next few hours then got up after eight, bleary-eyed, dressed and made my way to the kitchen to make myself breakfast and a coffee, hoping Anjoli wouldn't be there. I don't cope well without sleep, and the occasional long sultry nights in the UK do nothing for my clarity and focus. At least in India we had air coolers and fans.

I texted Naila to make sure she was all right, and she responded, *Not been strangled yet. On my way to college xxx.*

I smiled, but the flutter of nervousness remained. Maybe it was all the movies I'd grown up with where the heroine went into a dark house with insouciance and ended up being chased up and down the stairs by a masked man with an axe. But Naila was right: she couldn't live a life being spooked by shadows.

Anjoli stomped in half an hour later wearing a T-shirt that said *I want a hot man, not a hot planet.*

'I thought you didn't want a hot man,' I said, trying to lighten the mood as she made herself a cup of tea.

'Thanks, but if I'm ever looking for guidance on what's hot or not, I won't seek it from you.'

I didn't understand what she meant by that, but let it pass. 'So, what have you done about the homeless thing?'

She looked at me as if debating whether to continue baiting me.

'Well, I've not had much chance to do anything with you running around town with the Queen of Sheba, leaving me to do your job here. But anyway, since Tahir said he found nothing, I've obviously been wasting my time. Which is precious and in short supply. I've literally been banging my head against a dead horse.'

I didn't comment as she continued: 'I was just so upset about Yasir, I wanted to find a reason, I suppose. His going to all that trouble to escape from Syria then dying in the doorway of a mosque five minutes away from a hospital was more upsetting than someone killing him.'

She picked up a knife and, looking morose, slathered an inordinate amount of butter on a piece of toast.

'It's for the best, Anjoli. It was always unlikely. What are your plans for the day?'

'Neha's working for a homeless charity in Southall, and I'd fixed up to meet her there this morning. I was going to tell her about my . . . theory. Have good Punjabi food. It's a waste of time now, but I need to get out of TK for the day and I haven't seen her for ages.'

I was glad she was seeing sense and leaving her obsession behind; it had always been fanciful, this mysterious Jack the Ripper stalking the streets of London killing the homeless and leaving no trace. I was wiped and would have liked to stay in the flat eating junk food and watching rubbish TV to recharge, but I needed to get back into Anjoli's good books.

'Would you like company?'

'Not with Ms Green Eyes today?'

'No.'

She shrugged.

Not the most enthusiastic response, but I put on an eager face. 'Great. It'll be nice to see Neha again. And I've never been to Southall. *I'll* treat you to a nice Punjabi lunch.'

We got to Southall just after noon after an hour's train journey during which my fatigue got the better of me, head falling to my chin and jerking back every time we got to a station. Anjoli let me get my semi-rest, oversized headphones covering her ears as she played Candy Crush on her phone. The tension between us was pushing me to breaking point, but I didn't have a clue what to do about it. I was regretting coming and dreading lunch.

Due to see Neha at two, we walked down the Broadway looking for somewhere to eat. On the surface, Southall seems to have a lot in common with Brick Lane – Indians thronging the streets, jewellery shops, cash and carries, restaurants – but once you get under the veneer you can see a very different world. Instead of thobes, headscarves and burqas you see saris, kurtas and salwar kameez; the shops are bigger, more colourful and luxurious; there's a vibrancy about the people milling around you don't see in the East End. Southall is the exciting, flamboyant Punjabi cousin to Brick Lane's down-at-heel Bengali dowdiness – although, as a proud Bengali, I would call it Brick Lane's cultured understatement.

Bengalis have always looked down on Punjabis, seeing them as boorish, money-grubbing Philistines eating their fat samosas, as opposed to the learned gentility of the Bangla folks sipping coffee while debating communism in the coffee shops of Kolkata. We have auteurs like Satyajit Ray and art films while they create garish soap operas. We eat sophisticated fish dishes while they wolf down basic cauliflower and potatoes. We . . . you get the point. But Punjab has adapted to the modern India of industrialists and job creation and succeeded, while Bengal hankers after a lost world and sinks into an oblivion of unfiltered cigarettes and forgotten poets.

A longing for Kolkata, like a dying ember sparking, filled me. My home. I had been happy there. Never thought about leaving, like so many others had. I was going to work my way up to become commissioner of police like my father, get married and live a respectable life in a beautiful, big house. And instead? Here I was, a cook in London trying to make ends meet while waiting for a magical event to take me back to the trajectory of my previous life. And who knows how long I'd cling on to my job, given how many liberties I'd already taken with Anjoli.

I normally keep such memories and longings buried inside me, but the smells and tastes and sights of a different India swirling around in Southall brought them all back to the surface. All it takes is one tiny event, one fork in the road chosen without thinking, and your future is altered for ever. It's impossible to recognise these life-altering choices ahead of time; they don't come with a blinking road sign showing you two directions. It's only afterwards that you recognise those moments for what they were and the 'if onlys' come back to haunt you with thoughts of the futures that never were. Argh! Sometimes memories are like the mutton curry in the Jolly Rajah restaurant – wiser not to uncover what's underneath.

I was suddenly hungry for good Indian street food. We wandered into MOTI MAHAL, nestled between ROYAL SWEETS (not sure where the ROYAL came from, it seemed unlikely Prince Charles would stop by for his jalebi fix) and NARGIS JEW L RY. We grabbed a table in the tiny cafe and ordered vada pav, papdi chaat, pani puri, bhel puri and mango lassi from the bored waiter.

'So, what's Neha doing with a homeless charity?' I said as the food arrived a couple of minutes later. The first time I'd met Anjoli's best friend, she was queening it up as the wife of a millionaire on Bishops Avenue. 'Didn't think it was her kind of thing.'

'The arrest changed her.' Anjoli cracked the top of a crispy round hollow puri, filled it with chickpeas and tamarind water and ate it whole. I followed suit, the tart tamarind and the delicate crunch of the puri creating a symphony in my mouth. 'She got the insurance money and moved in with her aunty while she figures out what to do next. In the meantime, she's "giving back to society".'

It had only been six months since we'd got Neha off the murder charge, but it felt like an eternity, given everything that had happened in the interim.

'While she looks for another rich husband?' I spooned a piece of yoghurt-covered crispy papdi into my mouth.

Anjoli shot daggers at me. 'That's nasty, Kamil.'

I had gone too far. Again. 'I'm sorry. I didn't mean that. I like Neha. It was just a joke.'

'Well, it wasn't funny.'

This brittleness between us was unsettling. I longed for the easy banter and familiarity of the time we'd spent together working to solve the murder of Neha's husband. I thought we were back there after the conversation in my bedroom the other night, but no sooner had we re-established our rapport, I had gone and wrecked it.

'Look, I know I've annoyed you over the last few days. I'm sorry. I realise how tough it is running the restaurant and the difficulties I've caused with my absences. I'd like to promise it will never happen again, but . . . Naila told me something yesterday and I'm worried.'

She raised an eyebrow over her lassi, and I told her all about Imran and Naila's fears.

Her eyes went wide. 'Shiiiit! Ms Green Eyes is *married*! She kept that quiet. And she thinks he may be here?'

'That's what she's frightened of. It could explain the text and the call, if he's trying to frighten her into returning to Lahore.'

'And you think it's connected to Salma?'

'I don't see how. It must just be a coincidence. But if he is here, I need to help her.'

'I understand.' She bit into her vada pav, a deep-fried potato patty in a burger bun. 'Listen, it hasn't just been you. I've been under a lot of stress. What with Ma and Baba being away and trying to keep things going at the restaurant, I'm worried I might not make it work.'

'I know, I'm sorry. But as I said, I have faith in you.' I reached out and took her hand.

She pulled it away gently. 'No, it's all right. I'm sorry I snapped at you; I've been a cow. Do you want proper time off from the restaurant? To sort all this stuff out. I won't be able to pay you, as I'd need to hire someone else while you're gone.'

I mulled this over. It wasn't ideal to have no income, and I had no savings. But it was better than letting her down.

'Maybe that's not a bad idea. Can I think about it and let you know?'

'Yeah, of course. So, are you and Naila still a thing or . . . ? I mean, now you know she's married, right? So . . .'

'I don't think she's planning on getting divorced. And she has to go back when her course is over. I don't know. For now, I just want to make sure she's not in danger.'

The realisation hit at that moment: I'd lost Maliha, then Anjoli and now Naila. What the hell was wrong with me? Well, I'd never actually been with Anjoli but still.

It must have shown on my face as she looked at me like I was a dog with a thorn in its paw.

'You'll be fine, Kamil. You're a good guy. And . . .'

'And?'

'Well . . . I was never sure you were right for each other.'

'You said we were!'

'Well . . .'

'You think she's out of my league?'

'Well . . .'

I smiled. 'Piss off. You're the one who told me to ask her out. Anyway, I wasn't sure your boyfriend was right for you, either. You deserved better than a coffee wallah.'

'That's rich coming from a waiter-cook.' She laughed.

'What can I say? You're an amazing woman. Pity you're so anti-relationship. You'd have men queuing up.'

'Hardly.'

'You would!'

'Maybe in the future. I don't plan to die a spinster spending my days in Lady Dinah's Cat Emporium. Let me sort out my restaurant empire first.'

'Good plan. Look, we'd better go, it's almost two.'

I paid, and we walked back onto the Broadway. I felt lighter and wanted to laugh. I spotted something in the window of New Fashion House and said, 'Hang on a sec!' I dashed into the shop and came back a few minutes later. 'Stand still,' I said, and pinned the brooch onto her T-shirt. She squinted down at the little blue bird with *I fly on my own wings* emblazoned on its feather.

'Aww!' Joy broke across her face and she pecked me on the cheek. 'That's sweet.'

And I didn't need to say anything more.

We were okay.

Chapter 28

Monday.

The Guru Singh Sabha Gurdwara is a large ornate building in white marble that looks Islamic – white domes, arched windows, metal latticed screens. Anjoli and I walked in under the arresting blue stained-glass window with snaking grey curlicues that dominated the entrance and stepped into an atrium with an ice-white marble floor with a glittering chandelier hovering above it. I could see the main prayer hall through an inner door – a giant circular space with a domed skylight – which reminded me of the interior of the Baha'i Lotus Temple in Delhi, a space I had felt an immediate connection with when I'd visited as a child. I guess all religious buildings must create a sense of awe among the believers to put them into the right frame of mind to let the spirit enter them. Or, if I was feeling cynical, let donations exit them.

The resemblance to a mosque ended as soon as I heard music and singing from the prayer hall. I peeped in to see a few dozen people – men on one side, women on the other – heads covered, listening to a group of identically dressed Sikhs in white clothes, black turbans and long beards, equipped with harmoniums and tablas performing a religious song. At the end of the room was what looked like a giant's gold four-poster bed with another Sikh – who I assumed was their equivalent of the imam – standing behind it waving a metal rod with long feathers at the end in time to the music. You'd never hear this type of music in a mosque – an example of the Bangla/Punjabi dichotomy translated into religion.

'Anj!' I turned to see Anjoli enveloped in a tight hug by Neha, who released her and advanced on me to embrace and kiss me. 'And Kamil! I didn't know you were coming. What a lovely surprise.'

'Hello, Neha. You look well.'

'Thank you, so do you both! Come, come, it's wonderful to see you. Let's join the langar.'

She led us into a massive canteen. Behind the metal counter were half a dozen Sikhs, standing in height order – a gigantic guy over six foot six (including his turban) on the left and at the extreme right a tiny fellow who couldn't have been over five foot (excluding his turban) – doling out food to a queue of people.

'Oh what a pity, we've just eaten,' said Anjoli.

'What's a langar?' I said.

'We provide free food to worshippers and anyone who wants it. So our charity brings the homeless here when we can. Nicer than a soup kitchen and way healthier food.' She grabbed us a table, and we sat.

Neha seemed a different person from the perfectly dressed, perfectly made-up, perfectly coiffed socialite I had seen the previous year. Instead of designer clothes and a flawless complexion, she now wore a white kurta over faded jeans and had no make-up on, but there was a sparkle in her eye as opposed to the worry and pain that had taken root before.

'How have you been, Neha?'

'Great. I still can't thank you enough for what you did, Kamil. If it wasn't for you, I'd be rotting away in a jail somewhere. And now . . .'

'How do you spend your time?'

'I work with HSSH, look after Aunty, who's not so well, and just live, you know. It's good to live!'

'What's HSSH?'

'Hope for Southall Street Homeless – that's why you're here, no, Anj? You said on the phone you wanted to talk about it?'

'Sort of, but it's not relevant now,' said Anjoli. 'I wanted us to catch up anyway.'

'How did you get involved?' I said.

'I came with my aunty to the gurdwara one day and saw them feeding the rough sleepers. I asked what I could do to help and was told, if you see a homeless person on the streets, just say hello. Treat them like a person. That pierced me, Kamil. It's so terrible – normal people just end up on the streets by accident, and if they don't receive help, drug addiction or alcohol dependency sometimes follows. You won't believe the stories I've heard. We give rough sleepers shelter, food when we can, help those who need it with immigration. Even get them back to their home countries if they want to return. And what's lovely is the gurdwara set it up with the local churches and mosques. It's non-denominational and inter-faith. I volunteer three days a week and have never been happier. But why are you interested in this, Anjoli? Are you volunteering too? I thought the restaurant took all of your time.'

'It does,' said Anjoli, glad to get a word in. 'But a friend of ours, a homeless Syrian man, died last week, and I wanted to see if there was something we could do to help others in his situation.'

'How dreadful! We always need help – in fact, there is one thing you might help with right now!'

'What's that?'

'We're working with several groups in London to see if we can build a model to predict who might be at risk of homelessness, based on early trauma they have suffered?'

I could feel Anjoli's interest quickening.

'How?'

'We're working on an ACE test – I think it stands for adverse childhood experiences or something. Anyway, we ask questions about rough sleepers' childhoods to see if we can find a pattern of behaviour that might be predictive of future homelessness, then we intervene. It would be ideal for you with your psych degree to get involved.'

'Wow,' said Anjoli, excitement in her voice. 'So, you're trying to target those at risk *before* they lose their homes. Does it work?'

'We don't know, that's why we need you. Father Spence there is leading it.' She nodded towards a middle-aged white man in a priest's collar who was chatting at the next table with what looked like four rough sleepers digging into their food.

She called out, 'Father Spence, this is my friend I told you about.'

The priest came over and sat at our table. 'Anjoli here is a psychologist. I thought she could help with your ACE study. And this is her friend Kamil.'

He shook our hands and smiled, kindly eyes magnified behind his rimless glasses.

'Good to meet you both. We can use all the help we can get,' he said in an American accent.

'I'd love to hear more, Father,' said Anjoli.

'It's something they tried in Australia which seemed to get results. We want to see if abuse, family breakdown, domestic violence – things like that – can be modelled. If we can get good enough data to run through the model, we may prevent homelessness before it happens, attacking the cause, not the effect. We want to catch young rough sleepers early. Young women, for instance. It's dangerous for them on the streets. Half of them are single mums or have had their children taken into care.'

'Oh no!'

'It's terrible, Anj,' said Neha. 'We have to do what we can.'

'I'd be happy to tell you more, if you want to contact me at my office,' said Father Spence and gave Anjoli his card.

'Thanks, I'd love to.' She put it in her handbag.

I flashed back to the conversation I'd had with Tahir in the restaurant. 'Bit Minority Report isn't it, all this prediction?'

'That was about crime prevention; this is about averting a tragedy. Are you two involved with the homeless?'

'Not as such,' said Anjoli. 'A friend of ours died on the streets and then so did another man we knew. It was awful, and I wanted to see if I could help. I run a restaurant, so we are offering free meals every week, but I'd love to do more. Have you heard anyone talking about an unusual increase in homeless deaths around here in the last year?'

I shot her a glance, but she ignored me.

'Unusual?' he said, running the tips of his fingers through his greying goatee. 'No. Fewer than normal, if anything. We've been lucky, and I haven't heard of too many people passing away. I think we have been more vigilant at finding them and we bring them to shelter much earlier. Why do you ask?'

'A few shelters I spoke to said it looked like there had been a lot more deaths than expected this year in some areas of London. We were just wondering if it was a broader trend. But I think now I may have been going down a cul-de-sac.'

'No unusual deaths around here. Although it's hard to know what is usual. Some years there are more, others less. But last winter was mild. So we were lucky.'

'Oh well, that's good, I suppose. I was scared someone might be harming them.'

'Really?' said Father Spence.

Anjoli looked embarrassed. 'I don't know. It was weird, but both of the people who died had the same bottle of gin next to them, and one of them was teetotal – he was Muslim. So, I thought that—'

'Was it poisoned?' said Neha, agog.

'No, the police tested it. I just wondered and . . .'

'If that's true, that would be terrible,' said the priest. 'Although I suspect a lot would be quite pleased to accept a free bottle of gin. I'll ask around and—'

A voice from the next table said, 'I was attacked. By a guy who gave *me* gin.'

We turned to see an old woman, dressed in what looked like a tattered, moth-eaten dressing gown, with thinning grey hair. She was staring at us, her empty plate in front of her.

'What's that, Agnes?' said Father Spence.

'You lot were saying about a guy handing out gin. He attacked me.'

'When was this?' I said.

'Don't know. Last year some time? May?'

'What happened?' said Anjoli.

'Don't listen to her,' said an old man at Rogers' and Louis' table. 'She don't know where she is half the time.'

'You shut your mouth. I know what happened. I was there, not you.'

'Yeah, yeah,' the man subsided and went back to his dal and rice.

'Where was this, Agnes?' said Anjoli.

'Near Southwark station. I was having a kip, and this guy comes up to me and gives me a bottle of gin. He says he's helping the homeless to stay warm, like.'

'What did he look like?' I said.

She shrugged. 'Don't know. A man. White. Any road, he gave me the bottle and I drank it and went to sleep. Next morning I feel someone pulling at my arm. It's the same guy, and he's pulling at my arm, and I shout, "Hey! What are you doing!" And he runs away.'

'Are you sure it was the same man? Anything at all you remember? Beard? Moustache? Glasses? What he sounded like?'

'No. Normal-looking. Educated, like.'

'Any accent?'

Agnes paused and wrinkled her brow. 'American? Like him.' She pointed to Father Spence.

'Me?' he said, eyebrows rising in surprise.

'Well, I don't hear too well.'

Anjoli pulled out her phone and showed Agnes the video of the man giving the gin to Louis. 'Please look at this, Agnes; was this the man?'

Agnes peered at the video, then pulled out a pair of reading glasses from her pocket and looked again, Neha and Father Spence looking over her shoulder.

'Don't know,' she said, taking off her glasses. 'Can't see his face. But he was wearing a cap like that one.'

'Really,' said Anjoli.

'Why did you think he was attacking you, Agnes?' I said. 'Maybe he was just trying to check you were all right?'

'No. He was trying something, no question. The look on his face. Like he was frightened.'

'Frightened?'

'Yeah. Don't know. Scared of something. Maybe I scared him off.' She grinned, showing brown teeth. 'He didn't come back.'

'Do you know if anyone else has seen him since?' said Anjoli.

Agnes shook her head, then seemed to lose interest in us. She shuffled out of her chair and made her way out of the room, swollen ankles showing under her dressing gown, as Anjoli called after her, 'Thanks Agnes.'

'That was weird,' I said.

'I wouldn't pay too much notice to Agnes,' said Father Spence. 'She's a bit dotty.'

'She seemed sure about the gin, though,' said Anjoli.

He nodded and stood up. 'You know the ONS has all the data on deaths. Have you checked there?'

'ONS?'

'Office of National Statistics. The boroughs report all homeless deaths to them, and they keep a detailed record. I think it's all on their website.'

'Thanks, that's super-helpful!'

'Do you have contacts with other homeless charities in London?' I said.

'Of course. We all cooperate. Rough sleepers don't all stick to one patch, so if we want to track and look after them, we have to work together to keep them safe. Look, it was good to meet you, but I must go back to work. Take care.'

'Nice guy,' said Anjoli, watching him go. 'Kamil, that's the third homeless person to whom something bad happened after they were given a bottle of gin!'

'Once is happenstance, twice is coincidence, three times is enemy action,' I said, quoting James Bond. 'Maybe you're right. Tahir also said there were other instances of gin being found near dead bodies. Why don't you look into getting hold of that data and see if it tells us anything?'

'I will. Neha, this visit was really useful. I'll follow up on ACE. So how are you anyway? Have you seen Rakesh's family since all that stuff last year?'

'No, thank God. After the police released me, the family didn't want to have anything to do with me. They weren't happy I got the insurance money but couldn't do much about it. I have to say, these insurance people are terrible. It took ages for the cash to come through. Anyway, I'd be happy if I saw none of Rakesh's people again in my life. The way they treated me! Poor Rakesh, I miss him.' Her eyes saddened.

'So, what are you planning to do now?' I said. 'Will you be

with your aunty for the foreseeable future or are you going to buy a nice place somewhere?'

I had learned the best way to change the subject in London was to get on to the state of the property market. Neha was soon showing us online pictures of houses she was looking at. As she and Anjoli weighed up the merits of period houses versus off-plan new-build apartments in different areas of London, I glanced at my phone to see Naila had sent me a text – *Seeing Sir at 4.30. Want to join?* It was just after three. If I rushed, I should just about make it.

'I've got to dash, I'm afraid. You two catch up,' I said getting up.

'Aww, do you have to, Kamil? I wanted to chat with you,' Neha said in a little-girl voice and pouted – so she hadn't left *all* of her old behaviours behind.

'I'm sorry, I do, I'm sure we'll meet again soon. You should come to the restaurant. You haven't lived till you've tried my raan masaledar.' I reached over to kiss her cheek but she got up and enveloped me in a hug.

'Naila?' queried Anjoli.

'Yes. I have to interview someone with her. I'm involved in another case,' I explained to Neha.

'Naila is Kamil's girlfriend,' said Anjoli.

'Wow,' said Neha, eyes widening. 'Now we *have* to meet, Kamil, so you can tell me about this girl and your new case.'

'She's not my— Anyway, see you at the restaurant.' I ran out of the gurdwara as Father Spence gave me a covert glance that he converted into a wide smile and a thumbs up when I caught his eye.

Chapter 29

Monday.

On the Tube, I realised I needed a fresh approach with Mackenzie. I was still certain he had something to do with this whole sorry affair but realised my previous mode of questioning would just slide off him. To get any further, I'd have to either get him on my side or get under his skin, but I was finding it difficult to formulate a coherent interrogation plan. Every time I tried to map out an approach, Naila's revelations returned to haunt me. While she hadn't exactly lied about her relationship status, she had certainly led me on.

Why was I bothering with all this? I'd be better off throwing it in and letting the police deal with it; putting all my focus on being a cook and helping Anjoli make the restaurant a success. Maybe see if there was anything in this homeless business. I should let Naila go back to Pakistan after her course and live her life while I lived mine. Give up on my dreams of becoming a cop again and be happy with my lot. Millions had it worse than I did. The rhythm of the train caused my eyelids to droop, and I jerked awake just before we arrived at Waterloo.

I got to Naila's college at 4.25 and found her waiting for me in reception. Which Naila would I get this afternoon? The vulnerable young woman who had been trembling in my arms twenty-four hours ago or the cheery, professional nurse, which was her normal MO? We had texted but not spoken properly since the husband grenade had detonated, but I couldn't show her how much it bothered me, given she was still in danger and needed all of my support.

'You made it. Let's hustle – I don't want to be late. I told Alaya Aunty I'd be home early today.' No-nonsense nurse it was.

We rushed past more italicised aphorisms from Ms Nightingale (*How very little can be done under the spirit of fear*) and stopped outside Mackenzie's office.

'Any luck with his file? Any previous improprieties?' I said, trying to scope out the approach I'd take.

She shook her head as the door opened and a young blonde woman came out with Mackenzie following behind saying, 'Come back to me if you have more questions.'

'Hi, Emily,' said Naila to the woman. 'How are you?'

'All good, Naila. See you around.'

'Just in time, Naila,' said Mackenzie. 'Come in.' Then he clocked me. 'Oh, you're here too? I thought we were having our tutorial, Naila?'

'Yes, sorry, sir. I was wondering if we could just ask a couple more questions about Salma. Since we had the time booked already . . .'

He didn't look thrilled at the prospect and for a moment it seemed he might demur, but then gave an abrupt nod and stood aside to let us in.

I'd have to wing it with my questioning and see where we got to.

'Dr Mackenzie,' I said as we sat, 'I think I may be under suspicion for Salma's death because I found the body. I'm on a work visa and can't afford to put a foot wrong.'

Naila's head swivelled towards me with a *Where are you going with this?* look, while Mackenzie stayed expressionless.

Where the hell *was* I going with this? However, I continued: 'So I want to help solve the crime and find the actual killer.'

'I thought Ziad Aziz was the killer?'

'The police have let him go.'

'I see.'

'I think you may have crucial evidence and not even know you have it.'

'Like what?'

'Well, Salma reached out to you with her concerns. I want to know what else she told you. I mean, was there *anything* she said you missed out because you believed it seemed irrelevant? Because *that* might point me towards the true killer.'

He picked up his pen and started spinning it around in his fingers, then leaned back in his chair, an amused look on his face.

'Just what I told you. She thought drugs were being stolen and suspected Mr Aziz, the pharmacist. Doesn't that give you enough to go on?'

'We have spoken to Mr Aziz and the police have cleared him. Was there anything else?'

Spin spin spin – the pen was hypnotic.

'Nothing I can think of.'

He was blocking all my moves, such as they were. Time to change tack.

'Did you know someone has threatened Naila?'

He sat up straight and the pen stopped mid-twirl.

'Threatened? How? What happened, Naila?'

'I got a text and a call. I'm sure it's nothing.'

'It's not nothing,' I said. 'See, that's why I'm not sure it's Ziad, Dr Mackenzie. What reason would he have for doing that?'

'What did the text say?' said Mackenzie.

'Told me to get back to Pakistan. Or else. Horrible stuff.'

'Oh Lord. Must have been very upsetting to receive messages like that. Did you tell the police?'

There was something in his voice that made me take a closer

look at him. On the surface he was all solicitude for his student, but underneath it was almost as if he was trying not to laugh. This guy had a dark streak, no question.

I moved to another part of the board.

'Just to clarify one thing: when did you get the yellow hoodie you showed us?'

'On our away weekend last summer, as I told you when you turned up at my house.'

'But that's odd. Because the photo you showed us had you wearing it in the spring. With the bluebells, remember? That would have been before last summer.'

It was as if he had been expecting this and he said, 'The photo was taken this April. You must have misunderstood.'

'Are you sure? Your children looked much younger in the photograph than if it was taken just a month ago.'

This caused him to pause.

'Well, you're wrong,' was all he could muster.

'Could I see the photo again?'

'I obviously don't have it here and frankly I'm tiring of your insinuations. You have no official role, and I was just seeing you out of courtesy to Naila. Naila, you shouldn't have brought this man here. I think it's time you left. Naila, you stay and we can finish your tutorial; we've already wasted enough time as it is.'

He rose and opened his office door.

I remained seated and said, 'We heard that there have been allegations of inappropriate behaviour made about you from students over the years. Can you tell me more about that?'

This took him aback, and he slowly shut the door. His pause before responding spoke volumes. I could see him trying to work out if I was bluffing.

'What the hell are you talking about?' he said, looking at Naila. 'That's just not true. Who told you that?'

I had hit a nerve.

'Senior people we have been questioning said that there were things on your file. Is that true?'

'What senior people? If your intention is to besmirch my reputation, you can get out right now.'

'I can get the police to check the file, you know. I don't want to get you into any trouble, Dr Mackenzie, but we need to find the killer. I know it isn't you, but anything could help.'

'Is there *anything*, sir?' said Naila. 'We promise we will keep it quiet.'

'Look.' He sat down and picked up his pen again. 'We live in a strange culture these days when anything can be misinterpreted. Yes, there have been a couple of students who made allegations, but there was a full investigation, and they came to nothing.'

'Who were the students? Was Salma one of them?'

He looked at me in disgust. 'Jaysus, you don't let up, do you? No! How many times do I have to tell you I would never do anything like that.'

'I was just wondering why she chose you to confide in?'

'I'm her tutor. She wanted me to do something about her suspicions.' He pulled out his iPhone and gave it a brief look. 'It's time for my next tutorial. Naila, this has been a complete waste of time. Please don't ambush me like this again.' His voice softened. 'And keep yourself safe, understand? I want nothing to happen to one of my star students. I hope you've told the police about your caller.'

We walked out to see the same woman who had earlier come out of Mackenzie's office waiting outside.

'Did you want something else, Emily?' said Mackenzie.

'There was a quick question I had, if you have a minute?'

He looked at his watch. 'Okay, come on in.'

He shut the door behind them, ignoring us.

*

'Well, what did you think?' said Naila as we walked out of the college towards Waterloo station.

'There's something there. I can sense it. That yellow hoodie – he realised he had screwed up and pretended we had misunderstood. And when you told him about your threats, didn't you think his response was odd?'

'Was it? How?'

'I can't put my finger on it – just something off about his reaction. And we shocked him about the sexual harassment.'

'Yes. That was clever of you. Do you really think Salma was having an affair with him?'

'It would explain a lot. She could have been feeling guilty. Maybe she wanted to break it off, and he got angry. Maybe she threatened to tell the college, and that's what the dean's appointment was about.'

She shook her head. 'I doubt she'd have done that. She wouldn't have wanted her parents to know. And she just didn't seem the type. To have two men on the go at the same time? Salma?'

Naila was right. I couldn't see Salma doing that either. But what other explanation could there be?

'Maybe she caught Mackenzie doing something he shouldn't have. And he's trying to deflect the blame on to Mr Aziz,' I said.

We walked up two flights of stairs into the station under the clock, which was now showing 5:16. Just as we reached the top, she jerked her head around and scanned the surrounding people.

'Are you okay?'

'Just thought I saw something.'

'What?' Ignoring your instincts was dangerous; ten years in the police force had taught me that.

'I don't know. You know the creepy feeling you get when you think someone's watching you?'

I looked around but couldn't see anyone suspicious.

'It's fine,' she said, holding her backpack straps tight to her like a security blanket. 'Let's go. I'm just jumpy.'

This was a different Naila again. I saw a shadow of the young woman in Lahore with a violent husband waiting for her at home.

'Do you want to sit down for a bit?'

'No. I've got to get home. It's fine. I'm just being stupid.'

Waterloo's concourse was packed with commuters heading home, people waiting in front of the departure boards for their platform numbers to come up. We dodged our way through the throng to get to the Underground entrance. There was a shuffling queue of people at the top of the stairs after the ticket barriers. I joined the queue down for the Northern Line platform, and the crush of people carried me along. Just as I reached the bottom, I heard a terrified scream.

'Kamil!'

The people behind me turned, and Naila fell backwards, almost in slow motion, hitting her head against the step above her with a loud *crack*. The crowd froze except for one woman who tried to help her up. I fought my way back up the stairs.

She tried to sit up, then fell back again. The colour had drained from her face. She pressed a hand to her side, then removed it and looked at it, puzzled.

There was blood dripping from between her fingers, creating a startling red pattern on her white top. A bloody gash in her side.

I forced myself to damp down my rising panic. 'Put pressure on it,' I yelled. Was anyone running away? No. Just a circle of concerned faces looking down at Naila.

Instinct. Always trust your bloody instincts.

Chapter 30

Monday.

Naila's brow wrinkled as though she was wondering why she was lying on the floor of Waterloo station, blood leaking from her side and staining her backpack. Two Good Samaritans helped carry her off the steps, and I kneeled next to her, applying as much pressure as I could to the wound in her side as she looked at me, incomprehension in her eyes. The station and people around me vanished and my entire being was concentrated on saving Naila – her blood warm and wet under my palms. *Don't die. Don't die. Don't die. Don't die* bounced around my brain, the pain on her face tearing out my heart.

The paramedics and police arrived in double-quick time. They transferred Naila onto a stretcher, and I accompanied her, bouncing around in the ambulance as we barrelled down the road, sirens blaring, and reached St Thomas' in what seemed like an eternity but in reality was only a few minutes. Arriving, the paramedics rushed her into A & E.

I felt nauseous as the adrenalin washed through me and leaned against the wall, clutching on to Naila's bloody backpack. I took what felt like my first breath in the last fifteen minutes and straightened up. With her in safe hands, I allowed myself to feel again. A combination of overwhelming fear for Naila and vengefulness directed at whoever had done this to her flooded me. I burned with the need to reach out and hurt someone.

What did it mean? Who had targeted her? It must be Imran. It couldn't have been Mackenzie; we had just seen him with Emily. Ziad? His father? The college and hospital were both nearby. But why Naila and Salma? Two Muslim student nurses? There'd been so much in the news about hate crimes. Was that what this was all about? Or was I on the wrong track? My mind whirred around at full throttle, unable to get into gear, going nowhere, trying to understand what had happened and avoid thinking about what Naila was going through behind that swinging grey door.

I looked down at my hands, still stained with her blood, and found them trembling. I went to the bathroom to wash, and as the red water streaked the basin, a surge of guilt smashed into me. Why had I walked ahead of her? If I had been behind, whoever it was couldn't have reached her. Why hadn't I been paying attention? I knew she was in danger; why hadn't I taken better care of her?

I went back out feeling a weird sense of displacement. Everything around me seemed unreal – as if I was in a dream with no way to wake up. I sat down then stood up again to ground myself, to get some sense of what was material and what was not. I paced up and down in the blue waiting area alongside patients waiting to be triaged and relatives and friends anxious to be told what had happened to their loved ones, everyone perched on uncomfortable linked plastic chairs. I got myself a paper cup of warm water from the barely functional water cooler in the corner and waited. And waited.

I had to calm myself down. There was nothing I could do for Naila now. It was out of my hands. British doctors were the best in the world. She would be fine. Tahir. I should let him know. I called. He listened with no jokes, promised to check with the local police and tell me if they found anything.

About an hour later a nurse emerged, followed, to my immense surprise and relief, by Naila.

'Oh my God, they let you out? How are you?' I could barely breathe.

She gave me a wan smile. 'I'm okay. I was lucky. Got a bump on my head where I fell. The knife missed my vital organs because I had my backpack on – it caught on the strap and didn't go in too deep. The doctor said if I hadn't . . .' She shuddered, and I sat her down.

I shut my eyes and gave a silent prayer of thanks.

'I was so worried. I'm so sorry.'

'It's not your fault, Kamil. But I'm fine. Promise.'

'I have your backpack. Is it very painful?'

She nodded and winced. 'Ya. They gave me painkillers. Just said I needed to keep it clean and dry. The bruise on my head hurts more. It was a clean stab. Went in about two inches, but . . . oh God, Kamil, oh God.'

I squeezed her shoulders, not wanting to hug her in case it hurt. 'Are you all right to go home? Shouldn't you stay the night here?'

'As if they'd have a bed for me. Anyway, I can't tell Uncle and Aunty what happened – they will worry too much. I'll just tell them I banged my head at work and need to take time off, okay?'

'Of course. Whatever you want.'

My phone rang. Tahir.

'Tahir, I can't talk,' I started, but Naila interrupted, whispering, 'I'm okay – talk to him!'

I shook my head, but she mouthed, 'Talk to him!'

'Sorry, Tahir, please go ahead.'

'They've closed Waterloo station, there's a worry it might be a terror attack. They found a Stanley knife near the top of the stairs. The culprit must have dropped it when he ran away. They are checking CCTV and fingerprints, and they'll let me know if they find anything. How is Naila? They want to interview her.'

'She's in a lot of pain, but thank God, the knife missed her vitals. They've discharged her, and we're going home now. I guess the police can speak to her there?'

I looked at Naila and she nodded.

'Okay, that's good. I'll tell them. A Stanley knife isn't really a murder weapon – the blade's too small. So, it might be more likely that the perpetrator was trying to scare the two of you off, rather than kill her. Tell her that, it may help.'

It made me feel worse.

'Thanks Tahir, I'll keep you posted.'

'One more thing, before you go. You asked for the date Salma first called Mackenzie? It was two Sundays ago.'

'Uh huh,' I said, distracted, watching Naila fill in forms for the nurse. Then brought myself back. 'That's interesting. She called him on a Sunday again instead of waiting to see him in college. What sparked that level of urgency?'

'Don't know.'

'Are you able to send me a list of her locations for that week? iPhones track them, right?'

'I think so. Let me see what I can do. Wish Naila well.'

He hung up, and I told Naila what Tahir had said about the knife and the CCTV, ending with, 'He sends you his best. He's really concerned.'

'That's sweet,' she said, grimacing with pain. 'I hope the CCTV shows something. I'm scared, Kamil. I still can't believe it.'

'I'll look after you.' I squeezed her hand, knowing I had palpably failed to do so. 'Are you *sure* you want to go home?'

'I don't have a choice, do I? Where else can I go?'

She started to cry, and my heart broke at her helplessness. I felt impotent, with no idea how to comfort her.

'We'll get him,' was all I could say. 'It must be Imran.'

'I don't know.' She wiped her face. 'I can't . . . I can't imagine he would hurt me like that. Not Imran.'

'Can you be certain, Naila?'

She shut her eyes as another spasm of pain hit her. 'Sorry, my head's throbbing. No, I can't be sure, Kamil. But I don't think he would want me dead. He loves me.'

Looking at her beauty, even pale and drawn as she now was, I felt I could understand Imran's obsession. If he did love her, who knew what lengths a psychopath might go to to avoid losing someone under his control.

'Yes. They all say that,' I said. 'He probably didn't want to kill you – just scare you. He's trying to force you to go back to Pakistan.'

She shut her eyes momentarily. 'Thank you for being here. Come on, let's go – people are staring.'

As we waited at the cab rank, she leaned against me and said, 'What was all that about locations on iPhones?'

I was happy to take her mind off the stabbing. 'I asked Tahir to let me have Salma's locations for the week before she phoned Mackenzie. It might tell us something.'

'Can you do that?'

'Yes, the iPhone stores all your locations under its location services history.'

'Wow, that's scary. I didn't know that. You think it'll help?'

'Who knows? I learned it from a pal of mine in the police cyber cell in Kolkata. Very helpful to track bad guys if they claim they weren't somewhere. Although you can turn it off and delete it, and the crims are learning to do that now. Come on, here's a cab.'

This had all been my fault. I'd been too caught up in the mystery to believe it might strike close to home.

I *had* to keep Naila safe.

Chapter 31

Monday.

In the cab on the way home, Naila kept repeating she didn't believe Imran would do that to her.

'Who else could it be, Naila? There's no reason for Ziad or his father to target you. Mackenzie is the only other option, and he was with that Emily woman. Unless he left her and followed us?'

'I could call her and ask?'

'No, leave it to me. I don't want you involved any more, it's too dangerous. You rest and recover – you've just been through a major trauma.'

'Stop fussing, Kamil, I'm fine. I *have* to know if it was Imran. It's killing me to think he hates me that much. I'll call.'

She phoned Emily and after a few minutes' conversation confirmed that Emily had been with Mackenzie for a good twenty minutes after we had left.

'It can't have been him,' she said as she hung up the phone. Her face twisted. 'Imran . . . I can't believe it. It must have been Ziad or his father.'

She put her head against my shoulder and shut her eyes for the rest of the journey, her hand soft in mine.

When we got to her place, I helped her out of the cab and asked the driver to wait as I deposited her with Alaya, propagating the fiction that Naila had hurt herself at work. Alaya fluttered around her and took her to bed promising her a sweet cup of tea, the elixir that solved all ills in the minds of Indian mothers. I wanted to stay but Naila insisted she was fine, and I left reluctantly.

On the way back to the restaurant in the cab, to take my mind off Naila and my guilt I checked my email to see Tahir had sent me screenshots of the significant locations Salma had visited in the weeks before her death from her iPhone's system services. I'd been shocked the first time I'd seen how the iPhone tracked locations but had to admit it was useful for the police. Most of Salma's movements seemed innocuous: college, hospital, flat, college, hospital, flat. Nothing for her trip home to Leeds, but she hadn't had her phone then. I checked out the evening of her death – college, hospital, our restaurant, then home. Salma appeared to lead quite the pedestrian life for a student.

Then something popped out at me. The Saturday night before her first call to Mackenzie.

7.37 p.m.: *Roupell Street – arrived via a 12-minute walk.*

7.53 p.m.: *Coin Street – arrived via a 10-minute walk.*

Outside TK I paid the eye-watering cab fare and checked out Roupell Street on Google Maps. It was near Salma's college and appeared to be residential, with a language school and a couple of restaurants. It seemed unlikely she'd be going to the school on a Saturday night; was she visiting someone at their home? Eating at a restaurant? I looked up Coin Street, which was mainly restaurants. So, odds were that she'd met someone at their home on Roupell Street and then gone to eat at Coin Street with them. But who? Ziad didn't live there.

On an impulse I dialled him.

'Hi, Ziad, It's Kamil. Quick question. Where were you this evening around five?'

'At college, why?'

'You didn't go out anywhere?'

'No, I was working on a project with two of my friends.'

Out of the frame.

'Thanks, one more thing. Were you with Salma on Saturday evening two weeks ago?' I gave him the date. 'It's important.'

'Let me check. Yes, we had dinner together. It was a date night. I treated her.'

'Where?'

'A Greek place in Coin Street.'

'Oh, right. And did you go to Roupell Street before that?'

'How did you know? We were *supposed* to go to Venezia on Roupell Street – I reserved a romantic table and everything – but when we got there, she said she didn't want Italian food, so we went for Greek.'

'How come?'

'I don't know. It was embarrassing. The waiter took us to our table, I went to the toilet and when I came back, she had changed her mind.'

I pondered this for a second.

'Did Salma do this kind of thing often?'

'What kind of thing?'

'You know, you book a nice place and she changes her mind?'

'No, this was the first time. Normally she loves Italian food, that's why I booked it. But I guess she just didn't fancy it that night.'

'Right. And how was she that evening?'

'She was fine before dinner. But then said she had a headache and went home early. Why?'

'Just following up on something. Thanks.'

This was decidedly odd. Why would Salma leave a nice restaurant? Had she seen something that had spooked her?

Or someone?

It was almost 8 p.m., but this couldn't wait. I couldn't do anything for Naila now, but maybe I could avenge Salma and find the monster who had brutally attacked my girlfriend.

I jumped on the District Line at Aldgate East to Blackfriars and half an hour later was in front of Venezia. Excellent choice by Ziad; it was romantic – candlelit with flowers on each table, waiters dressed in stripy gondolier tops, evocative pictures of canals on the walls. The owner had a theme and by God he was going to stick to it. It was a quiet night, but there were a few couples inside eating. It had a very different vibe from Tandoori Knights, more cosy, warm and friendly. Maybe I needed to bring Anjoli here one day to inspire her. But first I needed to find out if my hunch was right.

Inside the door a liberally mustachioed man with a thick Italian accent welcomed me. 'Have you reserved, signor?'

'No. I wanted to know if I could book the restaurant for a party of twenty in a month.'

I knew what I was doing; *group* and *booking* were magic words which, when combined, transformed Anjoli from grumpy contrarian to super-welcoming hostess.

'Of course, signor, of course. Come in please. Which date did you have in mind? I am Stefano, the owner.'

I gave him a random date, and as he was checking, I dropped in, 'A friend of mine recommended it. Liam Mackenzie. Do you know him?'

He looked up. 'I am afraid I do not know that name. But we get so many guests . . . Ah, it is a Tuesday, yes? We can give you a nice table that night. Of course, you will have to pay a deposit.'

Had I just wasted my time? I pushed on. 'I hope I have the right restaurant. He said he was here a couple of weeks ago. Could you check your reservations, if you don't mind? I don't want to book if it is the wrong place.' I gave him the date when Ziad had taken Salma out.

'Certainly,' he said, flipping back in his reservation book. 'Mackenzie, you said. Ah yes – you are right. Dr Mackenzie, 7 p.m. Saturday for two. Table three. Our best table.'

Triumph flooded into me. I was right. Salma *had* seen

Mackenzie, then left. And called him the next day. That night had been the start of everything. I could feel every nerve in my body jangling.

'Do you remember who he was with?'

'I am afraid not, signor; we get so many people . . .' He threw his hands open in what was almost a caricature of an Italian.

'Wait, this is him.' I pulled out my phone, searched for Naila's college website and pulled up a photo of Mackenzie to show Stefano.

He stared at it, shook his head and narrowed his eyes, possibly realising I wasn't here to reserve a table.

'How about the waiter who was serving table three? Could I speak to him?'

'Marco is not here tonight. Signor, how would you like to pay your deposit, cash or card?'

'And you don't have CCTV?'

'No, signor, we are a small restaurant. But what is this about? You want to book my restaurant or not?'

'May I take a menu with me and I can call back and confirm?'

'Of course.' He gave me a takeaway menu, disgust at my time-wasting now dripping from every pore, and I dashed out.

I took the train back to Brick Lane, adrenalin coursing through me. I loved this part of a case, when pieces fell into place like a jigsaw in my gut.

Mackenzie was a liar. This didn't mean he had killed Salma, and it appeared he couldn't have stabbed Naila, but when you pulled on the right lie, you could get the entire story to fall apart. And I had found the thread.

I tried to piece it together. Salma had told the imam something had upset her six weeks ago, and that would have been a month before she had seen Mackenzie at the restaurant. Then two weeks ago someone made a fool of her. Was this that occasion? How could he have made a fool of her at the restaurant?

She *had* to have been having an affair with him. What else could have precipitated such a reaction? She had seen him with someone else at the restaurant and realised he was two-timing her. Three-timing her, if you counted his wife. So she called him the next day to tax him with it and kept calling for the next two weeks, culminating in her seeing the dean to expose him. And he had killed her to stop it coming out.

It all fitted. I just had to crack his alibi.

Naila's stabbing was separate – that had to be Imran. These were two separate cases.

Should I call Tahir? No. This was something I had to do myself. And there was no need to involve Naila; I couldn't put her in any more danger. I'd get nothing else out of Mackenzie, but it might be worth talking to his wife. What was her name? Roisin, that was it.

It was 9.35 by the time I got back to TK. The adrenalin had dissipated, and I was more than ready for bed. The thought of lying down and pulling the sheet over me was almost making me quiver with anticipation. My phone rang as I entered the flat. Naila.

'Hi, how are you feeling?'

'I'm all right. Tired,' she said. 'The police came round, and I gave them my statement. They want to talk to you too.'

'What did Alaya think about that?'

'She was really confused, but I told her it was normal for work-related injuries. I think she bought it. I'm off to sleep now but calling as promised.'

'Did you tell the police about Imran?'

'Yes. But I felt like I was betraying him.'

'Don't feel that. It was him. You need protection.'

'I'll be fine. Are you taking your Vitamin D?'

'Yes. Did you take your antibiotics?'

'I did.'

For a second I debated whether to tell her what I'd found, bubbling as I was with my cleverness. No. She would insist on coming with me to Mackenzie's, and I needed her safe.

'I've decided we need to leave this to the police. I don't want you getting hurt again.'

'Okay.' She yawned. 'Whatever you think. Mwah.'

Better she was out of all this from now on. I could handle things on my own.

Chapter 32

Monday.

Anjoli was sitting at her computer at the kitchen table, listening to Taylor Swift singing that she didn't want to live for ever because she'd be living in vain. She looked up as I walked in. 'Where have you been?'

'It's been quite a day.' I realised I had eaten nothing since our lunch in Southall and was ravenous. 'Have you had dinner?'

'Yes. There's leftover rice and keema in the fridge if you want it.'

I did. Rice and keema were exactly what I needed at this moment.

I put them in the microwave and told her what had happened to Naila. She looked at me in shock, slapping her laptop shut. 'OMG! How is she?'

'She says she's okay. The hospital said she was very lucky. The knife missed her vital organs.'

'Who do you think did it? Was it the husband?'

'I think so. We need to keep her safe. The other suspects seem to have alibis.'

'I better go see her.'

'She's resting now. We can go tomorrow. But I found out something else.'

I told her about tracking Salma's movements and my hypothesis about her seeing Mackenzie in the restaurant.

'Oh wow. So you think he was sleeping with Salma and she

saw him with his wife? Maybe she didn't know he was married? Is that why she was talking about sexual harassment? There was a teacher at uni who got sacked for having it off with someone in my class.'

'Could be. Mackenzie has form. Someone complained about him before, but they cleared it up. But he couldn't have stabbed Naila, and his wife says he was with her when Salma was strangled.'

'Go to the wife and verify that! Maybe she's protecting him, or she's got it wrong. I wonder if she knows about the complaint about him.'

The microwave pinged, I grabbed the food and dug in. There's something about leftover Indian food: the flavours infuse and become more intense. Sometimes I think we should just serve precooked microwaved food in the restaurant – we might get a Michelin star. The sweetness of the peas with the spicy ground lamb and the fluffy white basmati rice hit the spot, and my fatigue eased as I reached satiated comfort.

'Maybe the two of us can see her,' I said through a mouthful of keema. 'How was Neha after I left?'

'Good. It was nice seeing her again. We need to spend more time together. But it's hard with the restaurant and everything. But listen, I have to tell you something too. I've been busy.'

'Tell,' I opened a bottle of Cobra. 'Want one?'

She nodded, and I popped one for her.

'Come up to my room.'

Her bedroom was the usual mess, clothes chucked everywhere, books, magazines and six-month-old newspapers piled next to her bedside table. She marched to her bed, and I negotiated my way through her possessions, banging my shin on the desk, on which she had piles of white T-shirts, stencils, a screen-printing frame and different coloured inks.

'What's up?'

She had taken down the print of Frida Kahlo adorned with butterflies that lived over her bed and replaced it with a large map of London. On it were several yellow stickies scribbled with numbers.

'Expanding your restaurant empire?'

'I wish. No, it's the homeless thing.'

'Oh?' I leaned closer. The stickies had numbers on them and she had a sheaf of printouts in her hand.

'So, I did an analysis of homeless deaths.'

'I thought we'd given up on that?'

'I had but gave it one last shot after the meeting today. I went to the ONS website the priest guy mentioned, and they have loads on there. All kinds of data about the homeless in London, number of deaths by borough, causes of death, age – the lot! All in a spreadsheet you can download. They have years of data, but the latest stats were 12 months old. Anyway, I found a contact number on the site and spoke to a guy who sent me up-to-date info; they have it all but only publish once a year.'

'And he sent it to you? Just like that?'

'Yup. I told him I was researching an article about the home-less. I don't think the staff in the ONS get many calls, he was happy to help.'

'And?'

'And I've spent the whole evening crunching numbers and analysing them. Who would have guessed all the stats courses I had to do for my psych degree would come in useful?'

'And you found something?'

'Let me show you!'

She sat next to me and we bowed our heads over her laptop.

'This column has all the boroughs of London in order of the number of homeless deaths over the last seven years, till March this year – see? Camden has the most deaths and Richmond the least. Lambeth is second, Westminster third, and our very own

Tower Hamlets fourth. I've put them on the stickies on the map.'

'Westminster is that high? I thought it was a wealthy neighbourhood.'

'I know. Anyway, you can see the number of homeless deaths for all the boroughs for the first six years was steady. Camden averaged around 17 a year, Lambeth 13, Tower Hamlets 9. I even made a graph.'

She was right. Apart from a few variations here and there, the deaths were stable, some flat, others going down a bit. It was tragic to think each of the points on the graph was a number of dead people.

'Very nice work, Anjoli, but what have you learned?' I downed the last of my beer. All the carbs from my late dinner and the day's drama hit me at once, and I wanted my bed more than anything, but I didn't want to disappoint her.

'Then I added in the new data I got from my statistical friend for last year and for the first four months of this year. See what happens to the graph.'

She clicked around a bit and the graph changed. The steady line continued for all the boroughs with two glaring exceptions – the lines for Lambeth and Tower Hamlets jerked up like hockey sticks.

'What happened there?'

'That's my point! What the hell happened there? Over the last sixteen months there have been around *double* the deaths there should have been in those two boroughs – fifty-nine people dead instead of thirty. And the two suspicious deaths we know of – Yasir and Louis – they were in Tower Hamlets and Lambeth. As was that woman at the gurdwara who said she was attacked.'

'So, are you saying someone has murdered *twenty-nine* homeless people in these two boroughs over the last sixteen months? Someone is killing a person every *two* weeks? They would be the most prolific serial killer in the history of serial killers. And no one has noticed? Come on, Anjoli. The data must be wrong?'

'Kamil, nobody cares about these people! They are just an irritation for most: someone whose eyes you have to avoid on your way to work, or someone whose sleeping bag you have to step over. These numbers are *real*, not just what a few people in the shelters or the local authorities thought. This is hard data.'

'Why, though? Why would someone be targeting rough sleepers?'

'I don't know. But look, I've found out even more. The extra deaths seem to be of older men. There are around eight times more homeless men than women – thank God, it must be so hard for a woman to be on the streets, all the things that could happen to her.' She shivered. 'Anyway, so it's not surprising they are men that are dying. Most homeless deaths are men between forty and fifty, but the last sixteen months has seen the biggest number of deaths in men over sixty.'

'So, the killer, if there is a killer and this is not all a bizarre coincidence or data glitch, is targeting old men?'

'There *is* a killer, Kamil. And yes, they are targeting old men.'

'Does your magic spreadsheet show the causes of death?'

'It does.' She clicked on another tab. 'Look at the amazing detail they have. They must do autopsies on all of them.'

I peered at the list. She was right. It was very detailed, listing around seventy causes of death – accidents at the top, followed by suicide, liver disease and a large section headed 'Undetermined'.

'They say drugs and alcohol are the principal causes of death, but the spike over the last sixteen months has been in "Undetermined",' said Anjoli.

'Race? Any targeting there?'

'I don't know. They don't break the death data down by ethnicity. But it is possible. Most homeless people in Tower Hamlets are Asian, and Black in Lambeth. Do you think because Yasir was Muslim that . . . ?'

'I don't think anything at the moment.' I tried to put all the facts she had firehosed at me together. 'So, there's a guy murdering a homeless man over sixty every couple of weeks in Lambeth and Tower Hamlets using some mysterious means, and no one has seen him or suspects this is going on. Maybe for racial reasons. And all this started from a couple of random comments made in our local homeless shelter and ended with this analysis?'

'Yep!' She slammed her laptop shut, a satisfied look on her face.

I didn't want to rain on her parade but had to tell her what I thought. 'I don't know, Anjoli. The gin bottles hadn't been tampered with and the PMs found nothing untoward. It all feels a little . . . far-fetched?'

'Did people suspect Jack the Ripper was killing prostitutes across London? Or Jeffrey Dahmer was killing Black people? I mean, look at Harold Shipman, for God's sake! He killed over 200 of his patients and nobody suspected him! Even in India! Charles Sobhraj killed a dozen hippies with his accomplice Ajay Chowdhury, and nobody knew!'

'You've been busy on Wikipedia—'

'So what if I have? It *happens*, Kamil. And it's happening now. Maybe the gin bottle is a signature. And remember, Agnes said the guy who gave her the bottle attacked her. She must have scared him off.'

'I'm not sure about this signature business, Anjoli. Life isn't like the movies where a serial killer leaves strange clues taunting the police to catch him. Most murderers don't want to be caught and quietly go about their business until they slip up.'

'Or, in this case, till a psych graduate who's good at statistics noses around some numbers, because she supplied two of the people who had died with food. Kamil, if we follow this up and we're wrong, fine, we've wasted our time. But what if we ignore it and later find it was true? That someone *was* killing old homeless people. How could we live with ourselves?'

I couldn't argue with that. 'Okay, so how is he doing it? The police found no poison in the gin bottle and said the post-mortem found nothing either.'

'*I don't know.* That's what we have to find out. Are you going to help me or not?'

The weight that had been oppressing me returned. How could I deal with Salma's killing, Naila's stabbing, my withering relationship and now this? But I had no choice. This was Anjoli asking. I couldn't let her down again.

'Okay, I'm sold. Great work! Very impressive. Where do we start?'

'That's your department. I've done the analysis; now you need to take action based on the data I've shown you. I need you to flex your detective muscles and tell me what to do next.'

Great. Where do *I* start?

'Well . . . we should tell Tahir about this. Maybe he can get hold of CCTV footage around the area where each body was found?'

Anjoli took over the brainstorm baton: 'I guess we can get the word out to the homeless to be careful . . .'

'We can't wander around every night hoping to see someone murdering a homeless person. I mean, there must be loads of rough sleepers in these areas on any one night, no?'

'Ah, I have that info,' said the data queen, opening her computer again and pecking around. 'Yes, here we are. Not many. Lambeth around fifty and Tower Hamlets around fifteen.'

'I thought it would be a lot more than that!'

'So did I. Unless the data are wrong.'

'You just swore by it. You can't pick the data you like and leave out what you don't.'

'Why not? The Tories do it all the time. Anyway, even if it is only fifteen people around here, we can't guard them all. I don't even know how we can find them to warn them. Also, if we put signs or something up in the shelter, then the killer will just move on to another borough or change his MO.'

'That's a good point. Why is he targeting these two areas? Why not Camden and Westminster?'

'No idea. Although those are busy boroughs at night, so I guess he'd be more likely to be seen there? Lots more people passing on the streets. These two areas have a lot of homeless and there are fewer people around at night going to restaurants and things.'

'That would make sense. He'd need to find the right balance between the number of potential victims and the likelihood of being caught, and these areas fit.'

The beer was having its effect, and my eyes were closing. It had been a lot for one day. I gave an enormous yawn. 'Let's regroup tomorrow. Let me think tonight about what we might do.'

'Okay. I'll email the stuff to Tahir . . . And Kamil, thanks for believing in me.'

'I'll always believe in you, Anjoli.'

She looked at me then said, 'Come here.'

'What?'

She rose and gave me a hug, squeezing me tight.

'You looked like you needed that,' she whispered into my ear.

The stresses of the previous week overwhelmed me and out of nowhere, a dam burst. I sobbed in Anjoli's arms in the middle of her bedroom, surrounded by her possessions and the ghosts of the homeless.

Chapter 33

Tuesday.

I slept surprisingly well after my emotional outburst the previous night but the anonymous text I received the next morning made me feel like I had been kicked in the nuts.

THE STAB WAS THE FIRST WARNING. BACK OF COOK OR THE NEXT TIME IT WILL GO IN HER HEART.

I read and re-read it a dozen times before I could breathe again. This was not how I had planned on starting my day.

What the hell did this mean?

I had pretty much decided Mackenzie was involved with Salma's death and Imran had stabbed Naila to scare her into going back to Pakistan. What did the sender want me to back off from? Investigating Mackenzie or being with Naila? Was the fact that 'off' was misspelled significant? Should I tell Naila?

The last was easy – no. There was no reason to freak her out even more.

I showed the message to Anjoli in the kitchen.

'Damn,' she said as she stared at my phone. 'What are you going to do?'

'I don't know. I can't be responsible for something worse happening to Naila. The text must mean I should stop seeing her, I don't see how it can have anything to do with Salma's case.'

'No, me neither. So, are you going to stop? Seeing her, I mean?'

'I don't see I have much choice if that's what it takes to keep her safe.' As the words left my mouth, I felt as if *I* had been stabbed.

That's when I realised my heart had always known what my head didn't.

I was in love with Naila.

All my dithering over the last few days had obscured that fact. And now I had to give her up.

My face twisted. 'What do I do, Anjoli? I really . . . like her. It's going to be so hard.'

Her lips parted wordlessly as she saw my reaction and she put her hand on my arm. Then said, 'I'm so sorry, Kamil. I really am. I'll help as much as I can. You're doing the right thing. Throw yourself into your work, that's always best. Solve the Salma case and my homeless case. Naila will go back to Pakistan and be safe, and we'll have achieved something here.'

She wasn't wrong, but the cases were the last thing I cared about now.

She saw the reluctance on my face. 'You owe it to Salma and Yasir and Louis. I've emailed my info to Tahir and am waiting to hear from him. In the meantime, didn't you say you wanted to check on Mackenzie's alibi with his wife? And see if she was having dinner with him at that restaurant? Maybe she knows her husband sleeps with his students. She could crack the entire case open for you.'

Not wanting Anjoli to see my pain, I walked over to the sink and poured myself a glass of water. Then I pushed my turmoil somewhere deep into myself and brought my cop self to the fore. 'You're right. I need to see her. I don't know what work she does, but my best shot to get her alone is to meet her in the morning after Mackenzie's left for college. It might be easier to get her to talk if I have someone else with me, playing good cop to my bad. You're an excellent good cop, Anjoli. Will you come with me to Bermondsey?'

She hesitated. 'I need to be at the restaurant, Kamil.'

'Please. We can leave now and be back long before the lunch sitting. I need you there. I have to see if she's lying, and your psychological insight will be invaluable.'

'This is your thing with Naila; there's no point me getting involved.'

'I'm not seeing Naila any more, remember? And you *are* a founding member of the duskyteers. Please.'

She sighed. 'Well, all right. I suppose I need to be your chaperone now. But if you need to take a break from cooking to focus on this for a few weeks, let me know – I need notice to find someone to fill in for you.'

I had to figure out a way to juggle being a detective and a cook without letting Anjoli down but also needed to occupy every bit of my day now that I was giving Naila up.

A quick search on Google Maps showed us the quickest way to get there was by bus. As we waited at the stop, I called Naila to see how she was doing, my heart closing with the thought that I might never see her again. She'd taken the day off to rest, all the while insisting she was still fine.

'Are you okay, Kamil?' she said. 'You sound . . . odd?'

I cleared my throat. 'I'm fine. Just an awful night, that's all. Did Imran call you?'

'No, I haven't heard from him for a few days. We need to talk about what I told you about.'

'I know. We will.'

'I'm worried.'

'Don't be, I'll keep you safe.'

'Not about that. About us. Have I ruined everything?'

Conscious that Anjoli was there I said, 'Not at all. It's all good.'

'Are you sure? I don't want to lose you. I still want us to go away together. I know my situation is complicated but . . . oh, I don't know!'

'I understand. Just make a full recovery and everything will sort itself out. We'll see how you feel this weekend.'

'Okay, guess you don't want to talk now. I'll see you soon. Take care of yourself.'

'Love you.'

It slipped out and I didn't know if she had hung up without hearing.

After I disconnected, Anjoli turned to me and opened her mouth to say something, then shut it again.

Shit. *She* had heard.

'What? Go on. Spit it out.'

'I was thinking. You know how you said the knife missed all of Naila's vital organs?'

'Yes.'

'Literally, how likely is that?'

'What do you mean?'

'I mean – a crowded station, a quick stab. Must be a real fluke to miss everything?'

'The text said it was a warning. He didn't mean to kill her. If it was Imran that makes sense; he just wants to panic her into returning to Pakistan and stop me seeing her.'

'But the stabber must have known what he was doing. Maybe it *was* Mackenzie? He knows human anatomy, teaching nursing and all? Does Naila's husband?'

'What would be Mackenzie's motive?'

'Perhaps he wanted to scare the two of you off his trail because you're getting too close?'

That gave me pause. Naila said it was the knife hitting her backpack that had saved her, but still . . .

'You may have a point. Let me get Tahir to test Mackenzie's alibi again for the stabbing and for Salma's strangling.'

The 78 arrived, and we clambered upstairs to the very front of the top deck for a glorious view of London on what was now a gorgeous sunny morning.

The bus trundled over Tower Bridge with the Thames gleaming green-blue on either side and the Tower of London crouched above the river, glowing a fiery orange. Anjoli gave a massive sigh and said, 'I find it hard to believe in a city as rich as this with so much history and beauty we can't take care of our poorest people. I mean, what's the point of all of this otherwise?'

'Well, your country has always been pretty good at exploiting the poor and underprivileged around the world and extracting everything they can from them, to keep the rich in their big houses and champagne and caviar. And leaving destruction in its wake. Look at the damage done in Bengal.'

'What do you mean?'

'During World War Two the British seized land in Bengal to finance the war effort without thinking of the effect on millions of farmers. Over three million died in the resulting famine. Churchill did nothing and had the gall to say it was their own fault for breeding like rabbits.'

I took a breath as my eyes moistened. The thought of the Bangla famine always affected me – my ancestors had died in it, barely two generations ago. It was easy enough to say it was another time, another place, but I felt callous disregard for the poor was getting worse around the world and becoming far too acceptable.

'Anyway,' I said, recovering, 'the mentality of the poor being the "other" has not gone away. So, it's easy for the poor to become like that.' I gestured at her shirt, which said *The Homeless Aren't Invisible*. 'Because they are not "us". Believe me, I know. In Kolkata you never see the poor. They are everywhere, and if you noticed every little child begging at traffic lights or every person with no legs shuffling on crutches, you'd go crazy.'

'I didn't know you felt like that. I thought you believed I was bonkers and obsessed with the homeless thing,' said Anjoli as the bus arrived at our stop and we got off.

'Well, we're privileged. Even when TK feels like a sweatshop when the extractors aren't working, I have to remind myself of the fact there are people way worse off than I am. And your theory of a serial homeless killer may well still be bonkers. But –' I raised a hand '– I'm still helping with it. As you said, even if there is a minuscule chance you're right, we need to investigate because the consequences are too awful to think about.'

We walked down Lynton Road and arrived outside Mackenzie's bungalow just after ten. 'Oh good, only one car,' I said as I rang the bell and the familiar 'Greensleeves' melody sounded inside.

The barking of a dog was audible before the door opened and Roisin Mackenzie looked at us with questioning eyes. 'Yes?'

'Mrs Mackenzie. Hi, it's Kamil Rahman. I came to see your husband a few days ago. Is he in?'

'Oh yes, I remember. I'm afraid he's at college. Down Lulu!' The dog paused from trying to jump up at me and whipped her tail from side to side.

'Oh damn. I should have realised that. Okay, we'll try to see him there.'

Just as she was about to shut the door, I said, 'Could we come in for a glass of water? We've walked all the way from the bus stop, and it's boiling.'

'It is, isn't it? Sure, come on in.'

'Thanks. This is my friend Anjoli.'

'Also, may I use the loo?' said Anjoli.

Roisin nodded, let us into the house and showed Anjoli the way.

I sat at the kitchen table while she poured out two glasses of water. Lulu rasped her tongue over every inch of my hand, before lying at my feet, her tail giving the occasional excited wag as I leaned over and tickled her tummy.

'What did you want with Liam?' said Roisin.

'It's a delicate matter. Personal, to be honest.'

'Oh? To do with that poor girl who died?'

'Sort of. Do you know if she was close to your husband?'

'Liam said she was his student. Why do you ask that?' There was a definite edge in her voice.

Anjoli returned and said, 'Ooh, thanks so much,' and sipped her water.

'The thing is –' I leaned forward '– there is going to be a complaint. Against Dr Mackenzie. I'm sorry, maybe I shouldn't be telling you this.'

Roisin sat back and her face tightened. 'What complaint?'

Anjoli helped. 'A student is filing a complaint with the college about his behaviour. We wanted to give him a heads-up.'

Roisin's face turned to stone. 'That all came to nothing. They cleared him.'

'Yes. But this is new.'

'Well . . .' I took up the baton. 'He has been taking his students out for dinners, and nowadays . . .'

'With #MeToo,' added Anjoli.

'With #MeToo,' I agreed, 'it's become much more serious. So, we came to warn him and make sure he had his story straight. We're trying to help.'

'Why would you help him? Who are you again?'

'Naila – the woman I was with when we visited last time – is in his class. She's from Pakistan, and Dr Mackenzie has been great to her. She knows the girl involved and wanted to tell him.'

'That bastard,' Roisin whispered. 'Was it to do with that girl who died? Is that why she kept calling him? You said she was pregnant? Did they find out whose baby it was?'

'Salma. They're still doing the DNA tests. We're not sure if Dr Mackenzie was involved with her. This is someone else.'

'Who?'

'I can't tell you that, I'm afraid. I have to keep her name confidential.'

Roisin's face went blank. 'Well, I'm sure it's nothing.'

'Apparently, he was out with her for dinner two weeks ago at an Italian restaurant. On a Saturday. He wasn't with you then, was he?'

'Two weeks ago? No. He said he was at a work do that night.'

I felt a deep satisfaction as another fact got hammered into place. Mackenzie *had* been three-timing Salma. My money was on Emily being his dinner companion. He had seemed friendly with her, and she was his alibi for Naila's stabbing.

'I'm afraid he wasn't. The evidence is compelling. She recorded him on her phone at the dinner. He was pretty explicit about what he wanted from her to ensure she got good grades.'

Now Roisin looked shocked.

'Are you telling me that—'

'I'm afraid so,' said Anjoli. 'The accusation is he is trading sexual favours for good marks.'

'*Liam?* He wouldn't do that.'

'He has. I heard the tape myself.'

'All those nights he said he was working late and he was just up to his old tricks again. The bastard!'

'We think he was involved with Salma,' I said. 'Were you here when she called him? Maybe you overheard what he said?'

Roisin didn't appear to hear me, working herself up into a fine fury, pacing around the kitchen.

'This is not the first time he's done this. I warned him. I told him if he did this shit again, I was out of here. All those evenings he said he was out for work . . .'

'That night he came back after the event at the college, the night Salma died. You said he was home at 10.30. Are you sure?'

'Yes, of course.'

'How did you know the time?'

'He told me.'

'What do you mean?'

'I was asleep when he came back. When he got into bed, I woke and asked him what time it was. He said 10.30, and I went back to sleep. Why? Was he with her that night?'

'No, that evening he *was* at a work dinner. I was just checking. Does he drive to work?'

'Yes. He gets parking. But that week his car was being serviced, so he took mine. I *will* leave him this time. Enough is enough. The lying toad.'

'Do you know if he was wearing his yellow hoodie that night? The night of his dinner?'

'What?'

I repeated my question. She looked at me, puzzled. 'I suppose. He always wears it. Horrible thing. He even bought an identical new one when he left the other in a cab.'

Anjoli looked at me, eyes wide.

I was circling my prey – every sense on high alert.

'When?'

'Last week. Found it online. Look, I think you should leave now. I need to think.'

'I'm sorry, we didn't mean to upset you. Thanks for the water.'

We left and stood outside her house, taking in the morning with deep breaths.

'Wow,' said Anjoli. 'That was something.'

Triumph tasted like steel on my tongue. 'I knew there was something off with the hoodie! It *smelled* new.'

'*And* he could have been back much later that night and just told her it was 10.30!'

'Exactly! And he wasn't driving his car. So Salma was probably sleeping with him. She must have started their affair six weeks ago, saw him with Emily at the restaurant, got jealous, and that's when it all started. The baby must be his. She threatened to go public with their affair and he killed her.'

'Wow. I think you've solved it, Kamil.'

'I think we might have.'

I took another deep breath. I was close. So close. I looked at the car in the driveway and took a photograph of its number plate.

'Come on. It's time to tell Tahir what we've found. It's up to him now.'

Chapter 34

Tuesday.

I called the sergeant on speaker while we were waiting for the bus, giving him Roisin's car number plate to check on the CCTV, the information about the newly purchased hoodie and Mackenzie being at Venezia when Salma could have seen him with Emily. He listened in silence, then said, 'Good work, Father Brown. Let me check it out. We'll test the hoodie we found at Ziad's for Mackenzie's DNA. We also got the results on Naila's stabbing. The knife had blood on it but no fingerprints; the guy must have wiped it or been wearing gloves. We assume he dropped it at the top of the stairs as he made his escape. Given the crush in the station, the CCTV didn't pick up anyone suspicious, but we'll keep looking. I interviewed Naila at home, and she told me about her husband. We'll follow up on that.'

This was excellent news. We were getting closer, although it was out of my hands now. With a little luck, Tahir would find something on the CCTV or Mackenzie's hoodie and have enough to pull him in for questioning again.

'Did you get my email?' Anjoli asked Tahir.

'I saw you'd sent me something, I haven't looked at it yet. I'll get back to you.'

'It's urgent, Tahir. Please take a look.'

On the bus home she said, 'How do you think he got the hoodie into Ziad's house?'

'I don't know. Maybe he slipped it into Ziad's backpack during a tutorial or something? I'm sure we'll find out. He's our guy, I'm certain of it.'

She nodded and looked out at the line of cars ahead of us on Tower Bridge Road, the Shard in the distance, gleaming silver and stabbing the sky like a modern Stonehenge.

'What about Roisin?' she said.

'What do you mean?'

'Well, she was furious about his affair. What if *she* suspected Salma was sleeping with her husband and took matters into her own hands?'

'You mean drove to Salma's and killed her? I don't know, Anjoli. It's possible, but a lot of things would have had to fall into place. She would have to suspect Salma, and—'

'If Salma was calling Mackenzie, she might have heard something?'

'True. But then she would have to find out where Salma lived, and Mackenzie would have to be covering up for her. And it's even less likely she could have smuggled that hoodie into Ziad's house.'

'Why put the hoodie at Ziad's anyway?'

'To throw suspicion on him, I guess.'

It sounded weak as I was saying it.

'Let's see where Tahir gets to with Mackenzie and then worry about his wife.'

'*She* could have stabbed Naila,' said Anjoli.

This was the piece I was uncomfortable about. I was sure Mackenzie had killed Salma, but he couldn't have stabbed Naila unless Emily was in it with him. No, that must have been Imran. These were two separate cases that had become intertwined because of Naila and me.

'This is fun,' said Anjoli. 'I like this stuff.'

'Nice to be the dynamic duo again, Sergeant Chatterjee.'

'The old band reunited for one last gig.'

We jerked forward as the bus left the stop, and I put my hand on her arm to steady her. Just then Anjoli's phone rang.

'Yes? . . . Oh hi! . . . That's fantastic news. Thanks so much for calling. I appreciate it. Bye!'

I looked at her questioningly as she disconnected and said, 'OMG, that was Masika from Webber Street. Guess what! The council told her they found Louis' son, and he claimed the body and gave him a nice funeral. That makes me so happy.'

'I'm really glad.'

'I must do more to keep them safe. Do you think I should go to the press? Tell them what we think is happening?'

I considered this. While I was coming around to thinking there might be something in her statistical analysis, I didn't want her to make a fool of herself. 'Do you think they'd believe you?'

'I don't know, but I feel we need to warn the rough sleepers.'

'I doubt they engage much with the *Guardian*. Except to use it to keep warm at night.'

'You're doing it again, Kamil. Joking inappropriately.'

'I'm sorry. Maybe we can ask the *Big Issue* to publicise it? How about in the shelters? We can tell the folks running the shelters our suspicions. Maybe get them to tell their clients not to accept gin if someone tries to give it to them.'

'That's a good idea. Also, I wonder if we can track down who's buying half-bottles of gardenia gin. Maybe they buy lots at a time.'

Once more I regretted not having the army of constables and havaldars I'd had in Kolkata. They could have done the rounds of off-licences and corner shops in the borough to check it out. I doubted we could do the same. I knew the mind-numbing pavement pounding it would take and the hundreds of interviews and dead ends we would encounter as we tried to mine the nuggets of gold from the impenetrable rock of lies, false memories and sheer irrelevance most investigations unearthed.

'Maybe,' I said, as we got off the bus and walked down Whitechapel High Street towards the restaurant.

We walked in silence for a while, then Anjoli said, 'Look!'

Bending over the homeless man who had taken over Yasir's prime location in the entrance to the mosque was the priest we had seen with Neha in Southall.

'What do you think he's doing here?' she said.

'Let's find out.'

We walked up to him and I tapped him on the shoulder.

The priest spun around in surprise as the old guy he was talking with looked up at me, a blanket around his shoulders, an empty coffee cup in front of him containing a few miserable coins.

'Hello, Father Spence,' I said. 'We met in Southall the other day. What brings you to this part of town?'

'Oh yes,' he said, trying to place me. 'Neha's pal?'

'That's right,' I tossed a coin into the man's cup.

'I came to see Sheikh Masroor. We're starting an inter-faith initiative to tackle rough sleeping. And I was just telling this gentleman he should go to a shelter.'

'That's great,' said Anjoli. 'Thanks for that tip about the ONS numbers. I checked them out, and I was right. There have been quite a few excess deaths in Tower Hamlets and Lambeth.'

'Tell me more,' he said, stroking his goatee.

Anjoli explained her analysis.

'That's terrible. But why would someone be doing that?'

'Yesh,' the homeless guy slurred. 'Why?'

I'd forgotten he was there, glanced in guilt at Anjoli's T-shirt and tried not to react to the stench of alcohol combined with body odour emanating from him.

'I don't know. I'm Anjoli.' She held out her hand, and the homeless guy raised his to shake it.

'Sham . . . Sam.'

'Hi, Sam. I don't know why. But I'm sure there is something

going on. They found a half-bottle of gardenia gin near some of the dead bodies. I thought maybe the killer was giving alcohol to the homeless.'

'Ohhh . . . I'd like that.' Sam smiled, showing brown teeth.

'Have you heard anything suspicious in your . . . community?' I said.

'Comm . . . community!' he laughed out loud. 'Do you – do you think we hang out together in the pub and gosship? We're not one, one homo . . . homogenous group of people like, like . . .' He gestured to me and Anjoli, then added, 'It's not a choice I make, to sleep here. And if shomeone is giving me gin, I'll take it.' Even drunk, he seemed well spoken and intelligent.

'Why *are* you here?'

'Losht my job. Bailiffsh came.'

'A story I've heard too many times,' said the priest. 'Especially in London. You mentioned the gin when we met in Southall. Let me reach out to my contacts in these areas and see if they have picked up anything unusual. I'll tell them to watch out for gardenia gin when they check on the rough sleepers.'

'Thanks,' said Anjoli. 'Did you get the email I sent you about ACE? I'd love to get involved.'

'I did, yes. Come and see us in our offices some time, and we'll take you through the model.'

I looked again at Sam, who seemed familiar. Then it hit me. I glanced across the road – a shop selling Islamic books and clothes, the East End was full of these odd combinations.

'You were on the other side of the road that morning. The day Yasir died. In front of that shop.'

He looked away from me.

'Weren't you? I saw you, didn't I?'

'Yesh.'

'Did you see anything? Did you know Yasir?'

'Don't know.'

'Please,' said Anjoli. 'It's important.'

He stared at her. She reached into her handbag and gave him a fiver.

He grabbed it and said, 'This was his spot.'

'And that morning? Was there anything unusual?'

'Other than him being dead?'

'Yes.' I was getting irritated now. He was prevaricating and knew something.

'Please,' Anjoli repeated.

He looked from me to Anjoli to the priest. 'There was someone with him that morning. I saw someone talking to him.'

Anjoli couldn't contain her excitement. 'What did he look like? When?'

'No watch.' He waved a bare wrist at her. 'Seven? Eight in the morning, maybe? I didn't see too good, I was half asleep, had a terrible head. I think he was wearing a long dark coat with the collar up and crouching next to Yasir, talking to him. I went back to sleep and woke up when I heard the commotion, and he was dead. I left because it was none of my business.'

'And you didn't see what this person looked like, the one who was talking to him?' said the priest.

'No. I thought Yasir was being told to go. We keep being moved on because they don't like seeing us.'

This was interesting. The first concrete proof someone had been with Yasir before he had died. It could be a coincidence, but still . . .

'Can you remember anything? Tall, short, white, Asian?'

He wrinkled his brow. 'Medium height, maybe? Thin? I wasn't looking.'

Anjoli whipped out her phone and showed him the video of the man with Louis.

'Was this him?'

He squinted at it. 'Not sure. Maybe my man was thinner. Wasn't wearing a cap. I can't tell, to be honest. I was half cut.'

'Are you planning on staying here today?' said Anjoli.

'Why? Am I stopping you from getting on with your life?'

'No, I mean . . . I just . . . I can bring you food later, that's all. We own a restaurant around the corner.'

He shrugged. We bid them both goodbye and walked back to TK.

Anjoli's crazy theory was growing legs.

Chapter 35

Wednesday.

Three a.m. A rumble of thunder in the distance. Hot as hell. I opened the window as wide as I could, hoping for the slightest breeze, but all I got was the noise of Brick Lane at night. Strange shouts, rattles and echoes which transformed into a thunderstorm. I slammed the window shut and lay listening to the rain lashing against the glass. I still wasn't quite used to the concept of weather. In Kolkata it was always hot – baking before the monsoon and not quite so warm in winter. Sun and rain, that was it – the only thing you had to worry about was whether to carry an umbrella. Whereas in this country . . . overcoat or T-shirt? Jeans or shorts? Sweater or raincoat? Often for the same day. Sun, drizzle, thunderstorms, snow, sleet, clouds, hail . . . The British obsession with the weather was completely reasonable.

Desperate for sleep, my mind whirred, trying to keep my feelings for Naila at bay. I was sure we had cracked the case. We just needed the final pieces of evidence – CCTV of Roisin's car near Salma's flat, Mackenzie's DNA on the hoodie found in Ziad's house and proof that Salma's baby was his. I still wasn't sure about Naila's stabbing, but once Mackenzie was arrested, that might become clearer.

Dry mouth and raging thirst. Rolling out of bed, I padded downstairs to the kitchen and downed a glass of cold water, the lights of Brick Lane looking like an Impressionist painting through the downpour outside. Was Sam huddling in a sleeping bag at the mosque door, trying to keep dry as the rain slanted towards him, hammering down and soaking any part of him exposed to the sky? What had Anjoli said? Around fifteen people on the streets around here, all hoping for the rain to stop. How did they survive in winter in the snow? Maybe they went to the shelters on nights like that. I hoped they did.

I trudged back up the stairs. I needed to sleep – there was a big night ahead. A group of tech workers in Shoreditch had booked all of TK for a thirtieth birthday bash – around fifty people coming. Not something I was looking forward to, although it would be a set menu. I hated to cook industrial quantities of any dish. All delicacy and subtlety was lost – you had to go for the big three – chilli, garlic, cream. And the menu always ended up as English Indian cuisine's greatest hits – chicken tikka masala, onion bhajis, saag paneer, vindaloo, rogan josh.

Mind you, any decent British chef would be horrified at the atrocities committed in the 'continental' restaurants of Kolkata – cream of mushroom, cream of tomato, cream of spring chicken, cream of asparagus – all the soups were 'cream of something' and tasted the same – sweet and cloying. And the main courses were classic British dishes from the 1970s: pork cutlets stuffed with ham and cheese, chicken baked with ham and cheese, fish topped with cheese sauce and spinach. I didn't know which continent this 'continental' food had emerged from, but India appeared to be the only place where you could still get it. Some kind of throwback to the Raj. Was it the same in Pakistan?

Naila. Always back to Naila. I had to give her up to keep her safe? And I'd never even told her about the depth of my feelings. Which was probably a good thing. She didn't need my tumult while she was dealing with the shock of her husband stabbing her. Easier for her never to have known.

In desperation, I jammed my EarPods in and put on Nick Cave, who told me to bleed if I needed to. Great. Maybe I should have picked something cheerier. I must have fallen asleep because I dreamed of a girl trapped in amber – mouth open, screaming without sound for eternity.

The next thing I knew, it was a quarter past seven. I felt like I hadn't slept at all. Shaken up. Ears hurting. Head heavy. Mouth foul. Time to face the day. I texted Naila, *Call me when you're up.* To my surprise, my phone rang as soon as I completed the text.

'Hi,' I said. 'Can't you sleep? Are you in pain?'

'Not a great night. I'm trying not to take the painkillers. Don't want to get dependent on them. I've seen what can happen.'

'Stop punishing yourself, Naila. Unnecessary pain causes more problems. You don't want the wound to get infected.'

'Kamil, please, I'm a bloody medical professional. I know how to look after myself, okay? Anyway, what's been happening? Tell me, I'm getting bored here.'

Ignoring my throbbing head, I said, 'Well, Anjoli and I went to see Roisin Mackenzie yesterday and . . .' I told her everything that had happened, including my trip to Venezia, and ended with '. . . so I think Tahir will bring Mackenzie in for questioning today.'

'Wow. That's incredible. I wish I'd been there. So you think he did it? I mean killed Salma?'

'It looks that way. He lied about the hoodie, could have lied about the time he got home. Salma was sleeping with him and caught him two-timing her.'

'And you think Sir was the one who stabbed me as well? Why would he?'

'I still think that was Imran.'

Silence.

'Face up to it, Naila. It's possible he has followed you here and means to do you harm.'

'I know. But what can I do about it?'

'Be very careful. You won't go to college today, will you?'

'I was going to rest another day, but I can if you want me to.'

'No, I *don't* want you to. Please rest. I need you to recover so we can go away this weekend. I'd come and visit, but we have this big party at the restaurant tonight.'

'I know. Uncle was complaining about it all of yesterday. I'm fine. You do your cooking for the party and I'll see you tomorrow. Tell me what Tahir finds out.'

I took two Nurofen and crashed.

Chapter 36

Wednesday.

It was after lunch and I was busy getting things ready for the big dinner when Tahir called. I wiped my hands down and found a quiet spot in the alley behind the kitchen.

'You nailed it! Mrs Mackenzie's car was seen on CCTV in the vicinity of Salma's flat that night. We missed it because it was registered under her maiden name. Couldn't see who was driving. He's been a suspect since the beginning because of Salma's texts and with his alibi looking shaky, we have something now. We brought them in for questioning and they both swear they were nowhere near Bethnal Green that night. The wife was not at all happy. The DNA tests on the hoodie and Salma's baby will take time to come back.'

'What about the restaurant? Did you ask if he had been at Venezia?'

'He said he had planned to go for a work dinner but cancelled. We'll check with the restaurant.'

'Well, that was a lie. And Naila's stabbing?'

'That alibi's solid. Both his student, Emily and his assistant corroborated it. No sign of him on the CCTV in Waterloo either.'

Damn! It was unlikely they'd both be lying. 'Any chance he was in it with his wife? Could she have stabbed Naila?'

'She was picking up the kids from school when Naila was being stabbed.'

'Have you arrested Mackenzie?'

'We don't have enough to charge him. Yet. Let's see what the DNA says and if any other CCTV picked him up on the route. We are close. I'll let you know. Excellent work, Nancy Drew.'

Cheeky bastard. For the hundredth time I thought about my old job – leading the questioning; playing cat-and-mouse with a suspect; locating the flicker of a lie in their eyes. I'd convinced myself that cooking in the TK kitchen was my career path to nirvana, but I missed my original calling with a deep passion. It was the source of the authentic me. As opposed to Kamil's Authentic Vindaloo Sauce.

The back door of the restaurant from the alley led to a small storeroom where we kept all our staples: massive bags of rice, spices, dal; ten-litre kegs of cooking oil; the freezer with the emergency frozen food and the fridge with the food we needed to cook for the day. Anjoli made sure we kept the store spotless; the food standard inspectors could come at any time, and we didn't want to lose our coveted five-star hygiene rating.

Salim Mian was sitting on a chair, injecting something into his belly, which was wobbling over his trousers. He smiled at me and put away a pen-like object.

'My medicine. Diabetes, you know.'

'How often do you have to take it?'

'Four times a day, but I have to take other medicines too. It's very difficult to have this problem and work in a restaurant where there is always so much delicious food I cannot eat.' He gestured around the storeroom. 'Sometimes I cannot resist it.'

'Well, you must,' I said, feeling a surge of affection for this avuncular gentle giant who had looked after me so well when I had first come to this country, teaching me the basics of being a waiter. 'We don't want anything to happen to you.'

'Yes, Naila keeps saying the same thing. She looks after me well, that girl. It is good to have a nurse in the family.'

'How is she doing?'

'She is quite upset with her work injury.' He waggled his head. 'Silly girl, hurting herself like that.'

'Upset how?'

'She seems very nervous. Worrying about something. Always a little . . . what do you say, jumpy? Sitting in her room a lot. What really happened, Kamil? Why did the police come to the house?'

It wasn't up to me to tell him. But I took the chance to find out more about Naila's life.

'She told me about her . . . problem in Pakistan. With her husband.'

He looked at me, inscrutable as the Buddha. Then relented.

'She lost something after marriage. Very sad. But things will work out, inshallah. She is a clever girl, she will make it work. She still speaks to Imran every week.'

'What's he like?'

He grimaced. 'I never liked that man. Too smooth. Too clever. Not right for Naila. But he was her choice. What could I do? I am just her uncle.'

'I wish there was some way I could help her.'

'Better not to interfere in family matters. Just let her be. Here in London she is having some life; independence, you know? Alaya and I liked that when we came to this country all those years ago. Once you are away from your family, you don't need to tell them every little everything.'

'I get the impression Naila was always independent. She's nobody's fool.'

'She was such a merry girl growing up. Always laughing, always joking. You know, she would take in all the stray dogs and cats she could find and look after them in her home in Lahore, till her mother finally put her foot down! "But Ma, I am giving them a better life," she would say. And after marriage . . .

sadness. Oh, she would still laugh and joke when I went to see them in Pakistan, but under her eyes I could see the tears. I was happy when she came to study here and live with us. That's why it is so sad to see her go back to the way she was in Pakistan. She has been doing very well here for the past two years, almost like the old Naila again. But recently . . . It is good you and Anjoli are her friends – she needs friends.'

Salim Mian had been her saviour. Now I understood why Naila was so fond of him.

His story made my feelings for Naila catch fire again. Maybe I *was* the person for the next stage of her life. I couldn't fool myself any more. My rational mind might not want to be involved with a married woman but my emotions . . . Naila had said love was a drug; well she was now in my bloodstream and was as much a part of me as the insulin Salim Mian was injecting into himself. I wanted her, and I needed her. We'd make it work. She could settle here – her a nurse, me a cop. We'd take care of Imran. This was the West; she could get a divorce and . . .

Salim Mian broke into my flight of fancy. 'Come,' he said, heaving himself up from his chair. 'We have to get ready for the big party. It will be a long night. They are only starting at nine o'clock and it will go on till one, two in the morning. I don't know how I am going to go home then; I cannot ask Naila to pick me up when she is not well. And taxis are so expensive.'

'Just sleep in Saibal-da's room. I'm sure Anjoli won't mind.'

'Maybe. I will ask her. Okay now, come. We have work to do.'

Chapter 37

Wednesday.

A t 8.30 I was buzzing around like a trapped fly in the
kitchen, trying to get everything ready for the party when
there was a banging on the door of the restaurant. 'Can't people
see the sign,' sighed Anjoli, wiping her hands on her *The pavement is my floor, the sky is my ceiling – I am homeless* T-shirt (She
had been busy with her new line. When on earth did she have
the time to knock them up?) and heading out to tell the potential
customer to find another place to slake his yen for kababs and
beer this Wednesday evening.

Listening with half an ear as I tried to judge the right quantity
of salt for the massive potful of tikka masala sauce bubbling on
the hob, I heard her conciliatory murmur, then a furious voice
yelled in an Irish accent, 'Where is he? Where is that Indian
bastard cook? Come out here from whatever rock you're hiding
under, Rahman. Get your fecking arse out here, I want to talk to
you.'

Mackenzie!

'Look after this.' I handed my ladle over and rushed into the
restaurant to find Mackenzie towering over Anjoli, who had
planted herself in front of him at the door to stop him coming
in. His face was red, murder in his eyes.

'Calm down, Mr Mackenzie,' I said. 'What do you want?'

'Don't you fecking tell me to calm down, you bastard!' He

shoved her to one side and thrust his face towards mine and I was slapped by the stink of alcohol on his breath. 'What the feck do you think you were doing? Going to see my wife. Telling the police lies about me. You got some brass neck, you fecker. Where do you get off calling me a murderer?'

Salim Mian and the other waiters had now come out of the kitchen to see what the commotion was about, and they formed a protective ring around me and Anjoli. Mackenzie didn't seem to notice as he continued. 'And you,' he pointed at Anjoli. 'Were you the woman with him? Do you know what you two feckers have gone and done?'

'What have we done?' said Anjoli, calmed by her staff there to protect her, although she must have been petrified.

He slammed the table in front of him with his fist, causing the cutlery to fall rattling to the floor. Salim Mian bent to pick it up as Mackenzie shouted, 'Because of your lies my wife has left me. With my kids. Your lies about me having an affair. Your lies about me killing Salma. All lies.'

Tears streamed down his face as he mumbled, 'Bastards, all of you, bastards.' He seemed close to a breakdown.

'You killed Salma,' I said. 'You took your wife's car, drove to Salma's flat and strangled her because you didn't want your affair to come out. I saw you coming out in your yellow hoodie after you murdered her because she was threatening to tell the dean.'

His eyebrows knitted together to form a line. 'Affair? What the feck do you two know? I didn't kill anyone. And now, because of your lies, Roisin's gone. I won't see my kids again. I'll fecking make you pay.'

He collapsed in a booth and wiped his face dry with a napkin.

'You're better off telling the truth.' I sat opposite him. 'I'm sure you didn't mean to kill her; it was on the spur of the moment. You used her hijab, so it wasn't premeditated. Just confess and they'll go easy on you. Roisin told us about the hoodie. They are doing DNA tests on it and Salma's baby as we speak. They'll soon find it's yours.'

He stared at me, and for a moment I wondered if I'd got through to him. Then he looked around like a trapped animal and lunged across the table, grabbing me by my throat with both hands, pushing me against the cushioned back of the booth. He sprawled across the table, squeezing, squeezing with an immense strength. I raised my hands to grab his wrists, but they were like iron, locked on to my throat, and I couldn't move them an inch. I tried to breathe and all I could hear were choking noises. Some part of my brain realised they were coming from me. I felt my vision go. Then his grip was gone. I heard the crash of plates breaking and through watering eyes saw him being pulled off me by Salim Mian and another two waiters, who threw him to the floor, where one of them sat on him.

I staggered up from the table, which was a mistake as my legs gave way and I found myself on the floor next to Mackenzie.

'Call the police,' shouted Anjoli, which had the effect of calming Mackenzie down.

'All right, all right. Get off me, you bastard. I'll go. You don't need to call the police.'

The others looked at me for guidance and I nodded, getting up and standing with wobbly legs in front of Anjoli in case he tried anything else. The waiter got off him, and Mackenzie stood up, gave us a last vicious stare and left, slamming the door behind him, leaving the entrance bell chiming.

'Shall I phone police?' said Salim Mian.

'No,' I said. 'The guests will arrive soon. We can't have them see the police here. He won't come back. I'll report him after dinner. I'm getting used to being strangled.'

I looked around TK, which we had decorated to the

specifications we had received from the birthday boy's personal assistant – a shiny banner with *Happy Thirtieth Birthday David* stuck onto a wall; red, yellow and white balloons everywhere; fairy lights strung up and bottles lined up on the open bar, waiting for the festivities to begin.

'Are you okay, Kamil?' said Anjoli, touching my neck.

'I'm all right. I can see how he must have killed Salma. The same rage came over him, only that time there was no Salim Mian to stop him.' I nodded thanks to my rescuers.

Anjoli nodded. 'Come on, everyone, back to work. Put the music on. The guests will arrive soon.'

Just as she said this, the door opened, and the guest of honour came in, followed by four others. They stopped and looked at us standing around, broken plates on the ground surrounded by knives and forks, the crumpled tablecloth.

Anjoli took control. 'Happy birthday, David! Come on in. We just had a slight accident and will clear it away in a second. Please, come and have a drink.'

The waiters smoothed the restaurant into normality, and I made my way back into the kitchen, feeling a throbbing pain in my larynx. Mackenzie had killed Salma. The police would gather the evidence and he would soon be arrested and charged. But it had been Imran who had stabbed Naila, I was certain of that now. Was he going to come after me next?

Later. I didn't have the brain space. I had to put murder on the back burner and focus on my paying job to give David a memorable birthday dinner. I looked at the hob with my tikka masala sauce bubbling away and scraped at the bottom of the pot with a wooden spoon. If it was stuck fast, and I stirred, it would be impossible to separate the burned bits. I put what little energy I had left into easing the chicken off the pan.

Chapter 38

Thursday.

We staggered through the night, cooking, serving, clearing away dirty plates and mopping up spills; ensuring there was enough booze on tap to revive the party if the revel level wavered below 'best birthday party EVERRR'.

Whenever I prayed they were winding down, there'd be another order for more beers and more whisky and more snacks, and on and on into the night it went. My neck still ached from Mackenzie's attack, but I had to keep going. These tech guys (and they were almost all guys) could party – the cliché of nerdy, introverted computer programmers didn't seem to hold true. I was like a zombie by 1 a.m., and my colleagues weren't faring much better, although the thought of the mammoth takings for the night kept Anjoli perky. 'Think of the tips,' she said every time she saw one of us fading. The techies finally rolled out at 1.35, singing their way down Brick Lane, the bosses grabbing the cabs that had been waiting and the minions heading for night buses.

'Well done, everybody,' said Anjoli with a cheeriness that amazed me given she had been working as hard as the rest of us. 'We can leave the cleaning up for the morning; just soak the dishes and go home and rest. You can come in early tomorrow to tidy the place for lunch.' That's the thing about restaurants: the work is relentless. Cook, serve, clean, cook, serve, clean. The same dead march every day, six days a week, fourteen hours a day – just clawing our way to Monday, our breathing space, when we catch up on life's chores and grab what little rest we can, then get ready to service the next week's conveyor belt. Seeing diners on date nights and celebrations made me miss my leisure time, but a night of unbroken sleep was now a far more exciting prospect than any movie, bar or gig.

Shattered, I made my way up to my room via the storeroom stairs as Anjoli fixed a bed for Salim Mian in her parents' room. 'I'll keep the door open in case you need anything. Don't forget to take your injections.'

'I will be fine, Anjoli, thank you. I am very tired; it was a good party,' he said, the bed creaking its protests as he climbed into it.

I heard her come up the stairs and say outside my door, 'Did you call the police about Mackenzie?'

Half-dead, not having bothered to change, I mumbled into my pillow, 'Tomorrow.'

Vivid animalistic dreams filled the night. Snakes writhing around me as faceless men tried to hack at them with strange, old-fashioned swords. Then I was running and falling down a steep hill at the bottom of which stood a sixty-foot effigy of the demon Ravana, his ten heads and twenty eyes staring at me as the yowling mob under him set him alight. The flames rose higher and higher, and I could feel the fire get hotter and hotter, smoke creeping into my lungs until I heard a scream. I tried to shout back and choked as my eyes slammed open. The scream was real. Anjoli. The yowling mob was the fire alarm.

I fell out of bed and yanked open my bedroom door to see her standing at the top of the stairs in shorts and a T-shirt, smoke belching from the floor below.

'What . . .' I said, eyes still bleary from sleep.

'FIRE!' she yelled. 'Salim Mian's down there.'

The smoke choked us and made everything black as we felt our way down the stairs. I couldn't see the fire, but the shriek of the fire alarm filled my head and scrambled my nerves. 'Wait.' I ran back up, grabbed three towels from the bathroom, soaked them with trembling hands and skidded back to Anjoli, tossing her one to put over her mouth and nose as I did the same with another.

I couldn't see anything given the darkness, the smoke and my watering eyes, but we made our way to Salim Mian's room, which was filled with thick, black fumes, the floor hot under our bare feet. The fire must have been in the restaurant's kitchen below his room. He was unconscious in bed, and I put the third wet towel over his face as Anjoli and I tried to wake him to no avail.

'We have to get him out,' she shouted over the screeching alarm.

I nodded, and we tried to pull him off the bed, but he must have weighed over a hundred kilos and we couldn't budge him.

'Pull off the sheet,' I choked through my towel.

She understood what I meant, and, fingers scrabbling, we untucked the sheet from the mattress then pulled on it with all the strength we could muster until he dropped on the floor with a bang that shook the house but didn't wake him. Between us we dragged the sheet out of the door, using it as a sled, with Salim Mian on it, all the while trying to avoid breathing in smoke and keep our smarting eyes open so we could see where we were going.

I heard the wail of a fire engine in the distance over the howl of the fire alarm. We were at the top of the stairway to the flat's front entrance, which opened onto Brick Lane. The fire didn't appear to have reached here, and we somehow manhandled Salim Mian down the stairs and threw the front door open to smell blessed fresh air. A crowd of people had gathered outside, and when they saw us, three men ran up and took Salim Mian from us as we staggered down the front steps, holding the railing to prevent ourselves from collapsing.

Swallowing in huge lungfuls of the night air, Anjoli and I turned to look at the disaster unfolding behind us. The front of the restaurant was dark but orange flames leaped up towards the sky from the back, and a force field of shimmering heat surrounded the building, shielding the ongoing rampage of destruction occurring inside. No one could get close as it burned and burned. I couldn't hear the alarm any more, but the fire had its own sounds – growling and crackling and snapping like a terrifying or terrified wild animal rampaging through a forest of dead trees.

A fire engine screeched to a halt in front of us and two firefighters jumped out, pushing the crowd back while two more unfurled a hose with balletic precision. They aimed jets of water towards the fire at the back, the bursts getting stronger and stronger, the spray going in all directions and settling on us, providing cool relief from the burning air.

I looked at Anjoli, who was leaning over Salim Mian shouting, 'We need an ambulance! Someone please call an ambulance. Now!' Her face was streaked with ash, and I ran a finger across my cheek to find myself covered with sooty blackness.

I turned back to the fire to see it was subsiding as the firefighters did their job; the flames had died down, but black smoke was still jetting up into the clouds, creating an ominous pall over Brick Lane. 'Is anyone left inside?' one of them shouted, and I shook my head.

'No. We all got out.'

The caterwauling of an ambulance. Two paramedics jumped out, checked Salim Mian and moved him onto a stretcher with difficulty. Another came to me and asked if I was okay and, on my nod, moved on to Anjoli.

'You stay; I'll go with him to the hospital,' she roared at me over the sound of the torrents of water still being aimed at Tandoori Knights.

'I don't have my phone! Which hospital?'

A paramedic shouted, 'Royal London.'

It was only five minutes away, I'd find her.

Somebody must have put a silver protective jacket over my shoulders because I collapsed on the pavement, hugging it close to me, shooting between hot and freezing for the next half an hour.

The fear that had bubbled underneath hit me like a train – Anjoli and I had almost died. I found I couldn't stop shaking. Solicitous rubberneckers asked if I needed anything. When I stopped trembling, my only thoughts were of Salim Mian and Anjoli. How was he? What would Anjoli do if the restaurant was gone? What had happened? Had we left a hob on in the kitchen in our zombified state of fatigue the night before?

The rising smoke had subsided, and the firefighters were rewinding their hoses back into the truck, bantering about who had been the most accurate. One of them disappeared into the alley behind the restaurant and came out five minutes later.

'Anything?' said a colleague.

'Arson. Looks like someone poured petrol under the door of the restaurant and set it on fire. The kitchen must have been behind the door, and it went up like cotton in a furnace.'

'It was the storeroom,' I said.

'Sorry?'

'I work here. It was the storeroom. We store the dried goods and oils and things there.'

He nodded with a strange satisfaction. 'There you go then. Enough to fuel it. Did you have a fire suppression system?'

'I don't think so.'

'Always have one, that's what we advise all businesses. But this was deliberate. The police will deal with it.'

I knew who had done this.

He would pay.

Chapter 39

Thursday.

A wounded sun was rising as I walked over to the Royal London, the orange glow in the eastern sky over Whitechapel Road reflecting the night's devastating fire. The world continued to turn, ignorant of our life-changing trauma. I walked into A & E and found Anjoli slumped on a bench in the waiting area, the clock on the wall pointing to five minutes past five. When she saw me, she stood and fell into my arms. I held her tight, trying to give her the strength she had given me just three nights ago. She released all the sobs she'd been holding into my shoulder as I enveloped her with all the tenderness I possessed. I sat her down, and she collapsed against me.

'How is he?'

Her ash-covered face was streaked with tears and she shook her head.

All the air went out of my body. I pulled her to me. Salim Mian, dead. It was my fault. I was the one who had suggested he stay the night to avoid having to go home late. *No. No.* I couldn't bear any more of this. What would his wife do now? What would Naila do? That gentle man who had always laughed and been there for me, now snuffed out because of a chance suggestion I made in the very storeroom that had caused his death.

'We have to speak to Alaya Aunty and Naila,' said Anjoli.

'Sorry.' I wiped my face with my sleeve and realised I was still wearing my chef's shirt and jeans, now filthy with soot.

She looked at me, softness mingling with the grief in her eyes. 'Don't be. It was an accident. I must have left the door to the flat from the storeroom open when we went upstairs last night. It was my fault.'

'It wasn't an accident.'

Her eyes widened. 'What do you mean?'

I told her what the firefighter had said.

'Mackenzie?' she whispered.

'Or Imran. This is all my fault, Anjoli. I don't know how I'll make it up to you.'

Her face was stricken, and no words emerged.

'Whoever did it, I won't let him get away with it, I swear.' Another wave of guilt buffeted me. If I had called the police the night before, they might have arrested Mackenzie for assault, and he wouldn't have been able to do this. If it *was* him. Mistake after mistake, all mine.

The hospital said they would keep Salim Mian's body and gave us a leaflet on how to register a death. I put it in my pocket without reading it.

The sun was up now, and Whitechapel Road was shaking itself awake.

'I don't have my phone or any money,' said Anjoli. 'How are we going to get to Alaya Aunty's?'

'It's about half an hour's walk.'

'Kamil, I'm sorry. I can't walk that far. I'll literally die.' Then something struck her, and her face crumpled. 'Oh God, how am I going to tell Ma and Baba about the restaurant?'

I looked at her. She was staying vertical through sheer Anjoli willpower, her ash-streaked T-shirt saying, *I am woman, hear me roar.*

'I'll explain it to Saibal-da.' I flagged down a passing black cab and gave him Salim Mian's Brokesley Street address. For a minute I thought he might not let us in, given our condition, but he looked at the streaks of tears down Anjoli's face and waved us into the taxi. We arrived ten minutes later.

We stopped outside the front door and looked at each other, knowing we were going to change two people's lives for ever in the next two minutes.

'I'll do it. I've . . . done it before.'

She nodded, wordless, as I jabbed the doorbell.

There was no answer. I imagined Alaya jerked out of sleep and wondering who was at the door at this time of the morning. It was never good news, the phone or doorbell going this early. I nodded at the waiting taxi driver and rang again.

A couple of minutes later the door opened, and Alaya was there, dressing gown wrapped around her, and coming down the stairs behind her, Naila, in pale blue pyjamas, rubbing sleep from her eyes, hair tied back in a ponytail.

'Anjoli?' said Alaya, worry and surprise in her voice. 'What happened? Why are you all so dirty?'

'Can we come in, Aunty?'

Alaya stepped aside, and we entered. Naila looked at me, concern and worry etched on her face.

I borrowed money from her to pay for the cab as Anjoli walked Alaya into the kitchen.

'Where's Salim?' said Alaya, worry now at the surface.

'Sit, Aunty,' said Anjoli.

I flashed back to sitting in our kitchen with Anjoli six months ago, having to break the news to her that her father's oldest friend had been murdered. This was worse.

'I'm sorry, but I have terrible news. Salim Mian is . . . no more.'

Alaya stared at me. Her mouth cracked open. 'Heart attack?'

'Someone set fire to the restaurant last night.' Anjoli had

tears in her eyes. 'We couldn't get him out in time. I'm so sorry, Aunty. We tried our best, but it was too late.'

Naila looked at me, aghast. 'Fire? Who set fire to TK?'

I continued. 'The ambulance came and took Salim Mian to the Royal London, but . . .'

'I was with him in the ambulance,' said Anjoli, hoping it might help Alaya to know Salim Mian hadn't been alone.

'She was very brave,' I said.

All of us were weeping now.

'I was expecting something,' said Alaya. 'He was not well. His diabetes. He would forget to take his insulin, eat unhealthy food. But not like this.'

'He didn't suffer, Aunty. He wasn't . . . burned. It was the smoke.'

Alaya nodded, then focused on us. 'Look at the two of you.'

We looked down at our smoke-destroyed clothes. We smelled acrid.

'You can shower here. I'll give you something to change into,' said Naila.

'Thanks.' Anjoli cleared her throat, finding it difficult to speak. 'Salim Mian is at the hospital.'

I remembered the leaflet I had been given and placed it on the table. Alaya looked at it without seeing it. A bureaucratic document informing us in unemotional language how to regis-ter the death, get a certificate, organise the funeral and so on. According to Islamic custom, we had to bury the body within twenty-four hours.

'I'll call Imam Masroor,' I said. 'I'm sure the mosque will help organise everything.'

'I'll do it,' said Naila. 'Leave it to me, Aunty. Kamil, give me that and I'll make the arrangements. Oh. I have to call Daddy.' Her strength dissolved into soft tears as she thought of her father's reaction to his brother's death.

We walked up to her room. She wiped her face and said, 'What happened?'

I told her of Mackenzie's visit to the restaurant the night before and his assault on me, ending with, 'It was him or Imran. He was drunk and raving.'

Naila looked at me, shocked. 'No,' she whispered. 'I can't believe it.'

'I was asked to back off, and I didn't,' I said, showing her the text I'd received. There was no point in hiding it from her now.

She looked at it blankly. 'Who . . . who would send this to you? And why?'

Before I could answer, her phone rang. She turned to me, fear replacing the pain in her eyes.

'It's him. Imran. What should I do?'

'Answer it. Put it on speaker.'

'Hello,' she said.

'Naila. I want to see you.' A deep voice. Strong Punjabi accent.

'What do you mean? Where are you?'

'In London. I had to come for work and have just arrived at the airport. See me this evening after my meetings. I am staying at Claridge's.'

Her eyes darted to me. 'I can't. Something terrible has happened. Salim Uncle is no more.'

Silence. His voice softened. 'What happened, my Jaan? That is terrible.'

'A fire. He did not survive.'

'Are you okay?'

'Yes, I am fine. Come to Salim Uncle's house in the evening. We have to make arrangements.'

Pause.

'All right. I will text you. You look after yourself.'

She hung up, sat on the bed and exhaled. She looked shell-shocked.

'He's . . . here?' she said.

'Yes. The question is, how long has he been here?'

She shook her head and seemed close to tears, which brought the sobs I had been holding in closer to the surface. I wanted to hit someone – to batter Mackenzie or Imran till they were as bloody and as broken as I felt.

'If Imran has only just arrived, it must have been Mackenzie. I'm going to see him. Now.'

'Why?' said Naila, exhausted. 'What will it achieve? Just let the police deal with it.'

'I'll call Tahir about the fire. I should have phoned him last night when Mackenzie left; I'm cursing myself for not doing that. But I need to look Mackenzie in the eye and hear him confess it was him who firebombed the restaurant. I want to see his face when I tell him he killed Salim. Otherwise, he'll get hauled into the system and I'll never see him again. Before last night it was a crime to be solved. Now it's personal.'

'Then I'm coming with you. Salim Uncle was my—'

'No, you shouldn't be involved in this any more, Naila. Especially since Imran is here.' I hesitated, then continued: 'Listen, I know we haven't talked a lot since you told me about him, but . . . I've been thinking about things, and Naila, I don't care if you're married. I . . . care for you and maybe there could be something . . .'

She looked at me in a silence that seemed to last way too long. I felt a sudden surge of nausea. Why had I just said that? Did I mean it or was it the trauma I'd just been through? Maybe I was in shock. No. I cared for her, and she needed to know that there was an option other than Imran.

Then, 'Kamil. How can I stay here with you? I want to, but we are both on visas and . . .'

I felt like a fool.

'I must have a shower. The smell, it's making me ill. We'll talk later.'

I went into the bathroom, turned on the shower as hot as I could take it and stood under the stinging water, trying to wash the pain, sadness and guilt of the last twelve hours away from me. The black water curled down the plughole, taking the top coat of ash from my skin. But the rawness that was underneath remained.

I dried off to see Anjoli waiting outside the bathroom, towel in one hand, some of Naila's clothes in the other. She stepped in as I walked out, towel around my waist, the ash gone but the smell endured, if only in my nose. It felt like a part of me.

Naila was sitting on the bed waiting for me. She handed me a T-shirt.

'I'm coming to see Mackenzie. Salim was my uncle, and if he did this . . . I need to know.'

'I can handle it, Naila. You still need to rest.'

'No. It was my fault. I introduced you to him.'

'There's more than enough blame to go around, Naila. Please listen to me. It may not be safe.'

'Sorry, Kamil, you will not stop me. I've lived in fear for too long. The time has come for me to confront men like this.'

She wasn't going to budge. 'All right, if you insist. But leave the talking to me.'

'Wait for me,' said Anjoli from the bathroom. 'I'm coming too. The bastard burned down *my* restaurant. We can confront him together.'

I wasn't sure going mob-handed to confront a murderer and arsonist was the best idea, but it was clear there was no way they were going to be deterred.

I made a final attempt: 'I'm not sure we should leave Aunty on her own.'

'She wants to go to the mosque,' said Naila. 'We'll drop her on the way.'

So be it.

I nodded and got changed. It was time for the three of us to stop being passive observers and act.

Chapter 40

Thursday.

We arrived in Bermondsey just after 7.30, Naila driving as fast as she could to get us there. We didn't speak to each other during the entire journey, each of us preoccupied with the administrative and personal aftermath of sudden death. It felt like the end of a long day, not the very early morning of a new one. Naila lent Anjoli her phone and she called Saibal. I heard his shock and pain on hearing another of his oldest friends had been killed before his time and the restaurant he had spent thirty years building had been destroyed. It was too big a loss to bear. He didn't blame his daughter, of course, but I could see Anjoli felt responsible. It was her fault; she was in charge. Anjoli's uncle in Kolkata was in a bad way, so Saibal and Maya couldn't come for Salim Mian's funeral, which made it worse. I felt equally culpable – I had baited Mackenzie. Then, filled with trepidation, Naila called her father. She spoke to him in Urdu then hung up, staring out of the window, one hand on the steering wheel, the other gripping her phone as if to stop it escaping.

'How was he?' I said.

'Bad. He was very close to Salim Uncle. He will come for the funeral.'

She lapsed into silence and viciously swerved to overtake a slow-moving Volvo. Everyone's past follows them wherever they

283

go, a shadow you can't shake. And all our pasts weighed on us at this moment.

Then it was time for my call, the one I should have made the night before, which might have stopped all of this happening. One small slip-up, one moment of forgetfulness on my part and lives had been changed for ever. I took Naila's phone, found the number and dialled.

'Tahir? It's Kamil. I have information for you.' I told him everything that had happened, omitting the fact we were on our way to see Mackenzie. I didn't want the police stopping me from doing what I needed to do.

'I'll get a car over to Mackenzie's place and bring him in,' he said after I'd finished. 'I'm so sorry for your loss, Kamil. I'll speak to Anjoli later.'

No smart nickname for me this time.

'Also, we've discovered Naila's husband is in London. Can you look into that too? Regarding her stabbing? He's staying at Claridge's.'

'I will.'

We pulled up outside Mackenzie's bungalow. Only the Volvo was outside, his wife having presumably left with the children in her Golf.

'Leave this to me,' I said, grimly determined. Enough of playing games with this man. I would get the truth out of him today.

We marched up to the front door, which to my surprise stood ajar. We rang the bell anyway, but there was no response. I pushed the door open and shouted, 'Mackenzie?'

Still nothing. We walked into the kitchen. There was an empty bottle of whisky sitting in the centre of the granite-topped island, as if placed there like a kind of totem. My back felt icy as my spidey sense kicked in. Something was wrong.

'Look,' whispered Anjoli. On the floor of the kitchen was a large metal can. I bent and sniffed. Petrol.

'Wait here.'

I walked back to the entrance by the main door and turned into a corridor. I opened the first door – kids' room, colourful drawings on the wall, toys scattered on the floor, bed made up. Shutting it, I opened the second – master bedroom. Sheets rumpled but no one there. I heard footsteps behind me and whirled around, but it was only Anjoli and Naila, disregarding my instructions to wait in the kitchen.

There was one more room at the end – the bathroom, I guessed. The door half open.

I shouted once more: 'Mackenzie?'

I shoved the door with my foot.

The smell of whisky hit me.

And there he was.

In an empty bath. Wearing a T-shirt and boxers. Eyes open, face a rictus of pain, gouts of blood streaking the white porcelain and pooling around him in the tub. I took in the slashes up both his arms and the scalpel lying on the floor by the side of the tub where it must have fallen. A glass lay toppled on the floor, amber liquid soaked into a white bath mat and pooled around a bottle of Midleton Irish whiskey next to it.

Everything seemed to slow down as if a film was running at half-speed. I touched his face – cold. His shirt was emblazoned with a quote from the U2 song 'I Want To Run'. Did he choose that to die in? Do people about to kill themselves worry about things like that?

Then Anjoli was in the doorway, eyes wide, mouth open, no words emerging, Naila coming up behind her, peering over her shoulder whispering, 'Oh my God. Has he killed himself?'

I forced myself to speak, my words seeming to echo off the white tiles: 'Looks like it.'

Things sped up. First came fury. Why should this man be allowed to escape justice? I hope he suffered as he saw his life leaking away into that white bathtub. Did he think about what he had done, or was he so drunk he had no coherent thoughts?

Then suspicion. Did he kill himself or was this murder? It looked like a genuine suicide. But . . .

Then practicality. 'Don't come into the bathroom; we shouldn't contaminate the scene. He must have left the front door open so someone would find him. Look for a note.'

I went into the master bedroom and, sure enough, there was a scrawled sheet of paper on the bed. I read it to the others without touching it.

'I am sorry for everything. I can't go on. The guilt of killing Salma is eating me up. I had to do it because she threatened to expose the affair we were having. We had been together for some months and I broke it off because I could not lie to Ro any more. Salma accepted it but then changed her mind and threatened to tell the dean unless we got together again. I begged her to reconsider, but she was adamant. She kept phoning and texting and I went to her flat that night to implore her to see reason. We argued, and I saw red and strangled her. I regret this with all my heart. I tried to frame her boyfriend by planting the hoodie on him. I regret that too. He was innocent and didn't deserve that. I wish so many things had been different. I'm sorry, Ro. I love you and the children.'

'Shit,' said Anjoli. 'You were right, Kamil. About everything.'

Before I could respond, someone shouted from the front of the house, 'Hello, Dr Mackenzie? Are you in?'

'Damn, it's the police,' I said.

We walked to the front door to find Sergeant Ismail and DI Rogers.

'He's in there. He killed himself rather than be arrested.'

Rogers stared at me in disbelief. 'Mr Rahman, finding one corpse is unlucky, finding two could be an unfortunate coincidence, but three means you're a serial killer taking the piss.'

I gave him a weak smile and resigned myself to hours of interrogation.

Chapter 41

Thursday.

As I expected, Rogers and Tahir grilled each of us for ages before letting us go. Answering the same questions time and time again, my fury at Mackenzie escaping punishment for the murder of two people diminished. I was worried about Naila and Anjoli, but Tahir told me quietly they would go easy on them. He convinced his boss we had been trying to help and told him we had passed on several crucial bits of information, so Rogers let us off with a stiff warning not to interfere any further.

'Mr Rahman, you not only crossed the line, but you also painted over it so there was no line left any more. You're lucky I don't arrest you for obstructing the investigation.'

Tahir took us to where Naila had parked and told us they were satisfied Mackenzie had murdered Salma, started the fire and killed himself. His fingerprints were on the scalpel, the glass of whiskey in the bathroom, the suicide note and the can of petrol, and to put the fried onions on top of the biryani, they had found traces of his DNA on the hoodie the police had taken from Ziad's house.

'Do you think he was Naila's attacker? I saw a toolbox when we went to see him at his place – maybe he had a Stanley knife?' I said.

'His alibi was solid,' said Tahir. 'We'll check the tools but obviously we won't be able to tell if a knife is missing.'

'Can you check his mobile to triple-check his alibi? To ensure it wasn't at Waterloo at the time?'

'We haven't found his mobile yet; we're still looking.'

'Isn't that odd?'

'Guess he dumped it before topping himself.'

'Why?'

'Your guess is as good as mine. Maybe it'll turn up.'

'Can you get any messages he sent from his carrier?'

'Calls yes, maybe not messages. If it's Android, we can, but messages between iPhones only go through Apple's servers, so the carrier won't have any record of them. Real pain for us hardworking cops. Anyway, we have enough evidence to be sure he did it. We'll inform Salma's parents of our success.'

'So, he was having an affair with Salma?' said Anjoli.

'Looks like it. That's why he killed her and tried to frame Ziad.'

'Poor Ziad,' said Naila. 'He'll be devastated.'

'Yes,' said Tahir. 'Especially since the baby *was* Ziad's. The DNA test came back.'

'Oh no,' said Anjoli. 'That's terrible.'

'So why was Salma so keen on getting back with Mackenzie then?' I said.

'Maybe she didn't know who the father was? Come on, Dalgliesh, you helped solve a crime. Justice is done – enjoy the feeling!'

'Mm-hmm.'

'Naila, we're still investigating your stabbing. Kamil mentioned your husband is in town; we'll check on when exactly he arrived.'

'Thank you.'

'Anything on the homeless thing?' said Anjoli as Tahir turned to head back into the station.

'Still chasing that are you, Anj? I saw the statistics you emailed me, and they are interesting, but I'm not sure what we can do with no evidence.'

'We may have evidence. A witness.'

Tahir stopped. 'What do you mean?'

'Well, there's this guy – Sam – who's taken Yasir's place at the mosque. He was there when Yasir died and saw someone talking to him that morning, just before he died. You should interview him. Maybe get a sketch of who he saw.'

'I'll look into it.'

'Don't you dare fob me off, Tahir Ismail. Sam will be at the mosque as usual and may remember something under professional questioning.'

'If he isn't drunk,' I said.

Anjoli ignored me. 'Maybe you can look for CCTV along the street or something. Promise me you will, Tahir.'

'Okay, okay, I promise. You're like a dog with a bone, Anjoli! I'll speak to him.'

'Soon. He may move to some other place and then you won't be able to find him.'

'Soon.'

'Are you guys okay?' I said as Naila drove us to TK. 'Naila, I'm sorry you had to go through all that, just after Salim Mian's death.'

She shuddered. 'I . . . I don't know what I'm feeling. I knew Sir. I'm still trying to process the fact that he killed Salma and Salim Mian and may have tried to stab me.'

'I suppose he must have. Why would he lie in his suicide note? And it fits with what the imam told us. He said something had bothered Salma six weeks ago, but she had resolved it – that must have been when he broke off with her. Then she saw him in the restaurant with another woman and felt she had been made a fool of, got angry and told Mackenzie she was going to complain to the dean. All that makes sense, but . . .'

'But what?' Anjoli said.

'There are far too many loose ends for my liking.'

'Like what?' said Naila.

'Well, for a start, who sent those threatening messages and stabbed you? Why would Mackenzie do that? Who was he having dinner with that sent Salma off the deep end? And why did she care about Mackenzie if the baby was Ziad's?'

'Does it matter who? She thought he had dumped her for another student. She must have felt used and discarded. I can understand why that would make her seek redress from the dean,' said Anjoli. 'I mean, we don't know a lot about Salma. What other reason would he have to kill her? And, as you said, why lie about it when he was about to kill himself?'

'I don't know. But if Mackenzie wasn't the one who stabbed you, Naila, there's no reason whoever it was won't try again.'

'I'm sorry,' said Anjoli to Naila, 'but I think it must have been your husband.'

Naila looked ahead at the passing cars and stayed silent.

'Let's see how he is when he comes tonight,' I said.

'And Daddy comes tomorrow,' said Naila. 'They are going to drag me back to Pakistan now that Salim Uncle is no more. It was my fault he died. I loved him.'

Her eyes glistened.

'We loved him too, Naila. He was a good man, and I know he loved you very much. But it *wasn't* your fault. I suggested he stay the night, and I provoked Mackenzie.'

'I should have come and picked him up after the restaurant party; it was selfish of me not to.'

'You were injured and had to rest,' said Anjoli from the back seat. 'It was me who forgot to shut the door between the storeroom and the flat. And I told him to leave his room door open, so he could call me if he needed anything. I'll miss him so much too. He has been a presence all my life, always there, smiling. And since Baba and Ma have been away, he's been my rock.'

Tears were flowing now.

I searched for words to stem the flow and all I came up with was, 'Look, we can all blame ourselves. One action leads to another which leads to a third, and before you know it, the mosque has been razed. That's life. We would never do anything if we didn't want our actions to have consequences.'

But I don't think any of us were convinced.

Chapter 42

Thursday.

The restaurant looked bizarrely normal in the sunshine. In my imagination I had seen a burned-out shell with tendrils of smoke rising to the sky as people stood around and stared at the bomb site where Tandoori Knights had once been. We looked up at the windows of the flat and Anjoli said, 'That's odd – our curtains have disappeared. I didn't see any flames upstairs.'

I looked up, and where there had once been white lace curtains, I could only see blackness.

'I think it must be soot covering the windows,' said Naila, and as I peered closer, I realised she was right.

'How will we get in?' said Anjoli as I realised we had rushed out that morning without keys. I couldn't believe it had just been that morning – thinking about it caused a wave of weariness to run through me. We went around to the alley at the back where the fire had started, and here you could see the devastation. There was a strong smell of petrol and the street was still soaked with water from the hoses. Someone had boarded up the back door of the restaurant, which must have burned off in the fire.

Anjoli went to fetch the locksmith from down the road.

We sat in front of the restaurant in silence then Naila said, 'Poor Anjoli. She's being brave, isn't she?'

'She's a survivor,' I said as she reappeared, locksmith in tow. He opened the door to the flat and let us in, refusing any payment, saying in Bengali, 'You are one of us; this was a terrible thing that happened. I am happy to help you.'

We walked into the flat and Naila picked up and folded the sheet, now black like everything else, on which we had dragged her uncle down the stairs. She ignored her inky hands, and we climbed the staircase, the throat-scraping stink of burning all around. The walls were dark with soot and everything in the living room seemed to be painted black. Anjoli and I avoided Saibal's bedroom, where we had found Salim Mian, and continued up the stairs. My room seemed undamaged, just a fine layer of grey over my belongings. The Holy Koran on my bedside table had curlicues of soot on it, looking like Arabic characters. I moistened my finger and brushed them off, then changed out of the clothes Naila had given me into my own, which made me feel a little more myself again. I unplugged my phone from its charger, wiping the dust away with the T-shirt I'd just taken off.

I heard Anjoli wail from her bedroom, 'All my stuff is ruined!' I went in. She and Naila were surveying her wardrobe, which seemed to have been worse hit than mine. I realised I must have slammed my door shut when she called me out the night before, which prevented the smoke from filling my room. Anjoli had left hers open with predictable results.

'It'll wash out,' said Naila, consoling. 'I'll help you take everything to the launderette.'

Anjoli rooted around for her insurance documents and her mobile.

Naila looked at the map of London on the wall with the now dingy and sooty yellow stickies of the graphs of deaths by borough Anjoli had taken from her spreadsheet.

'What's this?'

'It's Anjoli's incident room. She's been trying to map the homeless deaths to see if she can find any pattern.'

'And have you?' said Naila, examining the Post-its one by one.

'I think so,' said Anjoli. 'Where *are* those papers? Lambeth and Tower Hamlets. That's where the killer seems to be most active. Look how the deaths rocketed over the last few years.'

'Wow! How did you find that out?'

'Statistics,' I said, proud of Anjoli. 'She analysed the numbers and discovered far more deaths in those two boroughs than the others. Tahir says he's looking into it.'

'That's clever.'

'I'm not sure he's taking me seriously enough, I may need to escalate it,' said Anjoli, as I explained the trend lines on the stickies to Naila. 'Ah! There they are!' She waved a folder marked 'Rest. Docs' at me. 'Great. We're covered for fire damage.'

I hadn't doubted it for a second. Anjoli, being Anjoli, would have ensured all the paperwork was in order. She may have seemed scatty on the outside but was meticulous when it counted.

'I can't sleep here tonight,' Anjoli said, looking around.

'You're going to sleep at ours,' said Naila, brooking no argument. 'Then I'll come and help you tidy up tomorrow after the funeral.'

We took what we needed for our overnight stay and made our way down to the restaurant through the inner door. Anjoli was right, she *had* left the connecting door between the flat and the restaurant open. It still gaped at us, soot covering the walls down to the storeroom, which was destroyed, the stench of the smoke made worse by that of burned food, spices and oil. The industrial cans of ghee we had stored there must have gone up first and then acted as a primer for the rest. To make matters worse, the entire room was sodden; black liquid squelched beneath our feet and soaked through my trainers. We picked our way through the debris and opened the door to the kitchen, which looked unharmed.

'Oh, thank God!' said Anjoli. The sturdy fire door between the kitchen and the storeroom had done its job. If the connecting door to the flat had been shut, we might have been spared the worst and Salim Mian would still be alive. The same thought appeared to cross Anjoli's face, and I gave her hand a squeeze. The main restaurant was untouched, cheering her up, and her gloom dropped away like an unneeded blanket.

'At least this is something. We should be able to reopen soon. I was scared it might need to be demolished. I must find someone to fix the storeroom and clean the flat. We must replace all our provisions, but the damage could have been a lot worse . . .'

The unspoken need to replace Salim Mian hovered in the air.

Naila winced and touched her side, her face white.

'Okay, Naila?'

'I'm fine. All this activity must have opened my wound. It's okay. I'll change the dressing when we get home.'

'Oh God, I forgot,' said Anjoli. 'I'm so sorry. Come. I have everything I need; we can go back to yours now. Thank you.'

Chapter 43

Thursday.

The rest of the afternoon was a blur of organising the funeral, looking after Naila's aunt, who was proving very resilient, and informing people about Salim Mian's passing. I could tell how sick Naila was feeling at the prospect of seeing Imran that evening. Various relatives arrived to offer their condolences, and Naila, Anjoli and I scuttled around making tea, offering biscuits and trying to make conversation with these people we had never met before, all of whom were solicitous and caring but wanted to hear all the details of what had happened to poor Salim Mian.

Just after 6 p.m. the bell rang. I opened the door to find a tall, good-looking Asian man outside.

'Is Naila here?' he said in a soft voice. 'I am Imran, her husband.'

So this was my rival. The savage, psychopathic spouse she had escaped from. He didn't look like a villain, but then they never did.

I ignored the proffered hand and led him to the living room. I felt a twinge as he embraced Naila and whispered something in her ear. She stood stiff, her eyes staring without expression into mine over his shoulder until he let her go and went across to Alaya to offer his condolences.

I kept him in the corner of my eye as I circulated, then saw Naila go upstairs with him to her bedroom. I was tempted to listen at the door but it would be hard to explain if I got caught. So instead, I got myself an orange juice and stood, discreetly watching for them to come down.

After ten minutes Naila followed him down the stairs, looking white and strained. He was grim faced as he walked past me.

'What happened?' I whispered to her.

'Nothing. I told him about the restaurant burning down. Then he got angry with me because I wasn't wearing my wedding and engagement rings.'

'Shit. What did you say?'

'That they got in the way at work. But I don't think he believed me. He ranted for a while and said he is going to drag me back to Pakistan whether I like it or not and I need to give him his ledger back or he'll make life difficult for me.'

'Do you want me to speak to him?'

'No. Please don't. It'll just make it worse. I'll think of something. I need to go – I don't want him to see us talking.'

She went into the kitchen as Imran came out. I went up to him.

'I'm Kamil Rahman. I cook at the restaurant Salim Mian worked at; he was very good to me.'

His face gave nothing away. 'Yes, I've heard of you. The policeman cook. Salim Uncle told me.'

'How long have you been in London?'

'I arrived this morning – why?'

'Oh, Naila said she had been trying to get hold of you earlier in the week and couldn't find you.'

'I was in Paris for meetings from Sunday.'

'How was Paris?'

'Tell me, Kamil Rahman. What do you, as a single man, want from a married woman?'

'What do you mean?'

'You know we are married?'

'Yes, of course. We are just friends. I'm also new to this country.'

His look said he didn't believe me as he got in my face and said, 'Stop sniffing around her like a dog. Salim told me everything about you. She is *my* wife. Stay away from her or I will not be held responsible for the consequences.'

And then he walked away.

As the guests dispersed, Imran said to Naila, 'Come to Claridge's with me and we can talk.'

'I can't leave Aunty alone here tonight, Imran. We'll talk tomorrow after the funeral, I promise. Daddy's coming.'

She was walking on eggshells around him, choosing her words as if she knew anything could set him off.

'After the funeral,' he said in a low growl and left.

Naila let out a shuddering sigh, went up to her aunt and said, 'Would you like to eat something, Aunty?'

'I'm not hungry, beti. You all eat. I will go to bed now.'

We hugged her goodnight, and Naila put out the food the visitors had brought for Alaya, as was customary. We picked at it and I let out what had been on my mind: 'Imran was in Paris. He could have come to London and found you, then stabbed you at Waterloo. To frighten you into returning.'

'I know,' said Naila. 'And it's working. I have to go back. I don't have a choice. I can't think any more, Kamil. I'm so tired, I need sleep.'

'I'll clear up,' said Anjoli. 'Naila, I'll sleep with you if that's okay. Kamil, I'll make up the sofa for you.'

I put the leftovers of the dinner in the fridge, and when I saw Salim Mian's medicines on the shelf next to the butter, a jolt of shame went through me as I remembered our last conversation in the storeroom. Naila's saviour, I had thought. And because of me, Salim, Naila's protector, was now gone. As was any hope of my future with Naila.

Chapter 44

Friday.

The next morning was sunny again. I'd spent a restless night on the sofa, strange protuberances digging into my back making sleep difficult as I thought of unworkable schemes to keep Naila in London, where she felt safe, and make a future for us. Try as I might, I could not find a solution.

Naila's father arrived at the house from Heathrow just after nine. 'Daddy!' She ran to him and fell in his arms. He was a tall man, immaculate in a suit and tie even after an eight-hour flight. Sporting a toothbrush moustache and tight grey hair, he had the bearing of an army officer and reminded me of my father. He stood, slightly stiff as Naila clung on to him, sobbing, then stroked her hair and whispered, 'Sab kuchh theek hai, bachha. Everything will be all right, my child. Sab kuchh theek hai. Come on, enough now. You must be strong. Enough.'

He gently pushed her out of his arms and, giving her a handkerchief, said, 'Wipe your tears now. Be strong. No need to cry.' She reluctantly let him go, took his hanky and dabbed at her face as he hugged Saleem Mian's wife, saying, 'Kaise ho, Alaya? How are you coping?'

She nodded and all she said was, 'Chai?'

He shook his head. 'No, I ate breakfast on the plane.'

'This is Kamil, Daddy,' said Naila. 'He was a cook in the restaurant with Salim Uncle.'

He shook my hand with a knuckle-crushing grip as I said, 'I'm so sorry for your loss, Mr Alvi.'

After a stop-start conversation on how the relatives had taken Salim Mian's passing, Naila, who seemed to have recovered from her earlier tears, said, 'We need to go.'

The five of us piled into her car and made our way to the East London Mosque. Naila's father reminisced about growing up with his brother in Pakistan, then said to Alaya, 'Ab kya karogi? What will you do now? Maybe the time is right for you to shift back to Lahore? We are your family there; we will look after you. What is there to keep you here now?'

Naila's face stiffened momentarily, before resuming a look of studied neutrality, eyes focused on the road ahead, hands tight on the steering wheel.

'I have been thinking that too,' said Alaya. 'Salim always talked about going back when we were old. Given all that is happening in this country, maybe now *is* the right time.'

'Pakistan is a lot better now,' said Naila's father. 'Less corruption, an easier life. You have to come back as well, Naila, of course. You can't stay on your own here.'

'We've arrived,' was all Naila said.

Imran was at the mosque waiting for us. Salim Mian's body had been transported to the mortuary in the mosque's basement, and the imam met us there. As Salim had no children, the washing of the body had to be done by his brother with Imran and myself roped in to help the professional washer the undertakers had provided, while the women waited in an adjoining room. Seeing Salim Mian lying on the washing table, covered from navel to knee in a simple sheet, choked me up. He looked peaceful, a slight smile on his face. The washer handed us rubber gloves, and we started with the ozu wash: hands and arms three times each, then the face followed by the right and left feet. The washer then took over for the torso, as we looked away to preserve Salim Mian's dignity. After being rinsed three times, the body was dried. We perfumed it thrice with attar, then all of us lifted the body, with some effort given his bulk, and placed him on top of the shrouds, the kafn, in his coffin. We wrapped him in the three pieces of the kafn, and my eyes went damp. He looked regal and peaceful lying there. He had been a good man in life, surely he would have a good afterlife. Allah would judge him well in the Yawm al-Din, and he would have eternal peace in Jannah.

The women came back in, stood at the back of the room and watched in silence as the imam recited prayers.

I walked over to Anjoli and whispered, 'You okay?'

She gave me a slow nod. 'You?'

The memory of Salim Mian's smile caused a stone in my stomach to melt, and before I knew it, tears were streaming down my cheeks. I felt like I was crying for Salim Mian, Salma, Yasir and Louis, as if my tears could make sense of all their deaths. Anjoli slipped her hand into mine and squeezed it as I tried to brush my cheeks dry. Naila's face twisted and silent drops rolled down her cheeks, and that set Anjoli off. I comforted her as Imran looked back at us from where he was standing with the men.

The imam continued his prayers; the body was readied for interring, then taken away to be transported to the burial site.

Naila sat down on a bench. 'I'm sorry. My wound, it's hurting.'

Imam Masroor walked over to us and looked at Naila. 'Are you all right, my child?'

'Yes, I'm sorry, Sheikh. I didn't think it would affect me so much. I loved my Salim Uncle.'

'We all did. Truly to Allah we belong, and truly to Him we shall return. Have patience, dear, mourn him. It was Allah's decree.'

'And was it also Allah's decree he be murdered by a madman, like Yasir was?' said Anjoli. 'Will his murderer be forgiven or get what is coming to him?'

'We don't know what fate awaits us in the hereafter, child,' said the imam. Then, looking troubled, he added, 'You still believe somebody killed Yasir?'

'More than ever, Sheikh,' said Anjoli. She explained about the bottle of gin and what Sam had seen.

'This is terrible. Do the police know?'

'Yes, but I'm not sure they believe me. They will question Sam soon. We also told the American priest who was here to see you the other day – he said he might help.'

'Father Spence? He is a good man. We work together often. Come, we must go for the burial now.'

'In a minute, Sheikh,' I said. 'Are you going to be all right, Naila? I don't want to leave you like this.'

She nodded. 'I'll be fine. Sorry, seeing Salim Uncle like that and then . . . Daddy and Imran. It just transported me back to the bad old days in Lahore. Then when Alaya Aunty started talking about going back to Pakistan, I almost had a panic attack in the car.'

'No one noticed,' said Anjoli.

'I'm scared, Anjoli. I don't want to go back to him. But if Alaya Aunty does, then I have to, and I won't be able to finish my course. He won't let me stay here on my own.'

'You can stay with us,' said Anjoli. 'We'll look after you.'

'That's so kind. But they won't let me. I think my time here is up. He has won.'

'Oh, Naila,' said Anjoli. 'You can't! This is what you've wanted all your life.'

'I don't know. I'm just so tired of it all. I thought nursing was the best profession there was – what could be more important than relieving people's suffering? Being kind, a kind word, a kind face – all sorts of kindness when they need it the most. But now . . . Salma dead, Salim Uncle gone, and for what? If I had never come here, he at least would still be alive. He was killed because I was helping Kamil investigate the murder. I can't stand it!'

A tsunami of guilt hit me, but I forced myself to say, 'You can't think like that, Naila. That wasn't your fault. Mackenzie was a maniac. You couldn't have saved them.'

'I know that, Kamil. And I'm not blaming you of course. But I really believed I was doing some good in the world after . . . after everything that –' she lowered her voice '– Imran put me through in Pakistan. He made me feel useless, and just as I was helping people here . . .' Her voice trailed away.

I felt helpless. The thought of losing Naila just after we had got close was intolerable. And if Imran was the one who had stabbed her, what was she going back to? Her life would either be in danger or be lived in psychological servitude. For a moment I got a glimpse of how trapped she must feel and how the classes and hospital here had been her lifeline, allowing her to blossom and follow her calling. And then Mackenzie had killed Salma, and Naila's life, through no fault of her own, had spiralled down and pulled her back into her husband's orbit. If I hadn't chosen to investigate the crime, things might have turned out differently. I needed to help her somehow, but what could I do? If I could prove Imran had stabbed Naila, maybe her parents would force through a divorce and she would be rid of him. But how?

'Come, Naila,' said Anjoli. 'Let's get Alaya Aunty and go home. The men have to go to the interment.'

Chapter 45

Friday

After we returned from the burial, Alaya received the mourners at home, all of whom brought even more food. Even Tahir came by to pay his respects, which I appreciated. As the evening ended, Naila went off with Imran to his posh hotel and, since Naila's dad was staying at Salim Mian's, we had no choice but to return to our smoke-engulfed home.

When we returned to the flat, the toxic, pungent air hit us in the nose, the acid burning our throats. The smell of smoke in the house pervaded everything, and even though Anjoli and I opened all the windows and sprayed industrial quantities of scented air freshener around, it didn't diminish. In fact, the combination of smoke and jasmine made it even more unpleasant, but the weird thing was after a couple of hours of living with it, I could no longer smell it.

Back in my bed I was unable to sleep even though every cell in my body craved it like an alcoholic lusts after his next drink. My life had reached another crossroads. Or a dead end, I wasn't sure which. Two weeks ago, everything had looked so different. I was making the most of my professional kitchen exploits; I had a beautiful sort-of-kind-of girlfriend, and springtime in London coated everyone and everything in fragrant, blossoming optimism. And now? Our home stank, the restaurant was wrecked, and my 'girlfriend' was heading back to her abusive husband. To make matters worse, the police putting the kibosh on my involvement with the murder case I had solved meant I would never tie up all the loose ends. That was the pistachio on my very fucked-up falooda, the taste of which would haunt my mouth for ever. And not in a good way.

I considered retreating to Kolkata. Opening a detective agency there and starting again seemed like a less dismal prospect than fighting with one hand tied behind my back in London. The one positive thing about the last few weeks since I'd started sniffing around Salma's murder was that I'd got my investigative mojo back and had cracked the case. I tried to push the fact my involvement had led to tragic consequences to the back of my mind.

My phone rang.

I picked it up: 11:23 p.m. Imam Masroor. What did he want?

'Sheikh? How are you? Is everything all right?'

'Yes, alhamdulillah. I am sorry to call you so late at night. We had just finished the Isha prayer at the mosque and I was going home when I saw Sam sleeping in the doorway as he does nowadays. I checked he was okay and noticed a bottle of spirits next to him. He said he found it there when he woke up. You had mentioned this, so I telephoned. What should I do?'

Jangling with excitement, sleep banished for now, I said, 'Nothing. I'll come and check up on him. Tell him not to drink it. Please go home.'

'If you are sure . . . Thank you. I can't have alcohol in the mosque.'

'Yes, thanks for calling. Please leave the bottle there for now.'

I pulled on my jeans and a sweatshirt and knocked on Anjoli's door. No answer. I knocked a little louder and got a sleepy, 'What? I'm asleep.'

'It's important, can I come in?'

I took her grunt as assent, went in and sat on her bed, the street lamp throwing its light on the wall opposite.

Her voice came out in a rasp. 'I'm so tired, can't it wait? What time is it?'

I switched on her bedside lamp, the brutal light banishing the soft darkness, and she sat up, eyes clenched shut. 'What the hell . . .'

'Wake up. This is important.'

She realised I wasn't fooling around and forced one eye open. 'Okay, I'm listening.'

I told her what the imam had said and now I had the attention of both eyes.

'Kamil! What should we do?'

'Stake him out. See if the killer comes back, and if he does, we grab him.'

'Shouldn't we call Tahir?'

'It's late. They won't do anything based on a gin bottle. They don't believe there's anything going on. And if it's a wild goose chase, I don't want to lose his goodwill.'

'Okay. I'm in. Give me five minutes.'

'Dress warm. It may be a long night.'

'Should we call Naila?'

'Better not; she's with Imran. Don't want to drop her in the shit with him. Or her dad. Just the dynamic duo tonight.'

A quick smile in response and I went to gather my things.

We took ten minutes to sort ourselves out, slipped out of the house and walked down the almost empty Brick Lane to the mosque. The street had a different feel at this time of the night, almost like the legendary Brick Lane from decades ago when the Irish, Ashkenazis and Bangladeshis lived cheek by jowl, each respecting the others' religions, customs, food and dress. These were people who had looked past the yarmulkes and hijabs and crosses, realising they had more in common than that which separated them – love of family, enjoyment of shared food, a deep drive to have their children succeed and knowing their gods would keep them safe. And now here were – Anjoli, Hindu Londoner, and I, Muslim Kolkatan – speed-walking to the mosque to keep a homeless, drunk, Christian Yorkshireman safe.

As we entered Whitechapel High Street a fox sauntered around the corner, stared at us with flaming eyes, shadowy under the street lamp, evaluating – threat or food – then turned and trotted off, its hindquarters twinkling in and out of the light till it was swallowed up by the darkness of a side street.

Sam was in his sleeping bag in the mosque's alcove as the Imam had said, a half-bottle of vodka lying next to him, empty. He didn't move as I leaned over him.

Anjoli's eyes went wide. 'Is he . . . ?'

I heard his stertorous breathing and shook him.

'Wha–what?'

I shook him again. 'Sam?'

'I'm going, I'm going.' He made to sit up then collapsed back down again.

'Sam, it's Anjoli and Kamil. Did you drink it?'

'It's vodka, not the same gin,' I said.

'Oh,' said Anjoli. 'What does that mean?'

'I don't know.'

Sam sat up, blinked the sleep out of his eyes, and seemed to work out we didn't mean him any harm. 'Go away!'

'It's important, Sam,' I said. 'Who gave you that vodka?'

'I don't know. I woke up, and it was there.' He shut his eyes. 'Go away.'

'Has he been drugged? Shall we call an ambulance?' said Anjoli.

'I don't think so. Do you feel all right, Sam?'

'Yes. I just need to sleep.'

I knelt next to him and slid a hand under his dirty coat sleeve to feel his pulse.

He jerked it away and screamed, 'FUCK OFF!'

I stepped back as he burrowed himself deeper into his sleeping bag.

'Listen, Sam. Anjoli and I are going to wait across the road, hidden under that shop entrance. If you feel bad or anything, we'll be there.'

'And if anyone comes to hurt you, we'll save you,' said Anjoli.

The sleeping bag gave no response.

Chapter 46

Friday

Anjoli and I sat in the shadow under the doorway of a shop imaginatively named Daily Essentials, the steel shutter behind us covered with graffiti. There was an unpleasant, unidentifiable smell I forced myself to ignore. We had an excellent view of Sam in the doorway opposite, although he was in shadow.

'I hope he's okay,' said Anjoli. 'If he's been poisoned, and we did nothing, I'll never forgive myself.'

'We may be wasting our time. This must be a coincidence. I think he's just drunk. But let's wait just in case. I'll check on him every hour.'

'Good idea.' I was hyper aware of her shoulder touching mine. 'This is exciting – my first stakeout!'

'Yeah, see if you feel the same way in two hours from now when you're exhausted, your eyes are closing, you need to pee, and you'd kill for a coffee. Believe me, stakeouts are not fun. Hours or days of boredom alleviated by occasional minutes of excitement. Don't get your hopes up; the odds are it's nothing.'

'Still, it's an experience, isn't it?' she murmured.

'That it is. Here, have a samosa. I grabbed them from the kitchen.'

'What a clever Boy Scout you are.' She bit into the flaky pastry.

'Let's see. It's just after twelve, and the place gets busy after seven, so we have a seven-hour window if he's going to come. Why don't you nap for a bit; I'll wake you and you can take over when I need to sleep? You can lean against me.'

'Okay, don't forget . . .' After a moment's hesitation, she snuggled against me, her head on my shoulder and, to my amazement, fell asleep within a few minutes. I envied her that ability. My non-sleep for the last week was now causing me genuine problems as every part of me seemed as heavy as lead. But I had to stay awake. This might be our only chance to catch this guy, assuming there was even someone to catch. While Anjoli's statistics were interesting, part of me still felt that a serial killer seemed fanciful – an idea that should be consigned to TV shows and movies.

My arm was growing numb, Anjoli was snoring into my ear, and my back was aching against the sheet metal of the corrugated shutter. I looked at my watch – 12:47. Whitechapel Road was quiet this time of the night. A few cars swished by, and there were no pedestrians. The mosque opposite glowed with an almost internal light, given there was no moon. I counted the shops opposite, my eyes growing heavier. I didn't dare look at my phone, for fear the glow would scare away the killer. How on earth did the homeless cope with boredom? This wasn't something I had ever considered before. We papered our downtime with media – books, TV, radio, Facebook, Twitter, the Internet – but someone on the streets? All they had to entertain them was rumination. Day after day, night after night. What went through their minds? Anger and resentment at the people with 'normal' lives who passed them without noticing? Memories of happier times that had now turned sour? Dreams of better times to come? A craving for their next fix, their next bottle? A longing for oblivion? Fear? I shivered and Anjoli groaned and shifted next to me.

*

The next thing I heard Anjoli was whispering in my ear. 'Look.'

My eyes snapped open. I hadn't even realised I'd fallen asleep. I looked at my watch – 3:24.

A fugitive shadow, barely visible, was flitting past the gym next to the mosque, trying to stay out of the street lights casting their yellow glow on the streets. Dressed in what seemed to be dark jeans and a long coat, face hidden under an upturned collar, he walked up to Sam and looked around to see if there was anyone watching. We shrank back into our little alcove and I peered to see if I could make out any features, but it was too dark. The figure kneeled beside Sam, then reached into the pocket of his hoodie to extract something that gave a transient gleam as it caught the headlight of a passing car.

'Now,' I whispered. Anjoli and I exploded out of our hiding place and sprinted across the road, my legs trembling from sitting still so long. Intent on what he was doing, the figure didn't notice us for the few seconds it took us to cross the road, then turned towards me as I put my arms around his waist and pulled him off Sam, who was sitting up, a confused look on his face.

The body felt slight in the grip of my arms, and as I twisted the man around, the light hit his face . . . *What?* No. It couldn't be . . .

Chapter 47

Saturday.

N aila?
I let her go as though she had given me a ten-thousand-volt electric shock, and she stumbled to the ground. Anjoli and Sam looked at her, utter bewilderment on their faces.

'Naila? What . . . what are *you* doing here?'

She looked at me, stupefaction on her face. Then she sat up and rubbed her side.

'Ow. Kamil, what the hell! What did you do that for?'

I couldn't get any of this to make sense. Why was Naila here? Had Anjoli called her?

'We thought you were the homeless-killer. I don't understand. Why are you here at 3.30 in the morning?'

'I couldn't sleep. Everything was swimming in my head: Salim Uncle, Imran, me having no more options, and I started thinking about what you had said about . . . Sam, is it?' She smiled at Sam, who was now sitting up, staring at us. 'I just wanted to check he was okay. All your talk of homeless people dying got to me, and I couldn't bear another death after all that had happened. Why did you rugby-tackle me?'

Anjoli whispered, 'What's that in your hand, Naila? Show me.'

My gaze dropped to Naila's right hand. For a moment it looked like she was going to demur, then she opened it, revealing a large syringe full of a clear liquid.

I didn't understand but said, 'Let me look after that,' and with the sleeve of my shirt over my hand, I plucked it out of hers and put it in my pocket, needle upwards.

'What's in the syringe, Naila?' said Anjoli softly. 'What were you about to inject Sam with?'

'Don't be silly, Anjoli. I wasn't going to inject him with anything. It was an old syringe of insulin I'd prepared for Salim Uncle.'

'You keep filled syringes of insulin with exposed needles in your hoodie pocket?'

'Not normally, no. But I'd prepared it for him the night he . . . died.' Naila's voice broke. But her eyes were watchful.

I was lost for words. Anjoli turned to look at me, and the clouds of my confusion parted. Naila's story about coming to check on Sam made no sense, so what was going on? I couldn't, wouldn't, believe Naila could have anything to do with the homeless killing. It was ridiculous. But we needed to sort this out.

'We're going back to Anjoli's to discuss this.'

'I can't. I'm glad Sam's okay, but I have to return to the hotel. Imran will be worried.'

'It won't take long,' said Anjoli, stone in her voice.

'I'm parked around the corner. I'll get a ticket.'

'You won't. Let's go.'

'What are you all doing?' complained Sam.

'Nothing,' I said. 'Go back to sleep, Sam. Let's go, Naila.'

Sam focused on Naila, then said, 'That's her! That's the person I saw with Yasir the morning he died. I recognise the coat.'

I felt like I was about to vomit as I gripped Naila's arm, and we walked in silence for ten minutes back to Anjoli's flat, where we sat in her ash-covered kitchen, dawn creeping over the sky outside.

'I need to get back to the hotel, Kamil,' said Naila. 'Imran will be angry when he sees I'm not there. I told him I was going out for a walk because I couldn't sleep. What were you and Anjoli doing there?'

I was finding it difficult to form any words. 'What would be the impact of injecting that much insulin into a non-diabetic?'

Naila paused. 'Why would anyone do that?'

'You're a nurse. Humour me. What would be the effect of doing that?'

Another pause. Then, 'Hypoglycaemic shock.'

'What's that?' said Anjoli.

'Severe reduction in blood sugar levels.'

'And what's the effect of that?' I said.

'Fainting.'

'No worse? We can check, Naila. I'm sure I can google it.'

She shrugged. 'Sometimes coma. Death.'

My heart broke like a promise. An iridescent bubble reflecting the sun vanished into an unremarkable set of disintegrating droplets.

Naila?

Why?

How?

Nothing made sense.

I forced myself to ask the next question. 'And is it detectable after death?'

'It's formed naturally in the body, so I guess not. Unless you're looking for it.'

'And they wouldn't look for it, would they? Why, Naila?'

'Why what?'

I had to come out and say it: 'Why did you kill those homeless men?'

She stared at me for a moment, then laughed.

'Are you serious? What are you talking about? I didn't kill anyone. Why would I? I told you I just came to check on Sam. Anyway, you saw the video – it was a guy. And that woman you met in the gurdwara, you said she told you a *man* had attacked her. Are you crazy? Why were *you* guys there?'

That gave me pause. She was right. The person in the video with Louis had definitely been a man. But Sam had identified Naila as the person he had seen with Yasir. Were there two killers preying on the homeless? This was impossible.

'We clocked the vodka bottle and figured the murderer would come, so we staked him out,' I said.

'Clever. You're a clever detective, Kamil. I always said so. Look how you solved Salma's killing.'

'Tower Hamlets and Lambeth!' exclaimed Anjoli.

'What?' said Naila.

'You live in Tower Hamlets and go to college and work in Lambeth. That's where the deaths happened.'

'I know nothing about that. What's got into the two of you? Do I look like a murderer? I'm a bloody nurse, for God's sake. I save people. I have to go now, Kamil. This is just silly. You'll be embarrassed in the morning. My side's hurting where you attacked me, and I need to check my wound hasn't reopened. Daddy and Aunty will be worried. I have to organise my trip back to Pakistan. Daddy and Imran are insisting I go back with them, and I can't refuse. Can I have my syringe back, please?'

She held her hand out towards me.

'No, I think I'll hold on to it for now. Naila, I am going to tell the police about this. They *will* go back and check CCTV around where the others died, and one of the cameras will have caught you.'

'They can do what they like. As you said, Anjoli, I live here and work there so it would surprise me if I wasn't on CCTV somewhere.'

'But why *Sam*, Naila? What did he do to you?' said Anjoli.

Then it hit me.

I turned to Anjoli. 'She thought he might identify her to the police! She was there when we told Tahir about Sam seeing Yasir's killer and you suggested he get a sketch. It must have spooked her. She was making sure he couldn't talk to Tahir. And she switched the gin for vodka because she knew we suspected the gin!'

Naila gave an unconvincing laugh. 'God, you two! These are crazy conspiracy theories.'

'She targeted old men because they were more vulnerable, and people wouldn't think about why they had died. They would have expected them to die, anyway. But why the gin Naila? Why leave them with gin before you killed them?'

'Guys, I don't know what you're talking about. Kamil told me you had this bee in your bonnet, Anjoli, and said you were a little crazy. But Kamil, you're a rational guy – can you even hear yourself? It was a man! Not me!'

I ignored Naila's attempt to drive a wedge between me and Anjoli. 'If they were drunk, it was easier for you to inject them. That was it, wasn't it? That's why you left the alcohol.'

'Just listen to yourself, Kamil. You know me. Is this what I would do? I'm doing nursing to help people, not kill them. I'm so disappointed in you . . . and you said you loved me.' She shook her head and put on her coat.

'Maybe she has something else in her pockets,' said Anjoli.

Before Naila could move, I thrust my hands into her coat pocket and extracted two 100ml vials marked *NovoRapid Insulin Aspart*.

'Also for Salim Mian, I assume?' I said, taking the syringe from my pocket and waving it at her, along with the bottles.

She grabbed at them, but I jerked my arm away.

'Fine, keep it,' she said. 'Have the insulin too. The amount of sweet stuff you eat, you'll need it soon.'

'You steal this from the hospital. I saw the fridge where it's kept in the ward. The key was in the lock. You used to get insulin for Salim Mian, anyway.'

'Poor Salim Uncle. Kamil, if only you had let him come home that night, he would still be with us. Anyway, don't blame yourself, it was his time.'

I ignored her barb, knowing it would smart later.

'Why, Naila? Why were you killing them?' said Anjoli.

Naila ignored her, looked around the smoke-streaked kitchen with a concerned smile on her face, then stroked my cheek. I grasped her wrist and shoved away her hand, trying to control my fury at her transparent manipulation. How had I never seen this side of her?

'What about the Hippocratic oath, Naila? First do no harm?'

'That's for doctors, not nurses,' she said and walked out of the flat as we watched, not knowing what to do.

'Are you just going to let her go?' said Anjoli.

I collapsed on the kitchen chair, all the strength leaving my body, feeling numb. 'What am I supposed to do? Arrest her?'

'There must be something . . .'

'I'll . . . call Tahir and give him the syringe and the bottles, I'm not sure what else we can do. I've got no power here, Anjoli.' I could barely remain upright. I leaned my elbows on the table and held my head in my hands. 'I'm so tired.'

Anjoli pulled up a chair next to me and swallowed. 'I'm so sorry, Kamil. I would never have imagined . . . ? I just don't understand.'

'She was so . . . matter of fact.' I could hardly get the words out. 'An answer for everything.'

'Psychopaths create their own reality,' said my psychologist boss. 'They bend the world to their will. They can be very convincing. Who knows, she may have thought she was doing the homeless a favour, relieving them of their burden.'

'She always went on about how she wanted to ease suffering. How many people did you say had died? Twenty-five? Thirty? It's unbelievable. I can't believe it. Naila?'

I imagined Naila setting out every two weeks on her mission of mercy, feeling the satisfaction of a job well done every time she extinguished a life. Did she look at them as they died? Hold them? Nurse them in their last moments, that caring look of Mary looking down at Jesus on her face?

'What are we going to do about it, Kamil?' said Anjoli, bringing me back from my reverie.

'Tell Tahir. I don't know how easy it will be to prove anything, though. She won't have left any fingerprints on the vodka bottle; she's too clever for that. Maybe they could check the bodies for insulin, but they will all have been cremated or buried by now. I can't see them going to the trouble of exhuming Yasir's corpse. And who knows if any traces remain after all this time. Maybe they'll find injection marks, but that won't prove anything.'

'*And* she's going back to Pakistan, so they won't be able to arrest her. Her father will make sure of that. But there's something I don't understand, Kamil. Who stabbed her? And why? Did that have something to do with these killings and not Salma's then?'

'I don't know. You were right though, Anjoli. There were at least two crimes – Salma's and the homeless murders. Maybe Naila's stabbing was a third – Imran wanting her to come home. And who was the man with Louis? I'm so tired I can't think. I need to give all this to Tahir. I'm done in. Let's try to get some sleep. Maybe it'll be clearer in the morning.'

I texted Tahir to call me as soon as he could.

'My God, Anjoli if it hadn't been for your doggedness, we wouldn't have caught her. I'm so glad you had that bee in your bonnet. And I never said you were crazy. I'd never do that.'

'Yes, you would,' said Anjoli and kissed my cheek. 'She was just doing what manipulative people do. Gaslighting us. I can't believe she fooled us for so long. I really liked her.'

'So did I.'

I found a transparent freezer bag, put the syringe and the bottles of insulin in it, placed them in the fridge and went up to my bed, weary and sick of life. Part of me wished Naila had injected *me* with that insulin. All I wanted, more than anything in the world, was to lie down, close my eyes and never wake up again.

Chapter 48

Sunday

I *really liked her.*
So did I.

The words rang round and round in my head like the son-
orous vibration of an off-key string. I felt like an utter fool. I'd
been besotted with . . . who? A cold-blooded killer. The embarrassment and hurt gnawed at my gut till my sides ached. How
could I have been so blind? What was Anjoli thinking of me?

What kind of detective was I if I couldn't spot a sociopath
right in front of my face? My mind traced over my every inter-
action with Naila. What clues had I missed? Where had I gone
wrong? Had she lied about *everything*? Imran abusing her in
Pakistan? No, Salim Mian had corroborated that. Hadn't he?
Could I have misunderstood? Was Naila innocent? Was it that
man in the baseball cap? No. I remembered the harshness in
her that had slipped out a few times the night before. I went to
the bathroom and threw up. Then got into the shower and tried
to wash everything off me – the soot, the guilt, the incompetence. But it would take a lot more than soap and water to rid me
of the stench of burned failure. What the fuck was wrong with
me and my choices?

A cold, savage rage came over me. *How could I have allowed
her to do this to me?* I felt something I never had before – a deep,
atavistic desire to hurt. To make Naila suffer for humiliating me.

For using me. I dug my nails into the palms of my hands, squeezed my eyes shut, buried my face into my pillow and screamed, trying in vain to expel the darkness I was feeling.

If only it were that easy.

'I've been googling,' Anjoli announced the next morning as I made my way down for a late breakfast, not wanting to face her in the state I was in.

'Uh-uh?'

'Insulin kills healthy people. There was a nurse in Canada – Elizabeth Wettlaufer – who killed eight patients with insulin between 2007 and 2016. Maybe Naila got the idea from her. I made a few notes. If the person is drunk, that masks the signs of hypoglycaemia and also reduces their blood sugar, so an insulin injection is more likely to kill. That's why she gave them the gin. Just one of those vials she had on her would cause coma or death in a non-diabetic. This NovoRapid is like its name – it acts fast. And because she was going after older people, they may already have high blood pressure or thyroid problems, which make death even more likely. And you don't need to inject it in a vein! Just a needle jab through a jacket into the upper arm of a sleeping homeless person would do the job. By the time they knew something had happened, she'd be gone.'

Every word Anjoli said was another nail in the coffin of my self-respect. It all made sense. Naila had planned the whole thing. I felt like I was falling down an endless hole, desperate to hit ground even if it flattened me.

Anjoli saw my face, stopped her pharmacology lesson and said, 'Have you heard from Tahir?'

'I need a coffee. God, this place still stinks! Do you think we will ever get rid of the smell? No, nothing from Tahir. I've left him another message. It's Sunday, so he may not be answering his phone. Must be with someone, knowing him. I'll keep trying.'

My throat was raw; the smell wormed its way everywhere. I made myself coffee and inhaled the aroma, hoping it would cover up the stench, but it was no help.

'I'm going to take all my clothes to the laundry today and see if that helps. Insurance should fix the storeroom and pay for the smoke damage,' said Anjoli. 'I hope they don't mess me around. Maybe I need one of those deep-clean specialists the police use on crime scenes. But forget all that. Listen, we have to do something before Naila runs away to Pakistan.'

'I know. But what? I'm even wondering if she was involved in Salma's killing. It just seems like such a coincidence. Salma's death at the hands of Mackenzie and these homeless killings, all at the same time. And then Naila's stabbing – who did that? Who was the guy with Louis? And those threats against her. There has to be a clue we are missing . . .'

'Maybe she made up the threats?'

'But we saw the texts.'

Anjoli started tapping into trusty Google on her phone. My phone pinged – I had a text from an unknown number: *See, you can literally fake texts to your phone.*

'Okay, but why? What did she have to gain? And she didn't fake the stabbing. I was right there on the steps of the station when it happened. And the police found the Stanley knife on the station concourse.'

'Do you think,' said Anjoli, eyes widening 'that *she* might have been Mackenzie's lover and not Salma?'

Silence covered us like a shroud.

Could that be it?

I had thought nothing could make me feel worse. I was wrong.

Was it possible? If so, they had concealed it very well. I

replayed the meetings between her, Mackenzie and me. Was there anything there? What had I missed?

'How could we prove it if she was?' I said.

'Her mobile? There would be messages and calls.'

'She won't hand it over to me. I could ask Tahir, I suppose. I wonder if they found Mackenzie's phone.'

We sat in silence as I chewed on a piece of toast and pondered. There was one way.

'Get dressed. We need to get to Waterloo.'

The manager at Venezia recognised me as we walked in just past noon. 'Ah, signor. Have you decided about your party now? Ready to book it?'

'I am a detective, and we are looking into a serious crime. Could I please speak to Marco, your waiter?'

'Marco? Why?'

'It's important. I'll explain later.'

He gave me a disbelieving look, but shouted, 'Marco, c'è qualcuno qui per te!'

A young man wearing a striped gondolier's shirt came running.

'Sì?'

'Marco, hi. My name is Kamil Rahman, and I'm a detective. I just need your help with something. Do you recognise this man? He ate here a couple of weeks ago.'

I showed him the picture of Mackenzie from the college website.

Marco squinted at it. 'Sì, I think so. He sit at one of my tables.'

'Do you remember who was with him?'

'A beautiful woman. Bella signorina.'

'Was this her?' I showed him a picture of Naila.

I waited, heart on pause, as he peered at the picture on my phone.

He smiled. 'Sì, sì. That is the lady. Beautiful green eyes. Very romantic couple. Very loving.'

I exhaled, unaware I had been holding my breath.

I had been played for even more of a fool than I'd thought.

Chapter 49

Sunday.

Anjoli and I stood on the narrow street outside the restaurant, hemmed in by the long terrace of houses around us. I felt like I couldn't breathe, even though I was out in the open, the sky as blank as my soul. Naila had been living a lie with me for months. Why? What had I done to her? Why had she played these games with me? I had initiated nothing. She was the one who had kissed me on that dance floor. I felt used. The blossoming relationship I'd felt so excited about was just a cover for her affair with a balding lecturer going through a midlife crisis. What the actual fuck?

We stood there as I tried to piece things together. My rage went icy and brought clarity.

'Salma was never having an affair with Mackenzie. She saw him with Naila that night at the restaurant. They were being lovey-dovey, and it shocked her. Salma was a straightforward girl, wanting to do the right thing. She threatened to blow the whistle on Mackenzie if he didn't break it off. Remember, she made an appointment with the dean for Wednesday morning.'

'Why didn't she speak to Naila?'

'She must have. There was something awkward between them at the restaurant.'

Anjoli thought for a second. 'You're right, they seemed a little off. And Mackenzie couldn't afford to have it come out, so he killed Salma?'

'And neither could Naila. She'd have to go back to Pakistan if it became known. And her life would be even more miserable than it was before.'

'My God, you're right. Naila must have known Mackenzie was going to see Salma when she was with us in the restaurant that night.'

'And when we went to give the phone back, Naila knew he was up there killing Salma. She must have texted to tell him we were on our way. *That's* why she didn't want Salma to come back to the restaurant to pick up the phone herself; she wouldn't have been home for Mackenzie.'

I felt sick as I contemplated Naila's Machiavellian behaviour. And then even more nauseous when I remembered us making out in the car. Had she *known* Salma was being strangled at that time? This was insane!

'Anjoli, this is too much. I need to sit down and have a drink.'

We went into the Kings Arms, an old-fashioned pub near the restaurant. It was busy, but Anjoli found us a table as I bought a packet of crisps and a pint of Guinness for myself and a vodka tonic for her.

I took a deep swig of the cold, velvety, bittersweet stout and wiped the trace of foamy head from my mouth.

'How are you doing?' Anjoli took a sip of her cocktail.

'I've been a fool.'

'It's easy to fall for someone trying to trap you. One downside of being a romantic.'

'*You* wouldn't have.'

'Well, I'm just a hard-headed bitch. Although . . .'

'Although what?'

'Maybe I was wrong about not wanting someone in my life.

Maybe it wouldn't be an additional burden; maybe someone could help carry my load.'

She fingered the brooch I had bought her. I didn't know if she was saying this to make me feel better, but I felt a lightening in my soul.

'As long as it wasn't a psychopath.'

'True dat.' She smiled. 'So, what does all this mean, then? If Naila was involved in Salma's death?'

I brought myself back to our immediate problem.

'If she was, then it changes everything. Let's work it out. She had to divert attention away from Mackenzie because she didn't want to be found out; it was as much about protecting herself as it was about him. In fact, the morning I went to interview Mackenzie with her, his assistant said something like "Nice to see you again." Maybe she was there that morning planning things with him.'

'Trying to frame Ziad?'

'Yes.'

Another insight struck.

'The hoodie! Shit! It was her! She must have taken it from Mackenzie because she knew I'd seen it. When we went to visit Ziad at his house, I asked her to leave the room because I wanted to talk to him alone. She must have planted it in his cupboard then. She knew that would lead the police to Ziad. And it worked. For a while.'

'But didn't the police find Ziad's hair in the hood?'

'She could have grabbed a few strands from his comb and put it there. We know her capacity for deception now.'

'And she could have sent those threatening texts to herself and invented that call to make it seem like a racial crime. What about the stabbing, though? Who did that?'

I tried to remember the sequence of events at Waterloo. Naila wearing her backpack, following me to the platform.

'She did it to herself. She must have.'

I shut my eyes and imagined the scene. Top of the stairs. Naila takes a knife out of her backpack, jabs it into her side where she knows the injury will be superficial, drops it in the crowd, then falls screaming down the steps.

'That's why they didn't get anyone on CCTV.'

'But why?' said Anjoli.

'To ensure Mackenzie was in the clear. We were closing in on him for Salma's killing. He made sure he had an alibi for Naila's stabbing. So if the police believed it was the same person who did both crimes, he couldn't have been Salma's killer. It sent us running off in the wrong direction, didn't it? If it hadn't been for Roisin, he would have got away with it. And when I mentioned Imran as a suspect, she let me run with it to muddy the waters.'

I looked at my phone again. 'Where the bloody hell is Tahir? You know, props to Naila. It takes guts to stab yourself in the middle of Waterloo station, then walk on as if nothing has happened to get a few yards away from the weapon. Got to admire her balls.'

Anjoli looked at me, shock on her face. 'She's a fucking sociopath, Kamil! What do you mean you've got to admire her! You had a lucky escape.'

'I know, I didn't mean . . . You're right. I'm an idiot. Sorry.'

'You sure you're okay? I mean . . . this must be awful, given how you felt about her and—'

'I . . . I feel like I've lost something. Something I'll never get back.'

She gave me a minute, kindness in her eyes.

'It wasn't real, Kamil. It's terrible, and I'm sorry, but there it is. It was an infatuation. You thought you were in love with an image of the perfect woman. You'd only known her for five minutes.'

I felt like an idiot but couldn't deny her words. It had been a weird rebound from Anjoli, if you can actually rebound from a relationship you haven't had.

'You're right, of course, but still . . .' Then something struck me. 'If she was so close to Mackenzie, I wonder if *he* was involved with the homeless killings? Maybe they were doing it together? But no. Agnes said the guy who attacked her was American.'

'OMG! Yes! Mackenzie *was* the man on the video. An Irish accent *can* sound American! *He* would give them the alcohol and she would administer the injection! That would explain her desperation to keep their affair quiet. If that got out, who knows what else might have. It wasn't just an affair they were trying to hide, it was the fact they were both murderers! When he tried to burn the restaurant down, she was terrified he was losing it and would drop her in it. You know what? She must have been relieved when he killed himself.'

'You're right. She didn't seem at all upset by his death.'

'Or maybe she killed him! I wouldn't put it past her.'

I considered this, then shook my head.

'That's going a little far. We found him together, remember. We were with her in Salim Mian's house the night before. I doubt even she could have sneaked out to Bermondsey in the middle of the night without both of us noticing, staged a suicide leaving no forensic traces, come back, washed up, crept past me on the sofa and got back into the bed she was sharing with you. Even you aren't that deep a sleeper.'

'She probably drugged us,' said Anjoli darkly. 'I wouldn't put it past her. The bitch.'

'I think we'd have known. I bet she took Mackenzie's phone when we were in the house, though. She was alone in his room when you found the body. And read his note to ensure she wasn't incriminated, or she'd have taken that too. He said he was having an affair with Salma to protect her – even before he died, he was looking after Naila.'

The power she had over men – Mackenzie, Imran, me – made me shudder.

Anjoli drained her drink as the enormity of what we had just deduced came over us. 'But she wouldn't have risked keeping hold of the phone, would she? She must have got rid of it by now.'

'I guess so.'

'Those Vitamin D tablets she gave you! Do you think that maybe . . . ?'

An icy snake crawled up my back.

'No . . . Why would she? Fuck.'

'Have you been feeling okay?'

'I think so – just exhausted. I'd better give them to Tahir to analyse. Where the hell is he, anyway?'

'With one of his conquests, where else? Last night was Tinder night.'

I tried him again and this time he answered.

'What do you want, Kamil? It's my day off. And . . . I'm not alone.'

'Sorry, Tahir, it's urgent. You'll have to get rid of her. Can you meet us at the restaurant in half an hour? We've found the homeless killer . . . No, I can't tell you over the phone . . . Thanks. See you soon.'

Sitting next to me on the train, Anjoli said, 'Wow. She's a bloody criminal mastermind. I'm just wondering what I could have achieved at twenty-one if I'd had half the initiative and nous she's shown.'

I gave a grim laugh that came out like a snort. 'Well, you weren't half as desperate as she was. The biggest worry you had at that age was handing an essay in on time and how to increase your alcohol tolerance.'

I wished the train would go faster. I was worried Naila would abscond any time now and regretted not going to the police station the previous night. 'Anyway, they weren't that smart. They were desperate and making it up as they were going along. The hoodie to frame Ziad turned out to be a terrible idea. The stabbing and the threatening texts confused matters, but the confusion didn't help them.'

'Can we prove any of this?'

'I don't know.'

'Maybe we should have let her inject Sam, then we'd have proof.'

'Anjoli!' It was my turn to be shocked.

'We could have got him to a hospital in time to reverse it or whatever. Now we literally have nothing. I can't stand the thought of her getting away with it. What if we told her father?'

'He'd protect her. Any father would. Imran will too.'

'Imran. She was good at putting suspicion on him for the stabbing. Poor guy. Why do you think she was doing this, Kamil? Why prey on the homeless?'

'I really don't know, Anjoli. But remember what she told us at Salim Mian's funeral? How she was doing good in the world and now she had to go back. She often told me she couldn't stand seeing people in pain. But maybe I'm just making excuses for her. Come on. Tahir will know what to do. We are going to get her; I can feel it in my bones.'

Chapter 50

Sunday.

'Not too bad,' said Tahir, looking around the restaurant as he sat down. 'Get rid of the smell and you're in business. This had better be important, Miss Marple; you screwed up my Sunday morning. I think she was the one, and I had to tell her I was on a big case so had to rush off. She wasn't happy.'

'I'm sure the big-shot cop impressed her doing big-shot cop things. Did you show her your massive truncheon?' said Anjoli, bringing out three Cobra beers.

'Wouldn't you like to know?'

'It is important, Tahir. Thanks for coming, we appreciate it. Listen . . .' I laid out all we had learned. He listened without interrupting, sipping his frosty beer.

A long silence after I finished. Then, 'That's quite a story. Your girlfriend! I'm sorry, Kamil.'

'Yeah, well, I was stupid. Not any more, though. Here's the syringe and the insulin we found on her.' I handed him the baggie.

He toyed with it for a few seconds, saying nothing.

'So, do you think you have enough to charge her?' said Anjoli.

He thought for a second. 'Take her in for questioning, for sure. Charge her? I don't know. There's no direct evidence. It's all circumstantial.'

'Well, everyone who could give direct evidence is dead. Almost thirty homeless people, Salma, Mackenzie, Louis, Yasir . . .'

'Sam identified her. And you could check CCTV footage around the homeless deaths,' I said.

'Going back eighteen months? I doubt it. Most of it is probably erased by now.'

'We think Mackenzie may have been doing the homeless killings with her.' I explained our theory.

'Interesting. We found a receipt from a wine warehouse for twenty-four half-bottles of gardenia gin in his house. We thought that was odd. They were the same as at the homeless deaths.'

'That proves it! He did it with her,' said Anjoli.

'It's a link in the chain,' said Tahir. 'But it proves nothing.'

'Maybe we can get her to confess to us somehow. You could wire us up and swoop in when she does.'

'The old, "It's no good, John, he knows. Let me spill the beans." That only happens on TV, Anjoli. It's rare that anyone confesses like that.'

'You're not being very helpful,' I said.

'I'm being realistic. Look, I'll take her in and lay all this out and see if she lets anything slip. But if she's as smart as you say she is, she won't. We need something to physically connect her to the crimes. It'll take time to get a warrant, and she must have got rid of anything incriminating by now.'

'Maybe I can search her house when you take her in?'

'I didn't hear that. What did you say?'

'He said—' started Anjoli.

I interrupted: 'Oh nothing, I misspoke.'

'Well, no time like the present. Let's go.'

'Don't you need to tell your boss?'

'It's Sunday; he'll be golfing. I don't want to disturb him. I can handle it.'

Tahir was hungry for glory. He wanted the kudos of being the maverick cop who collared the killer. I could tell; I'd been there.

As long as he stopped Naila, I didn't care any more if it was through my sweat that he won his glory. I'd be happy for him.

Naila didn't look at all surprised when Tahir, Anjoli and I turned up at Salim Mian's front door. I couldn't bring myself to look at her.

'Ms Alvi,' said Tahir, 'we have a few questions for you. Could you please accompany me to the station?'

'So formal. What's this about, Tahir? I'm alone here; my father and Aunty have gone to see her relatives.'

'Please come with me. We can talk at the station.'

'Have these two been wasting your time with stories about last night? I told them it was perfectly innocent – I'm not sure what I can tell you.'

'That's fine. I'm sure we can clear it all up there. Please get your things. Can you bring your mobile phone as well?'

'I'm sorry, Sergeant. I'm afraid I lost it.'

'Oh yes?'

'Yes, I think I dropped it in the mosque when I became dizzy at my uncle's funeral yesterday. You remember, Kamil, don't you? I got stabbed as you know, officer, and it was all too much for me. But ask the mosque, and if they find it, you can have it; I have nothing to hide.'

'Did you call the imam to ask if he has it?' I said.

'No, I haven't had time. Would you be a darling and check for me?' She gave me a loving smile that renewed my rage.

I controlled myself as she accompanied Tahir to his car. Anjoli said, 'Oh, I need to use the toilet. You take her to the station Tahir; I'll shut the door when I finish.'

Naila grinned at Anjoli's amateur theatrics but got into the car with Tahir, leaving us in the house.

'She knows there's nothing for us to find,' I said. 'That's why she was fine with us being here.'

'She may have missed something.'

We went up to Naila's bedroom and searched her cupboard ('Nice clothes. She has style, your psycho girlfriend'), drawers ('Her room is so neat, not a pigsty like mine; she must be a Marie Kondo fanatic') and under her bed ('God she even hoovers under the bed').

After half an hour we realised we had nothing. Naila had been careful. If there had ever been anything incriminating, it was gone now.

Anjoli flopped down on Naila's bed, said 'Ow,' then reached under the covers and pulled out the MacBook she'd sat on.

'Aha!'

I sat next to her as she opened it to see a pretty picture of waves breaking on a beach, fishing boats in the background. The thought of the weekend by the sea I'd organised for us thrust into my heart.

In the middle of the picture, it said *Naila Alvi* with a blank box for a password.

'Go on, lover boy. What's her password? This is our last chance.'

'How am I supposed to know? Try "Password".'

'Doubt she's that stupid. Nope, she isn't. Any other guesses? When's her birthday?'

'I don't know.'

'You don't even know your girlfriend's birthday, no wonder she went psycho.'

I was getting annoyed. 'She's *not* my girlfriend. Look, here's her passport. Knock yourself out.'

Anjoli entered various combinations, to no avail.

'Favourite pet?'

'No idea.'

'Husband's name?'

'Imran Akram.'

'Nope, that doesn't work either. Neither did Kamil Rahman, I'm afraid. Favourite movie?'

In films they made this look easy.

'She said she liked Bollywood movies. And film noir.'

'Figures. It would be hilarious if her password was "Psycho". Damn, it isn't.' She tried a few more, murmuring under her breath. Then, 'Okay, I give up. I'd be a shit identity thief,' and she slammed the laptop shut.

A memory came to me. A kiss under a mirror ball. *This is my favourite song.*

'Try "Survivor".'

'She is that. OMG! I'm in! How did you guess that?' She high-fived me. 'Even her bloody computer desktop is tidy. I have a thousand and one documents on mine. Let's start with browser history. Hmm, very vanilla, your girlfriend. Nope, nothing dodgy. Expedia, few newspapers. Okay, let's try her Gmail account. Same password, no sense of security, Ms Murderess. Expedia again. Oh look, she's booked her ticket back to Pakistan. Leaving tomorrow. We have very little time. She's emptied her deleted mail folder.'

'She may have outwitted us. What were you hoping to find? A folder called, "My Favourite Murders" with pictures of her victims? A shoebox under the bed full of amputated fingers?'

'At least I'm trying. Here's an emailed receipt from Royal Mail. Looks like she mailed a package to Lahore this morning. Addressed to her dad. Are post offices open on Sunday?'

'I think some are. Does it say what it is?'

'Nope. I bet it's her mobile.'

'Maybe. Don't see how we can get it, though. Check her photos. Maybe something there.'

Anjoli checked. Nothing. Naila wasn't much of a photographer. Mouth twitching, Anjoli showed me the selfie Naila had taken with me in the club before we had kissed. When I didn't rise to the bait, she clicked around more but just found home-work assignments and various nursing references.

'Shit, nothing.'

'That's why she didn't care if we stayed. She's got rid of every-thing. I bet it's all on her and Mackenzie's phones. But their iPhones are at the bottom of the river or on their way to Pakistan.'

Anjoli's head jerked up. 'iPhones . . . I wonder . . .'

She tapped around. 'Kamil, look.'

Hidden away in the computer she had found Apple's Messages app.

'What's that?'

'Apple backs up all your iPhone-to-iPhone conversations on the Mac if you're signed in with the same account. Naila must not have known. *Look!*'

It was all there.

Messages from Naila to Mackenzie.

From Mackenzie to Naila.

Arranging to meet. Explicit messages from her telling him what she wanted him to do to her. Nude selfies. She had him smitten enough to do her bidding. Then, from the night of Salma's murder: *K and I have to come and deliver S's phone. Try to persuade her and get out. I'll delay as much as I can. Good luck. I hope she's sensible.*

Ok

He's on his way up

It was all there. Forget a smoking gun, this was an exploding howitzer.

'We've got her!' said Anjoli, wonderment in her voice.

'Yes.'

But I couldn't feel anything any more.

Chapter 51

Sunday.

An Uber rushed us to Bethnal Green police station, where we asked for Sergeant Ismail. The man at the desk told us he was busy and couldn't be disturbed but Anjoli persuaded him it was vital, to do with the suspect he was interviewing, and he would want to see us.

Tahir came out five minutes later and shook his head. 'No luck. She has an answer for everything. I tried. She wouldn't even admit to having an affair with Mackenzie. Said she had dinner with him but that was innocent. I'm sorry, I don't think we can hold her.'

'We have something,' I said. 'Look.'

His eyes widened as he saw the texts. I also told him about the plane ticket to Pakistan and the package she had posted.

A shark smile crossed his face. He closed the app and snapped the laptop shut. 'I could kiss you! Right, leave it to me.'

'Any chance we can watch?'

'No way. That's against all the regs. The guvnor would have my hide.'

'Come on, Tahir,' said Anjoli. 'We've given you *everything*. You owe us. You'll get your inspectorship out of this, you know that!'

He looked around. 'If you ever say anything . . .' and took us through into the observation room with the one-way glass next to the interview room where Naila was sitting, looking at her nails as if she was waiting for a manicure. 'Not a word,' he whispered and went in to her.

He restarted the tape recorder, put the computer on the table between them and said, 'For the purposes of the tape, I am showing Ms Alvi a computer. Ms Alvi, do you recognise this laptop?'

'It looks like mine. Where did you get it?'

He dodged the question. 'Would you mind if we looked inside?'

She hesitated, and I could see her working out what might be on it. Then she appeared to decide she was safe and said, 'No, not at all. I have nothing to hide.'

She opened the laptop, tapped in her password and handed it to him.

Tahir took his time. Opened her Gmail account and said, 'You're leaving for Pakistan tomorrow?'

'Yes,' she said, getting comfortable on her chair. 'With my uncle's demise, my father and husband want me to go back with them. I'm sad I won't get to finish my course and will miss all the friends I've made here, like Kamil and Anjoli.'

She looked straight at the mirror on her side of the room and Anjoli and I flinched. There was no way she could know we were in here. But still . . .

'And what was in this package you posted to Pakistan this morning? The receipt is in your Gmail account.'

She stiffened. 'Some personal possessions.'

'Why not take them with you since you're going tomorrow, anyway?'

She seemed at a momentary loss. Then, smooth, 'Can I be honest, officer?'

'Of course, Ms Alvi. It's always best to be honest.'

'See, I have bought a few pieces of jewellery as a present. And Pakistani customs charge a lot of duty on things like that. I didn't want to declare the jewellery so posted it.'

'I see. And can you prove that?'

'Certainly.' She fumbled in her handbag and passed him a piece of paper.

Tahir glanced at it and said, 'For the tape, Ms Alvi has handed me a printout of a Secursus insurance receipt for a package to Pakistan sent by Royal Mail. It says "Jewellery" under description.'

Naila leaned back, a catlike smile on her face.

'Shit, she is smart,' said Anjoli.

'Wait for it . . .'

And sure enough as if he had heard me, Sergeant Ismail then said, 'And how do you explain these messages?'

He turned the laptop towards Naila.

She looked at the screen. Her mouth opened, but no words emerged. She reached for the computer, but Tahir was too fast for her and pulled it back. He kept the screen pointed towards her as he scrolled through, reading out a few choice messages.

She gazed at the mirror. I could see her calculating, face a complete blank. Anjoli had been squeezing my hand with the power of an industrial vice, and it hurt. But Naila's beautiful face hypnotised me as she was staring through the glass into my eyes, as if she was saying, 'You did this to me. And I thought you loved me.'

'Ms Alvi? Anything to say?'

She looked back at him and said, 'I'm done here. I need to go back to see my father. You said that I could leave whenever I wanted. Well, I want to leave now. May I have my laptop back? I don't know how you got it, but I didn't give you permission to bring it here. They stole it from my room.' She held out her hand.

'You gave me permission to examine it, Ms Alvi. I have that on tape. And I'm afraid you can't leave yet; I have many more questions for you. You see these messages not only make you an accessory to Salma Ali's murder, they also implicate you in the murders of many homeless people around London for the last –' he scrolled down to the last few messages '– eighteen months.

You and Mr Mackenzie were busy. You may have posted your phone to Pakistan, but you didn't know Apple tries to be helpful in case you lose your phone. Here's an interesting one, the night of Ms Ali's death, from Mr Mackenzie to you: *Saw a sad homeless guy in front of Mosque on way to S. I think he needs your Mercy. Gave him GG as a present.* I assume *GG* is gardenia gin?'

Her usual equanimity cracked, and fury moved over her face like a stain. I had never seen this display of emotion from her before; it was fascinating to behold.

'And, on the day of Dr Mackenzie's death he sent you a text: *My love. I am so sorry for all I have put you through. I couldn't lose you and I did what I did to her for you. I can't bear the thought of you going back to Pakistan to your wretched control freak of a husband. I don't know what to do. I can't go on any more. I have put you in danger. Ro and the kids have left me. If I can't be with you, I am done and can't see any way forward except to end it all.*

'And your reply: *I understand my love. Do what you have to do. My love will be with you for ever in this world and the next. Find peace my Jaan.*

'Convenient for you, wasn't it?'

'My laptop, please,' Naila repeated, her voice controlled but beginning to crack.

Tahir shut the laptop and said, 'Naila Alvi, I am arresting you for the murder of Yasir Abadi and for being an accessory to the murder of Salma Ali. You do not have to say anything. But it may harm your defence if you do not mention when questioned something which you later rely on in court. Anything you do say may be given in evidence.'

Abadi. I didn't know Yasir's surname had been Abadi. A faint memory came back from my Koranic lessons – eternal. That's what Abadi meant. Now he could spend eternity knowing we had brought him justice.

Chapter 52

Three weeks later. Saturday.

A banner hung over the front of the restaurant:
TANDOORI KNIGHTS – GRAND REOPENING – SPECIAL TASTING MENU!

I was back in the kitchen preparing the special tasting menu, the first I had designed from scratch. It had five courses, starting with tiny fried puris topped with spiced paneer with cashew nuts to open up the palate. I followed this with steamed dhokla squares, fragrant, sour semolina cakes with fresh curry leaves, mustard seeds and coconut ice cream. Third came mackerel – Bengali style – cooked in mustard oil with sweet potatoes. The penultimate dish was wild mushrooms sautéed with Indian garam masala, and I ended with my take on mishti doi, a sweet, unctuous dessert with the consistency of condensed milk and the taste of the fresh paddy fields and wide open skies of Bengal. I had spent days practising, and we were full tonight so I couldn't afford to mess it up.

I was sporting the T-shirt Anjoli had made for me: *Good Waiter/Great Cook/Amazeballs Detective*. I wasn't sure about *Amazeballs* but would take it. We were pleased Ziad, his father and Salma's parents were all joining us for the dinner. The police had told them about our help in identifying Salma's killer, and they had phoned me to express their gratitude. One of the

343

best parts of being a police officer had been bringing a sense of closure to victims of crime and their families.

Tahir had called round that morning.

'We learned a lot from their texts. We've worked out that Salma saw them after hours in Mackenzie's office in some compromising position, and that's what kicked it all off.'

'She told the imam she had seen something six weeks before,' I said.

'Did she? Well anyway, they told Salma it was over, and she believed them. But then she saw them again at the restaurant and realised they'd lied; that's what made her determined to expose them.'

'So, we've got Naila?' said Anjoli.

'I'm not sure we can tie her to anything. She's not talking at all. She wasn't involved in Salma's killing because she didn't know Mackenzie was going to murder her, although she perverted the course of justice by covering it up. And we still have no proof she did any of the homeless killings, although . . . let me show you something.' Tahir pulled out his phone and cued up a video.

'We went back to the CCTV at Webber Street – remember where you saw Mackenzie give your friend Louis the gin bottle? Well, if you'd looked a little longer, you'd have seen this.'

On the video a figure in a black coat went to the sleeping Louis and leant over him. It was dark so we couldn't see who it was, but they knelt next to Louis and held his upper arm with one hand as he slept. There was a glint in the other hand as they injected something through Louis' coat. The homeless man jerked upright, but the person whispered something to him and he relaxed back down again. They then sat and spoke to Louis.

'Naila,' said Tahir, 'sat there for an hour, watching him die.'

He fast-forwarded the video, and we saw her cradle Louis' head and shut his eyes. With what looked like extreme tenderness, she covered him with his piece of cardboard and walked off.

'She had her back to the CCTV all the time so we can't prove it was her. We're checking other CCTV on the route to see if we can spot her, but at the moment we have nothing.'

'Shit,' said Anjoli. 'If we had just watched the CCTV to the end that day, we'd have seen her. Why didn't we?'

'I think Naila hurried us off to see Tahir before we got to that bit,' I said.

'OMG. She must have been shitting bricks as we were looking at the video. And she was so cool. Unbelievable.'

'That she is,' said Tahir. 'Oh, those tablets you gave me *were* just Vitamin D – she really was concerned about your health, Kamil. At best we have her as an accessory after the fact to Salma and maybe attempted murder on Sam. But he's vanished so we don't even have him as a witness.'

Anjoli's face fell. 'You're kidding!'

'Let's see. We're still digging. But her father is kicking up a massive fuss, and the Pakistani embassy has been on to us demanding her release – I didn't realise she was so well connected. So far, the higher-ups are giving us time to finish our work, but the pressure is building. I shouldn't have taken that laptop from you. It's vital evidence and they are claiming illegal search and seizure; that the evidence could have been planted. Although we retrieved her and Mackenzie's phones from the post office, and they corroborate what's on the laptop, so that's helpful.'

'We *had* to get the laptop to you,' said Anjoli. 'Otherwise, she'd be back in bloody Pakistan by now!'

'I know that. I'm just telling you the tack her lawyers are taking. I got my knuckles rapped for it.'

'Well, sorry about that, but we didn't have a choice. Anyway, it's good for your maverick reputation. Do we know how many homeless people she and Mackenzie killed?'

'No, but we've set up a major investigation team to work on it. As long as she's not talking, I'm not sure we ever will know how many or even who they were or why they did it. As they say, serial killers are either famous or good at their job.'

Anjoli shut her eyes. 'It's terrible, those poor people who died before their time. Now in paupers' graves. And she may get away with it.'

'Through your stats we have a rough idea how many died,' I said. 'It was a hell of a lot, Anjoli, and if you hadn't been so bloody-minded, there could have been more.'

'Yes, marvellous job, Anj,' said Tahir.

'I still don't understand why,' said Anjoli. 'Why did she do it?'

I gave a deep sigh. 'I don't think we'll ever know. We're taught about looking for means, opportunity and motive, but the more I've seen, the more I'm coming to realise that motives are slippery. Take the murders last year – Asif Khan and Rakesh Sharma. I'm not sure I really understood the motives for those. I mean,' I said, warming to my theme, 'do we really understand *why* we actually do anything? Or do we just rationalise our actions after the event? Maybe we are like a fly on an elephant walking through the jungle: the elephant goes where it wants but the fly thinks it is steering it. So we do things out of our deepest impulses but our mind then tries to explain them away.'

They looked at me blankly and I added sheepishly, 'Anyway, that's what I think.'

'Thank you, Deepak Chopra,' said Tahir. 'Anjoli, can I get a table for two for dinner tonight? Name of Maverick.'

'Of course. I'll fit you in,' said Anjoli, glancing at me. 'New girl? Who is it this time? Is this the love of your life you found the other night?'

'That didn't work out. But this one I've got a good feeling about. She's Icelandic.'

'I'll cook my herring curry for her,' I said.

'Hilarious, Inspector Clouseau. Talking about inspectors, I told DI Rogers about the help you gave us, and he said you should apply to the Met. They can fast-track you, given your previous experience, so you would not have to start at the bottom as a constable, and as long as you keep your philosophising about motives to a minimum, you can help increase the BAME representation.'

'I'll think about it.'

A month ago, Tahir's words would have filled me with joy and sunshine mixed with rage at the possibility Naila might get away with it. Now I was . . . calmer. I didn't need to prove myself, and Naila's fate was out of my hands. Part of me still hoped she had really liked me and it hadn't all been an act but deep down I knew it probably had. Well, I would know not to fall for green eyes and a warm smile again and with time my fury at being gulled so easily would subside. Now I could enjoy cooking, the creativity of inventing new combinations of heat, salt, fat and acid to transform raw meat, vegetables, spices and herbs into something that hadn't existed ten minutes ago and would cease to exist ten minutes from now. For me it was a deep dive into mindfulness, taking me out of my head and into pure creativity – there was something beautiful about the sheer ephemerality of it. Maybe my jihad was over.

I glanced at Anjoli, across the kitchen, haranguing the new waiter we had hired to replace Salim Mian, whose picture we had put up in the restaurant, garlanded with sandalwood flowers. She raised a hand to push her hair back from her eyes, and I felt a deep surge of affection, respect for her insistence on doing the right thing and admiration for her tenacious pursuit of a killer who only her intuition and penchant for statistics told her existed. I had the chance to work with her every day, seeing her grumpy in the morning, tired in the evening, smiling when she saw an Instagram post she liked, frowning when she read a tweet she disagreed with. I wasn't sure I wanted to give that up. She had met up with Father Spence and was helping the ACE people, happy she was flexing her psychology muscles and her restaurateur ones.

I went back to filleting my mackerel, the skin silky against my fingers as the crackling aroma of fried cinnamon, cloves and bay leaves suffused my senses. Feeling nostalgic for a world I had never known, I saw our old cook Suresh, his family gathered around him, tending to a pot bubbling on a fire in a village surrounded by lush emerald fields in Bengal, as the lavender evening drifted down and the wheeling and swooping black mynah birds over the green river cried *home home home.*

Epilogue

Later. London.

The sea around Churna Island was body-warm. Daddy held her hand, pulling her along as she looked under the crystal waters, hoping her mask wouldn't fog up this time. There it was! She tugged at Daddy's arm in excitement and pointed at the sea turtle, moving with majesty through the blueness below, weightless despite its heavy, grey, mottled shell. The joy she felt couldn't be described – everything at that moment was just . . . pure happiness.

She'd never felt it again.

She missed Daddy's hand in hers.

That's the trouble with the happiest time of your life: you never know it at the time, you always think it's ahead of you. It's only later you realise you've let it slip away, unmarked, unnoticed.

A clanging outside her cell.

Her back ached – the thin mattress provided no support during the hours and hours she spent on her bed. If you could even call it a bed. But she would be out of Bronzefield Prison soon. Her lawyer had told her Daddy and Imran were fighting on her behalf. They would sort out this mistake, and everyone would see it for the miscarriage of justice it was.

Salma. It had all started with Salma. If only Salma hadn't seen her with Sir that day in his office . . . He had been having second thoughts about the humanitarian aid they were providing to the homeless. She had knelt in front of his chair and . . . almost bitten it off when she heard the scream and Sir leaped up. And there was Salma. Hand over her mouth. Standing at the door. Staring at them in disbelief.

It scared Sir; he couldn't afford to have another complaint on his record. So they had to promise Salma it would never happen again; it was a one-off. And later when Salma had asked her if Sir had forced her to do *that*, she had looked away with a 'What was I to do?' expression painted on her face. But no, Salma mustn't complain to the dean. Naila would be sent back to Pakistan. It would be a scandal.

Of course, she couldn't explain the real reason, that she and Sir were doing important work, and there was no way they could stop. There were so many lives to be saved. And deep down she had to admit to herself that not only did she need Sir's help in her mission, she liked the way he looked at her, the longing in his eyes when they entered a hotel room, how she'd make him wait.

Then Salma had seen them in that Italian restaurant.

It was terrible of Sir to have done what he did. She hadn't believed her eyes when she saw Salma dead on the floor of her little flat. She tried to revive her and correct Sir's mistake, but it was too late. He was supposed to have *persuaded* Salma not to report them. Bribe her with good grades, not *kill* her! He had seen red, he wailed. Salma was being so obstinate. He couldn't lose his Naila. Didn't she *understand*?

She'd been furious with him. His stupidity had brought her to this predicament. To quench the blinding rage, she had eased the burden of suffering on Kamil's friend Yasir. But it hadn't worked. She didn't feel the calm fulfilment she normally did when she moved their souls to a better place. She'd tried again with the black man in Waterloo after Sir had given him the gin. But that hadn't worked either. That's when she realised if she didn't free them out of love, then it didn't count. That's what she had done wrong. Let anger overcome love.

It had taken ages to persuade Sir the only way they could *really* help the poor homeless was to relieve them of their suffering. He was sympathetic to people who used Dignitas and euthanasia – why was this any different? A rejection of pain in favour of . . . oblivion. She'd had to show him how – and he was supposed to be *her* teacher. But he failed. Trying to kill that old woman in Southwark while she watched and scurrying away when she shouted. But all she felt was compassion for him; not everyone could do what she did.

Salma had not deserved to die. Nor had Salim Uncle. Neither of them had been suffering.

Salim Uncle had been so good to her. His death was another product of Sir's weakness. Two unnecessary deaths because of his inability to control his urges.

Her eyes filled with tears, and she brushed them away with an impatient finger. How could she show them she wasn't the unfeeling psychopath they were painting her as? Her problem was she felt *too* much. They would never understand how she sat with her wards, cradling them in her arms till they passed on. It was so much better for them to breathe their last enveloped in love than alone on a cold, heartless street. How could anyone deny them that? How could that be evil?

Finally, after Sir had been arrested and called her, sobbing, she'd had to tell him it was over. She needed to protect herself so she could continue her work. He could understand, couldn't he? She still loved him. Just like he loved her. Now he must release *himself.* But she hoped he hadn't suffered too much. Cutting his own wrists must have been painful. She hadn't realised it would hurt so much when she'd stabbed herself. Some nurse she was. Lying there on the floor of Waterloo station, Kamil staring at her in pain at *her* suffering. That was an odd feeling.

She had hoped Kamil would understand what she was trying to do. The goodness in her. She had loved him too, just as she had once loved Sir. Kamil had given her what Sir couldn't, a connection to her life back home. He understood her in ways that Sir didn't. She wished she had gone away with him for that weekend. It would have made him happy, and she enjoyed making people happy.

Even Imran. He believed he'd had all the power over her but eventually he'd succumbed. After she had told him she had the ledger, all it had taken was for her to lead him to her bed and . . . But he would save her now, after Kamil had disappointed her. Maybe he *was* the man for her, after all. That would be ironic.

Jo ho gaya, so ho gaya. What was done was done. She'd be back in Lahore soon. She had done nothing wrong and would settle back into Lahore society. Be a good wife. A good nurse. Continue to love the needy and release them with the steady fingers of her beneficent right hand. A slight scratch and it was done.

A shoal of angelfish flickered through the water, dozens of individual fish moving as one, snaking and twisting as they shimmered away, silver melding into the blue. *Poof!* Gone, as if they had never existed.

She squeezed Daddy's powerful hand.

Acknowledgements

The intensely moving stories about rough sleepers in Britain in Maeve McClenaghan's *No Fixed Abode: Life and Death Among the UK's Forgotten Homeless* educated me on the many unjust and sometimes unavoidable pitfalls in life that can lead to homelessness. It inspired some ideas in *The Cook*, and Ms McClenaghan's book should be required reading for anyone with any interest or influence in health and social care.

Thank you to the superb team of editors and marketeers at Harvill Secker – Jade Chandler, Anna Redman Aylward, Sophie Painter, Hugh Davis, Dredheza Maloku and Kate Neilan. They have been a great support during my fledgling writing career. I wrote *The Cook* before *The Waiter* had even been released and just knowing this team was behind me made it that much easier for me to yield to the creative process.

Many thanks also to Laetitia Rutherford, my agent at Watson Little, whose comments help me shape the story and generated ideas that improved the book no end; and to Dan Mogford, whose beautifully designed and evocative covers undoubtedly caught the eye of many readers who may not have heard of these books otherwise – I'm convinced this contributed greatly to their success.

Thanks to Georgia Kaufmann, brilliant novelist and my good friend, who went through my manuscript with great care and made invaluable recommendations, which I am grateful to have received and incorporated in the final draft.

Thank you to Caroleena Bhojwani who gave generously of her pharmaceutical and medical knowledge to help me work out the mechanics of how the murders might have been perpetrated. And to Anthony Khatchaturian who corrected me when I went horribly wrong on police procedure. And to Islam Uddin who helped with Islamic religious rituals; his Global Development Foundation is a charity that works towards the relief of poverty and the improvement of living conditions in socially and economically disadvantaged communities, with a particular focus on Bangladesh and the Bangladeshi community in the UK.

The inspiration for Tandoori Knights came from the restaurant I have been frequenting for thirty-five years – Akash Tandoori in Maida Vale (500A Edgware Road, London W2 1EJ). Abdul Majid Choudhury started it in 1977, and it still serves the best lamb dhansak in town. He was kind enough to take the time to sit down with me on one of his rare mornings off and answer all my questions about the running of a busy Indian restaurant.

And of course, my family. I owe a great debt to my mother Indira, who fed me so well when I was growing up and inspired my love of cooking good Indian food, and to my sister Nandini, who has always been a great cheerleader and who gave me valuable feedback which made the book better. I've always received great encouragement from my daughters Layla, Eva and Tia, and the writing of this book was no exception. My wife Angelina is my greatest champion. She provided a much-needed sounding board for me when I was chewing over plot threads and forced me to confront potential difficulties. She also pored over every draft, helping to imbue the characters of this series with humour, warmth and authenticity. Thank you, Angie.

Read on for an exclusive extract
of *The Detective* . . .

Prologue

East End of London.
Wednesday, 31 December 1913.
Eve of the Great War.

'HE DIED FOR YOUR SINS!'
Determined to be heard above the hubbub in St Katharine Docks, the preacher tilted his head back and his voice rose above the racket. 'God will damn you all to hell unless you embrace our Lord and Saviour Jesus Christ. This is your last warning.'

'What is he saying, Papa?' Leah's sticky hand wormed its way into her father's as she skipped along to keep up.

Avram pulled down his fur hat against the late-night fog creeping in from the Thames. The cold in London was nothing compared to what he had experienced growing up in Pinsk. It was the damp he couldn't stand. It crept over you like a malaise till you felt you would never be warm again. Kneeling to button up the coat his daughter had kept open to show off her new white pinafore with its pink sash, he muttered, 'A meshuggenah, Leah.'

She looked at him, little face questioning. Avram smiled and switched to halting English, the language with which he wanted her to grow up. 'Come, quick, or we will miss the bells.'

Over his shoulder he saw Malka pushing the perambulator, baby swaddled and asleep, oblivious to the surrounding tumult.

He raised an eyebrow, and she nodded she was fine, tucking a stray lock of hair back under her headscarf.

They made their way through the hordes, avoiding the entreaties of the gutter merchants selling stripy hooters and the hawkers with their sweetmeats. The fog seemed to thicken, and they found themselves near the oil-black Thames where a young girl's voice sang a plaintive air above the crowd's excited chatter, until a stentorian 'Chestnuts, get yer hot chestnuts!' drowned her out.

'Papa?' Leah's enormous eyes did the trick, and Avram handed her a farthing. She dashed off, returning with a bag that she tossed from hand to tiny hand, squealing, 'Hot! Hot!'

As if a switch had been pulled, the pack went mute, the old year seeming to exhale its last breath. Then the first bell chimed from St Paul's and a murmur began. The buzz of the throng grew in intensity as people started counting down with a single voice, Leah joining in. Seven. Six. Five. Four. After the final 'One', the crowd erupted with fireworks, blaring trumpets and clanging pans, welcoming in 1914, kissing anyone who might be in their vicinity.

The little girl took it all in, four-year-old face rapt as she munched on a chestnut. Glancing at the pram, she stood on her toes and, almost toppling into the buggy, kissed the baby, saying, 'Happy New Year, Miriam!'

'Leave her, Leah,' said her mother in Yiddish. 'Let her sleep.'

Avram's love for Leah rose as a warm sea inside him as he saw her excitement. 'May HaShem make you as Sarah, Rebecca and Rachel.'

As the crowds pushed, threatening to pitch them into the trembling water, he gazed downriver, stung by the memory of the stinking boat that had brought him and Malka from the Pale of Settlement eight years ago, their small suitcase of belongings in hand. Those days were over, the pogroms but an echo haunting their dreams; but even now, Malka would toss and turn at night, sweating, whimpering; Avram holding her till she quietened. He saw Leah's eyes shining in the dark; her children would not experience that suffering. He had done well by his offspring – Baruch HaShem.

He called in Yiddish over the singing, 'Maybe next year we will go upriver, with the rich people on Westminster Bridge, not here with . . .' He waved an arm at the assembled pedlars, tanners and beggars.

'They will never let a Jew there,' Malka shouted back as a group of revellers wearing colourful hats and playing tin whistles marched down the street, the throng parting for them as the Red Sea had done for Moses. The music faded as she added, 'Be happy with what we have, Avram.'

'We shall see. Anything is possible. We must believe things will be better for the Jews. They cannot get any worse.'

'Everything can always get worse,' she grumbled. 'You should realise that by now. Be content.'

'Be optimistic. Come, let us go home. It is raining. Leah should be asleep.'

An organ grinder whipped up a tune, and merrymakers sang along as the family weaved on, dodging the horse dung that littered the cobbled streets. As they walked up Christian Street, the crowds thinned and Leah, chestnuts tight in hand, ran ahead, the bottom of her swaying dress a sliver of white in the darkness. The perambulator rattled over the slippery cobbles, the infant immune to the bumps, jerks and the bangs of the fireworks in the adjoining roads.

A voice.

'Pinsky?'

A figure emerged from the fog in top hat and tails, silhouetted against the light from the gas lamps.

Malka stiffened as Avram shot her a warning glance and said, 'Mr Pennyfeather.'

The man swayed towards them, hairy hand clutching a bottle of Krug. 'How are you, Pinsky? This is your family?' Pennyfeather's upper-class accent contrasted with Avram's rough Slavic tone.

Avram gave a curt nod and walked away as Pennyfeather called after him, 'Liking our English New Year's Eve celebrations?'

Avram's inbuilt politeness forced him to stop and wait for Pennyfeather to catch up. 'Very much. And are the festivities to your satisfaction?'

'They are, they are indeed.' Ruffling Leah's hair as she shrank into her father's side, Pennyfeather peered into the pram and said, 'Ah, the new child. I heard. What is her name?'

'Miriam,' said Malka reluctantly.

'A beautiful name for a beautiful girl. Congratulations, madam.' He tipped his hat to Malka. Tickling the baby's head, he turned to Avram, who flinched at the stench of alcohol assaulting his nostrils.

'So? Have you reconsidered, Pinsky?'

'Mr Pennyfeather, I have already told you many times. My business is not for sale. I must go now. My children are tired.'

'Of course it is. Everything is for sale with you people. I am a patient man, Pinsky, but I need an answer.'

Not responding, Avram picked up his pace, pulling Leah along with him as Pennyfeather trailed behind them up Fieldgate, passing the Great Synagogue that was shrouded in darkness. The lamps were out again, and the small side street was ill-lit and empty, save for the smell of the leather factories and raw soot. A hansom cab swept by, horseshoes clopping on the cobblestones in syncopation with the ever-present fireworks. The driver kept to one end to avoid the black hole of the construction site where Pennyfeather was expanding his department store. The carriage turned the corner onto Whitechapel Road and Pennyfeather said, 'Well, Pinsky?'

Avram's name sounded like a curse, emerging from Penny-feather's fat red lips. They were outside their small house now, the windows dark. Avram said, 'You have my answer. I am sorry. Malka, go upstairs.'

Pennyfeather's eyes glittered. Draining his bottle, he dropped it together with any pretence of civility. As it smashed on the street, he grabbed Avram by the throat and slammed him against his front door. Avram's hat fell off and rolled into the sewer, and Pennyfeather hissed, his face an inch from Avram's, 'Listen to me, Yid. Sign those papers tomorrow or I will make sure they throw you and your family back to whatever shitting country you came from.'

Leah screamed at the sudden violence and Miriam wailed as Avram struggled, trying to prise away the excruciating grip from his neck. Malka grabbed Pennyfeather's arm and sank her teeth into his hand, drawing blood. Pennyfeather shouted, 'Hellcat bitch!' released Avram and spun around. He punched Malka on the side of her face. She fell back. Her head cracked against the pavement's edge with a sickening thud. Blood gushed from under her sheitel.

'Mame!' Leah screamed and ran to her mother as the baby screwed up her tiny face, her cries filling the street.

Avram dropped, knelt beside his wife, and shook her. 'Malka? Malka?' But there was no response. Her eyes were open. Unsee-ing. Avram unwrapped her scarf and lifted the edge of her wig to see a crack in her skull weeping gore. Looking up in horror at Pennyfeather, he said, 'What . . . what is this you have done? *Hilf!* Someone. *Hilf!* Help!'

Pennyfeather stared at Malka's dead body, then at Avram and Leah, panic on his face. He turned to run, then paused and glanced around the darkness of the empty street. Swivelling, he pulled a derringer from his pocket and pointed it at Avram with a quivering hand. Avram looked up at him, uncomprehending.

Pennyfeather muttered, 'I'm sorry, I can't let you—' and fired, hitting Avram point blank in the head, the gunshot causing the baby to stop crying.

The sudden rain-drenched silence of the street was broken when Leah whimpered and hid her face behind her hands. Fist shaking, Pennyfeather turned the gun on her and, shutting his eyes, squeezed the trigger once more, the shot lost in the rat-a-tat of firecrackers in the distance. Her moan was cut off. Seeing her lying dead on the road, he fell to his knees and vomited.

He stayed kneeling for a minute, then stood. He passed his arm over his mouth and dragged Avram across the street to the rim of the construction cavity. With his foot poised on Avram's hip for purchase, he tipped him over the edge, the corpse falling twenty feet, swallowed by darkness. Another concerted effort, and the bodies of Malka and Leah followed their patriarch into the pit.

Breathing hard, he walked over to the pram and stared at Miriam. She gazed back up at him with huge dark eyes, silent, as if she realised something momentous had taken place.

Pennyfeather hesitated, saw he was out of bullets, and put away his gun. He snatched Miriam under one arm and rolled the perambulator into the hole. A final brief look around, and he vanished into the night with the baby.

The rain washed away the blood and vomit and soon there was nothing to show that anything of note had happened, except for a sodden fur hat in the gutter, a smashed champagne bottle and a scattering of chestnuts on the cobbles.

PART I
The First Week

There was of course no way of knowing whether you were being watched at any given moment. How often, or on what system . . . It was even conceivable that they watched everybody all the time.

George Orwell, 1984

Chapter 1

London.
Today. July. Monday night.

I t sounds like the start of a joke.

An imam, a restaurateur, a constable and an inspector are having a curry. The imam says to the constable, 'Congratulations on your life coming full circle, Kamil. With two Muslims in the police, we can finally establish the Brick Lane Caliphate.'

The three of us guffawed. 'Great idea, Sheikh,' said Tahir. 'Then Anjoli will have to exchange her personalised T-shirts for a burqa and always obey Kamil.'

Anjoli mopped up the last of her Iberian pork belly in a chilli sauce with a corner of naan and looked down at her T-shirt that read *Distant Socialising Goddess*. 'I'll fight tooth and veil to keep my T-shirts. I'll have you know Kamil does *my* bidding. I'm his boss, remember?'

'*Used* to be my boss.' I emptied my glass, relishing the last drops of the cold Cobra. 'Anjoli imposes *She*-ria Law!'

Another round of laughter.

'Very funny. To Detective Constable Kamil Rahman!' She raised a glass and waved my shiny new Met Police badge in the air. 'He'd like to thank me for everything I did to get him here. He couldn't have done it without me.'

'What is it they say?' said Tahir. 'Behind every great man there is a . . .'

'Woman cleaning up his crap. Sorry, Sheikh!' Anjoli grinned and clinked her glass with Tahir's.

My celebratory dinner was turning into a roast.

'I also know a joke like that,' said the imam, a smile escaping his full beard. He took a sip of his nimbu pani and said, 'Why do women walk five paces behind the Taliban in Afghanistan?'

'Why?'

'Landmines!'

He roared with laughter, the topi on his head bobbing up and down.

'Lol, Sheikh!' Anjoli fanned herself with a menu. 'Waiter! My glass is empty.' She waggled it at me, and I went to the bar to top her up in a final tip of the hat to my old job.

The imam was right about one thing – I *had* come full circle. A cop in Kolkata five years ago, then a waiter and cook in Brick Lane and now a detective again. In *England*. The spark of pride that flamed inside me was at once doused by contrition. Why was my recruitment into the Met a greater glory than getting into the Indian Police Service? Was it because I had dragged myself back up after hitting bottom? That I'd erased the disgrace of being fired from the Kolkata force? Or was it just that Indians have always had daddy issues about England?

Either way, here I was in Tandoori Knights, the restaurant I knew better than my parents' kitchen, being feted by the three people dearest to me – Imam Masroor, my spiritual guide; Anjoli, my landlady; and Tahir, my closest friend and now, boss – in the hottest week London had experienced for a decade.

And the last few years had felt like dog years. The twenties had a dismal beginning, as we tried to take the panic out of the pandemic. When Saibal and Maya, Anjoli's parents, died of the virus while they were in India, Anjoli was inconsolable. We couldn't attend their funeral in person, so we watched the livestream of their bodies on the cremation pyre – it was heart-breaking. I swallowed my grief to support her – holding her up as she sobbed herself into oblivion. That these were just two of the millions of unnecessary deaths that had occurred around the planet and fires like these were burning twenty-four hours a day didn't matter – this was *our* family – not points on a graph.

And poor orphaned Anjoli. Her pain wrapped around her like a shawl, she slogged hard, so hard, to keep the restaurant afloat. The terror of losing the business built by her parents, which was not only their legacy but also our livelihood, kept us going; and we just about survived. After the abrupt ending of my last relationship, Anjoli was my support and a genuine friend. I realised how well we fit together. It felt right, the two of us in our tiny bubble. We slipped from sharing meals on the kitchen table to sharing cuddles on the sofa, to . . . nothing. Every night ended with a closed door between us. I tried to talk to her about why I was perennially in the companion zone, but she would always bat it away with 'It would be too much, Kamil – working together and living together and sleeping together. You know how I feel about you, but I need some space.'

The problem was, I *didn't* know how she felt about me or how to give her the space that she said she wanted. So, we remained flat mates and best mates, drifting like two goldfish in our bowl, always circling and never quite meeting, with me waiting for us to connect and Anjoli waiting for . . . something.

On sleepless nights, hearing her bed creaking just metres away from mine through the wall as she struggled through her dreams, I'd think of what might have been. What was Maliha, the love I'd left behind, doing in Kolkata at this moment? And Naila . . . the other woman I'd fallen for in London four years ago? No. I still couldn't think of her green eyes drilling into mine without being overwhelmed by feelings of shame.

I had to move on.

Then the lockdowns lifted, the restaurant hummed, and business boomed. Anjoli gave up her side hustle selling T-shirts on Etsy, hired Chanson, a new Indian chef who had trained in molecular gastronomy (pretentious name, pretentious shaved head and even more pretentious food), revamped the menu, and left little for me to do as a cook. On Tahir's urging, and with Anjoli's encouragement, I'd applied to the Met and spent my two pandemic years at the University of East London's Detective Degree Holder Entry Programme, still paying my way by cooking part time, chafing under Chanson's charlatanry.

But my days of chopping onions, grinding peppercorns and peeling garlic were behind me. As of today, I was Detective Constable 20097 in the CID division, on the princely salary of £33,500 per year. And it *was* princely. Four times what I'd made as a sub-inspector in Kolkata and higher than the £27,500 (pre-bribes) that my father had reached as a top rank commissioner in the IPS. This hike in my earnings also saw the return of my self-respect – no longer was I dependent on Anjoli's largesse – and it felt like another new beginning.

I gave Anjoli and Tahir their drinks and sat down as he said, 'So, top of your year, eh? You Kolkata cops have sharp elbows. I'm going to have to watch my back!'

'You'll soon be reporting to me.' I winked. 'I come, I see, I conquer!'

Anjoli snorted. 'Veni, vidi, vindaloo, more like. You came, you saw, you cooked!'

Tahir guffawed. 'Good one! Do you know how many strings I had to pull to get them to assign you to my unit?'

'Yeah, yeah.' I polished the crown on top of my badge with my napkin. 'What you fail to mention is that you only got your promotion to inspector because I handed you a murderer on a plate four years ago and you took all the credit.'

'Hey,' Anjoli elbowed me hard. '*We* handed him the killer. No way you could have done it without me.'

'Sorry. Of course, you were an integral part of the team. Any tips for my first day, boss?'

Tahir considered this.

'Focus on the work. Don't feel you have to be a nice guy. The cops in CID are a good lot, but remember you're not looking for new mates, you just want their respect. And, as the sheikh said, you and I will be the only brown faces.'

'How do the goras regard you, Tahir?' asked the imam.

Tahir grimaced. 'Well, I was the first brown guy to make DI in Bethnal Green nick. When I got promoted, some started calling me Diversity and Inclusion Ismail behind my back. So, yes, Sheikh, institutional racism is a thing, but it's improving. When I joined, it was much worse. The coppers would joke about me being a terrorist, shout "Allahu Akbar" and pretend to duck when I entered the squad room – now it's more subtle and you have to brush it off. But you still must be way better than your white colleagues to make it up the ladder.'

'You'll have to teach him, Tahir,' Anjoli said. 'Kamil doesn't recognise racism. He floats along in his own little world.'

'Oh, believe me, I experienced discrimination in Kolkata, being a Muslim,' I said, nettled. '*And* had to deal with accusations of nepotism.'

'Well, you may face the same here, since I wangled you in as my partner,' said Tahir. 'I *should* have a sergeant reporting to me, instead of slumming it with a newly minted DC.'

'How are the others going to take that?' I asked.

'It'll put a few noses out of joint. But I've cleared it with Superintendent Rogers – told him that given we are in a Bangladeshi area, we can interact better with the locals as a team. And I'm not sorry you're replacing Protheroe. He's a fucking bongo. Sorry, Sheikh.'

'What's a bongo?' said Anjoli as the imam gave Tahir a vague smile. She giggled and said, 'Bingo Bango Bongo. Kamil you're a Bong Bongo.'

'She's out of it, isn't she?' laughed Tahir. 'Yeah, Protheroe just books on, never goes out. He's more interested in making himself look good than doing the hard graft. I've had to redo his work half a dozen times – he's missing in inaction. You provided an excellent opportunity for me to get shot of him.'

I wasn't sure how to take that; I'd rather Tahir had picked me for my skills than someone else's incompetence; but to hell with high-minded principles. If I had to show I was twice as good as the others to make it, well, that's what I would do.

The imam popped a last saffron-infused gulab jamun into his mouth and said, 'I must go now. Congratulations again, Kamil; I am very proud of you. You are a true inspiration to our people.'

'Thank you, Sheikh. Your guidance helped me get through the hard times.'

He patted my shoulder, and wheezing, raised himself from the table. Tahir followed suit, giving Anjoli a peck on the cheek and winking. 'Well you don't have to hear Kamil diss you anymore, Anj. He's my problem now.'

She started to clear the dinner table. 'Who knows, I may miss his dissing.'

'Not a chance. Anyway, nice new haircut.'

Anjoli blew her fringe out of her eyes. 'Good of you to notice, unlike Bingo Bango here.'

I protested, then realised I *hadn't* noticed. 'You always look so lovely . . .' I began as Tahir interrupted: 'I'll expect you at the shop nice and early tomorrow, Constable Bingo. You need to learn how to do *all* my paperwork.'

'I know, I know, Inspector. You're the lead singer; I just stand at the side of the stage, banging my bongos.'

The imam embraced me, and the scent of his rose attar

followed him to the door, the bell tinkling behind him and Tahir as they left the restaurant. Anjoli locked it, took my hand, ran the tip of her tongue over her lips and whispered, 'Come. Now that you don't work for me, let me show you another "ing" we can do besides dissing.'

My heart leapt. 'What did you have in mind?'

'*Rinsing* – bring the plates and glasses.'

Rolling my eyes, I followed her uproarious laughter into the kitchen. This policeman's lot was not a happy one.

Credits

Vintage would like to thank everyone who worked on the
publication of *The Cook*

Agent
Laetitia Rutherford

Editor
Katie Ellis-Brown

Editorial
Sania Riaz
Beth Coates
Elizabeth Foley

Copy-editor
Hugh Davies

Proofreader
Sally Sargeant

Managing Editorial
Leah Boulton
Sabeehah Saleq

Audio
Oliver Grant
Han Ismail
Laura Ingate

Contracts
Laura Forker
Gemma Avery
Ceri Cooper
Rebecca Smith
Toby Clyde
Anne Porter
Design
Dan Mogford

Suzanne Dean
Stephen Parker
Kris Potter
Matt Broughton
Rosie Palmer
Lily Richards
Ros Otoo

Digital
Anna Baggaley
Claire Dolan

Finance
Ed Grande
Jerome Davies

Marketing
Mollie Stewart
Sophie Painter
Chloe Healy
Kate Neilan
Helia Daryani

Production
Konrad Kirkham
Polly Dorner
Hayley Williams

Inventory
Georgia Sibbitt

Publicity
Anna Redman-Aylward
Bethan Jones
Zainab Mavani

Ivan Robirosa

Sales
Nathaniel Breakwell
Malissa Mistry
Caitlin Knight
Rohan Hope
Christina Usher
Neil Green
Jessica Paul
Amanda Dean
Andy Taylor
David Atkinson
David Devaney
Helen Evans
Martin Myers
Phoebe Edwards
Richard Screech
Justin Ward-Turner
Amy Carruthers
Charlotte Owens

Operations
Sophie Ramage

Rights
Jane Kirby
Lucy Beresford-Knox
Rachael Sharples
Beth Wood
Maddie Stephenson
Lucie Deacon
Agnes Watters

Thank you to our group companies and our sales
teams around the world

penguin.co.uk/vintage